A PATH OF DARKNESS

Copyright © Marnie L. Norton, 2021

All rights reserved. No part of this book may be reproduced in any form on by an electronic or mechanical means, including information storage and retrieval systems, without permission in writing from the publisher, except by a reviewer who may quote brief passages in a review.

This is a work of fiction. Names, characters, places, and incidents either are the product of the author's imagination or are used fictitiously. Any resemblance to actual persons, living or dead, events, or locales is entirely coincidental.

Illustrations copyright © 2021 by Marnie L. Norton

A PATH OF
DARKNESS
AND
Runes

by

MARNIE L. NORTON

MARNIE L. NORTON

*In loving memory of my grandad, Jack.
I believe in magic because of you.*

And to all the broken, beaten, and shattered souls - let us heal together.

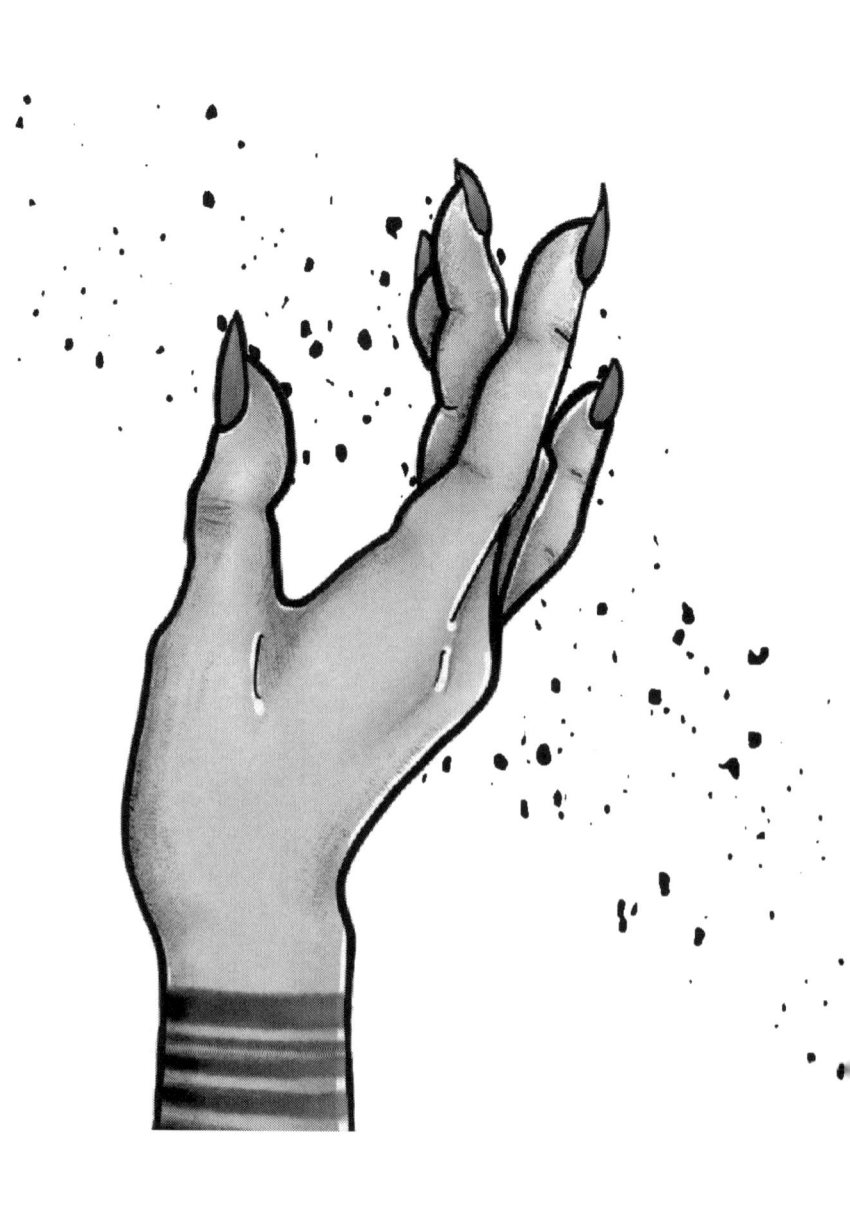

MARNIE L. NORTON

A PATH OF DARKNESS AND RUNES

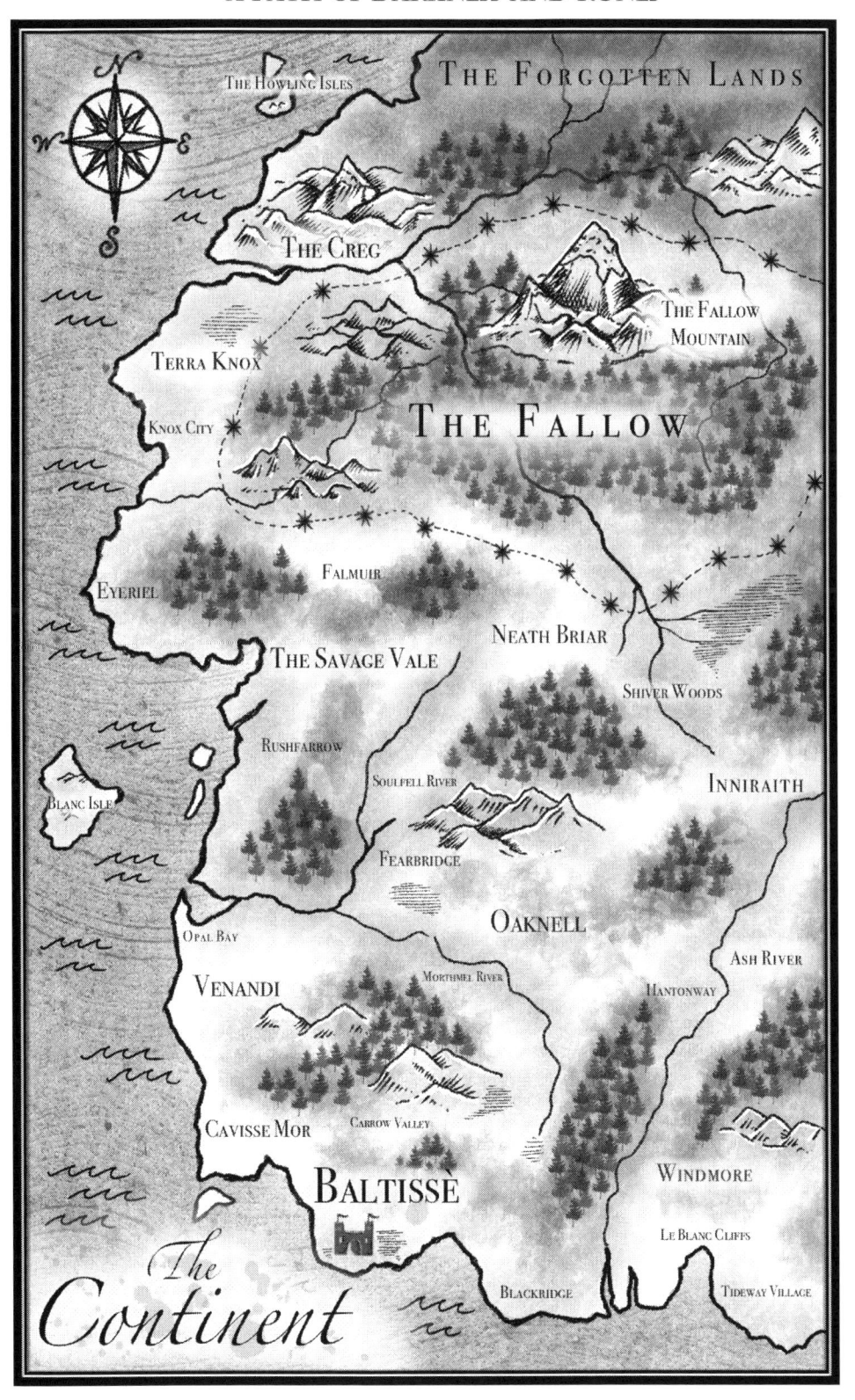

MARNIE L. NORTON

Prologue

"Slaughtered, all of 'em!"

The farmer had been slurring his words for the past hour, hiccupping and growling to each and all who had gathered to listen. The tavern had been filled that night and the ale was flowing freely. The news of old Will's missing sheep had been whispering about town all afternoon. The men of the village had gathered at the tavern that evening to hear the tale from old William himself. They all stood around the farmer in front of the open stone hearth, gossiping like the village women on market day. The village baker had gasped, the butcher had growled, and the blacksmith had seemed simply dumbfounded, as did the others. Spluttering and sloshing his ale, old Will had told them of his horror at dawn that very morning.

"Eight I counted. Eight of 'em they've taken from me." Old William sniffed. "Filthy beggars. I thought it was me eyes at first. But when I looked again, I was right." The old man seemed to sag against the beaten chair he was sitting on. "Thieves, murderous thieves they is, all of 'em!" he bellowed.

"Murderous?" the holy priest asked, worry lines forming on his brow, looking around at his flock. The men gathered looked at each other in turn at the priest's question. Confusion marred their faces at the old man's words.

"That's it, you see. Never bothered with 'em before but ... me sheep. Eight taken from me, eight from me herd over Dunning Hill. I went looking, you see, this morning. Try'na bring 'em in with the cold weather coming. But when I knew some were missing, I took old Bess up to look for the other eight." The old farmer rubbed a calloused hand over his weathered face. His arms and jug hand trembled. "She found 'em, me dog. Led me straight to it." The men seemed to tighten their formation at his rasping words, spines tense in waiting.

"It was by the tree line at the edge of the wood. Bloody Bess wouldn't stop barking when she found him." The old farmer took a long swig of his warmed ale, a stream dribbling down his whiskered chin. The roaring fire shone off the tin mug and his long nose and cheeks were pink with the heat and ale. He stared, dazed and haunted.

"Tell us then, Will," the baker almost laughed, "what did old Bess find?"

Old Will's watery eyes raised from his mug to meet the bakers, his mouth pursed in a withered line as he sighed heavily through his large bristled nose. "One of me lambs that came early this year. Whole jaw were missin'. Tongue hanging out, with half it body gone. Blood and guts everywhere."

The group of men seemed to exhale together, chuckling at the farmer. The baker, large as he was, shook his head in disappointment at the old man.

"It was probably foxes that did it, you old fool!" the baker bellowed, scoffing into his own mug of ale.

Some of the men walked away from the old man shaking their heads, back to the bar for another pint, the tension evaporated from the old man's worthless story. Card games that had been paused continued once more and other stories chirped up again, filling the tavern with soft chatter. The baker and the postmaster rolled their eyes at the farmer, who just sat there in his chair, stone faced.

"It wasn't foxes that done this, foxes are animals. What done this wasn't natural." The old farmer piped up over the dim chatter. Everyone seemed to halt again, expectantly. "No fox rips the meat and muscle off of bone, does it? No fox leaves half a body with its spine sticking out, does it? With claw trails the size of pitch forks!"

The crackle of the fire was the only sound as the men fell silent. The priest's throat bobbed, and the baker's thick brow crossed.

"All eight were like it in them trees. Shredded. Like something ate 'em when they were alive."

Disbelief was carved on the baker's face as he sat across from the farmer. The men poised for more of the story.

Old Will took another mouthful and ale dribbled down his chin. "I know's what foxes can do to a sheep. Raised sheep all me life!" he spluttered, pointedly looking into each of the men's eyes. "It wasn't foxes who done this," he finished, sitting back in his chair.

"Wolves could have had them, Will," the iron master stuttered, the hairs on his arms raised at the old man's words.

"There haven't been wolves this far south in years, Jon," the baker replied to the iron master, "and besides, wolves would have eaten the animal. Bones n'all."

There was a hushed murmur of agreement from the group, and all attention swung back to the farmer.

Old Will's heavy brows crossed as he said, "I know's who done it."

All eyes shot to the farmer.

"Them *'unwanted'* camped up near old Fenton's field." His pint of ale sloshed as angry thrusts matched his words.

None of the men said a word.

"Slaughtered them they did, disgusting heathens!" he spat, guzzling another mouthful of the bitter. "I've had enough. They don't belong here, never have."

Murmurs of agreement greeted the old farmers' ears.

"They stole a chicken from Peter's farms not a fortnight ago," he carried on, and again a chorus of agreeing harmonies answered him.

"Aye, Will, but it was just a young traveller boy who stole it. His father brought it back to Peter and apologised for the boy," the priest admitted to the gathered company. "Travellers couldn't do this, surely. It seems too savage."

"But they have that she-devil who travels with 'em," the baker spat. The fire spluttered as another log was thrown onto the flames and orange sparks scattered up the stone shoot. "She could have done it."

No one opposed the baker's statement as they contemplated his words, minds now teaming with ideas.

"She came to the village a couple of days ago, try'na buy milk with her trinkets and palm readings," the baker hissed and the farmer nodded profusely from his chair.

"Yes, it must'a been her. They say she's a Witch. With her palm readings and devil cards," Old William hiccupped, covering his drawn mouth and reddened nose with a large rough fingered hand.

The baker showed his teeth, and a growl seemed to ripple at the farmer's words.

The postmaster downed his own ale, wiped his broad hand across his mouth and burped loudly. "Are you saying a girl ripped those sheep apart?" he sneered at the old farmer and the baker.

The priest's eyebrows knitted together, and he crossed his arms. "She is just a child. I doubt she could have done something so...so..." The priest couldn't find the words to finish his admonishment.

"So sinister?" the baker bellowed, his plump cheeks and jowl quivering. "So evil? Believe me, Father, I wouldn't put it past her. They ain't like us. They ain't people of the faith. They ain't churchgoers. I'd bet ten coins it was her. Casting a spell 'cause none of us bought her devil trinkets!"

The baker's breath was thick with ale and his eyes seemed bloodshot in the fire's glow. They continued talking late into the night around the dying fire in the tavern. Another barrel was brought up from the cellar and mugs were glutinously refilled. The ale gradually turned their words sour, until hate coated their tongues. Even the priest, near the end, was raucous towards the travelling troupe with every passing gulp. The men rattled with conspiracy, planning their actions that night in a chorus of loud hollers and shouts. The decision was made, and the men gathered what weapons they could find and lit torches aflame. The barkeep could do nothing to stop them as the haze of drink shrouded their judgement. The men gathered their sons and horses, readying to go to the traveller's camp up on old Fenton's field, to rid them of the *'unwanted'* once and for all.

Chapter 1

The surrounding woods were filled with the sound of creaking wheels and ponies' hooves. The snaking line of decorated travellers' carts made their way across the snow-streaked dirt road. The last in the long line of the carts was the smallest. My cart. My home. Its floral paintwork had faded and now frosted with the biting winter wind. The oil lamp at my driver's side rocked from side to side as the wagon stumbled over the devoured land. This path, blanketed in white, was unusually quiet. The closely packed trees cast dark shadows over the underbrush and no animal tracks could be seen in the freshly fallen snow. My horse occasionally whinnied at the nipping wind, but no bird song or scattering of animals could be heard over the rustling of frost-bitten trees and the creaking of wooden wheels and spokes.

I was the driver in the last wagon, right at the very back, heaped in furs and blankets, all of which were a small mercy against the painful chill. The reins of my horse were clasped tightly in my mottled blue hands and plumes of mist floated in the air from my breath. I shivered violently, following the clan as we moved further north, away from the southern villages and unfriendly folk. The same monotonous road and landscape burned my eyes. The constant white was glaring, and I was exhausted; exhausted from the road, exhausted from always fleeing. A shudder wracked my jaw and my teeth chattered painfully. A flicker of movement in the shrouded woodland caught my eye. A gleam and shimmer of unnatural light. Not white snow or grey woods. Something else. I eased the reins, slowing my horse, Balthazar, from his trot and into a careful walk as I stared at the creases in between the trees. No other glimmers emerged in the gloom as I sat, motionless in my seat.

An icy trail began creeping up the nape of my neck, as though someone's breath and lips lingered there. Balthazar nickered, agitated at our clan moving further away up the road. The beast was anxious here and it made my stomach tense. I paused a second longer, glaring back at the trees, searching. I knew why he was so agitated. I could feel it. Feel the hidden eyes of something. Something not wanting to be seen. But there was nothing. I saw nothing.

Clucking my tongue, Balthazar takes up pace once more. My fingers ached with the onslaught of the winter wind. I burned to move them and muttered to myself about purchasing a pair of gloves in the next town.
Please let us make camp soon.

My lank hair was crisp with frost, the thick scarf shrouding most of my face, except my eyes, was dusted with ice. A muffled shout from the front of the wagons filtered down towards me and I sagged, relief ebbing its way down my aching form.

Finally.

We had found somewhere to make camp, somewhere safe and off this endless road. I clicked my neck, rustling my spine to sit straighter. The fabrics covering me were stiff and crackled as I stretched, trying to get sight of where we were moving to. The awakening moon hovered over the nearby trees and I could see a clearing off the road, surrounded by woods.

I slowly reached the entry point, the snow in the clearing had been untouched before our arrival and the towering oak and birch trees looked like they would give us good cover. The wagons rounded into the clearing, all sizes and shapes, creating divots and streams in the carpet of white. Each of them stationed themselves closely in formation. Always together, always safe. Living so closely together was protective and yet frustrating. Every person surrounding you left their imprint on your thoughts and soul. My clan and others like ours followed that tradition. They found it comforting and stable. I, however, found it suffocating.

But it was better to stay together as we moved north. Travelling away from the south, away from the capital and it's kingdom, always held its problems. But we had outstayed our welcome down south and now we were on the move again. My people have faced many struggles these past fifty years, experiencing hate and malice for a life which they know not of, nor understand. The people of this land had slowly, over the century, turned on us and regarded us with disdain and hostility, and I knew first-hand how they loathed us.

The Kingdom, and stronghold of Baltisse, was to the very south of the Continent, with the King and Queen ruling over all twelve territories viciously. However, the Continent was too large for the King and Queen to rule solely, so they allowed men of wealth and title to rule in their favour across those lands. Duke's, Lord's and Earl's governed unchecked and with the ability to enforce laws and rules of their own devising. That was the case in the end for the villagers near the Blanc Cliff's. They made their opinions quite clear as they ran us out of the field we had been living in for nearly four months, causing us to journey across the land to reach Windmore.

Steering Balthazar into the middle of the plane, my large ebony beast shimmered bronze in the dying light. The clan were already offloading trunks and tents to set up for the night, readying themselves for a few days rest in the peace of this quiet corner of trees.

Another shiver wracked me, causing my bones to creak, but it was nothing compared to the slithering sensation crawling over my skin from the eyes within the trees, watching us from deep within the fallen foliage. I strained my eyes, seeking out what vexed me.

"Rhona!"

My name being called pulled my focus back to the camp.

"Rhona!"

A heavy breath escaped me at seeing my brother, Roman, a short distance away unfolding his wagon's canopy. A smirk tugged at my lips at his dark furs and coat deforming his shape into another creature. He looked like a towered black bear. Catching his eye, he pointed at the spot closest to his own wagon. I did as he indicated, steering Balthazar onwards to the small patch of untouched snow next to his caravan. Scanning the copse, I noted the distance of our two wagons from the fellow carts. My brother had thankfully placed us away from the gaggle and noise of the other caravans and tents, how we preferred it.

Balthazar huffed with an appreciative whinny when we finally stopped and I smiled to myself, seeing his black muzzle nodding. Groaning with my own relief as I jumped down from my driver's seat, the snow falling from my winter cloak, landing in heaps around us. My breath clouded in the chilled air as I rubbed my hands together briskly, needing the friction to revive my fingers, when I noticed Roman looking at the treeline, his eyes tense and searching.

It's not just me then.

Roman helped dismount the horse from the wagon, unfastening the fore carriage and lowering the bracing struts into the snow. Grasping Balthazar's bridle we both walked my towering beast over to the other horses, all huddled together in a large makeshift pen already set up, sheltered in a small copse of low hanging trees. I rubbed Balthazar's nose. The beast's breath warmed the cold set deep into the bones of my fingers and his nostrils and lips twitched, seeking the treat I had hidden. A fallen apple. Cold velvet lips and teeth gently pinching against my palm as he chomped on the less than fresh fruit, making me smile.

"You spoil him too much," Roman grumbled, settling his own horse. I ignored him, watching his large hands unbuckle the harness and straps. I smiled up at my Balthazar, rubbing his forehead with an affectionate scratch of my nails.

"He's worth all the fuss. Aren't you?" I replied.

The horse nudged my palm in response. He was right, I did spoil Balthazar. But he had been my constant companion these past few months, and the only creature that held my full trust that I could speak openly too, even if those quiet exchanges had been on the road or alone in a forest. Balthazar listened and he understood. Roman chuckled as he looked at me, observing the small smile on my lips that was rare these days.

I dropped the smile from my mouth, afraid of the look now passing over my brother's face. "I saw you talking to Merci earlier," I probed, with a quick glance back at my brother.

His eyes sharpened at the mention of the girl's name. Anything to wipe the pity off his face.

"Still trying to persuade yourself that the match is meant to be? That she hasn't been saving herself, just for you?" I dared, watching his features transform and darken. I had hit a nerve. **Good.**

I had seen him on the road, talking to the girl. Everyone in the line couldn't help notice the bored nonchalance of his face as she rode next to him. A smirk grew on my mouth, knowing exactly what my brother would have said to her, or not said; Merci had been the one doing all the talking. She had taken the opportunity to talk to him where he couldn't physically run away into a town, or go off hunting or patrolling. It had been plain to see on his face that he did not like or want the match made for him and Merci to marry.

Roman was barely twenty and four years, four years older than me, but he was old by our traditions of when to take a wife. It wasn't uncommon for a man to marry in his late twenty years, but it had been expected of him to marry earlier than this. As it was equally expected of me.

To her credit, Merci was pretty, gentle and quiet; everything I would have wished for my only brother. But I knew him. I understood his heart wandered elsewhere, away from our brethren and camp, away from the traditions that sometimes forced the children into things they did not want for themselves. Arranged marriages being one of them.

Roman's mouth quirked to the side and relief washed over me. "I'd break too many whores' hearts if I strayed from the path of the wicked. You know how much of a catch I am."

"Only to the pigs and dogs," I quipped.

This was how it always was. How we loved each other, by being verbally throttled.

"And there was me thinking you left your savage tongue back at the village," Roman chuckled, wrenching an arm to brace around my neck.

"Never. My tongue only saves the foulest things for you and you alone, brother."

Little did my brother know exactly what I had left behind in that southern village whilst he and Elias had been away. They had been gone for over three months, trading with a rival travelling troupe. I had been left alone with our brooding uncle, elders and women. There were many of us, journeying across the continent but on this occasion, Baja had tasked both Roman and Eli and a few other men to do this duty of haggling silks, potions, and new wives. Thankfully both my brother and our friend Eli, had returned unhitched and without women in tow. I had missed them. I had missed this, the way we talked and played. I had missed my brother. I had missed…

I stopped myself.

"I'm such a lucky fellow to have such a beast for a sister. Fate plays cruel games, for it blessed me with the looks and you with the mind." He dramatised his words, tensing his muscled arms.

"Poor pretty thing you are," I snickered. "It is such a shame that I have you for company and you only me. I dare say fate made you quite stupid as well as pretty." I wrinkled my nose at him.

"I am as clever as a fox. Not everyone can swipe four purses of coins whilst brawling." He looked thoughtful. "Maybe the great Mother gave me both looks and brains."

"Do not kid yourself, and don't look so pleased. I have no trophies unfortunately, only hurt pride," I said, shuddering at the memory.

His eyes softened slightly and creased at the corners. "They hurt you?" he asked and his mouth twisted at the question.

"Not really, a few bruises and a cracked knuckle. That was one of the worst we have suffered. Well, for me anyway; I lost my footing and the bastard began to choke me."

Roman's eyes widened at my words and his hands whipped up quickly, trying to peel away layers of wool that were wrapped around my neck, to the bruises underneath. This I would share with him, but he would become overbearing if he knew about the cracked ribs I was also nursing.

"I'm fine. Eli got to me and hauled me from the fight." A blush crept up my cheeks. I hated the fact I had been hauled away like a child, away from the fists and kicks I was ready to deliver, but I was clumsy in that fight. The shock of it all had rattled me. If it hadn't been for Eli, I may not have walked away with my life. "I landed a few cruel blows, though. Let's just say the baker from Blackridge won't be making love to his wife for a month," I said, with a wicked smile.

Roman's hands withdrew carefully, his tension easing as he accepted that I was fine and a smirk returned to his mischievous mouth.

"You wicked thing. Pray tell, did you do anything this time to warrant such hysterics from the villagers? Or was it just fear alone that brought them to our campsite late in the night?"

I swallowed down the lump in my throat, the conversation from the night before clawing at me, of the lambs and sheep that had been slaughtered.

"It was a good job myself, Eli and the others returned when we did," he offered, brow raised.

His comment struck a nerve and my hands fisted. Honestly, it was a good thing Roman and Eli had returned the morning before the night raid, and yet, I could only scoff at him.

"Apparently, it was Mutza who ventured into town this time. I was hunting with uncle. And besides, I recall you being the reason for a raid last year?" I said exasperated, waving my hands in emphasis. The sores and crusted blood cracked on my knuckles.

Roman and Eli were known for boxing. Both were betting men, who arranged fights, with themselves as the main contenders. They were both experienced, avid fighters, however, last time Roman rigged the fight. It wasn't long after the people in Cavisse Mor realised they had been conned.

"It must have stung you to return to our boring little troupe. All those ladies' hearts, you must've broken." I made an unladylike sign with my hand and caught a whiff of myself. I needed to wash. My brother's eyes betrayed him, but he distracted me quickly, inadvertently guessing my exact thought.

"Yes, you stink. Hurry up and wash, and then you'll be as pretty as your old brother," he said with an amused gleam in his dark eyes.

A distraction, and I was thankful for it. Another smile spread across my face, warm and inviting, chasing away the ransacking our clan had experienced nights before.

"Vein arse," I retorted, giving him a vulgar gesture with my throbbing hand.

"Witch," he chuckled back, and I had to reach on my tiptoes to grasp a clump full of his hair, yanking it roughly.

"And what of your betrothed?" Roman dared, eyes squinting in pain as I pulled at his scalp harder than I intended.

I stilled, releasing his hair and turning abruptly back to unbuckle Balthazar's harness. His answering laugh made my blood boil. I, like my brother, was not interested in marriage. I despised the tradition, as I despised that our mother was forced to marry our cruel father. The idea of being betrothed was something I repeatedly repressed, and yet Roman reminded me of the fact often. I was betrothed and it tightened my stomach into knots. I had been betrothed since I was a child and the knowledge of this had never really bothered me, until my mother's passing. The promise had turned sour and the tradition haunted me. It was not just the marriage that caused nervous shudders or a sickening of the gut, but the bitter understanding that no man would have me. Not now. Not if they knew.

A darkness began creeping into my mind and I locked it away, vaulting it back into the nothingness of old memories. Our traditions within travelling families and those who followed our way, were not something I nor my brother coveted. Girls were married off to young men in other clans or other families, they were honoured with such things, to be married and bear children. But I would not consider it. I couldn't. I wouldn't, on principle, even though my intended was not a cruel man. He was a good man. He was our childhood friend, my brother in arms, and he did not like the idea of a match between us either. We had both made our opinions clear to one another many years before, when I was eight and he, twelve.

"I would never force Eli into marrying me, and neither should tradition. It's not right for him to marry me," I said quietly, more to myself than to my brother. Even as the words tasted bitter on my tongue, I knew it to be true.

Roman eyed me cautiously, a question growing in his dark blue eyes.

"We both do not want the match. I know he is a good man-"

"The best, Rhona," Roman interrupted.

"I know he is Roman. But I cannot give him what a marriage inherits, like he could not give it to me. He is…" My breath caught in my throat as Eli walked past, seemingly oblivious to our quiet conversation.

His broody face and eyes were darting about the campsite, unaware of me or Roman.

"-is like a brother," I finally whispered, my throat bobbing and struggling at the sight of him stalking away.

The lie was strained and sounded unnatural, and I knew Roman saw and heard it. I cleared my throat quickly, bringing my attention back to my mount and bridle. My eyes followed him as he walked across the camp to a caravan in the circle. When Eli's snow dusted form entered his cabin out of sight, I finally met my brother's piercing stare. Roman's thick brows were raised, another question forming on his lips.

"I will not speak any more of this, Roman. He doesn't love me and I do not love him. Why do you think we haven't taken our vows?" I gushed angrily. "They haven't forced us because even Uncle thinks that the match is wrong." My heart felt like it was lead in my chest. "Uncle hasn't forced you into it for reasons I'm not privy to," Roman retorted. It was like a slap in the face, but I kept up my guard. A mask of feigned boredom in place once again.

"And besides, do you see me as a whimpering wife, attached to her caravan and rearing five children? Or do you see me for the rogue mouthed heathen of a sibling, who can whip you senseless?" I teased, trying to sound as if his blow wasn't something that kept me up at night.

Thankfully, the conversation was over, even with the lingering question in Roman's eyes. I could only cross my arms in emphasis and Roman, begrudgingly, held up his hands in surrender.   Leaving

Balthazar with the other clan horses, we began setting up our wagons for the night. Our fellow travellers and family were all wrapped in animal furs and fleeces, woven blankets and thick leathers, trudging about, clearing the snow. Soon the snow would be cleared within the centre and several fires built to keep warm, while the fiddles played and the old blind Mutza told stories to those who dared to listen.

I did not need help setting up my station for the night. My aged wagon was small and homely, built solely for one, and yet Roman took it upon himself to assist me with its dismantling at every stop. I blocked the wheels to stop them from rolling and released the wooden steps until they fell with a soft thump in the snow. I sighed looking high above; the moon was nearly whole and glowed pale in the slowly darkening sky. The twilight twinkled with mist that crept over the nearby forest and the temperature was dropping by the hour.

"Are you not setting up your canopy?" Roman asked, confused.

I had not opened any shutters on my wagon and was untying the brass oil lamp from its hook.

"It will freeze tonight and cause problems tomorrow." My words felt sharp in my mouth. There were clouds a few miles away waiting to unleash a cold storm upon the hill and its woodland. I could feel it in my bones; one of the only gifts left to me in our watered-down bloodline.

"I best inform the others then." Roman began to walk away, but I stopped him.

"No," I said firmly, my dark brows crossing, teeth beginning to chatter from the cold.

"But if the night is foul, they will begin to..." His words trailed off as he swallowed. "You know, see you as the seer you are."

Roman's words sent a shiver down my spine and I fisted my hands. The words caused cold to spread in the depths of my belly, sending ice-fire through my veins. One mistake. A horrible mistake that had turned mine and Roman's life upside down and I was never looked at the same by my clansmen again. All had shunned me but Roman, Eli and my uncle Baja. I was not my mother and I was certainly not a seer.

I bared my teeth. "Fine, but it came from your lips and not mine." I dismissed him with a hand and turned my back on him.

A bit too forcefully, I opened the door to my home and the smell of old oak and rosemary filled my nose. I stopped at the threshold and looked back to the tree line across from the caravans. The forest and surrounding woodland was quiet and resting and I frowned, searching for movement in the shadows and found none. The unease building was not something to be ignored. I turned and made my way to help my uncle and his men set up their tents, my mind as restless as my limbs.

***

After an hour, we had erected the tents and a roaring fire was now crackling and spitting at the centre. As the head and king of our traveller troupe, my uncles tent and fire was placed at the head of the small copse. We did not follow the standards and ruling set for us by those in power. We lived by our own means, sleeping under the stars, and never owning land. We followed the wind and the earth, never being ruled by those who would prefer to see us in servitude and chains.

I sighed as a bowl of spiced oats and meat were passed to me. It was then that my stomach growled, along with my muscles. I was ravenous. I devoured the meal quickly, licking my fingers appreciatively. My uncle was already in his tent for the night but the sky was still light and I couldn't bring myself to be confined in my wheeled home just yet. Some men remained around the fire, allowing the warmth to sink into their bones, as I was also trying to do. My body still shook from the bitter ride we had endured this past week. My brother was nowhere to be seen. He'd probably passed out from exhaustion in his cabin. Or was out in search of the doe-eyed Merci. I rolled my eyes at the thought, stretching my hands out closer to the fire's heat. The men murmured across the campfire and I heard them talk of the ruckus that caused our camp to travel with haste away from the southern village.

"How did you fare, Rhona? In the fight?" It was Darius, one of my uncle's men. He was slightly older than my uncle and the skin around his eyes and brows was wrinkled from too many summers of sun. His long dark hair, streaked with slate grey, was pulled back from his face. I looked across the flames at him. His nose had been broken again and an eye was puffy, the bruises not yet fading.

"As well as one can be from a midnight raid," I said, rubbing my healing knuckles. "How's your nose?"

He smiled a toothy grin. "I like that it now faces east and not west." That brought a bubble of laughter out of me and the other men around the campfire.

The laughter eased as Taren, Darius' son, asked, "do we even know what caused them to turn on us? Did anyone do anything that we know of?" All eyes looked to Taren, his young face worried, his high cheek bones highlighted in the yellow and orange of the firelight. His long dark hair was unbound and nearly as long as my own. He was three years younger than me but held a cold light in his eyes like that of a man thrice his age.

"Not to my knowledge. I heard Baja say a farmer got drunk and accused us of butchering his flock." I said.

The men hissed in distaste. From what we had gathered, foul rumours were spread about the town and caused the group to rally in the night. I chewed the inside of my cheek; my anger rising with each pulse and beat of my heart. The pain was a welcomed source of focus.

"We'd been living among them, beside them, for nearly four months!" Taren spat. "How could they tell such lies?"

We had dwelled on the outskirts of the town for longer than usual. We had made trade, created connections, and had made a point of trying to be useful, sharing our practices, being hired for labour, and healing when the town's doctors had been too expensive to folk. I, myself, had hunted and sold pheasant and foul to the market men, as well as braided baskets and foraged for herbs to sell to the village woman.

I had even made an acquaintance, Malik, a farmer's hand who had purchased baskets from me one balmy day in autumn. He had begun to fill the void that Roman and Eli had left when they had travelled. He had been kind and not mocking, quiet and in ways, peaceful. We had spent many days together, talking, labouring and hunting. Until one day, I had gathered enough courage to rid myself of the fear that my memories pressed against my skull every day. We had amused ourselves with each other, in short guttural exchanges. The sex had been a short-lived education. I had mainly used him. He would exile the terror and build up the trust again with my body until all the fear had faded and a small part of me had gathered itself together again. I realised now I would not see Malik again for quite some time.

"Because it was true," Darius sighed, rubbing his bruised hand about his neck.

I looked up, shocked.

He only nodded and continued. "No traveller tore the sheep apart. None of our people could ever have done it. But something did. We were the ones they chose to blame for it." Fear coated my tongue and my meal rolled about uncomfortably in my stomach.

"What do you mean, Da'?" Taren asked, his own face mirroring the shock and confusion on my own.

"The farmer's flock were ripped apart. Flesh from bone. Some sort of wolf or creature did it. No human could have done that. I saw with my own eyes as we passed his field that morning. I even offered the old git help."

A shiver crept up my spine. The idea of such a beast, in these lands, was unheard of. My lips moved before my mind could register what I was asking. "What creature could have done that?"

I didn't realise my uncle was standing behind me until his voice rumbled deep and low. "A creature for you not to worry about, Rhona."

I jumped, startled, and was rewarded with heat flushing my cheeks as he stepped around me and sat down next to me on the log.

"Whatever it was, it is long gone. Feasted and fled. It was likely to be wolves."

I watched Baja as he looked pointedly at his men across the fire. They began muttering about the journey here, commenting on the harsh snow and cold. I rolled my eyes and faced my uncle. His lips were split, and dried blood coated the corner of his mouth. There was shadow under his eyes and his usually shaven chin was bristled with dark hair. He looked exhausted.

"You don't have to protect me from such things," I whispered, eyeing the men across from me.

"But I do and I will." His voice was firm as he looked into the fire. His hair was loose and unclean, the only bright thing about him was the gold hoop earring that glinted in the firelight.

"I'm not a child anymore. I can look after myself," I retorted, running my fingers through the tangle of tresses.

"No, but you will always be a child in my eyes." His voice was soft although it held an edge.

My throat felt tight and I pursed my lips together trying not to let memories and my recurring nightmares show on my face.

"I know," I said. "But you made me strong. Trained me, to fight, to survive. You can't keep protecting me. Sheltering me." My throat contorted and my voice strained. "I'm not a little girl anymore. Time has passed, and I am healing and growing every day."

Baja looked at me, his eyes betraying the thoughts rallying in his mind. My breath was heavy as I shook my head, understanding what haunted him.

"Are you healing?" he asked, his voice below a whisper. I knew he could see through me, to the broken pieces deep within my soul. But I lied, nonetheless.

"Yes."

"Get some rest, Rhona. You need to sleep," was all he said as he stood and walked back into the darkness of his tent, leaving me alone with the fire and the burning image of his haunted face.

Chapter 2

In the sky, the grey clouds moved at speed against the blackness above as I walked back to my wagon. When I opened the door, the hinges creaked their familiar squeal and I sighed, looking at the space, so small but comfortable. The oiled wood ceiling glittered with silver chains and trinkets collected by a dead woman long passed. Books lay in piles up next to the bed, supporting candles, while others lay scattered across the threadbare rug disturbed from their bumpy journey. A broken mirror hung to the left above a wooden cabinet that Roman had crafted for me, three summers ago. It was enough for me, more than enough.

Closing the door against the winter night, the small cabin fell into darkness. Walking over to the candles that were weeping down the wooden shelves and cabinet, my footfall did not stumble. Even with the cabin in deep shadow and its contents hard to distinguish, my hands led me to the discarded flint, and I struck. The new flame illuminated the small space and I quickly lit the candles evenly spaced, filling the cabin with a warm glow.

Turning to face the fractured mirror, I saw my distorted features in the jagged cracks. The mass of long dark hair that hung limp from the melting frost, the dark blue eyes that seemed almost black in the candlelight and the high cheekbones, and straight nose that were red with cold. A scar cut across my right brow, breaking the growth of hair with a sliver of shimmering skin. The scar, and the memory that accompany it, were a daily reminder of the girl I once was. My lips, sore and cracked from the weather, formed their usual stubborn line as I measured myself.

My skin was pale and did not hold its usual honey colour. The southern coast had not been as warm this winter and smudges of purple crept under my eyes from all the sleepless nights, spent wondering about Roman and Eli, and what they were doing, or what the next day would bring. The band of yellowing bruised flesh was visible around my neck, as I stared back unflinchingly through the cracks. I looked like my mother. That fact caused my chest to heave and I blew air out steadily, open mouthed.

My mother had been the clan's seer and a painfully accurate one too. She could speak of the future, whether it be minutes, days or years. She remembered the past as though it were a drawing in a book or a reflection in a mirror. She saw things no others could see and her voice would change when another became present. Those memories scared me. There were times as children when her eyes would glaze and her voice would wrestle with a new tone, another's voice from the grave. Although those memories were not the darkest in my mind, I was proud to have been her daughter.

Without my mother, I had grown up quickly and learnt to understand things faster. I had knowledge girls in our clan didn't necessarily learn and wore men's riding trousers because skirts got in the way when hunting. I saw the beauty in such feminine things, but I couldn't bring myself to wear them, refusing to dress myself up to make myself seem womanly. I chose to hide those attributes, so others wouldn't look and take notice. But I had my reasons, and made my choices, to ensure I would never be a child again. I was at peace with it. In some ways.

I shut my eyes tightly against the images trying to resurface in my head, as my battered and numb fingers quickly unfastened the thick layers of furs and winter woollens. My heavy woven shawl sprinkled droplets of water on the floor as I hung it from a nail on the wall. Still staring at my reflection in the mirror, I reached knowingly for the pail of water at my side and drank quickly. It was as cold as the snow outside and caused me to shiver as it sank into my belly. I poured the rest into the chipped porcelain wash basin, before sitting on the disarray of my bed. The layers of straw, fleece and knitted wool were soft on my behind. Beaded glossy fabrics hung from the ceiling to the floor around it, obscuring the view of the cabin. I untied the laces and tugged at my boots, being careful to remove both the hunting daggers hidden in my calf brace and thigh strap. They were once my mother's but now mine by inheritance. I set them down carefully on a stack of books beside my bed, both glittering dangerously in the candles glow. The flames dotted about the cabin were warming the space and soon the slight heat was easing my stinging cheeks.

My hands wrestled with the layered bedding until I grasped my comb, looking at the intricate detail, viewing its strange shape and teeth. It was such an unusual and hideous thing to cherish. It was not ornate or gilded in silver or gold, it was ethereal in design, but no jewels or stones decorated its handle or shaft. The comb was slim toothed and long in my outstretched palm. Its pale ivory surface was darker in places and no one would have known until closer inspection that it was made from bone. My mother's bone. But that was our way. We burned our dead, so their body and soul blew away with the travelling winds, so they could continue wandering the earth free. A family member would take a bone and have it made into something mundane. Something to be with us for the rest of our lives. I had been that person to receive it, but not out of personal choice. Baja had gifted it to me.

My thumb grazed along the carved handle, thinking of a time when smiles were given freely, and her deft fingers would weave my hair with ribbons and wildflowers. Those days were long gone, and now my scarred and scabbed fingers braided my long tresses every night with the remnants of a woman long gone.

I washed my face and splashed my neck as carefully as I could with soap before my blood began to thread and swirl in the water. It was blood from cracked, clotting knuckles. The cold water coaxed and then numbed the persistent sting as I washed them clean. I looked over the skin covering my fingers and hands, both decorated in tiny white scars with a treasure trove of new wounds across the knuckles and wrist. More added to the collection.

The water was no longer good for washing as the colour churned a murky red. The tension in my neck cramped and I forced my spine to straighten and click, hissing suddenly from the pain of my cracked rib. I would have to treat it soon. The skin around my throat was still tender with dustings of faint purple and yellowing brown, thanks to the lynch mob from the southern town before. My mind raced back to that night, to the raid we had been victims of, and the memory came crashing back with clarity.

I had been tracking boars that were roaming in the forest next to the fields nearby and I was crouched, knees and boots caked with pungent mud and leaves. The forest and trees were thick with heavy limbs and rotting fruit, perfect for the beasts to feast on during the winter. My trap had been set, the darkness of night hiding me in the thicket near their group. I was barely breathing as they snuffed and growled about the sodden floor, the moonlight highlighting the thick bristles and leathery hides.

It had been a strange evening, especially as the crescent moon was ringed in a faint haze of red. Blood on the moon, we would say. An omen. But we had seen many and not paid heed to the blemish of scarlet on the moons in the past. None of our camp had realised that warning had been for us. I had watched the moon through the sprays of dying leaves in the canopy above, contemplating the brightness it was shining on this night. That's when I heard some of the women begin to scream.

Soon a distant haze of yellow appeared, lighting the sky above our field not half a mile away. I had sprinted from the thicket, branches and vines snagging on my coat and hair as I pelted towards the camp. I heard a disturbance in the trees as several shadowed forms hurtled through the entwined trees after me. Roman and Elias. I'd nearly stumbled as I jumped over a fallen tree where the foliage grew sparse nearest the field, and my legs pounded the ground hard and fast to get back to camp. I could see now, see horses charging at the women, with torches blazing with spluttering flames, as the unknown men rallied animals and people alike. The sight made my blood run cold.

Denif and his family's caravan was being rocked this way and that, as other men threw putrid smelling liquid over one of the wooden homes. Flames burst and erupted, and the caravan was soon ablaze in towering angry flames. The caravan was soon a crackling heap, spitting embers into the starlit night. There were screams and men's raucous laughter echoing across the field. Before me, on horseback, a fat-faced man was holding a girl's hair in a vice-like grip, dragging her behind him. The cold that was running through my veins turned icy and a steely calm settled over me.

At my feet lay two large stones beaten into the dried earth. I grappled with them quickly and began to run towards the man on his dapple-grey horse. The beast's backside was to me as its sluggish rider tried to haul a young girl onto his mount. I hissed and with all my might I threw the stone at the horse's rump. It smacked the skin with a satisfying whipping sound, causing the horse to rear in a cry of alarm. The rider yelped as he struggled to stabilize his steed, but to no avail. The horse hollered and bucked the man to the ground in a heap of sodden mulch and I shouted to the girl, Mira, to run. My ears were ringing with the hateful ruckus around us. Another fire blazed with an almighty bang that rang out and I ducked, swivelling on the spot, looking around eyes wide in horror. No bodies, no unmoving travellers murdered yet. Murdered because outright hate filled these men's hearts. Hate for crimes we didn't commit.

I saw another man, one with a round gut and a torch, skittering after one of the camp elders, Mutza. I stood sharply and threw the second rock still clutched in my hand. The stone flew through the air, arcing high above, until it landed with bone-cracking accuracy to his temple. The wretch stopped, stunned, falling limp and out cold onto the ground.

I smiled at that, with cruel satisfaction. **Take that, prick**. But my smile was wiped away as I heard men's voices behind me. I had been cornered as the ruckus of a night time raid sounded out.

"She'll do," one of them had spat at me through crooked, blackened teeth, his burning torch blooming in the dead of night.

I could hear more women in the camp screaming and my mind whirled, my heart hammering, as that black hole opened in my mind as another woman's screaming filled my ears from long ago. I spun looking at the fires, at my people, unable to tamper down the rising terror filling me. The horses huffed and nagged from the confines of their pen, as the village men began rounding all up, with wooden staffs, pitch forks, knives and makeshift weapons, causing my brethren to be in chaos.

"Let's see if there is black magic inside this one," a red-faced balding man slurred, with a butcher's cleave held aloft in his thick fingers.

My stomach flipped, anger and fear clawing its way up inside me and over my skin. I felt penned, caged like the horses. That memory, like death's cold breath on your cheek, began to pool in my mind but I wouldn't let it take hold, not when I needed my wits about me. I clenched my fists, digging my nails into flesh, painfully forcing that darkness to choke back into the hole I locked it up in.

Whilst inhaling a lungful of cold winter air, I surveyed my position. I was cornered, forcing my steps to be light and calculated as they approached me on all sides. North, south, east and west. I heard my name being bellowed from across the chaos and briefly remembered my brother barrelling through the men, trying to reach me. One of the fiends lunged with ruddy hands, so I dived and rolled to the ground. My hands swiftly grabbed the hunting knife strapped to my thigh, as my knees jolted sharply with the force of standing from a crouch. I brought my knife hand up, smashing the dagger handle into the nose of the heavy-set man with the butcher's cleave. Blood cascaded. The satisfying crack of his nose and cheek bone soothed my blood into something calm and lucid, thrumming vigorously as he fell to the floor, eyes streaming, his howls deafening. It only spurred me on further. I rounded on the second, to the wiry old fool, who had originally cornered me. His eyes were wide in the campfire light as I kicked, my foot falling heavily on his exposed groin.

He fell with a hoarse yelp and I took advantage of his falling frame, punching him square in the jaw. My knuckles barked in pain as the skin split against his own stretched and sallow cheek. I stalled, shaking my hand and wrist against the pain of impact and the moment had cost me. The third of my attackers grabbed me from behind, with a thick arm and elbow crushing my windpipe. I gasped at the force as the man sent a fist into my left side, stunning me. The breath was knocked out of my lungs and I collapsed in on myself, wheezing.

His rancid breath flickered against my ear, and his saliva splattered on the exposed skin of my neck as he said viciously, "you'll get what's coming to you, *unwanted* witch!"

I flinched at his words and tried my hardest to kick out, to struggle and contort in a way he would be forced to release me. My fingernails tried with force to tear at his flesh but to no avail. My lungs burned and my throat was raw with the assault, as my windpipe was pinched and restricted entirely. I tried to punch blindly behind me, hoping to catch his nose or mouth with a quick unexpected fist. He was growling as he tried to restrain the wild creature in his arms. His friends were still rolling on the earthen floor as he freed a fist and sent another stealthy punch to my ribs. I felt the snap of a rib crack under the block like fist, causing black to encircle, my vision as my arms and legs flailed about to break free.

There was a sudden jolt which made me and my attacker careen forwards, head over heels. His arm released the now agonising flesh around my neck, and I fell, heaving and gurgling as my lungs finally drew down icy air. Thick calloused hands grabbed at my waist and hauled me up with impressive ease. My rib cage barked at the sudden straightening, causing me to gasp and cry out as my vision was blurry with shadows. Figures and burning shapes ran from left to right, as I struggled to focus on the form crouched before me. My knees gave out and I crashed painfully onto the uneven field. The hands then moved down, and a broad shoulder gently fitted into my abdomen, lifting my weak and gasping form over their shoulder.

"Roman?" My voice broke as my vision cleared enough to distinguish the ground moving below me as my captor ran, the rocking and uneasy movements of being hung upside down turning my stomach.

They did not answer me, but I tried again and my voice box rattled painfully and I quickly closed my mouth. I was laid down in the tree line, carefully. The same strong hands supported my weight as they rested me in the thicket. I slowly sat up straight, as unimaginable fear chilled me and my heart battered within my bruised body. I winced, hands going to my ribs. The pain throbbed across my chest, but I couldn't focus on that now. Eyes wide, I rounded on my captor, knife out ready to gut them from navel to nose.

One brown eye and one blue eye met mine. My heart stumbled at those familiar eyes and his shadowed face contorted, giving me a once over. **Elias**. My hand cupped my broken rib, the throb and ache causing my teeth to clench and my throat to growl. Then he was gone, running back in towards the thickest of the fight to find my brother and help the other unwanted drive out the villagers.

The memory faded and shame blossomed in my cheeks as I looked at the swirling crimson water in my basin, now back in my wagon. I knew I should not have dismissed my blind side so easily during my battle. I was lucky, I supposed, to be able to fight and hold my own like any man in this camp, lucky that I had my brother and Eli, both of whom had taught me for years how to block, duck and punch. Also to have my uncle teach me to defend myself with a dagger, and how to hunt with a knife and bow. However, too many raids, too many fights and too many shadowed attacks had taught me to be more than prepared.

I rose to open the sky light on the roof of the wagon, needing to feel the open air on my skin. The moon was nearly whole and cast a pillar of light down through the small opening. Golden and white light glittered across the room from the collection of coins, medallions and metallic charms that dangle on silver chains, string, rope and leather cord from the ceiling. Memories crashed in and I sighed, eyeing the charms that had been passed down to me. Saints, symbols, gods and goddesses, creatures of myth and legend were carved, moulded and polished into their once shiny surfaces. *'All of them have a purpose'*, my mother's voice echoed in my mind. All were found and saved for the protection that they had promised.

But now the array of myths and medallions hung limply. Unused and dull from dust. None of them saved my mother. None of them protected her or protected me for that matter. Something oily and black swelled within me, and I had to shut my eyes tight.

Not now, please not now.

I swallowed the darkness down, like an acrid foul tonic and fell back on my bed, unable to shake it. Something wasn't right as the feeling would not shift, and I knew it was not the oncoming weather. There was a lump to the left of my head; the straw stuffed pillow was covering something which was causing me discomfort. My hand searched the hay and fabrics, finding a leather drawstring pouch, and I was relieved by the brief distraction that was anything other than my thoughts. I pulled it out, observing the marred skin and fraying knot. It contained my mother's runes. Runes that were now mine. I could not read them, Mother above knows I've tried. No matter how many times I called upon them or tried to read the scatter of stones, or the rune marks themselves, I got nothing. My mother had been the seer, I was not. Guilt grabbed me and I stuffed the pouch quickly back under my pillow, avoiding the reminder. I lay still, concentrating on my sore muscles and aching back, and glad to be laying in warm and soft bedding.

Chapter 3

When I awoke, the morning light crept in through the open hatch above, causing my eyes to burn. My breath clouded in plumes in front of me and dew covered the furs and thick blankets.

Shit.

I had slept with it open all night.

The sound of my uncle's cockerel crowing across camp stirred me further and I sat up slowly, my aches and pains causing me to wince as my coverings fell away and the cold morning air nipped at my warm torso.

There was a darkened wet patch on the small rug below the hatch light and I swore loudly, mentally kicking myself for leaving it open. Standing hastily, I stretched, clicking my spine in a favourable manner and adorned my worn military jacket. I made swift work of fastening my boots before grabbing a thick shawl and wrapping it twice around my neck and shoulders. In a basket, I packed a clean shirt, trousers, soap and clean bandages, and a jar of valerian and witch hazel. I would need to tend to my ribs and bruised neck. But when opened the door, the small amount of heat within the wagon evaporated, as cold morning air swelled into the room. I swore, again, knowing too well I would be sleeping on damp bedding that evening.

The camp was covered in a light dusting of glittery frost, just like I had predicted and a smug pleasure enveloped me as I stepped down with a crunch. The air had chilled but no grey clouds covered the sky. It would not snow today, thankfully.

I found a small stream in the woods, relieved that it was still too early for anyone else to be stirring in search of water or a wash. I was pleased I had some time to myself, to clean and redress my wounds. My ribs were dark and patchy, with bruises indicating a cracked or broken rib. I would need to go steady and ask Mutza for a draft of healing tea. As I washed, dried blood flow down the stream, disappearing into the crystal-clear water. The bruises and scars that littered my skin were normal, from sparring, hunting and fighting. The usual. However, there were others that I knew of, and could pinpoint their exact locations, as though I had a mental map of my skin. It was a map of my own doing. Pain was a welcomed release. It was consuming and cleared out the emotional pain held in my mind. I was not proud of them, the healed and scarred cuts. It was a simple tradition of mine, where rather than facing the onslaught of thoughts, I would rather face and feel physical pain.

Once cleaned and tended, I braided my hair once again and packed up, heading back through the trees to my wagon. Some of the women were about now, tending fires and preparing morning broth and tea for their families. The camp was subdued, with many still sleeping and unaware of the fresh morning that now stirred the woodland around them. The horses nickered and rustled in their pen, eager to walk about and be fed. After stowing any evidence of my bath and the bloodied bandages back in my home, I walked up to my brother's wagon, stationed a few feet from my own. I had barely raised my hand to knock on his door when its brass hinges creaked open.

Roman stood there expectantly, in his hunting gear. His long brown jacket that was secured at the waist by a black leather belt and he appeared less threatening, compared to the piled furs and blankets that distorted his form the night before. He too had bathed, but where I did not know. I mentally noted to wrangle the river location out of him later. His beard was short and tidy, no longer hiding his jaw and mouth, and his dark hair was scraped back into a knot at the back of his head. Mother above, Merci would be drooling when she saw him. Roman wiggled his dark brows at me as he stood proud in the small frame of the door.

"You look positively female, Rhona."

I had to hide my smile as I retorted, "funny brother, I was about to say the same thing about you."

He chuckled as he turned back towards the inside of his cabin, pulling out his trapping wire and hunting knife. His crossbow was already strapped across his back, the leather brace and gold buckles gleaming from underneath a brown lapel.

"Why don't you let your hair down every once in a while?" His tone was light and amused, but his eyes sparkled with jest.

"It gets in my eyes when I hunt and fight," I replied, matter-of-factly, clenching my jaw. For a long time, I had tried not to show my femininity. I had hidden it in men's trousers, oversized shirts, and coats. I had had my reasons, primarily to hide the shape of my body, but now I'd learnt to manage my fears. I had grown into this woman's body carefully, equipping my mind to deal with the passing glances and eager jeers.

"Hunt and fight? Dear sister, do you intend on causing more havoc for our poor brethren?"

I scoffed. "No, Roman, I only save it for you, and especially if you insist on baiting me."

"You have awoken in a delightful mood, haven't you?"

"Seeing your face puts me in such a mood," I quipped. "And besides, what's wrong with my hair being braided?"

"Nothing at all, just you look more like a woman with it down."

My hand instinctively flattened my hair. The comment stinging and causing a pang of unease. "I am a woman."

"Barely," he huffed, mockingly.

"Oh, bugger off, if you intend on annoying me."

"But that is what I live for." He wagged his eyebrows again, in that insufferable way of his.

I smiled, wagging my own eyebrows. "And there I was thinking you lived for hunting, fighting, thieving and the occasional whoring?"

His smirk was imperious. "Only on a full moon."

We both erupted with laughter, the air filled with Roman's throaty roar and my snickering. I aimed and punched him with playful force on his shoulder and he dodged out of the way with ease. He was more agile than me, something I cursed daily, but as he swerved his body, coming down the steps of his caravan, and I managed to land a swift kick on his backside.

"A kick on the arse for a complete arse," I taunted as I danced my way back to my wagon, its faded floral paintwork peeling in the morning sun. I quickly collected my own knives and traps and proceeded to catch pace with Roman.

We walked side by side towards the tree line that arced around us. The clearing was sparse, but the surrounding woodland was thick with winter washed trees of white and grey. The frost covered the remaining leaves, and all the way down the trunks to the undergrowth and thickets. Tracking would be easy this morning.

I scanned back at the waking camp, my eyes looking for the third member of our trio, Elias.

Your betrothed, the voice in my head said and I mentally batted it away.

"Is Eli still sleeping?" I asked, my eyes scanning for his hooded head and deerskin coat.

"He was up before the cockerel shit this morning. He is probably already scouting."

"He still isn't sleeping well?"

Eli hadn't slept contently these past six months; I could tell from the dark circles that sometimes showed under his blue and brown eyes. I sometimes stayed up late myself, thinking about what could be keeping him up. Was it the accident haunting him, or training and fighting? Perhaps he'd found a girl, and had been sharing a bed with her... I twitched, the muscles in my shoulder twerking, but I couldn't put my finger on why.

My brother only nodded at my assumption. The unease from the conversation the night before seemed to swell in me and I bit my lip.

"He is well, Rhona. He is his own man," he said with a cock of his brow. "Are you unsure?"

I scowled at him, worried. "A little, as should you be," I said as we walked into the trees, the snow coated twigs and leaves crunching under our boots.

The waking sounds from our camp were quieting with every step into the thick coverage of elm, birch and ash. The trees were even silent this morning with no wind stirring the arms that stretched high above, and no birds twittering their morning chant. The smell of damp earth was musty and familiar, as small wisps escaped my mouth and nose. My skin felt the chill as we crept through the wood, and it was colder here than it was in the clearing. The winter sun, though weak, couldn't penetrate the clawing cold or than canopy of trees.

There was a snap and rustle ahead and I halted, raising my hand to stop Roman, but he had heard it too. I looked to my left, the outline of Roman becoming clearer as he moved silently beside me. His footfall was noiseless as he searched the canopy above. The muscles up my back and neck tightened, and I shivered, slowly looking up, my eyes following the glittering bark of the tree ahead of me. Another snap of twigs above and I stilled my body completely, my pulse quickening and breath becoming shallow.

There was a loud crack of sudden movement and air stirred my braid from behind me. It was followed by a heavy thump and I whirled, to the fallen thing behind me. My heart was thundering and my ears were deafened by the blood pumping in my veins. My knife was in my hand in a flash of shining silver, raised and ready to lash out. But there was nothing there.

A rock lay at my feet, leaves and earth dusted the ground from its impact. I looked to Roman, a hidden smile creasing his eyes as his lips trembled from holding in his laughter. I straightened, knowing it was not a threat at all.

Elias.

I looked at my brother, his lips pursed, straining to hide his smile. Sheathing my knife with a loud sigh, I looked up, searching the trees above for our mute friend. Dead leaves fluttered down from their branches above, but there was no sign of him. My brother snickered like an adolescent boy, and with my hands on my hips, I arched a brow at him. It was far too early for games.

"Come out, Eli," I shouted at the trees.

There was another whoosh of debris and as I turned towards the sound, there he was. He landed almost soundlessly in my personal space. Meer inches from my face, his mouth and jaw hidden with a piece of dark fabric, his different coloured eyes, glittering. He pulled the fabric down from his nose and mouth revealing a boyish grin. My eyes darted across the pale scars running down his cheek, across his jaw and throat, scars that were mapped went further down under his shirt and coat, and across the top of his chest. My stomach fluttered at that smile, and the joyful glint in his curious eyes. That feeling soon disappeared as Roman doubled over, spluttering with laughter. Suddenly annoyed, I ground my teeth taking in both men in front of me.

They were both so different. One was silent as the dead of night, the other as loud and obnoxious as a goat. I hissed, my pointed finger already jabbing Eli in the chest.

"I could have hurt you," I said, already regretting waking this morning.

Eli's eyes crinkled in the corners, his smile widening. Roman scoffed and clapped Eli loudly on the back as he came up beside us.

"I would bet a good coin you could best him, Rhona. I bet Uncle has been training you viciously whilst we've been away. Care to wager, Eli?" Roman asked, eyes dancing.

Eli looked towards my brother, and then back to me with the briefest flash of annoyance. I huffed and crossed my arms, inhaling sharply at my bruised and cracked rib. Thankfully neither noticed. **Men and their money**.

"Two coppers says I can have Eli flat on his arse in six moves," I wagered.

Eli's eyes widened with something I didn't recognise. He didn't speak, mute and cool as always. Nor did he revise the bet we were currently orchestrating. But I watched for his reactions wondering what was truly under the surface.

There was no reaction, and this only spurred me on. "Make it five."

I looked at Eli fervently, waiting. We hadn't scrapped or wrestled for a while and I wondered if he would partake in our little wager. His eyes flashed as he shrugged, indifferent.

Roman's only answer was a cocky grin and the swinging of a leather pouch of coins, no doubt stolen during the brawl from the last village. Eli seemed to straighten. The furs and leathers creaked with the full extension of himself. He was a head taller than me but that wasn't the point. I inhaled slowly through my nose, licking my lips as I contemplated his height. Eli's head tilted as he watched me and I could feel my skin blanch as he looked at me. I could only raise a defying eyebrow. The bet was on it seemed.

He only stood there, and I waited, my muscles coiled to pounce and strike. He didn't even flutter his eyelids as he stared me down and I realised he was faltering. Courage flared in my chest.

"You won't hurt me, but I can't promise the same for you," a feline smile spread across my mouth as I spoke.

His jaw twitched, and the stark scars against his olive skin flickered ever so slightly. He lunged and I dived into a forward roll to get out of the way. I had not realised I had been staring at Eli until the very last second. A chill seeped through from the snow clinging to my back and hair and I whipped around, forcing all my weight into a right-handed punch, which was quickly blocked by his thick hand. His fingers gripped my arm, twisting and turning me as he swivelled us, until my back was flush to his chest, my arm pinned between us. His knee dipped into the crease of my own, forcing me to fall forward, knees crashing into the snowy earth. My arm was locked behind my back, but his fingers didn't dig in and his grip wasn't harsh enough. He was going easy on me and anger flared in my gut. Gone were the days when he treated me like an equal, when we were children it seemed.

Wriggling, I saw my opportunity. My heels were positioned adequately in between his legs, and a prized shot would have him reeling. A small chuckle escaped my lips and I swiftly kicked up with my heel, his crotch in aim. But he reacted quickly, protecting what all men deemed precious, but that was my cue. His brace on me slackened as he dodged, freeing my arm completely. I leaned forward with all my weight on my palm, the frosted ground and dying leaves rough on my skin. I twisted, bringing my leg around, knocking his own legs out from underneath him. As his back hit the earth and I promptly pinned him, my sodden knees on his shoulders, my hands pinning either side of his head.

Clapping echoed behind me, followed by the jingling of coins being poured from a purse. I smiled, victorious. I was panting as I looked at Eli, my smile causing my cheeks to ache.

His face gave away nothing, and there was no flicker of bruised pride or incredulity. He was unreadable, blank in the eyes and mouth, watching me. It sobered me and sudden awareness edged its way throughout my body. I was a breadth away from his face, almost sharing air. **Enough**, was my only thought.

I began to rise when his foot and ankle tangled tightly around my outstretched leg and he rolled us, flipping my body onto my back as he followed, pinning *me* to the floor. The air whooshed from my lungs and my ribs throbbed in pain, causing me to wince, as air gushed out between my clenched teeth. My gasp of protest and pain was drowned out by Roman's thunderous laughter.

I could only hiss as I forced cold air back into my lungs.

Fuck. Damn the five coppers and my brother.

Blinking and inwardly cursing myself for such a falter, I sighed, "thank you for teaching me humility."

His weight shifted and he hauled me up with him, one hand in mine, the other on my lower back. I gasped again, feeling that my rib must truly be fractured. Alarm formed on Eli's face as he saw my hand clutched to my ribs. He came closer towards me, fear in his eyes, but I stopped him with my hand. I brushed off the leaves and freezing mud that now covered my only clean pair of riding trousers, annoyed I would have to wash these and my other pair back at camp. But that didn't stop the worry lines on Eli's face as he assessed me.

"It's not from you. I received a few punches to the ribs in that fucking raid." I said, my teeth still clenched.

Roman brushed past me and pulled Eli's slack hand from his side, placing five copper coins into his awaiting palm. "You owe me five coppers, Rhona. Maybe one day you will best him. I think you just need to realise his weakness and then ..." he trailed off, as Eli stealthily hit him in the shoulder, silencing him with a darkened look.

"Have you finished hearing the sound of your own voice?" I chided. "We've probably scared off most of the hunt for at least two miles now," I said, looking through the trees and its quiet inhabitants.

A flutter and snapping caught our attention ahead in the trees and my pain and hurt pride were momentarily forgotten. Pheasants skittered out of the bushes and I picked up my discarded pack quickly, unaware of my shawl falling from my shoulders. Eli caught it before it fell in the snow and placed it gingerly back around me. His eyes didn't meet mine as he did so and a questionable flutter erupted in my stomach. I turned away in time for him not to see the blush that heated my skin.

Chapter 4

The fires were roaring when we returned to camp, the distant clouds mere whispers of dark grey in the twilight. The snow had not yet melted, and our breath still caused magnificent plumes as we walked among the caravans and tents of our travelling troupe. Eli had taken our meagre bounty to his grandmother to add to tonight's cooking pot, allowing Roman and myself to take a seat at our family's hearth. Our uncle's fire was the largest, with only room for direct family and his council to sit. The same men and women had gathered around the traveller King's campfire since my childhood and all were my family and brethren.

We sat on a dead trunk that had been hauled over from the nearby woodland and the heat soon licked at my cold sodden skin, the flames soothing my weary body. The familiar cracking and snapping of logs eased me out of the day's cold grip.

Baja was bemused as he talked to his companions, his streaked hair glinting in the fire light. His gravelly voice bellowed over the roaring flames at us to ask, "not a good kill today?"

My brother answered, "No, not for four miles due south. All tracks led that way, so we followed."

"Ay, seems the snow has spooked them into hiding or caused them to burrow deep enough underground," Baja replied. "The nearby farm, a stone's throw east of here, is empty, save for a few weathered sheep and a bastard cockerel."

A few of my uncle's companions laughed and muttered to each other at that. Baja's caused me to swallow and I was reminded of my mother. He was my mother's only brother and the man who had raised us through our childhood and adolescent years, after she died. Her face flashed in my mind, like it often did, and I swallowed the hard lump in my throat.

"The farm was abandoned?" Roman asked.

"All but the animals, yes," Baja replied, before swigging dark liquid from his broken bottle, aged and green. Whiskey most probably. Lethal stuff. "We took the sheep. Mira is shearing them as we speak. And the cockerel."

There was another rumble of men's laughter.

Mutza, Eli's blind grandmother, tapped the cooking pot with a worn wooden spoon. "I'll be spitting feathers for a week! That beast put up a fight, I tell you. It's not right leaving beasts like that to the weather, alone!"

I laughed wholeheartedly, finally feeling at ease with my family and council, the memories forgotten. All around the fire laughed, and even more so as Mutza glared, her pale, blind eyes darting around the campfire.

"The people must have upped and left a few days ago," Denif muttered, he was my uncle's right hand man and he rubbed his rough jawline thoughtfully. A single gold hoop was pierced through his right ear and his dark hair was covered by a blue linen scarf, knotted tightly at the nape of his neck. Even with the fires raging, we still sat heaped in winter coats and furs. I did not know if it was the cold that caused my sudden shiver or Denif's words.

"Anything valuable?" Roman asked, that feverish glint in his dark eyes.

Baja only tutted. "Your mother and I raised you better than that boy."

The remark had stung, hitting its mark as Roman receded slightly. ***Stupid idiot.***

I dug an elbow into Roman's side, rolling my eyes and watched from the corner of my vision as he played with his silver ring, twisting it around his finger. It was his tell, for when he was ashamed or upset.

The billowing steam of the stew pot caused my stomach to growl loudly, but it stopped mid roar as I saw Miriam stirring the steaming contents. Miriam was my uncle's new wife. She was round with child and only a few years older than myself, but she was not skilled with the cooking. In fact, her meals in the past had been downright disastrous. Roman caught my eye and he too looked displeased, and nearly nauseous, at Miriam cooking. He grimaced, sticking out his tongue. I had to cover my mouth, to hide my snort.

"Who has prepared tonight's food?" Roman asked, and everyone around the fire quieted.

Miriam turned to face him, her expression frustrated as she replied, "Mutza has cooked this evening."

There was a mass sigh of relief and Baja seemed to flinch.

"Mutza has cooked every meal these past two weeks, in fact," she said eyeing us all.

A few men tried stifling their coughs and snickers and I bit down on my lip, remembering the turmeric and rabbit pie she had made. However, it hadn't been turmeric, but pure mustard seeds ground to a pulp, causing my mouth to burn for days after. Roman leant towards me, feigning to pass a skin of water.

"At least it will be edible," he murmured, eyes twinkling.

"I heard that," Miriam snapped, as she suddenly passed behind us, smacking Roman over the head with a wooden spoon and raucous laughter rolled out of everyone. Thankfully something edible and utterly delicious was passed around; root, rooster and pheasant stew was eaten greedily by each man and woman. The single rabbit we had returned with was to be dried and used for meat later the next day.

Comforted and satisfied, I felt myself relax further, with a small smile on my face. Roman took out his small water skin again and from the smell, it was not water. He swigged, wriggling his eyebrows, and passed it to me. The liquor smelt rancid and peppery, but it didn't dissuade me as I took a sip, the liquid burning my lips and my tongue. I nearly gagged, spluttering the drink down my chin.

Eli chose that moment to sit next to Roman, amid my spitting and coughing and I flushed, quickly wiping my chin. I was never good with whiskey. Well, I was never good with any strong spirit, but great Mother above, that was humiliating.

Eli's side smile only made my cheeks darken and heat even more as I glimpsed him from the corner of my eye. Roman proceeded to beat me on the back, feigning worry at my spluttering and I smacked him hard across the knuckles with my hand, my throat still burning from the whiskey.

Bastard.

"What in all the darkness is-" I managed, wiping my chin.

"Denif's new concoction, made with grapes and hops," Roman said with a slight shiver.

"Aye," Denif spoke up from across the fire, swigging his own mugful. "It will put the hairs on even a babe's chest!"

We all laughed as he even began spluttering.

Mutza coughed, silencing the gathered circle. Her unseeing eyes looked to the heavens above and all quieted as we prepared ourselves.

The sky above was an abyss of unending black, littered with white glowing stars and clusters of beautiful light. I watched, searching high above for a glittering streak or shimmer, but the night was still, with only the unmoving stars in the fathomless black.

"A story? One for such an auspicious night, that is this very eve?" Mutza's rasping voice was the sole focus of my concentration, as it seemed to be for everyone around our campfire.

Others had gathered from smaller campfires to hear her tale. I took another swig from Roman's skin, bracing myself for the burn, but it slid down my throat easier this time, the liquid filling my belly with its fiery taste.

"These tales of old, as you all know, were passed down from my mother, and her mother before her and so on, back to the very first travelling family; from those that chose the unsettled path, and that chose to walk the Earth with kin and beast alike, and to not settle or find a true home that wasn't the wild."

Her words filled me, reaching that place of knowing deep within my soul. My eyes caught something, Roman, recounting her introduction word for word. Her stories had always started this way, from as far back as my memory would allow.

"We travellers do this for one reason and one reason only. Although our bloodline doesn't sing the chorus of the wild as it used to, there are still those that walk among us that are blessed with the old songs, quiet and almost unheard."

Again, my brother chose that moment to look my way and something tugged at my heart as we shared a smile.

"We folk have always seen those that are not there to the normal eye..." This wasn't a new story, but one we had not heard for a long time. "And why should we not. We, who sleep under the stars and bathe in natural wells. We who sleep under stars and follow the winds like a compass of life. We have always been kin with the very earth we walk on. We have always been a friend to those who share this land," she took a breath, her blind eyes searching in the direction of the gathered crowd.

Even more of our clan had huddled around our fire to hear and my gaze fell on all who had gathered. Contented smiles were stretched across faces and there was a lull as we settled in, soaking up the fire's warmth. As my eyes roamed, my uncle's expression caught me off guard. He looked perturbed. His brow was crossed and riveted, and there was sadness in his eyes as he looked at the old woman, recognising the tale she was about to tell. Usually he was joyful and enraptured when Mutza told stories about his campfire, and I chewed my bottom lip, wondering what could have disturbed him so. His eyes darted and caught my own, and he held me in a look that sent a shiver over my skin. He swallowed, his face illuminated by the amber glow of the fire and looked down, defeated.

My heart sank remembering our conversation the night before. Was he still irked by our talk? By the lie I had told, so transparently? Had I displeased him? Many thoughts swirled chaotically in my head and I dug my blunt fingers deep into the palm of my hand. The pain and pressure, centred and focused me, bringing my attention back to Mutza and the beginnings of her tale.

"Although, with some beings it is not reciprocated. But we dwell where other folk care not to. We walk during the day and the night and see the wonders of the world under the sun and the moon. We see and help all creatures upon this earth, as it was once our duty and right. The gift of our sight held a price and we have battled the darkness as much as any other soul. However, the burden is greater with us travelling folk. We know of the others who share this earth, ethereal and evil. We do not hide from such creature and beast. We walk alongside them."

Only the crackling fire could be heard over Mutza's words as the flames spat, devouring another log in an array of golden sparks.

"There was a time, long ago, when a manner of darkness spread across the world. It was a darkness so great and terrible, that from its unfitting reign over this world, spawned mysterious and foul beings alike."

My heart pulsed hard against my ribs at that moment, as I began to remember this story from long ago.

"And it started with the love of a woman."

This story had been heard many times by our people, but every time Mutza told it, we all gathered, whispered and made awed noises. Thinking back, I realised the last time I had heard this story was that of my fourteenth year, an entire year after my mother had been killed. That had been over six years ago.

"But we all know how the story begins. You see, the Sun God and Moon Goddess had watched over this earth before feet walked upon it. In the beginning they saw that with every passing century, darkness seemed to seep, like ink in water, over the very world they had strived to light. The Sun God rid the earth of shadow during the long hours of the day and the Moon Goddess shone light over all in the deepest night. They saw how powerful the evil had become, and how much it hungered to devour and eliminate that light, so the Sun God and the Moon Goddess created seven children. The seven daughters who embodied the very powers that moved the world into life. But after a time, darkness and evil found its way even into one of their hearts. It warped her, twisting her very face, body and soul; a physical representation of the manner of evil that dwelled far beneath. We all know whom I speak."

A wind caressed my cheeks, and the flames suddenly engorged with the wind in answer to Mutza's words.

"The darkness, this great evil from worlds beyond our own, had stalked the sisters. It watched these blessed beings blossom with gifts more powerful than any. The darkness knew what these women could be capable of and it wanted to vanquish them from the earth forever more and claim this world as its own. No one knows exactly how the darkness turned the first sister from her blessed path, but this tale tells it to be love. Love made that one sister abandon the very gifts the Sun and Moon had so graciously bestowed upon her and the darkness beseeched her, turning her into everything she and her sisters were created to protect against. They had been granted these gifts for one purpose only, to rid the earth of such darkness. This story begins with the oldest sister, the first daughter forged, Armelle.

Old words say Armelle's mind was a force to be reckoned with and that she had a heart as strong as the northern wind. Her power lay with the air and sky high above us, for she could control the winds and weather. For Armelle was the Sun and Moon's aid, moving and shifting the skies to bring about the light in the day and the dark of the night. But she had been the first forged from the earth and had walked a lonely path, until her sisters had been crafted. The darkness saw her fear of loneliness and played with her worry at becoming lonesome again.

The darkness tempted her in the form of a man. A man who promised she would never walk alone in this world. She became twisted by his love, becoming false and unfeeling. It broke her into submission and it, or should I say 'he', became her bedmate. She became the Fallen Sister." Mutza paused. The flames suddenly withdrew then rose in a billowing furnace of sparks again and all of us eased back at the sudden roar of unexpected heat. Mutza only smiled her knowing smile.

I glanced at Eli and a small smile touched my lips at seeing him enraptured in his grandmother's tale. His pale scars gleamed slightly, as his throat bobbed and as if on instinct, he looked towards me and I hurriedly looked back to old woman, swallowing hard.

I inhaled deeply, feeling the soft buzz of the alcohol beginning to soothe my aching limbs and restless mind.

"There were seven sisters, as this story began with, and I will not focus all my attention on the Fallen One. Her sisters, the souls and guardians of this very earth, have just as an important part to play as she. After Armelle was created, the magnificent Sun and Moon created and brought to life the second sister, Iria. Iria brought life to the ground beneath our feet and she provided the colourful landscape we are so fortunate to walk and ride over."

There was a low rumble of agreement and a soft murmur of noise from us all.

"Then there was Sarine, the creator of the oceans, lakes and streams that run like life-giving veins across the world, of which we humbly use and seek out. Following Sarine, they created Javhara, who brought to life the animals and beasts we share this land with, and who we walk beside, master and eat. We give praise to her creations every day. The twins Wylista and Raina came to life next. Wylista's creation brought to this quiet silent world the sounds and songs of nature and voice, of which I treasure daily, as a storyteller. When the moon birthed Raina, she stole knowledge and words, something Wylista couldn't exist without. Both Wylista and Raina are a path to knowledge, of listening and learning, to better oneself. Something we, all travellers, strive to do in this world."

All around the campfire knew what was coming. The story changed along with my breath and I handed the drinks pouch back to Roman, my belly fired and warm from dinner and the alcohol. I looked at my brother smiling, feeling the peacefulness of this moment.

"And then came Falin. The only sister gifted by both Sun God and Moon Goddess with all that they could not do on this earth, and that her sisters were not gifted with before her. They gifted her with the ability to walk amongst the darkness and shadows. She was in darkness herself but with the inner light from the moon. The Moon Goddess had sacrificed some of her very essence, her very light against the endless night. The Moon gave up her ability to shine her glorious white light, every night and gave it to Falin, to allow her not to fully fall into shadow. Since the gift of her light to her daughter, the Moon only shines fully whole every twenty-nine days."

We looked up at the waxen moon, shining in a haze of pale light, lonely and hollow, accompanied only by a few stars.

"Falin, who was also made from the darkness, saw it for what it truly was. She saw how it had debased and violated her sister."

A shiver crept its way up my spine.

"After a time, with the darkness deep within Armelle, whispering in her ear, the sisters finally began to see what their sister had become. The skies had darkened, and foul weather encased the earth, stopping the Sun and the Moon's light from filtering through and the land began to die. The creatures and beings began to wither and decay. Armelle, through the darkness that had twisted her, began to steal the essence of each sister, to fuel the need of the ever-absorbing darkness. Together they created creatures and beings of our darkest nightmares, so evil and depraved, that for a millennium, their ancestors still haunt, hunt and plague this very land. The six remaining sisters, seeing the beasts ravaging the earth, created their own beings to battle those that were not natural to this once beautiful land. But it was not enough. Armelle was growing in power and hatred every day. They saw what she had now become; she was a creature of darkness and evil."

I inhaled, filling my lungs, as my ears strained to hear every detail.

"Her sisters, Iria, Sarine, Javhara, Wylistia, Raina and Falin, realised what their sister had become, and they knew they needed to act. Armelle's power dominated the sky, allowing no light upon the earth, and they could not conquer that, so the sisters came about a plan. They could not defeat the darkness, as no matter what, it would still linger long on this world, after they were gone. But they could separate their sister from it. So, they chose to trap her in a prison of oak and elm. In a great tree, grown by Iria from the centre of the earth. Sarine watered and fed the tree, empowering it to grow and strengthen. Javhara, created beings who would forever walk the earth and guard the living prison. Wylistia and Raina worked together, encasing Armelle in silence, so the darkness could never breathe or whisper in her ears again."

I stilled as a familiar twinge took form in my gut.

"Its roots drove deep into the earth and branches high into the sky, as though straining for freedom. They had trapped her in what we now know as the Fallow lands, by the Fallow Mountain."

A hushed whisper of awe circulated around the campfire. We had grown up hearing stories of the Fallow, and of the creatures who dwelled within. The Fallow had always played a part in our childhood.

Mutza took a staggering breath and the firelight distorted her face, causing me to take pause. "But even imprisonment was not enough, for the tree could not keep such evil within forever. So the sisters guarded Armelle's prison as it grew and or a thousand years, they stood and protected this land, this world from their sisters foul creatures, until they became part of the forest themselves. They became trees, guarding their fallen sister from ever escaping. But this fate was not for all."

Roman knocked my leg, his enjoyment evident on his face. This was one of his favourite stories, that had been told to him and our clan, long before I was born.

"Falin, the last child of the Sun and the Moon, who was made from the shadow itself, could not become a tree, for she was between the light and the dark; she was the balance. She created the wards. The wards that, along with her sister's tree's, guards the continent and its humans from the creatures within. She lived for many years, watching the world turn and birthed many children of her own. We can still see Falin's lineage and imprint upon the dirt that we walk, the forest we pass and the sky we sleep under. We can see her bloodline within women that walk amongst us today, in the descendants of the children she bore long, long ago. The witches, of white magic and black magic. The balance between the light and the dark, good and evil."

Mutza's words seemed to weave a tapestry of unease about me, just as a soft wind rustled the nearby trees, sending sparks to float and flutter from the campfires. The fire snapped with a mighty crack as a log disintegrated in the flames causing all to jump, yet again. A murmur of laughter went around the gathered circle, all shocked and engaged by the story.

I had heard this story before by Mutza, but tonight's telling set me on edge with an untold cold that was set deep into my bones. My mind wandered back across the past ten years. We were all too familiar with witches; our last encounter was some time ago, when a witch killed three of our men. Well, butchered more like. The witches were scarce and did not publicly show themselves anymore. Too many were hunted down and persecuted for magic or untold crimes, good and bad.

I looked across the roaring flames to see Mutza's blind eyes directed on me and a pang of unease rippled across my skin.

Unnerved, I looked to Roman and asked, "when was the last time you saw one of the magic folk?"

"Three years ago...yes, three. That was the last. We all know how that ended." Roman's face paled at the memory. "But nothing since. No passing tales or gossip, or that of any other creature for that matter."

It was true, we had not heard or encountered a thing from village folk or fellow travelling families and clans.

"And so it goes; we travellers were placed on this land to rid the world of the filth and Bastards of the Broken, blah blah blah," Baja hiccupped, the whiskey slurring his words. He rubbed at his face and I gripped Roman. Baja rarely got drunk. The king of the clan, usually a pillar of responsibility and sound mind, was drunk. I gawked, clinging to Roman. He only looked at me warily in response.

"Our bloodline, Baja, is that of Falin," Mutza spat, her face twisted. "We travellers were born from one of her children. You should not scuffle my words. Your own father was of mixed blood, as was your sister Chrizta," Mutza blurted out, over the fire.

Everyone went silent. This was common knowledge, but it was only ever discussed in whispered tones. My grandfather was of mixed blood. His mother, my great grandmother, had been a witch, and white or black, we did not know. The tale was only known to our family, but she was not of our clan. She had been a witch on the run, and my great grandfather had given her a safe haven. From that moment, he had fallen in love with a witch, married her, and together they had birthed and raised their only son, my grandfather, father to Baja and my mother. I had never known my grandfather. Roman had, but all I knew was that he had died before I was brought into the world. They say magic can only be passed through the female and that is why all white and black witches are women, and that it is uncommon for them to even birth males. But nonetheless I would have liked to have met him. I would have liked to have known him, and to have heard his stories of the witch that became an 'unwanted'.

Shame flitted through me at the thought, as my mother's face paraded across my eyes. My throat closed, lungs tightening. Instinctively, my fingers pinched the soft skin at my wrist, hard enough to leave a bruise. The pain shot up my arm. It took a few moments for me to settle my thoughts and bring my focus back to the fire and all who sat around it. Their faces caught me first, dumbstruck, and wary and watching the battle going on between Mutza and my uncle.

"Quiet, woman! We will speak no more of this. They haven't got a drop of magical blood between them." Baja waved at me and Roman.

I straightened, realising the topic of conversation.

Roman leaned in close. "Thankfully," he ushered under his breath.

I hadn't realised he was passing back the skin of whiskey and I took it, taking another long fiery swig. It didn't burn as harshly this time or cause me to cough and wheeze. As I downed it, I saw across the flames such an unease in my uncle, a restlessness that I had never witnessed before.

"There hasn't been a beast to flay or a daemon to kill in nearly thirty years. The folk haven't sought us out in over a decade. Non-travellers haven't heard or witnessed their kind for a lot longer. And the creature, the black witch, we endured three years ago was diluted," he said, rubbing his hands in his face again. Miriam, stood behind him, scowling at Mutza and my heart warmed as she touched my uncle's shoulder and rubbed it soothingly.

Both were correct. My uncle Baja, and the traveller king before him, had rarely encountered any mythical beasts or creatures of which our ancestors once had. However, Mutza and my mother had still taught me as a child what they were, what they looked like and what they could do. Their lessons were always something I had enjoyed and looked forward to. When my mother died, was killed, was murdered... I physically shook myself. When my mother died, Mutza had taken over my lessons, but as I grew older, they began to decrease. They stopped entirely when I came of age, and I was left with no teachings, other than my uncle, brother, and Eli's guidance.

"Thank the great Mother she was!" Mutza continued as some of our people about the campfire found other topics of conversation to talk of. "Falin's bloodline still lives and breathes today, as do the other children from when they were of monstrous form. They may have slunk back from the darkness in which they came, Baja, but they are still there," Mutza spat. She looked over to me and Roman, a strange line set across her withered mouth.

A look passed between my uncle and Mutza, as a battle of will and determination creased both their faces. Something aired between them and both looked away from the other. Mutza looked blindly to the stars above and my uncle continued to stare into the roaring flames.

"But that was a millennia ago," Mutza began again, diverting the conversation and I was thankful for a change in topic.

My skin prickled and I realised I was still being observed and that the eyes upon me were from others around our fire. I squirmed under their scrutiny, unable to stand it.

"The Sun and Moon still guard us with their light. The sister's guardians and Falin's wards still protect us from those that were banished to the Fallow, from those that reside in the north."

I leaned in close to Roman, "have we ever travelled that far north?"

His eyes shot to me and I watched him lick his lips. "Not in my lifetime. We've never ventured further than Tarra Knox. That's the furthest I have travelled, and I was still a babe."

I didn't realise he had travelled so far north, even as a baby. The furthest of the Continent I had travelled was to the Savage Vale, but no further.

"What do you think is past the Fallow?" I asked.

"They say the Forgotten Lands, where the witches and other creatures live. But I wouldn't know. I don't think I want to, to be honest," Roman replied, eyes distant.

I rubbed my hands, imagining what land lay past the Fallow in the north. From the maps I had seen as a child, the Fallow *was* the north. I had never thought there could be something further than that. The idea didn't sit well with me and I chewed my lip absently, thinking about what could dwell in the furthest reaches of this strange land we called home. Whether it be witches or other creatures, we didn't know, but the thought caused me to shiver.

"We haven't worked with or had dealings with witches for what, ten years?" I watched his features scrunch, as he raked through his memory.

"Not for at least fifteen years. Since the last ascension," he said, gruffly.

I thought back as far as my mind would allow. It was true, I had only been a small child, when we personally had met with a witch. It had been during the pagan ascension. When the death of the Crone rebirthed the cycle of the Trinity, and a new witch was chosen, to then ascend, and become the Maiden. The former, growing and evolving into the Mother and so on. It happened every one hundred years. The birth, growth and end of the cycle. Falin's last lineage.

"Enough old one," Baja bellowed, and I brought back with crashing clarity to the fire and the argument still ensuing. "No more stories tonight. We are safe and sound, together once again, under the stars. Let us give thanks for that tonight, at least." And with that, a shrill tuning of a fiddle rang out and the crumpled Brovnik began to play an upbeat melody.

A hand beaten drum commenced its rhythm and the cold that had begun to creep and set spines, eased with the music. Within mere minutes the disquiet had vanished, and all seemed merry again. My uncle played his guitar and Denif played along with his flute. All the talk was forgotten, as the music flowed and pulsed with the roaring fire. Fresh logs were dumped upon it, spurting new heat and life as the flames swelled and rose high into the sky. Drinks sloshed in cups as the dancing started and our folk songs and voices rang out into the quiet night.

This was how most nights began, on such 'auspicious nights', as Mutza would call it. I drank, as did everyone else, until a haze fogged my clarity. The fire was loaded with more wood and the snow had nearly disappeared from the heat and stomping feet. Denif stopped the flute and my uncle played solely on his guitar, with the odd accompanying thump of a drum beating rhythmically to the sweet and gentle melody.

I cursed under my breath, recognising the tune. It was the traveller's courting dance and my kin joined in pairs to begin their caper. Couples old and young began the intricate steps, timed to the beat and pluck of each guitar string. I saw Merci get coerced into the dance with Taren, her sullen eyes trailing Roman as he sat next to our uncle and drank obliviously. I smirked, watching the bodies create patterns with their movement and limbs and I was happy just to watch for a time. Suddenly, something caught at my senses and I felt familiar eyes appraising me. I knew who it was and found myself feeling this sensation more so than ever before. Since Eli and my brother had returned, it was something I couldn't ignore, and like a distant thrum in my veins, I knew where to expect him. I could feel Eli within the camp and anticipated wherever he could be. He was my betrothed, technically, although we were not. Could it be, now that I was of age, I was just more aware of him, knowing him in the way that a sister looks for a brother? I couldn't place my finger on it. But I knew, his eyes were upon me, as if this dance now gave him the fidgets too.

"Eli, take Rhona for a spin!"

I froze at my brother's holler across the crowd. His eyes weren't the only ones on me. Cursing under my breath, I called him every foul name under the sun in my head. ***Insufferable bastard swine.***

"Yes, Eli, your betrothed awaits." Taren's voice echoed across the music and laughter that bubbled, as he and Merci twirled beside me. I looked around the fire and bodies dancing, as my betrothed began stalking towards me. Eli's face betrayed nothing, stonelike as always and I swallowed.

His coat was off, with his chest and scar peeking above his linen shirt and I silently marvelled at his broad shoulders. It felt like an eternity for him to walk over to me, as I once again, looked over to Roman as he conspiratorially whispered to my uncle. The sight of them together smirking at me made my blood boil. If they wanted a show, they would get one.

After removing my military jacket with vigour, I un-braided my hair, and my mass of dark waves tumbled around me.

Fuck Roman and his games.

By the time Eli had reached me, I had unclasped my hunting knife and was physically ready. But when I felt the heat of him, come up behind me, my lung locked and my mind spun dizzyingly. His calloused hand outstretched before me, waiting and I inhaled deeply, unlocking my lungs. He was waiting for permission to touch me, and my heart thudded hard in my chest. Ever the silent gentleman. Trembling, I brought my hand up and placed it upon his. His fingers squeezed mine and the light in his eyes sharpened, as a brief smile tugged at his mouth. That smile soothed away the tremors and I grinned at him.

"Let's give the prick a show," I said, mischievously, and Eli returned it with his own wicked grin.

He swung me round, catching me off guard, causing me to squeal like an adolescent girl. His smile only bloomed as we began the dance we had once had to do as betrothed children. I heard Roman and Baja's laughter as we partook in the steps, an entanglement of arms and stepping of feet. Spinning around and around, changing partners every twelve steps, until we came back to one another. The alcohol in my belly eased my mood into lucid enjoyment and I began to smile and laugh at the dance, joyful and carefree. I couldn't relax completely though, as my stomach dropped every time Eli's eyes caught mine. Each time his hand gripped my waist as we moved closer, heat pooled in my core and as his hands entwined in mine, flutters erupted over my skin.

The music ended and my back was slick with sweat. Eli bowed low and I began to curtsy in my riding pants and boots, smiling even more broadly when I turned it unabashedly into a bow. There was a cheer and the clapping of hands around as all the dancers bowed and departed.

Eli's eyes lingered on my mouth as I stood, heaving cold air in my lungs. Loose curls fell across my eyes and I wrestled with my hair, trying to tame it once again onto a braid.

Roman met us and clapped a heavy hand on both of our shoulders. "I say we marry you both tonight, before sanity crashes down upon thee."

Every warm and joyful feeling was washed away then, as cold ran through me at his words. I wanted to pull away with a hiss as the darkness began to creep in and I physically shook myself. Neither noticed and I managed to school myself.

"Trust you to ruin a nice thing," was all I could manage with a false smirk, before stumbling away.

I was unable to face them after that and walked back to the log and sat watching the merriment continue. More drink was passed around and other dances commenced at the new melodies played. I couldn't bring myself to enjoy it after my brother's words, so I sat silently, with glazed eyes, pretending to watch the festivities. No one could see or hear the flashes and screams that rang out like haunting echoes in my head. I tried to keep my resolve composed, but it was no use. So, I drank more and more, until the fire before me swirled and I became finally comfortable in my solace. The darkened memories disappeared with each glug and swallow of whiskey and after a time, the music began to lull until only a slow, lonesome tune filled the night air. In my befuddled state, I recognised that tune. Like a painting of smeared brush strokes, the memory came into life in vivid colour. My mother and her voice echoed in me. The lyrics were sad, but beautiful and the words creeped upon me and I could feel my mouth moving, forming each sorrowful sound. I sat staring into the flames, the tune filling my very lungs as each line poured out of me.

"*I am stretched out in the heather fields, and I will lay here under the moon,*

If only your hands were in mine, why did you have to leave so soon,

My sun, my moon, my brightness. It is time we were together,
As you are all I dream of, as death takes you forever..."

The song surged up my throat with each slow incline of Brovnik's fiddle, until the words and verses ended, and in my haze, I was greeted by silence and a company of wide eyes. Roman sat staring, his eyes glazed with unshed tears. All were watching me, that sorrowful memory in their minds, thanks to the song and my drunken singing. Baja looked upon me and I couldn't recognise whether it was love or shame that plagued his face.

"You sound just like her," he rasped, across the fire.

I stumbled upright, my footing off and balance, but Eli caught me, leaning across my brother to steady me. He stood, both hands on my upper arms holding me still as the world about me seemed to spin, and I closed my eyes against the onslaught. My knee gave way, but firm hands caught me, lifting me. And then everything went black.

Chapter 5

I awoke groggy and aching, my stomach wretched and mouth tasting like arse. ***I had danced***. I had danced a lot. My sore feet and twinging muscles complained, and my head spun. I yawned and nearly gagged, my dry throat cried out for water. I looked about the space, trying to find my basin and pitcher of water, and my stomach dropped as I realised I was not in my wagon.

My heart began to pound as the surroundings came into sharp focus. I was nearly sick, panic ebbing its way up my throat in liquid form, when I finally recognised the smell. It was Eli's wagon. Relief coursed through me, though my heart was still beating hard from too much drink the night before.

My hands patted down my body and I was thankfully fully clothed but in his bed. I looked at the candlelit space and took in the details flickering before me. Eli's home was small and nearly empty, with only the essentials placed about the wooden box cabin. One wall held hunting knives, traps, arrows and his crossbow, and the other held three full bookshelves, nailed directly to the wall, secured with leather straps. There were so many books; I had not known Eli was such an avid reader, that a part of me felt displeased he had not told me. Everything was clean and free of clutter, without candle wax residue pouring down the sides and onto the floor, like it did my own. Everything was simply in place. The smell of leather, salt and sage filled the room, smelling distinctly of Eli.

I looked around the small space, but he was nowhere to be seen. A blanket lay folded in the corner on a small chair, but there was no evidence he had stayed the night in his cabin with me. I moved the covers and stepped out of the bed, rubbing my aching neck. I opened the caravan door and the light nearly blinded me, causing me to hiss as I squinted, looking about the open area. The sun, though covered by clouds, was high in the sky. It was past noon. I stepped out of the caravan, inhaling a breath so fresh and cold; it stirred the fogginess into painful clarity. I inhaled again, trying to ease my stomach from hurling its contents onto the floor.

Roman greeted me first, as I walked unsteadily back to my caravan a few paces away.

"How are you feeling?" His tone suggested worry which brought about a sudden annoyance, like a flint infighting a flame. I could only glare at him. "Well you look like shit, so I thought I would be genuinely polite and ask," he scoffed. He wore his hunting clothes, with thick fur against the day's chill. The snow around wagons and tents was still solid but all through camp there were sodden, muddy brown pathways from our people, milling about.

I hissed, feeling the cold bite my clammy skin.

"Alright, alright," he said, already sensing my mood. "Do you realise this is what fun feels like the morning after?" he said, and I groaned.

"No wonder I don't do this. This is why," I chided, cracking my neck and wincing at my cracked ribs.

"You'll get used to it. I've been up since dawn. But Eli and I caught nothing."

My face flamed at his name. "Did Eli-"

Roman finished my question with a slight smirk of his mouth. "-Put you to bed because you were too drunk? Yes." I groaned again. "Your wagon was locked and you're a lump, so he had to lay you to rest in his.

Poor sod, he had to sleep on the floor," Roman finished and I sighed in utter embarrassment and shame.

"It's called having fun, Rhona. Something we all know you're not good at." It was true but it didn't stop me from slapping him sharply on the arm. He stumbled dramatically, pretending to be in pain, his face creasing.

A smile tugged at my lips. "I feel awful," I confessed, noticing that my clothes smelled of campfire, sweat and whiskey. It was enough to bring acid to my throat.

"Mutza will have something for that. And the voice. You sounded like a dying cat last night." My mouth went into a horrified "O" as I remembered singing. Singing my mother's song. Roman saw the alarm on my face. "I am joking. You did sound like her though. You were good." His features turned solemn as he looked at me, "you should sing more."

My chest tightened and it took everything in me not to wince at his words. "I'll go see Mutza and take a long cold bath in the stream," I managed before walking away.

Roman's only reply was, "good, you look and smell awful."

After a few tonics and food, I began to feel relatively normal. I bathed and washed with great effort in the freezing stream. It woke me, bitterly, but took the edge away from the nausea that still rolled my gut. I kept telling myself the steady unease building in my stomach was from the onslaught of drink and dancing and nothing else.

There had been nothing to hunt for four miles, Roman told me later, and they didn't dare venture too far from camp. Eli was scarce as I wandered about camp, distracting myself by seeing to Balthazar and helping where I could. I would not be drinking tonight. Or tomorrow. Or the foreseeable future.

In the early afternoon, I sat by the fire watching the children play near the tree line. The cold seemed to scratch me today, causing my skin to prickle up and down my arms and legs. I couldn't get warm, even by nestling closely by the blazing fire, wrapped in my coat and woollen shawl.

The log creaked beside me as Eli sat down and I felt myself straighten. His scarred hands were in front of my face, handing me a chipped China cup of broth, its steam billowing and inviting. I took it gladly, a small shy smile tugging at the corner of my mouth. I inhaled the wisps of warmth and then recoiled, nearly gagging as my stomach twisted and nearly heaved. Another tonic.

Eli grunted, nudging the cup with his calloused hand, urging me to drink. I thinned my lips at the silent command, whilst Eli watched the flames in the cold afternoon light. Words tumbled out before I had a chance to chew on them.

"Thank you. For last night, I mean."

He just continued to look into the fire.

It only spurred me on more as a sudden agitation crept over me, causing me to twist and wring my hands, and the skin on my neck and cheeks to turn hot. "I feel like death walking today." That got a smile from his lips and like a wave, my agitation washed away. "I don't know how Roman can be so fresh after such liquor."

He finally looked at me, his blue and brown eyes focusing. Fidgeting, I tried tidying my unruly hair, no doubt a mess of bedraggled curls and fly away strands. I licked my lips, hoping I didn't look as pathetic as I felt. My mirror had shown me the peaky skin and shadowed eyes unkindly this morning.

Firelight flickered over his scarred neck and jaw as he swallowed. He gracefully signalled with his hand, fingers retracting and shaping, going to his throat, signing to me. '*You sang beautifully.*'

My cheeks and neck flared with heat again as an agonising blush crept over my sallow skin. I was never drinking again. I remembered the song, its words creating blurred ripples in my mind's eye. Me singing, my mother humming it as a lullaby, my mother singing to the fiddle as the melancholy sounds of the bow and strings simpered with her ageless voice. I shuddered.

"It won't happen again," I said, unable to tolerate the lyrics, singing and spinning in my head.

I saw his brow crease in his usual manner as he looked back to the flames, to our people going about their business. Anywhere but me. I didn't blame him, but he did not know, nor understand how much those words haunted me. How my mother's voice haunts my every waking moment. My lungs seemed to contract, and I couldn't, wouldn't, be that person today. So I twisted next to Eli, my neck cracking with the forced stretch. My body was in a pitiful, tiresome state. I yawned widely, unable to look at Eli, knowing the redness was still evident on my face. Eli, stone-faced once more, signed for me to sleep and I nodded, in thorough agreement, and made my way back to my cabin, feeling his lingering eyes tail me all the way.

***

I slept for a few hours, nestled deep within my blankets, but I was awoken by a memory of a hissing voice in my dream that chilled me to my core and brought sweat all over my skin. The sound of my screaming as a child left me as soon as I opened my eyes and I gasped, almost thrashing. The smell of home filled my nose and not of a roaring fire and blistering skin. I willed my heart to slow as I steadied myself upright to look at my home.

My caravan was warm and dully lit. Some of the candles were smouldering stumps of feeble light, that flickered soundlessly. I stretched, feeling my muscles creak and abase the stiffness as the dream slowly faded to my reality, relieving me of my past. Inhaling deep, I felt better, my body now rested and limber and I sat for a time, staring, and allowing the darkening shadows that clawed at my dreams to finally disappear.

I made myself get up from my pile of blankets, the cold raking its fingers over my skin so I could light new candles, leaving the old, desecrated ones in their places to smoulder and die. The medallions and trinkets twinkled and glittered in the new warming light and my wooden floor creaked under my steps as I moved about the cabin, washing and taming my hair. My head had begun to throb, and I hastily sat back on my bed, looking about my small home, rubbing my temples slowly. The stacks of books beside my bed, beckoned me and began pulling at the dusty book sleeves and covers.

My fingers found warped bindings and fragile papers. It was a book of recordings, of predictions, from one of my mother's ancestors, as old as a hundred years. I carefully opened the aged parchment, aware that the coarse spine barely held the pages safely together anymore. There were no pictures, just words from hands forgotten long ago. Some writing was in ink made from clay and coal of the earth, others scrawled in blood; the writing of women that came before me, of my mother, and even my grandmother who I had never known. Each woman's words described predictions for members of my past family, the Lords and Ladies of the realm from long ago.

I remember the first time I received it. It was handed down to me, like it had been to the women of our family. It detailed, to my surprise, different creatures encountered by our people over the years. I scanned through the rest of the ancient books and journals, looking for newer coverings and bindings to find the words of my mother. I found an unblemished book, well used but without the smell of aged paper and ink. I flicked over the handwriting, reading and skipping retellings until I finally found what I had been looking for; my grandmother's flourished words were scrawled in long lines across the page. It told the story of a night long ago, when my mother was a child, when our clan had stumbled across a black witch. A single woman walking the road alone at night. A black witch who enchanted their campfire into a walking creature of flames. My grandmother called it the 'Burning Man', the explicit letters a mess of blotted black ink. I read the slope of each word, penned quickly and it was as though I could taste the fear in each letter and symbol. The next words I read made my blood run cold.

My brother, my Nikosth is now gone, forever. The Burning Man devoured him. The witch with ivory skin and hair like honey, only laughed at me, as I coveted the medallion of Nefferia at my heart. Protection against flame and ash, protection against the children of the Fallen one.

The children of the Fallen One and her sisters were both good and evil and Mutza's story from the other night swirled in my mind, a story we had heard so many times around our campfire with old and new brethren. I closed the journal, looking about my home as I had done hundreds of times, for the one volume of predictions I wanted to read the most. My mother's last ledger of predictions. I had never found it. I had purged the cabin from top to bottom several times, but to no avail. I did not know where on this forsaken earth it could be and the haunting realisation always bit at me. It was lost to me, just like my mother.

There was a rapid knock on my cabin door and a yelp betrayed me. Heart hammering, I quickly opened it, the twilight air greeting me with a cold nip to my cheeks and neck. Mutza stood waiting on the wooden steps. I stood dazed, staring for what must have been a while. Her head tilting at me, jolted me into action.

"Come in, Mutza."

A little stunned, I quickly helped her up the last step and into my cabin. Her white eyes and foggy pupils darted all around and I had the sudden urge to organise and move my possessions about, the restless feeling dragging me about my small home in a fumble.

"Have you been reading?" she asked. Her aged voice seemed too loud for my ears and I winced at the pain in my head.

I froze as I digested her words. "A little?" I stammered, looking at the books scattered across my bed.

"Good," she replied, inhaling deeply. Her blind eyes travelled up towards the tinkling mass of coin, medal and medallions pinned to the wooden ceiling, and I questioned if she could actually see. "Wear that of the three faces," she whispered, pointing with a bony finger to a silver medallion dangling above her head. My stomach seemed to drop several feet. I had never worn one, never even conceded to touch one.

I stepped over to her, to the coin shining almost gold in the candlelight and to where her gnarled fingers miraculously touched one, amongst the mass. My breath hitched as my fingers unfastened it from the piece of leather used to hold it up high. In the yellow light, the features of the medallion were just visible. It was the moon, in three phases, imprinted on an uneven silver circle. Crescent, full moon and crescent again. The metal was cold on my palm as I studied the smooth, beaten surface.

Mutza's weathered, wrinkled fingers closed my hand around it. "I never gave you a reason as to why I wouldn't finish your mother's teachings all those years ago. I know you must have felt so lost."

I stiffened, keenly aware of my shallow breath. It was true, Baja had asked Mutza to assist in my learning, after my mother's death, and she did for a time. But as the years passed, they stopped entirely and I never progressed onto learning about runes, or the voices of the grave. I never learnt how to read the signs or what to look out for. Mutza had taught me other things, she taught me how to mix and gather herbs and treat wounds. She had taught me to read the skies and the weather and taught me all manner of beasts and creatures which we have encountered over a millennium. She had even allowed me to be taught how to hunt and fight by Baja. However, she had never trained me as a seer.

"You must understand, it was not my place to take over your mother's teachings," she rasped, and I was suddenly aware of how old Mutza really was. She must have been in her eighties; an age most never envisage reaching. "And understand this," she continued, still clutching my hand under her papery thin skin, "it is not the way you were supposed to learn them, through me."

My blood was icy in my veins. I couldn't say anything and didn't move as I watched her wrinkled form observe me, unseeing in the dim candle that flickered hauntingly across her face and my own.

"Your mother…" She paused, biting her puckered lips with browning teeth. My fists clenched awaiting her next words, but none came. "Wear it tonight, Rhona. The full moon. And every night after that." Her unseeing eyes found the open vent behind me and her lined features furrowed, as shadows crept into the crevices and weathered plains of her face. "The winds of fate are changing."

Chapter 6

Mutza left me in a rush of words as she hobbled out of my wagon and into the night. The building turbulence heightened within me and I couldn't overcome its onslaught. I did as she commanded and found an old silver chain and threaded the medallion on it, placing it over my head with tribulation and a sense of foreboding.

My dreams that night were plagued with screeching and the rallying of wheels, racing over disturbed roads. Shadows nipped in the corners of my dreams, teasing the fear that restrained my limbs. But everything was unclear and unfocused; faces appeared murky and unrecognisable, and voices were a chorus of howls and stuttering words. Banging sounds erupted, suddenly pulling me out of my strange nightmare. I shot up quickly. The hollow thuds came again from outside my cabin and I hurled myself from the covers, grabbing my hunting knife, placed next to my bed.

I swiftly unlocked the dead bolt, ship iron lock and wooden barrier, securing me in my little home. The sky was still an inky black, smeared with the faintest purple from daybreak as dewy night air filled my lungs. Eli stood atop my steps, fully dressed in his hunting leathers and furs. There were murmurs from a few who were on the night watch, with Roman standing with them. Baja was walking towards them, dressing himself as he went. I looked back to Eli, finding his intense stare hard to keep, as a chill swept across my neck suddenly and I looked down. My thin night shirt was unbuttoned in a V down my chest, exposing pale skin and the tops of my breasts to the early morning chill. My hands scrambled to cover my chest but Eli deftly pulled off his fur lined cloak and stepped up to place it about my shoulders, covering me. The warmth was instant, on the inside from his kind gesture, and physically from his body heat that remained on the heavy fabric.

"Thank you," was all I could manage, averting my eyes.

I stepped down the wooden steps, my bare feet scrunching at the cold wood. I didn't mind being barefoot, especially after such a suffocating dream, but I stopped short on the third step. Surrounding the base was a puddle of mud and ice, a slush of cold grimness. I turned, about to grab my boots from inside my cabin, when strong solid hands wrapped around my waist, hauling me weightlessly. I quietly gasped as Eli picked me up, arms around my waist and under my bare legs. I was a chaotic mess of arms and limbs, unable to comprehend my current situation. I wrinkled my nose as he placed my feet on the frost barren grass, a few paces away. I wrapped his fur cape tighter around me, suddenly aware my hair was a mass of flyaway tresses coming loose from its long braid.

"Erm, thanks," I said, my voice a rasp, as I tried to tame and tuck my hair behind my ears. "Eli, what's going on?"

He started to walk towards the group, with a brief nod of his head insisting I follow. I did, with my breaths were coming out in a thick mist about me and I clenched my fingers in the furs, glad Eli had so obligingly wrapped them around me. We reached the small gathering of my uncle's men and I wished I was dressed fully. They all stood in the dawning light, the night was slowly transforming with a blue film covering the sky, trees and nearby hills. They were all looking north, and my uncle Baja was speaking in hushed tones with Roman, Denif and Varris. Eli left my sight as I waddled up to hear the commotion, wondering what on earth could have drawn everyone from their slumber in the dead of night.

"What's happening?" I asked, suddenly chilled.

Baja hushed me and pointed to the road. The hills and grey mountain scape far away were like a mirage of morning vapour. I squinted, finally seeing what was of concern. Moving at a great speed over the furthest hilltop was a swarming shadow, moving south towards us. I stilled, holding my breath at the sight of so many horses moving fast.

"Carriages," I voiced, "in such haste?"

"Aye, following the southern road. But why at this hour?" Baja asked, his clothes dishevelled and oily hair falling around his lined mouth.

We watched as the party travelled closer to us, until the hurried hooves and horses echoed ominously along the road. The road passed near where we had made camp and we hurried to its sodden side, the snow and ice a wash of pale blue in the early hours. My feet were frozen, my legs prickling with goose pimples and my teeth chattering profusely.

"Why aren't you properly dressed?" Roman demanded beside me.

"Because I was asleep. Why else do you think!" I retorted. There were muffled steps from behind us and Eli came into view, holding out a pair of boots. My boots. He placed them on the ground at my feet.

"At least someone cares enough to see you dressed properly," Roman said, and I could do all but stick out my tongue at him.

I mouthed yet another thanks to Eli, as I forced my stone-like feet into the soft worn leather. There was a scrape and flash of light as Eli took flint to stone and lit an oil lamp. The lamp blazed and was a beacon on the road side.

The horses thunderous galloping was drawing closer and the sounds of carts, wagons and carriages thumping and crashing over the uneven road stirred more from our camp awake. Men on horses passed in a blur of frenzied shapes and disturbed dirt. Carriages with wooden trunks and boxes flew past, the strained wood and ropes creaking at the fast pace. Faces peered out from the carriages and atop the carts. Pale faces of women and children. A long parade of people. I clenched my fists, the hairs on my neck standing on end. These people were fleeing.

Baja stepped out onto the road, waving an arm. A black horse and rider bolted past, beside the line of carriages and carts. The rider slowed his steed, turning back to gallop towards us. The end of the line was nearing, the gusts of wind and air stirring my hair and Eli's cape. The rider skidded to a halt in front of Baja, pulling down a balaclava from around his nose and mouth. He was around the same age as our uncle, early fifties, with faint red brows and beard. There was a long healing cut running across his nose.

"Why do you flee, friend?" Denif asked cautiously from behind my uncle. We were all poised, waiting on the stranger's answer as his horse reared.

"Something fowl reaped death over our village. Five days north on horse. We had to leave." His voice was gritty, exhausted from the ride. "It followed us for a day. Then it seemed to move east. But we are travelling far south, as far away as I can get these people."

I instinctively moved closer to Roman and Eli, my shoulders brushing theirs.

"What was it, friend?" Baja asked, looking around at us warily.

"We do not know, but it slaughtered six families in the dead of night," he huffed, his expression turning pained. "You folk should be careful. It was not a creature we have come to know. Whatever it was, liked the taste of man."

I shivered and a murmur went through our men, as they shifted on their feet.

"Move south away from here. Keep clear of the north. It has not been the same these past few months. Something is stirring." The man nodded to Baja, authority recognising authority, and sped off after the last wagons, racing away from us. I swallowed hard, watching the shadow of the man fade into the distance, aa everyone turned to Baja, our king, awaiting instruction.

"We stay here another night, two at most. Then we leave. Don't tell the women and children." His eyes then turned to me, and realisation dawned on him. "You should be in bed, Rhona. This is a matter for the men," he admonished, wiping a rough hand over his hair.

"She's more man than woman. Even you must admit, uncle," Roman gibed and I scowled at him.

Prick.

I sent my right fist into the side of Roman's shoulder, sending him staggering and I was rewarded by his oomph of pain and wide eyes. He pivoted and a smirk was already on his cocky face.

"See what I mean," he said.

"I can handle myself," I seethed, pointedly looking back to my uncle, daring him to state otherwise.

Eli huffed and chuckled beside me. I looked at him dumbfounded. I had not seen him laugh for a time.

"I know you can," Baja retorted, "but if our friends' words were true and a beast lurks north, then it is a task for the men. Not the women." He looked above at the stars shining, the last of their light fading against the turning sky, unwilling to look at me.

"I've known a lifetime of monsters, Uncle. I can handle myself." My words were breathy, hiding the lingering pain. But Baja caught my gaze finally and I schooled my features into bored neutrality, something my uncle had come to recognise as a defence. Roman approached me, his hand lightly resting on my shoulder, questioning me with a look. I couldn't bring myself to acknowledge my brother or Eli as shame coiled in my gut and strangled my throat. But I did not lapse and kept eye contact with my uncle, unwilling to be badgered into submission. Not over this.

Baja stiffened at my words, understanding filling his eyes. He only nodded once and walked away, his men in tow.

I watched them walk back to camp in the shrouded morning mist, back to their beds and women and families. Inhaling deeply, I closed my eyes, wrapping the cloak and fur around me. The wind nipped at my ear and tugged on my internal compass and I knew how to distract the others from this moment. Roman hadn't removed the hand on my shoulder, and he turned me to look at him. I shook him off, trying to be imperious in our usual fashion. I plastered a false smirk across my mouth, blinking away the burning in my eyes.

My voice didn't break as I mocked excitement. "Meet me in an hour, we need to hunt," I said, decisively allowing some freedom to that internal tug that insisted I surrender to it.

Both Roman and Eli looked at me, a wicked smile on each of their lips.

Chapter 7

We were out in the woods and heading north before the sun had begun its slow rise above the mountain peaks. I had rushed back, to wash and change into my hunting clothes; my usual attire of fitted riding trousers, my grey military coat and a mixed wool shawl wrapped around my neck and shoulders. I had quickly braided my hair into a messy rope like plait, off my face and down my back. I adorned my hunting knife to my thigh and my hand knife was buckled and strapped to my calf. I had also acquired Denif's crossbow for the journey. The crossbow was thanks to Roman's quick fingers as we skulked out of camp and into the shadows within the trees. I would return it to him when we returned. Roman had his knives and crossbow, whilst Eli had his own crossbow, a long cutlass and his staff, which was a gnarled wooden stick, as thick as my arm and stronger than oak. We headed north, over the hilltop, towards the peak of the road. Looking back out onto the valley below and behind us, the woodland and surrounding fields seemed bare of life and silent in the morning light, however our camp teemed with activity as they readied breakfast nearly a mile away.

"They'll know where we have gone by now," Roman said, watching our brethren busy themselves tending fires, making breakfast and talking about the night's development.

I looked at my uncle's tent, the largest in the settlement and saw no activity or alarms being called. He had not stirred or walked out amongst the camp yet, as he was probably still hosting council with his men and Mutza, discussing the warning and what creature could have caused such horrors. Mutza could know, she would have the knowledge, read the runes and signs. But I couldn't wait for that.

"They will think we are out hunting for food," I replied, hoping it would be so. Baja would give me an earful if Roman was right.

"Well if they don't and I am right, I'll be blaming you as I always do," Roman goaded with a smile plastered across his face. "They won't blame Eli, they never do. The poor mute gets away with everything," Roman said and Eli grunted and rolled his eyes.

The sun gave an unfamiliar warmth that we hadn't felt for a time, with the blistering cold and snow, and I could hear the teetering and twitter of birds overhead. We walked for two hours, following the wheel tracks along the road. No other carriages passed, nor farmers on their way to market.

It had been ten days since we ran from the southern village that had been our home for nearly four months. We were settled there and feeling at peace with the neighbouring woodland of beautiful bay trees in autumnal oranges and reds. The snow had not yet begun to fall and the air to the south was fresh and salty from the port a few miles away. The village had allowed us to stay, with the guarantee we would not venture into town often. We only traded with those who were brave or unwitting enough to venture out to us. We made do.

Denif shod horses for farmers who couldn't afford the blacksmiths high coin prices, and Miriam weaved baskets and sold them to farmers wives for half what they would sell at market. All of us had a purpose. Roman, Eli and I hunted game, which consisted mainly of pheasant and rabbits, and sold them to the poorer families within the village, undercutting the butcher's prices. That was until Mutza stumbled into town and tried bartering something for palm readings, no one knows what she had been asking for, to this day it was a mystery. I could only imagine the stir of irrationality she caused there, all haggard, blind, and blazoned in her fine spiritual medallions, bells and beads. That night the men, seething and bloated with the stink of ale, galloped in, chasing, and beating anyone they could lay their hands on. My neck seemed to ache and pulse at the memory.

Eli was in front of us, his staff clattering with his steady steps as we made our way along the road. The weather had turned slightly warmer as the sun stretched over the grey blue sky. The wind still rippled with a shivering bite, but it was a nice reprieve from the snow and ice that had hounded the land for nearly a month. I listened to our sloshing steps as we made our way along the roads, the dark mud and brown ice melting on the path. The trees along the road were grey and near lifeless, keeping a firm hold on the last dry leaves that still clutched on. I inhaled looking ahead, surveying the land on either side of the road.

Eli's staff stopped clacking, and then seconds later so did his footsteps. I halted, somewhat with a stumble, but found my feet moved quickly once more, wanting to close the distance between me and him. But I stopped short, a foot from him. I watched his broad back, covered in a dark grey woollen coat with brindle rabbit fur lining the collar, stiffen and straighten. I saw the muscles in his neck stretch as he held up his hand and looked to the canopy of trees to our left. The wood hadn't moved or bustled with movement the whole time we had been walking and I silenced my breathing as Roman crept past me to Eli. The hairs on the back of my neck rose to their full attention and I assessed the road ahead.

Roman whispered something to Eli and my ears strained but failed to hear. There was a distant crash, like trunks ripping and breaking from a tree, and my brow gathered as I searched the woodland. The sky above the tree line suddenly filled with crows, as black as night, cawing and flapping in shifting waves as they flew high above and then away. There was another cracking rip from deep within the wood and I hurried to follow Roman and Eli as they edged to the side of the road, the sound louder and closer than the one before. They ducked, squatting behind the larger trees at the edge, squinting through the thicket of twigs and trunks. With haste I followed suit, going to squat behind Roman, only to have Eli grab me and pull me behind him instead. I crouched, aware of my thighs and arms resting against Eli's back, as his strong legs braced my uneven footing when I nearly stumbled. I peered over Eli, bracing my hands on his shoulders as I looked deeper into the trees. He smelled of morning dew and mint, and the nearness of him flooded my every nerve. The crows chorus of cawing echoed in the distance as we watched them fly fast overhead once more.

"What do you see?" I whispered to Eli, watching his face tense as his eyes roved the forest floor.

There was another cracking sound of breaking wood, as though large, aged trees were being ripped from their roots and we all flinched, the sound nearly deafening. My nails dug into Eli's coat, as my heartbeat frantically beat against my rib cage. The woods were still once more and every muscle in my body eased a fraction, until Eli silently stood, placing his staff quietly on the floor of fallen leaves. I watched wide-eyed as he stepped away from me and deeper into the tree line. His footfall precise and quiet as he walked to a large, mangled tree covered in moss and earthly vines, its low hanging branches were a puzzle of bracing arms. He began to climb, the only sound being the quiet moan of a branch under his body weight. My pulse quickened and I could feel my whole body go taught again as brown leaves fluttered down from his ascent. I looked to Roman, saw his eyes trained on the forest floor, on any movement ahead. Something didn't feel right as my gut clenched and I looked up again, seeing no sight of Eli, now high above. The cold wind nipped my right ear and I looked over my shoulder at the road a few paces away. The leaves stirred and whirled, blowing in a storm of dead colour. They whipped towards me and into the trees and I suddenly felt cold and my fingers tingled with numbness. The same splintering shiver crept up my spine and I could not ignore that familiar nudge.

"Roman, get into the trees and away from the road!" I hissed, scrambling into the brush and behind a tree. Roman followed wild-eyed.

Out of nowhere there was another thunderous smash, the sound of splintering wood closer than it had been before. Roman skidded feet first under a low hanging bush a few yards in from the road, mud and snow spraying as he went. I ran, finding the widest tree and hid behind it. My heart was frantic, and my breath raged down my throat. Leaves began to flutter again above me, and I stilled, holding my breath. There was a soft thud and whoosh of air as Eli landed in front of me. I nearly screamed but he quickly brought his hand up to cover my mouth as he pushed and angled my body behind the tree, his broad shoulders and arms enveloping me. I tried to complain and push away until I noticed his face. His wide eyes were frantic, and his forehead beaded with sweat, as he scanned the forest warily. I clenched my fists and he looked at me, removing his hand from my mouth, leaving a finger over my lips as his nostrils flared, and our noses almost stroking. I nodded, as a tremor ran down my legs. I was thankful for being pinned against the tree and Eli, as it gave me no room for my knee to weaken. The crashing continued, only louder, and I strained my neck around the trunk, clamping my lips together.

There was a rumbling and cascade of broken branches flying. Another battering crunch sounded, and I flinched, turning back to Eli. He was focused on the foliage, yards away from us. I watched his pupils follow the loud rustling and cracking of trees, and saw the black dots grow larger, then subtract as they finally beheld what was making such chaos. His body went rigid and what little space there was between us vanished. Wood and bark flew, trees and splintered branches fell with each step.

Whatever it was it left destruction in its wake.

The shape moving through the trees was a blur of noise and bulk as it bashed and battered its way through and onto the road. We silently shuffled around the trunk, hiding our bodies fully from the view. My heart stopped as I finally beheld the creature.

A giant troll, taller than four men, with long gargantuan arms, and skin like rotting wood and shattered flint charged and smashed at a nearby tree. It's hunched back and small round head, was adorned with twisted angular antlers, and it sniffed the air stirring around it. A memory stirred within me, of scrawled words on a page, describing such a beast. I tried to grasp the name, but terror kept it from my lips until it roared.

"Knarrock troll," I whispered.

Eli's strange eyes darted to me, then to my mouth, then once again to the road, as I heard him swallow. There was a rippling growl and it stalked to the other side of the road and into the opposite trees. The crashing echoed across the land as it went, leaving a trail of mutilated and ravaged trunks behind it.

We waited, and my breathing suddenly became fast and heavy. The roar of my pulse was loud in my ears, and my neck ached from straining around the tree trunk, but we didn't dare to move until it was far enough away. More crows scattered in the distance as the creature continued to move slowly away. The strain in my neck was too much and I had to turn back, burying my face in Eli's coat. I inhaled a shuddering breath, trying to tame the muscles down my back to relax as the adrenaline had wound me into a stiff and hypersensitive state. We stayed like that, entangled against the tree for what seemed like a while, waiting anxiously to be able to move, to make a noise and to speak. I waited, waited for Eli to move first and push me away, but he didn't and I was very aware of how long I had been in his arms.

"That was close," I muffled in his furs, trying to break my train of thought. "Too close for a Knarrock troll to be raging through woods, south of the Fallow Mountains," my voice scratched out as I finally lifted my head meeting blue and brown eyes.

The beads of sweat trickled down the side of Eli's temple, meeting the scar that reached up from his collar bone to the corner of his mouth. Eli didn't move away from me as he mouthed, breathily, dipping his head.

"I'm fine, spooked but fine," I replied, dazed. "The beast has travelled a long way. But I thought they were trapped by the wards in place. All of the ...creatures," I voiced, still aware of Eli surrounding me against the tree.

I gulped as he suddenly moved away, taking the growing heat with him. There was a scrape and rustle as Roman crawled out from the bush and stood, his knees were sodden with thick mud.

"Was that what I thought it was?" he asked, now standing next to Eli, who nodded. I walked back and forth, restless and playing with my braid, trying to answer the many questions now swirling in my head.

"Knarrock trolls are known to dwell in the Fallow Mountain's. Why would one be so far south of the northern border? Of the ward's even?" I quizzed, before pausing to look around at the surrounding woods. "We haven't seen any animals for a few days. All the tracks made their way south. Those villagers were running from a creature that tore their town to pieces," I said thoughtfully.

"That Knarrock could have been the reason for it?" Roman pondered, brows crossed.

Eli muffled a whistling breath, and he signed with his hands, answering Roman. Pointing to his chest and mouth as he did. *'They do not eat men'*.

Eli was right of course; Knarrock trolls weren't man eaters.

"The rider said the creature that terrorised them liked human flesh?" My skin prickled as I said the words. "Eli is right. Trolls eat bark, stone, and other trolls. Not men. They stay together, where there is an abundance of it in the mountains. They are slow-witted creatures, but they protect their territory and those within it. Why would one be here, away from all of that?"

Eli grunted, signalling with his hands north.

Roman nodded. "The rider said they came from four or five days north."

I knew where this was going, and my stomach did a little flip. We could travel along the road to see what destruction was left. It would be easy, just like a hunting trip, but we had minimal food and animals were scarce. Except for the crows, which would not make a good meal.

"Baja would kill us if we are gone for more than two days," I said. "We cannot venture there without proper supplies and horses. The clan will be moving tomorrow, and we would not know where."

"Then we go back, make our intentions known. Know where we can meet the clan when we come back. We take others with us also in case we run into trouble." Roman shared a look with Eli who hoisted the crossbow, he had been carrying, over his shoulder.

Eli seemed to ignore it and went to retrieve his staff. My skin still seemed to crawl with a cold itch as I looked back down the road. I had never seen a Knarrock troll, other than in scribbled pictures from my brethren of old. Even then, the pictures could not have prepared me for the creature that had come upon us. I chewed my lip thinking over and over why one would be so far from its home in the mountains.

The sun's pale light was slowly fading behind thick grey clouds and a wind rippled my hair, pulling strands free from my messy braid. I had not realised Eli was beside me, until he gently pulled a twig from the mass of hair around my face. I bit my lip, shying away from his gaze as he meticulously removed debris bit by bit.

"So feral, Rhona," Roman smirked with a wicked gleam in his dark eyes. Eli straightened as he quickly threw the last twig away. "It's settled then. We go back, tell Baja of the troll and travel north with the horses, to see what those villagers were truly afraid of, and see if we make our ancestors proud, finally hunting monsters again," he finished, his mouth still holding his smile.

I huffed a laugh. We travellers were not monster hunters anymore. "Agreed," I replied, forcing my legs to replicate the long strides of both Roman and Eli as they started walking.

The woodland was once again eerily quiet, the troll now nearly a mile or two east. There was still a sense of unrest that clung to me, like a haunting grip that stroked my spine every now and then.

"Did you just agree with me?" Roman mocked, staggering in the path, bringing my attention back to him.

"It doesn't happen often," I retorted, smiling.

"Never is more like," Roman said, still feigning shock. "I think this is a moment I will remember for the rest of my life, sister," he said, grabbing me around the shoulders in a side embrace. Eli looked back at us from ahead, smiling. "There's hope for us both, Eli." Roman then huffed a laugh.

Chapter 8

We reached camp as twilight turned the sky a haze of purple and blotchy grey. Thankfully Baja had chosen to reside here another night, otherwise our disappearance could have caused a stir. Heaps of snow could still be seen but most of the camp was no longer covered nor surrounded in white. There were splashes of vibrant colour from wagons and tents that distorted the pale scape. Night-time fires were already roaring about camp and our people milled around, talking, doing laundry and cooking for their families. A baby seemed to be crying in the distance, its wailing muffled by tents and wagons. I walked over to the horse pen and began seeing to Balthazar. I gave my beast a few affectionate scratches, conscious now of spoiling him, and an apple for leaving him all day. My ebony horse ignored me at first until I produced the piece of fruit as a peace offering.

Whilst walking through the mill of people, I found more than the usual number of eyes watching me, eyes of my cousins, extended family, and neighbours. As I passed, voices shushed and tutted, lips sneered and chatted hurriedly. I gulped, suddenly feeling breathless, toying with my braid, rethreading strands into a more presentable weave. I eagerly looked for Roman and Eli but did not see them as I rounded the corner towards my uncle's tent.

When I reached Baja's fire, I saw that he was surrounded by his men, deliberating. All eyes were suddenly on me and I stopped short.

Mutza and Miriam were fussing by the cooking pot, whispering to each other as I approached. Mutza blindly fumbled with herbs as she stirred the pot's contents, whereas Miriam gently soothed her large round belly and my smile dropped as she turned to me scowling.

Baja sat in the centre of the circle on a stool in front of his tent. He watched me under heavy brows, his hair wet and tied behind his head. His gold earring glimmered in the orange glow, as did the knife he was holding, and I gulped loudly. I held my breath, unsure of where to look as my stomach twisted, and I knew I was in for a thrashing. Baja was carving a small wooden log, pieces and shavings littered the ground at his feet.

"Where did you go today, Rhona?" His voice was not raised but the grim paternal edge made me swallow again and my palms suddenly became clammy. I looked around the fire, not seeing Roman or Eli still.

Shit.

I slowly took the seat to Baja's left, aware that all conversations had ceased.

"Speak girl, where did you run off to today?" he demanded as he continued to carve the piece of wood.

"I went north, along the road and into the valley." The truth would be better; however, a lie was on my lips ready. His expression did not change, so I dived in. "There was a sign and I wanted to see for myself," I stammered, rubbing my hands together in front of the fire. Barely a lie, it was more a feeling than a sign. I looked at my uncle, and saw his brows raise indignantly at my words.

"And did you find anything?" There was a lethal calm to his voice, one I knew too well from many scolding's as a child.

I swallowed, feeling the weight of his words riding me. "Yes," I replied, biting my lip and looking around.

The men and Denif were silent and watching my every word. Well, this was expected; the clan were here to see and hear my berating. It was typical of Roman to be elsewhere during such a thing. I sighed, trying to taper down my anger and humiliation.

Mutza chose that moment to bang the wooden spoon against the pot, making it clang loudly. I flinched, feeling positively helpless against my uncle's quiet rage. But Mutza began to speak and words surprised me. "She took Roman and Eli with her. She was not alone, Baja. She cannot solely be blamed for this."

Miriam hissed like a cat at the old woman, as she grabbed the wooden spoon out of Mutza's wrinkled hands. "It is not your place, Mutza," Miriam warned, resuming stirring the stew.

"Quiet, old woman. She is *my* niece and *my* ward. I will ask questions as to why she decided to go on an adventure without telling me. Even if she isn't solely to blame," he spat. I clenched my fists, biting the skin on my lips again, the winter had not been kind to my skin it seemed. "If Rhona and the other two had been on watch like they were supposed to have been today, this would not have happened."

My palms had grown steadily slick and my stomach dropped at his words.

"What's happened?" I croaked, wringing my hands now, feeling like a small child, under my uncle's glare.

"What did you find on your adventure, Rhona?" he asked, the vein in his temple flickered in the fire light.

I swallowed, trying to plan my next words carefully. I had told my uncle things before. I had never intentionally lied to him, but the look in his eyes made me reconsider myself.

What in the darkness had happened?

Relief flooded me as I saw Roman and Eli walking over, conversing purposefully. That was until they saw me squirming under Baja's watchful gaze. Roman looked at me wide-eyed and stopped short a few paces away, I scowled at him.

Ruddy coward.

Eli tried to move closer to me and my chest ached a little, watching him, but he halted to a stop at Baja's seething look. Eli's worried expression made me rethink the lie I had waiting, so I told the truth.

"We found nothing at first. The woods were quiet, and the road was unused. We thought we would find more food due north, but we ran into something else entirely." I trailed off, skulking under my uncle's foreboding crossed brow as his eyes darkened.

Eli made a noise and tried to sign at Baja, who held up a silencing hand and turned his glare back to me. I looked to Roman, who looked as though he too felt like an insolent child, again.

"We came across what we believe was a…" I paused, realising every eye was on me, and I couldn't help gulping loudly. That familiar tingle, traced idly up my spine and danced with hairs at the base of my neck. The feeling, strange yet strengthening. A guiding touch. I paused, feeling myself straighten. Lifting my chin, I squared my shoulders. "A Knarrock troll." My words were firm and clear as I looked my uncle straight in the eye.

Shock registered in his eyes, which then darted all over me. The men gasped and began speaking all at once. Baja's was still searching for any signs of hurt or blood on me it seemed as relief finally flashed and he sagged with it, but it was quickly replaced by that lethal calm and annoyance.

"It was on its own, going east. It did nothing to us." Again, that strength gave me clarity, so I continued, ignoring Roman gawking beside me. "We thought it may have been the creature who had caused destruction to the northern village, that the rider spoke of." I spoke the last bit quietly; aware it was not common knowledge to all in the camp.

"They come from the Fallow Mountains, but one was scrambling through the woodland. Alone. It should not be this far south," Roman interjected to my surprise, but I was thankful as it gave me time.

"After we encountered it-"

Roman was cut off by Denif, disbelief colouring his voice. "What do you mean?" He looked wary as he shared a look with Baja. The knowing look shared between friends, that I had seen many times. The same Roman and I shared, and sometimes Eli. My skin chilled again at that look. Something else had happened and the Knarrock was not what the problem was here. Baja flared his nostrils in annoyance, before he rubbed his stubbled jaw and he turned his attention back to Roman, waiting.

"We heard it crashing through the wood. We hid from it obviously. We know not to disturb or ambush such a creature, even if it was alone. We did nothing to make it aware we were even there. We kept down wind. And besides, Eli and I took a shift last night, because Denif was ill with drink," Roman retorted, puffing his chest and looking thoroughly agitated.

Denif began spluttering, but Baja held up a silencing hand. Mutza tutted and tusked her weathered lips. Miriam only placed her hands resolutely on her wide pregnant hips at Mutza's impatience, still scowling.

"They do not know, Baja, and they were not to blame for this, or to have even known," Mutza rasped over the cooking pot, as her pale eyes and tanned skin glowed in the billowing steam.

"What happened while we were gone?" Roman asked, keenly aware.

"You were supposed to be on watch today. If you had, I do not know... maybe we would have known. Mind, it could have been you, my own flesh and blood," Baja started. All the men around the fire shared a quick glance, a mournful one that set my teeth on edge. "Nickos is missing. We found his things shredded two miles from here. Looked like something had grabbed him. There was blood and a gold tooth." Baja paused, his lips thinning, and my stomach flipped. "His gold tooth near a tree." Uncle finished with a deep swig of warmed whiskey.

"That Knarrock was moving east, towards Windmore. It could not have come here so quickly. Besides they do not do that to men," Roman's voice quavered. "Do they?"

"It wasn't a troll who did this." All eyes found the old woman again. "It was a skineth. A Flesh Peddler," Mutza replied with finality. There was another rustle of whispered conversation.

"Skineth!?" I blurted out. "Here? But they can't be. They shouldn't be able to leave the Fallow."

Fear gripped me deep and true. Skineth's were foul and evil creatures who hunted humans and creatures alike to steal and manipulate the flesh unto their own. The thought made the hairs on the back of my neck stand and my skin stretch with shivers. My mind reeled; they were contained deep in the Fallow, by the wards. All those creatures were. It was written long ago that they had been herded into the boundaries of that land, to be imprisoned along with the other monstrous creatures, Armelle's spawn.

Eli sat down beside me, in disbelief. He signed to Baja, *'are we sure it was one of them?'*

Baja nodded and leaned across me, passing Eli the bottle of whiskey. Eli took a long deliberate swig, and I rolled my eyes, the thought of whiskey again made my gut roll.

"It must be. Nothing else could have done what we found," Baja said, rubbing his face again. He turned to me now, no more anger in his eyes. "Skineth's cannot absorb that which is not living, the tooth, being gold," he paused, eyes closing. "That is the conclusion we came to. I thought it was you or your brother when we found the blood."

My heart ached and I placed my hand on his, knowing the anguish he must have felt. "I am sorry, Uncle. Truly." My lungs felt heavy and I took a shaky breath. Closing my eyes, I sent a silent prayer into the new night for Nikos and a prayer to keep both the skineth and the Knarrock troll from finding our camp.

"Strange that two creatures are within reach of this place. To be out in the world now, after such a dormant time. Do you think the skineth was the creature who did that to the rider's village?" Denif asked.

It was true. For years, our paths had been quiet and undisturbed by any creatures, especially since such creatures should have been trapped and contained within the Fallow. Few stories were passed about camp now, of creatures and folk being in passing. The travellers were always aware of what lurked in the shadows, after our livelihood as hunters and bearers for the kin of creatures was taken from us by the wards a thousand years ago; we had observed and been the keepers of secrets of the world hidden. Now it had seemed hidden from even us. Silently sleeping. Even the creatures who had not been trapped by the wards and still lived freely on the Continent were scarce.

Baja frowned, rubbing a rough calloused hand over mine, bringing me from my troubled thoughts. "I do not know. But one thing is for certain. These beings should not be here." His throat bobbed.

"What shall we do? Do we leave tonight? All knew we were to leave in the morning," I asked, quietly hoping we would leave this place and the pressing horrors behind. But to move south again towards the hate and wrath of the southern villages and towns, seemed just as horrible.

But that incessant tug took me by surprise, and I found myself saying, "do we go hunting for the creature? Make sure it cannot harm anyone or anything else." I sounded calmer than I felt.

There were murmurs about the group, and Denif started talking to Baja about the dangers of such a quest. Mutza began rambling about the traditions of travellers and how it was our duty of care to the folk and creatures of this land. Voices started to deafen my ears as rambling discussions were bellowed back and forth across the fire, some for and the majority against it.

"You have no idea, girl, what we would be up against," Henris spat at me, an older man of blood relation to my father. "You women have caused enough trouble this month," he snarled but then grimaced in pain as Mutza hit him harshly over the head with the wooden spoon.

"What about the women? You can't leave us all unguarded. If the creature came back, we would be defenceless," Miriam warned, meeting her husband's eyes across the fire, men chorused in agreement.

"Enough!" Baja shouted and all went silent. His dark lined eyes fell on me as he spoke to those gathered. "We do nothing for now. Our paths have crossed too many creatures these past weeks to take the decision lightly." He looked to Mutza resolutely, the blind old woman's milky eyes creasing at him from across the cooking pot. "We pack up and move at first light. Nikos was taken westward; that's what the tracks indicated. We continue north, towards Oaknell."

Chapter 9

We packed up the camp with haste that morning, choosing to travel by daylight rather than moonlight. Everyone was in a worried frenzy as they unpegged tents and packed up the wagons and caravans. The horses were saddled and harnessed ready to travel. News had spread to the entire camp of the skineth being in the area and all sprang into action, without question. We left only tracks behind in that small clearing and reprieve we had called home for a few days. But the road was really our home, along with the wild.

Baja ordered many of the women to drive during the day, allowing the men to drive during the night. Eli, Roman and I took turns driving both mine and Roman's carts, resting and closing our eyes for a few hours at a time. Eli's cart was being driven by Taren and his mother, further down the line. When our group did break it was for minutes at a time, enough to eat and relieve ourselves.

For two days and two nights we followed the roads east, until the horses, mules and other beasts could not go any further without proper rest. Baja's theory was that east would be best, even if the Knarrock had moved that way. We could easily defend ourselves against a troll, but not a pack of skineth's.

We harboured ourselves in the shelter of a valley, giving all a good night's rest including the animals we tended to and cared for. The morning of the third day, we set out along the road once more. The snow was nearly gone in these parts, our caravans and wagons running easily along the beaten sloshing roads. The weather was brisk, with the sky a grey smudge above us, but it still held the winter cold nip. By the look of the day, there would be no more snow for a while and yet I still had my winter furs and woollen shawl wrapped tightly over my heavy coat.

Thunder began to rumble ahead in the late afternoon and the heavens opened and poured icy rain. Watery sheets cascaded upon us, making the road a mess of mud and river-like puddles. Balthazar whined at the weather as he pulled me along, my home in tow. I was not at the back of the long line of caravans for once. There was a call from the front, Denif's voice, interrupted by the splattering rain and thunderous rumbles above and we stopped the wagons. I looked around, seeing Roman's sodden form jump down from his driver's seat; his wagon was behind me in the queue. Eli's horse was tethered to his caravan, and after untying it Roman climbed onto Ovi and they galloped past us, splashing waves of murky muddy water.

The rain was heavy, blurring the figures and shapes ahead. Eli strode through the puddles and muck, over to my seat, his dark curls plastered around his face and neck.

"What do you think it is?" I asked over the rain's onslaught, squinting to see ahead.

Eli climbed up to my driver's side, sitting next to me on the bench. His tanned skin was flush from the cold and heavy droplets ran down in streams over his forehead and thick eyelashes. His scarred throat huffed and rasped as he grunted, moving his hands to sign. *'There is a bridge to cross.'*

I nodded in understanding. I was soaking, the layers of leather, wool and furs a sodden heap around me. My hair was in lank streams about my face.

"Why go to Oaknell?" I asked, spitting rain, "Why not go back down south?"

Eli's eyes glinted in a lightning flash. His hands moved then, picking up my own, tightly gripped around the reigns. He pulled my fingers free, turning my palm over this way and that. My cracked and bruised knuckles were painful, slow in healing from gripping my knives and riding.

He grunted again, pointing to my hands, signing again in answer. *'Because it's not safe for us anymore.'*

I watched the rain fall on my pale bruised fingers, clasped in his tanned ones. Warmth crept over me and I felt dazed in the moment. Lightning flashed again and Eli's eyes blinked against the downpour at me, unwavering. Static seemed to tingle under my skin as thunder crackled a few seconds after. I tried to speak, my mouth filling with rainwater but the sound of galloping hooves rushing to us stopped me.

"The Hantonway Bridge. Apparently, there is a toll for travellers," Roman spluttered in anger, now skidding to stop beside us. Eli let go of my hand, his face thunderous.

"What kind of toll?" The rain was hammering now, and I had to shout.

"Anything valuable," Roman spat. "I have to tell the others. Find something we can pass off as valuable," he blared before trotting down the line behind us, calling the toll price.

I gave the reins to Eli and climbed into the back of my wagon. It was dark but dry, the usual scent of dried rosemary mixing with the damp wood. I sparked a candle to life and looked at my small trove. The medallions and coins glittered high above me, tinkering a quiet melody. I would never hand over any of those, even if they hung limply and unused, I was to attached. I looked in my coin purse, finding only coppers and a few silver lint's. It wasn't enough and I ground my teeth, as a pang of anger edging its way to the surface. Of course, there was a toll for travellers. I grabbed a freshly brewed tonic for digestion from my shelf, along with a healing salve. Both new and untouched, prepared for me by Mutza. I looked to my bed, the flowing gossamer, and glittering fabrics of orange and red hanging richly. I yanked at one, folding it into a pile that shimmered with fiery cobwebs. I looked about for anything else, only finding my sopping reflection in the cracked mirror. Gold glinted in my reflection and my hand quickly pulled at the one of the two gold hoops that were pierced through my ear. Real gold. This should be enough for Eli, Roman and myself as passage.

"I have something for all of us. It should be enough," I called out, then jolted with a start as the caravan started to move forward. My footing and legs nearly buckled as Balthazar walked forward. I swivelled seeing Eli beckoning me out. I grabbed an old hand basket, broken and splintered and placed the items inside it, before crawling through the small door to the driver's bench.

Eli looked at the basket, his brow furrowing. He pulled out his money pouch, heavy in coins but I held up a hand.

"We won't give these people money for passage. It's not our way. Besides, save it and buy us a pint of ale each in the tavern if there is one," I said, smiling. A hearth fire would be needed to dry ourselves this eve. The clouds above were still as thick and dark as smoke. This rain wouldn't pass for a few more hours. Eli studied the collection of items in the basket, his face unreadable. "Go steer Finne's, I'll worry about the toll. Just promise me that ale?" I smiled, pushing him out of the seat.

Eli whirled a playful smile on his own lips and held up two fingers.

I chuckled, shouting in the downpour, "aye, two ales are better than one!"

***

The rake of a gatekeeper accepted our passage fee, taking the salve's and gold begrudgingly in the roaring downpour. The glittering fabric however was tusked and tutted at, but taken, nonetheless. He knew its worth. Every wagon and caravan were allowed passage, thankfully. One at a time, wheels sloshed over the small stone bridge that crossed the wide Hanton River. A small boy, dripping and sodden in a fraying cloak directed us to a field at the back of an older, less favourable inn. We rallied behind its stables, where the innkeeper courteously said we could make up camp for the night or two. From his dishevelled appearance, it was apparent he was eager for a few coins. I looked about the small, sparse town, being beaten and hounded by the rain. A few curious faces hovered in the windows, watching the large party of unwanted arrive. All seemed out of pocket. From the tatty curtains, to the lack of candlelight from within, Hantonway Town seemed poor, relying solely on the coin of travellers, market sellers and merchants passing through. When I had looked to the innkeeper beckoning us to his nearly empty tavern and with all this rain, I was sure we would oblige.

The stables were small and clean, and the horses seemed to be in the care of the young stable hand. He was barely ten, with a face full of auburn freckles and tawny red hair. I talked with the boy briefly, asking the usual fair of questions. I asked when they had last had visitors and merchants pass through the inn. He had informed me through whistling, gappy teeth, "three weeks, Miss, since the last lot came 'ere." He had whistled Miss and his accent was poorly schooled. From his narrow nose and waned skin, he and his family hadn't eaten well for longer than three weeks. I advised him with a sceptical brow of Balthazar's imperious and stubborn nature, crossing my arms at the small child, looking unconvinced. I nearly choked when my beast nudged the young boy affectionately. The boy smiled at me, showing me his lack of teeth. I flipped him a silver coin, hoping it would be enough to buy him and his family some food for the next few days. He whooped and whistled in awe as I strode out into the rain.

I strapped only my hunting knife to my thigh and slid my usual blade in the calf trap in my boot, then locked my wagon, not trusting any curious passers-by. Hantonway was a small town, made for road-goers and travellers passing through. You always hear stories of robberies along the road. **Why would it be any different here?**

I stalked into the tavern, untangling my dripping hair and wringing it out as I went. A few of our folk, all men, were already seated at tables, flagons of warmed ale in their hands. I noticed I was the only woman, as I walked over the threshold and into the warmth and dryness. I looked down at my rider's trousers and boots, not the usual flowing skirts these villagers had come to expect from our kind. In the corner, by the roaring hearth, sat Eli and Roman. Six flagons of ale shone in the fire light. I smiled broadly, feeling the heat envelope me as I walked to their table.

Both men had shed their coats and thick furs, hanging them from hooks near the flagstone fire. Steam billowed up in plumes from the wet garments. Looking at the stone walls and busy tables, it seemed most of the men of our clan, save my uncle and his council, had done the same. I hung my own up on a spare hook and took the seat in between both Eli and Roman. Picking at my tatty white shirt, its embroidery threadbare, the garment was sticking to my arms and chest like a second skin. I was glad to be rid of my coat and shawls even if my breasts showed through the slick material. I quickly scraped my long tangles of hair back, twisting it tight and high on top of my head, aware the skin of my neck and shoulders were now on display. I crossed my arms across my chest, hoping to hide my womanhood.

The fire's heat soon began to dry the beads of rain that still dribbled across my flesh and I slowly started to relax. I ached from my neck, to my rump, to my feet. The cold and rain did nothing good for my already strained muscles. I slumped slightly in the chair.

"Thank goodness for Hantonway Town," I sighed, as Roman smiled over the rim of his ale.

Eli merely looked at me with curious alight eyes. I blushed, feeling conscious but picked up the ale and began drinking deeply. Both men laughed at me as I wiped the drips and froth from my upper lip in appreciation. The ale was on the verge of being stale, but it was ale and it was better than the concoctions of whiskey my family brewed, which were acidic and fiery, and gave one the worst case of head pains the following day.

We sat there quietly, allowing the fire to chase away the last of the thrumming cold in our blood, as the ale caused a familiar, delightful haze. The barkeep and innkeeper served ale and roast mutton with baked bread for a few copper coins. All was devoured gratefully. When our bellies were full and our clothes were nearly dry, more ale was brought to our table, courtesy of Roman.

"Thank you." My voice was husky as the lull of sleep began to caress me.

The barkeep came over to collect coin and Roman was paying him in silver with one hand, politely asking about the weather and surrounding area. My stomach gave a lurch as I noticed my brother's other hand. I ground my teeth, seeing the other stretched out lazily, stealing coins from the barkeep's back purse. Huffing through my nose, I looked away, ashamed. I searched the tavern, waiting for a warning or shout to alert the barkeep. None came. All eyes and mouths were busy in their own conversations and companions. I looked back, finding Eli watching me intently. I raised my brows, sucking on a tooth. Eli's mouth thinned into a strained line. He knew what my brother was doing, which angered me more. I blew at a fallen curl on my forehead averting my eyes again.

The barkeep, an aged man with bloodshot eyes and a crooked smile, was more than welcoming. He smiled in thanks at Roman's payment, unaware of the theft happening to himself. I pulled out my own purse, the leather pouch only holding a few coppers and a silver lint or two. Nothing I could give as extra, to compensate for my brother's swift thieving fingers. Eli cleared his throat as the barkeep was about to walk away. Interested, I looked back to see Eli pull another three silver coins from his own purse. He placed them on the table, pushing them towards the old man. Eli's eyes were solely on me as he did so, his lips and jaw flickering. A grateful surge rose up in me and I graced him with a small, indebted smile.

"For your trouble at hosting such a large crowd this evening," I finally contributed, looking back at the old man, fully aware of my brother's dumbfounded expression. "Not many taverns would take in 'unwanted'. No matter what with the weather," I finished, smiling at the barkeep.

He nodded, hesitating before taking the coins off the table in haste.

"It's no trouble, Miss," he spluttered, giving us all a brown-toothed grin. "It's hard times now and we have always welcomed folk such as yourselves. With all goin' on up north, tis' nice having a tavern filled," he replied in earnest, rubbing his nose on the back of his grubby sleeve.

I nodded again, my smile genuine at his kindness. Kindness our clan hadn't received for a long time.

"Can you tell us news from the north? We've heard strange things on the road and seen even stranger. What have you heard from folk passing through?"

The barkeep's watery eyes looked over us and his bottom lip trembled. I sat up straighter in my chair as did Eli.

"We've been 'earing terrible things. An entire village was slaughtered. Creatures stalking normal folk that shouldn't be 'ere. A witch tried passing through, travelling with a carriage a fortnight ago.

That's the fourth one this month. Can tell it's a witch just by looking at 'em. Same silver eyes, hair unnatural in colour. These are troubled times we are seeing and for all we know there is more to come," the old man whispered, as worry lined his eyes and mouth.

I shivered at his words. "Witches? Passing through here?" I asked hushed, trying to suppress my unease.

"Aye, passing. Fleeing more like it. You'd all do well to stay here a few nights, off the road, if you get my liking. Thank you again, Miss," he said with a little bow and walked back to the bar with our empty flagons.

As a shiver crept up my spine, I kicked Roman hard under the table, earning me an array of foul profanities.

"What the fuck was that for?" Roman hissed, eyes watering.

"You should choose your victims more carefully!" I spat at him. "We don't get such kindness everywhere we go. You stealing his hard-earned money is a damned way of making sure we don't receive such hospitality again!" I crossed my arms tighter, blood boiling. "Give Eli back what he paid extra for *your* stupidity."

Roman pursed his mouth. Eli's hard-skinned fingers lightly rested on my forearm and he slowly shook his head, signing to me. *'Don't worry about it.'*

"You should not have to cover for his ignorance, Eli. He can be a pig, even at the best of times," I whispered, leaning in close to him, near the fire. Roman hiccupped his drink indignantly, raising his eyebrows. "Well, you are," I retorted, tossing the strands of curls from my forehead and eyes.

Eli removed his hand, and I was aware how warm it had been on my skin. Roman pulled out three silver pieces from his coat pocket and gave them back to Eli. I made a vulgar gesture with my hand, whilst poking my tongue out at him. Roman only smirked wickedly and rolled his eyes.

The fire crackled and snapped, sparks flying up the flume. I watched the embers dance about in the grate, my body heavy and relaxed. Our brethren slowly filtered out of the tavern, back to their wives and children, until Roman, Eli and myself were the only travellers that remained. The tavern was quiet, with only a few other merchants and people sitting, chatting in groups and drinking heavily. The majority ignored and took no notice of us. I watched the men laugh and bellow, spitting beer and ale, clapping hands on tables at jokes or hunch over for news. My eyes darted about but stopped at two pairs of eyes who watched me intently from the corner of the tavern. Whispers passed between both men's lips, their eyes never leaving me. I awkwardly averted my eyes, turning back to Eli and Roman signing to each other in silent conversation. Eli was giving Roman a telling off of his own, which I watched with smug satisfaction. I heard the creak of wood and the scrape of a chair from the far corner, knowing all too well who was vacating their seats. I bit my lip, fisting my hands. My nails digging into my palms, the pain centring and grounding me.

"Here we go…" I said under my breath, but Eli caught it nonetheless, his brow gathering instantly. The blurred hulking shapes in my peripherals told me the men were coming over.

"You, traveller woman." a gruff voice said, as I looked up into the black bearded man's face. His dark watery eyes were glazed with drink. "What gives you the right to think you can drink in here with these men?"

I noticed Roman fidget, his hand moving slowly to his side. Eli went rigid beside me, his face darkening at the threat in the stranger's voice.

"Unless you're here to sell your wares?" the other sneered. This man was rat-like, with a pointed nose and chin and thin arms too long for his body. "Traveller whores aren't worth as much as normal whores, so what's your going rate?" the ratty man goaded, rubbing himself in front of me.

I gulped down the bile that began to rise up my throat. A darkened moan and scream whispering in the chasm of a locked away memory. I heard the unsheathing of blades either side of me and felt, rather than saw, Eli's rage. He was almost quivering with it beside me. I held up a hand to both my companions. My own rage and disgust, writhing under my skin.

Brazenly, I raised my leg, flexing it and resting it leisurely on the table, keeping my face neutral. Both these bastards blinked in surprise, the bearded one flaring his nostrils, while the other licked his teeth. I caught Roman's eye before I smiled, as seductively as my temper would allow, and leant forward, pulling my hunting knife from my calf strap. It glinted in the fire and the ratty man hissed.

I played with the blade, my fingers stroking up and down the cold steel. "I'd rather fuck the pigs." My voice was soft and wrathful as I stroked the blade, my eyes never leaving the rat-like shit's face. "Call me a whore again, scum, and you will have no cock to use on another woman again."

My eyes glittered, the malice sculpting my lips into a cruel smile. Roman pulled out his own blade, stabbing the point into the tabletop with such force that the wood splintered. Eli stood to his full height, standing behind me, face full of cold invitation.

The rodent of a man took a step back, his toothless smile curdling my stomach. The bearded man only looked over our party and spat at me. His warm phlegm hit me across the nose and cheeks. There was a crash and stumble, and Eli had the bearded man by the throat and had slammed him down to the flagstone floor. The heavy thud and smash of bone was too loud in the quiet tavern.

"Oi! We'll have none of that in here!" the innkeeper bellowed, his flagon and aged polishing cloth motionless in mid-air.

The kind barkeep staggered out from behind the bar, eyeing both men with a dissatisfied glare. Eli's temple flickered and twitched, the restraint in his face and arms wavering as he pinned the brute to the floor. He abruptly stood, letting the man go and holding his hands up in surrender to the barkeep, before walking back to sit down by my side, breathing heavily. He handed me a handkerchief from his pocket, and his eyes darkened as he stared down the retreating men. That stare gave me chills, deep within my very core. I took the fabric and wiped my face quickly, shame heating my cheeks, causing my hands to shake. I cringed; all eyes were watching us. The barkeep finally hobbled up to our table, looking us over. I clenched my fists again, waiting for his dismissal and refusal of service. Another place to leave in haste.

"You two have outstayed your welcome 'ere. I'll give you back your coppers for tomorrow's stay, but you're to leave first thing at dawn. You hear me!" he ordered at the two men. Breath whooshed out from my lungs. "Shame on you for spitting on a lady."

I looked up at the quivering old barkeep, grateful for such decency and benevolence. The men gave us another rotting sneer and left the tavern. I held my breath as the door slammed shut behind them. My heart was hammering in my chest as I looked at the barkeep, mouthing my thanks before I finished wiping the spit from my face.

"They're rogues, Miss, take no heed in their appalling behaviour. I won't stand it 'ere. Yous' are all still welcome to stay," he offered, his watery eyes looking at myself, Eli and Roman. To mine and Eli's amazement, Roman pulled out another two silver coins and placed them in the old man's hands.

"Thank you. Like my sister said before, we are thankful for such welcoming hospitality. We promise not to cause you or any trouble here," he said, shaking his hand in solidarity. My heart swelled at that moment.

As the barkeep walked away, I watched my brother. "Were those...?"

"No, I only stole three. Those were my own and worth paying him for what he just did."

I smiled weakly at him. I placed the handkerchief on the table in front of me. "I will wash this for you, Eli." My stomach twisted, lips trembling, trying my utmost to not look at him.

There was a creak of wood and then calloused fingers traced the side of my face. I turned, startled. Eli's fingers gently wiped away more of the scums spit I had missed. I stopped breathing, as his eyes traced my face for any other signs of it in the firelight. My heart thundered at his touch and his eyes finally found my own, wide and beholden.

For what felt like minutes I did not breathe, entranced by his blue and brown eyes. I placed my hand over his, on my cheek, finally filling my lungs. Roman cleared his throat and I flinched. Eli dropped his hand immediately, picking up his handkerchief and wiping his fingers. No longer looking at me. My brother sat across from us, his ale tanker trying to hide his cat-like smile.

Chapter 10

We didn't return to the tavern the following night. Word had spread to Baja of what had occurred, and he forbade me from returning. The haunting memory had been present in his dark eyes as he told me to stay at camp. I wouldn't fight him on this and knew too well the dark conquests of men, even if I was not the child, he still saw me as. The rain had subsided, and night was clear enough for our brethren to make campfires. We sat with Baja and his council. The fire licked and devoured the fresh logs, as the damp wood smoke and vapour caused us to cough and choke occasionally. Spiced mutton stew was ladled out and passed around, followed by apples and dried meat. The innkeeper had sold us a mutinous old sheep, with barely any meat on its aged frame, for a tin of spices, a sack of wild garlic and two bottles of my uncle's own distilled whiskey. It had been more than a fair trade; the spices were half real, and half dyed flour and the wild garlic was pulled from a field not far from the inn itself. I felt sorry for my camp's trickery but could not say anything for fear of being moved on before we needed to.

The oblivious innkeeper had spluttered when he tasted the fiery gold whiskey, his eyes bloodshot as he hiccupped. He slapped my uncle on the back heartily, before taking another swig. He chuckled and explained he would sell this for a few gold coins to the richer folk. He even snickered and divulged about labelling it exotically for the extra coin. My brother's eyes brightened at the innkeeper's secret and, with a knowing glance at Eli, there was another plan brewing between them.

Baja, to my surprise and that of the camp, gave the innkeeper a horse. Horses were prized high amongst travellers and the honour of such a gift was uncustomed. Everyone discussed and whispered their questions as to why, but I knew. It filled my heart with fierce loyalty and devotion as my uncle willingly gifted it to the man. It was thanks, for me. For keeping me safe from those men.

After the exchange, I had ransacked my caravan, trying to find something extra to give the innkeeper and his old colleague as a thank you. I found an old, printed book, detailing the uses of herbs and ointments for ailments, and proceeded to give it to them. The innkeeper's eyes were wide as he beheld the book, holding it gingerly.

"It's not witchcraft," I spluttered, fear coating my tongue. "It was from a physician in the Abstillion Isles. We have our own copies from our people long ago. But they are the same. Please take it. As a thank you, for last night."

The innkeeper received it reluctantly but smiled warmly as he finally understood. "Thank you, my daughter wishes to become a midwife. So, I shall pass this gift to her."

I smiled broadly, then walked back to the fire. With the sweet lull of the flames, everyone talked while they ate, discussing the weather and news that had been shared by the barkeep the night before. But more than once I heard hushed conversations about the new arrivals that had come to the small town that day.

A few carriages had pulled up midmorning, with heavy crates and emblazoned trunks with gold filigree. But it was the tall black slim carriage, with a small window of iron bars, that peaked everyone's interest. I didn't see them get out of the wealthy transport when they arrived, but from the mutters and conversations around our camp, they were fancy travellers with heavy purses.

The innkeeper had asked politely for us not to stumble into the bar that evening and due to his courteous manner, these past two nights, we obliged. We were not far from the tavern though, only a stone's throw away in the back field, but close enough to the back door that the barkeep could roll us out a barrel of stout. There was no music tonight, only roaring fires and talk. Everyone seemed to be at peace considering the upheaval we had endured this week. We were far east, away from the strangeness that seemed to be developing. Far enough that the gossip and whispers were from the west and the north. Hearsay and idle chatterings of travellers and merchants. But still, when I paused and recounted all that had happened, that heaviness in my chest ebbed and deep within me I could feel the threads of fate pulling at me.

***

We stayed in Hantonway for four nights, feeling settled and pleased with the warm reception we'd received. The small town was thankful for our custom and trading, and those who were brave enough to socialise with us, held firm the friendly welcome. So much so that on our last night, two of the town's families joined us for dinner one being the innkeepers' own family. They talked and danced with us in merriment on our last eve in Hantonway. On the morning of the fifth day, we shook hands with the innkeeper and barkeep, who both willed us to visit soon. I embraced both elderly men, thanking them profusely for their hospitality and welcoming nature. It was a kindness we wouldn't forget anytime soon.

As we began trailing our carts and caravans along the road away from the town, further east to Oaknell, I finally spied the wealthy carriages the camp had been spying on since they arrived. It was true, the owners must have been heavy with gold and silver coins for such finery. The tall black carriage gave me pause, as we trotted slowly away. It was an iron box with studded sides and iron bars. A cage, or portable prison. A shiver crept up my spine as I beheld it from my driver's seat. It was monstrous and dark in the bleak morning light. I couldn't take my eyes from it as we passed.

I inhaled sharply as ivory fingers suddenly gripped at the bars. From the depths of the prison's darkness, pale silver eyes shone.

Balthazar skittered, bringing my focus back to the path ahead of us. I was suddenly cold to the bone, even in the new dawn's light.

Chapter 11

We spent four days on the road travelling north over the snow-covered land. The weather was turning, and the sun was looming longer in the sky each passing day. The cold was becoming bearable. When we finally reached the borders of Oaknell, relief settled the anxiety throughout the group. This land, Oaknell, was a haven for travellers and 'unwanted' alike. There were fields and forests to camp on, all free and unoccupied, on the outskirts of Terre Voss, the city bordering Oaknell. It was a sacred place to us, and a place my brethren had made home many times on the road. All of Oaknell was vast and beautiful, where the feet could wander, the mind could capture, and the heart could love. It was a home of sorts. But our road was our true home and Oaknell, as beautiful as it was, bordered the lands closest to the Fallow. Here, we would be five, maybe a ride of six nights and days from the Fallow, but instinct told me that wasn't far enough.

As we travelled off the road towards a large forest of pine, oak and elm, we watched the horizon for fellow camps and travellers, but all seemed quiet and undisturbed. The camp had found an area and had begun unpacking and setting up before the last caravan had entered the protection and cover of the forest. The trees spaced well enough that some were camped under the branches, whilst others camped in the small meadow. Camp was settled quickly, in the dying winter sunlight that filtered through, with all scrambling together to assist our family and neighbours.

I washed thoroughly in my caravan, donning an old pair of Roman's riding pants and tucking the loose fabric into my laced boots. I threw on an old woollen jumper, ignoring the wool that was fraying and unravelling at the neck and wrists. New clothes were a luxury, and I was more than happy with my brother's hand-me downs.

I grabbed my grey coat and stepped out into the evening air. I scouted for Roman and Eli about camp, but they weren't anywhere to be found.

Walking past tents and caravans, the sight of fires burning, and food being passed around made my heart swell. The memories of my mother always surfaced; her cooking pot boiling, steam billowing and the smell of flat bread charring on hot coals as she sang to me and my brother under star flecked skies. Her smile and scent of rosemary gave me reason to smile. Then the screams rang out. Lately, the memories were always followed by screams and gurgling, as the darkest of my memories pounced. My feet stumbled on the solid ground and the nausea rose with bile in my throat. I closed my eyes tightly, steadying my shallow breaths, clawing at the memory to leave me as quickly as it came. My heart ached and tears burned my eyes. I filled my lungs with cold air and forced my eyes open, looking at the camp around me, to rid myself of the memory trying to surface and wreak havoc. They were coming thick and fast recently. Stinging and biting at me. But I couldn't, wouldn't, delve into that pool yet. I wasn't ready to fully face it. I didn't think I would ever be. So I forced my feet to move towards Baja's tent and fire, keenly aware of the eyes watching me as I walked past.

Roman and Eli weren't sitting around the fire with my uncle and his men. I felt suddenly lost, overwhelmed by my memories and lack of their nearness. I craved company, but not the sort the council would provide. I needed Roman. I needed Eli. I looked around the fire and the faces in its light; all were in deep discussion whilst Miriam and Mutza prepared the evening meal. Thankfully, no one paid me attention as I sat, stretching out my hands towards the fire. My breathing was normal again but the ache in my chest from the memory lingered.

"Where are Eli and Roman?" I asked, picking up a stranded twig and drawing symbols in the slush of melting snow.

"On watch tonight, girl," Mutza's rasp answered me, across the dim of male chatter. "They are south of the forest, near the road. Maybe you could take them some meat and broth when it is ready." Her blind eyes wandered idly around the circle as her gnarled, wrinkled hands rubbed and broke herbs above the large pot.

"Of course," I replied, watching intently as she threw them in with accuracy. I leant forward, retrieving another stick to draw with, making the silver medallion fall from the confines of my jumper and coat. The metal glinted in the fire light as I examined it closer. It was old, the metal's edge worn smooth. Only the barest lines of the three moons cycle was visible on its surface.

The silver was warm in my hands from my body, as I placed it back beneath my layers, adjusting the chain around my neck. Milky eyes meet my own across the fire. Mutza was focused on me, or so it seemed. Those unseeing eyes pinning me above the roaring flames of gold. I swallowed, afraid to look away. The old woman was known for her blindness, and yet on occasion, unnervingly, her eyes could somehow pierce you motionless. Mutza was wise and earthly in ways all our clan wished to be. She sometimes knew of events before fate whispered them into life and could see things our normal mortal eyes could not. And it was this otherworldly sense of self in her that caused my pulse to quicken. She had been my mother's teacher, for mother had been gifted with the same ability. I believed she knew about the past as well as the future and this frightened me most of all. Scared that the memory was somehow radiating off me, I fisted my hands and tried to focus, the stick snapping as I grounded myself, not allowing a flicker of the darkness to show on my face. Her eyes averted to the sky and I huffed a heavy sigh, glad to be rid of her gaze.

My uncle's gravelly voice caught my attention. "...this far east. But why the crates and the prison in tow?" He was discussing the travellers we had encountered in Hantonway. I continued to listen, pretending to draw, unobservant as he spoke in hushed tones to his men who sat closest.

"Caleb, the barkeep, said it was a woman in there. Locked up. He heard a woman's voice as he helped unload the carriage when they arrived. The folk said nothing of it to him though. Unyielding he said, but rich," Denif croaked. "But he did not see anyone in it. Just heard."

"They were from north of Oaknell past Fearbridge and the Savage Vale, apparently. I'd say near the northern pass. Neath Briar perhaps or Falmuir?" Taren suggested.

I watched Baja with lowered eyes and a hidden face. He watched the flames contemplating what his men were saying.

"I haven't seen a prison cart like that for a decade or so. It was pure iron. Black as night and thick as oak. Whoever was in it, wasn't getting out. So few people too, in such a party travelling on the road. Two carriages, one cart and a prison. Not normal," Tamer said gruffly, his dark beard and dark eyebrows shadowing his face.

"Aye but who or what were they transporting. And why?" Baja voiced, his eyes distant. "A prison like that isn't for a normal criminal. Not a human one at that."

"Could have been not human. The past few weeks, days even, have been uncommon in our lifetime. The skineth, the Knarrock troll," Zeek said, eyeing me across the fire. He was a few years older than Roman and the oldest son of Denif. "A woman, you say, Father? A black witch? Let us be glad she was being carted off to her end," Zeek replied in answer.

Baja's brows rose at that. My arm was tingling, and I realised I had been as still as the dead during their discussion. I began moving the stick in the slush again, drawing moons and stars.

"If it was a witch, that would explain such a cold cage. But none of us heard a scream or manner of ruckus. Black witches cannot abide being caged or contained even at night. White witch perhaps. Something is churning the balance. I don't like it." Baja's voice was strained and in that moment his eyes locked on mine. My shoulders tensed, my hands now clammy.

Uncle Baja rubbed his beard as the fire played tricks with the shadows across the sodden grass at my feet. I let the night air fill deep in my lungs, feeling that familiar unease set in once again. Things were happening, unusual things. They could not be ignored. Resolutely, I knew that if Baja was worrying about this, then I should be too. Before I could broach the subject, a voice stirred and called to me.

"Rhona, take these to my Eli and Roman, will you, girl?" It was Mutza, her pale eyes homing in on me.

Standing on wobbling legs, I walked over to collect the two mugs of broth and wrappings of meat. My stomach gurgled loudly at the inviting smell. I walked to the watch point, no torch or lantern lighting my path. I knew Roman and Eli would be in the trees, watching. Eli would be high above, balancing gracefully like a lethal wild cat with his eyes trained on the distance. Roman would be at the base, scouring the undergrowth, forest and roadside. Both ready to raise any alarm if need be. I walked softly, being careful where I trod in the grass, dissolving snow, listening to the soft crunch of frosted earth under each step. The stars and moon above shone white on the tree line making everything have an otherworldly glow. Roman walked out from his spot, meeting me and taking his cup of broth.

"Baja is worried," was how I greeted him.

He sipped the steaming cup, wrapping his hands around the metal for heat. "Why? We are fine here. I have my knives and a crossbow," Roman fussed, rolling eyes. It was like a second reflex of his. A crooked smile and an exaggerated eye roll.

There was a rustle in the trees and Eli fell silently from above, landing behind Roman. A warm shudder rattled me as he walked out of the trees. He took the cup from my outstretched hand and gratefully gulped down the dinner.

"Anything tonight? I saw no tracks walking over," I asked, trying to sound nonchalant whilst looking around the tree line, my own eyes curiously searching the shadowed woodland.

"Nothing. Not a rabbit nor an owl," Roman confirmed, in between sloppy mouthfuls.

The road was visible in the moonlight from the slight slope at the base of the forest. The trees were shrouded in darkness and nothing stirred or rummaged from deep within. I held my breath straining my ears.

"Don't you both think that's abnormal? No birds, nor fowl. No mice or owls to hunt them. No rabbits or deer to stalk either. For days we've seen tracks leading south or no tracks at all. Don't you think that's odd at all?" The unease was evident in my voice as it rose an octave higher. Both men look at me eyebrows raised and all of us seemingly sharing a look of joint fear. A fear that had been building for days in the pit of my stomach.

"Baja is worried you say? Has Mutza said anything to you at all?" Roman directed at Eli, who only shook his head. "We shouldn't start worrying until Mutza foresees any trouble ahead. Or is warned from beyond." Roman voice was gruff, but I sensed the angst in his composed words. Eli held my gaze unfaltering causing my stomach to flip.

"I don't know, Roman. All three of us know something is amiss." The winds picked up at that and cascades of dead leaves rippled around us. The trees were in a chorus of scraping and rattling branches, fighting against the strong pull. The light of the moon and stars casting an eerie glow over the skeletal trees, seemed to dim. But still nothing scuttled or skittered in the darkness and gloom.

I gasped as what felt like a cold finger ran down my entire spine. Eli's eyes widened at my outburst as I turned to face the wood. In the watery darkness, two small white lights darted about the winter coated woodland. They zoomed, at such speed, moving erratically from within the wood towards us and the open plane and road ahead. I froze, transfixed. Roman cursed and Eli dodged in front of me, shielding me as the small flickering balls sped past in a dizzying blur. We watched, their light still burning my eyes as they flew ahead, past the hills and down the valley. Both lights were heading south.

I moved around in front of Eli's broad shoulders, my legs eager to follow, to chase them. But Eli's solid hand gripped my waist, halting me. His warmth centred me still, to my core. My skin seemed to prickle at his touch. Wonderment rippled through me at the sight, causing my mind to race along with my pulse. I turned, knowing the shock and awe was still etched across my features. Eli and Roman were too, in their own way, amazed.

"Were they...?" Roman whispered, his eyes searching the distance.

"Yes," was all I could put into words, as my eyes too searched the distant darkness for any sign of them.

"Spirits of the Fallow?" Roman questioned again, barely a whisper. As though he was frightened to voice them into reality.

"Yes," I breathed as my awe was suddenly replaced with a weight in the centre of my chest. My ear tingled as though a soft breath was about to murmur and hush me. I straightened my spine, suddenly feeling the familiar tug from deep within. That familiar twist of my stomach and sizzling of nerves.

Eli noticed me first, how I do not know. The night was at its darkest and the moon's light did not shine its brilliant haze upon me. He moved into my line of vision. He grunted, raising his hands to my shoulder. His blue eye shining dimly against the shadows cast over his face.

"What is it, Rhona?" Concern marred Roman's words and his brow creased with shadow.

"Spirits of the Fallow should be within the Fallow. Not out of it. They protect us, the humans and folk from those that should not pass through. Two were here." The cold was gripping at my throat, but I pressed on. "They are heading south." That weight in my chest clanged in recognition. I looked north at the small, darkened mountain scape, a jagged shadow on the horizon, to what was far, far away. The wind roared in my ears pulling swathes of dark curls from my thick braid. I swallowed, tasting bitter cold. "Something is coming."

Chapter 12

I ran back to the camp whilst watching the forest and woodland for any hint of movement or sign of oncoming threat. I ran to Baja's fire and found it empty, all men back in their tents for the night. I tried to call Baja from outside, raising my voice as loud as I dared. But nothing. All had drunken themselves into a deep sleep. So, I did the only thing I could do, just in case. I sat on the outskirts of camp, posting myself facing the canopy of winter-wrought trees, all of them sparse in life and leaves, waiting. Nothing came. Even as the sky began to turn from inky black to a shimmering purple, hours before dawn, still nothing came. My legs ached from the cold. My hands were numb from feeling and my lips cracked, but my eyes stayed trained on searching the deep shadows within the trees. The stars began disappearing with a pink turning sky as the sun slowly crept into the new day. I saw the shapes of Eli and Roman walking down the hill, returning from their watch post for the night. Both looked exhausted, as if their nerves had been riotous the entire night. They looked at me grimly as they walked into the quiet camp.

"Nothing, Rhona," Roman said wearily. His eyes, although shadowed with sleeplessness, showed pity as he looked at me. "Go to bed, Rhona. All seems well here," he said with an agitated sigh and walked past, dismissing me entirely.

I bit my cheek, stopping myself from the simmering anger that suddenly gripped me and stalked silently back to my cabin. I slept all day and did not dare venture out of my confines when I finally awoke.

***

The camp outside was restless with night-time whispers and the chattering of Mutza's stories over the campfire. Brovnik's fiddle tempted the night air with a symphony of melodramatics. I could hear the children playing hide and seek in the shadows of the nearby trees, then being scolded by Miriam and other mothers, telling them to stay clear of the wood. The sudden raucous laughter of the men drinking and reliving past lives caused the distant scuffle of hooves. I could hear the ponies and horses playing in the moonlight of their pen. I had not moved from my cabin or bed all day, the shame of the night before, constantly recurred. The memory of their faces as they regarded me. Roman and Eli's faces, who matter most. Another prediction and another failure. I bristled in my bed, hiding my face from nobody, and sighing heavily. I was so adamant, as though footsteps of whatever was coming were in sync with my heart. I could feel it. Whatever it was, drawing nearer. Pulling me. And then nothing. Nothing but another look. Another look of sympathy from Eli, the type of look that dried my mouth and causes my teeth to grind. And the look of annoyance from my own brother. A look I've received many times from him. It made my blood boil and my white knuckled fist to strike the pillows and bedding around me. I threw myself back, breathing in the crisp night air filtering through my hatch, willing the cool to settle the heat roaring through my veins.

My eyes searched the moon and stars that peered through the rooftop hatch. It seemed like I had lain here for hours, sleep evading my eyes and my restless mind. The children had stopped playing and the gaggle of voices was growing steadily quieter. The strong and pungent homemade rum and whiskey seemed to slowly numb their tongues. All seemed well outside, the sounds of talking and the occasional outburst of laughter whispered into my cabin from the night. But the gnawing sensation from last night was hard to shake.

It was like a shiver that would not pass or a smell that became stronger by the hour. I couldn't surpass the feeling, so I grabbed my mother's pouch of runes from under my bedding. They felt foreign in my hand. They would never be mine, as though my mother still clung to the stones. Irritated, I quickly threw the runes to the threadbare rug. They were stark white in the candlelight; smooth ovals of polished stone, all engraved in black. The language and symbols on them had not been spoken for an age; they were old tongues, a language only few travellers could read. But nothing was happening. I couldn't interpret anything from the old black lines or the composition of the fallen stones. It was so frustrating.

Nothing was clear to me anymore and I felt the burning of tears behind my eyes begin to threaten my personal illusion of strength. If only my mother were still here to trust in me, to hold my hand and guide me through the fog like she did many moons before.

Sometimes a sickness rolled through my stomach when I believed I was beginning to forget her. To forget how her smile was infectious, how her voice could lull me and Roman into a restful sleep, and even how her presence calmed Baja's fitful rages. It was difficult. Sometimes I couldn't recall her face. It was as though a haze blurred out the beautiful features that I promised myself I would never forget.

But then looking at the blue-black eyes that stared back at me through a cracked mirror reminded me daily. I have everything around me to remind me of her. Not just my eyes, which are my mother's in shape and colour, but my hair, the curve of my jaw and lips. My face is her face.

I know she is with me here in this wagon. She is the medallion's that twinkle and glitter above me each night. In the aged books that lay misused and scattered all over this wagon. Her very body is with me. My comb, made from her scorched bone, taken from the dying embers of the fire that killed her, carved, and smoothed into a fine-toothed comb and ornately detailed in death and fire. My mother's death told in the deep score marks on her bone. I shivered and I averted my eyes from the pale handle that was just visible atop my wash bowl and jug.

The runes that lay unseeing before my bare feet laughed at me, riddled with stories and memories I am unable to grasp and read coherently. My mother was teaching me runes before she died. Since then I have not sought to finish my learning. Although I had no one to assist me with it anyway after Mutza had refused.

Shame still burned at me and I hissed, grabbing the runes frantically, my shaking fingers forcing them into the leather pouch from which they came. I should never have tried to see. My cheeks flushed angrily, my blood pumping with angst as my throat swelled viciously. Tears now cascaded down my cheeks. I was as useless as the runes. I threw a pillow, relishing the force and anger. I threw another at the wall and my mirror fell. Shattering completely.

Controlling the scream that wanted to rip free from my pursed lips, I exhaled, all air rushing out of my lungs, as a small rune slipped from my fingers. It crashed to the floor, spinning in a perfect circle for several long moments, until it shuddered to a complete stop. I froze. Every muscle tensing as my lungs seem to fail and my breath caught. My heartbeat roared in my ears as I went cold, fixated. The oval stone spun so precisely, so unnaturally.

The rune lay finally still. Its soft edge seemed to glow from the moonlight leaking down into the cabin. A thrill suddenly electrified every muscle and I eagerly struggled out of the blankets.

Three marks engraved on the smooth pale surface were my awakening. A black three-pronged fork. As though a small bird's foot had left an inky print. Chills ran up my spine and the air in my cabin seemed to turn colder. Eyes blurring at my cabin wall, not seeing at all, I tried to focus. My ears pricked at the distant snapping of branches from deep within the wood, behind my wagon. The faint crashing grew louder and more erratic, and then the dogs began barking frantically.

Chapter 13

A faint whistle grew louder and closer. Heart pounding, I hurtled up, grappling to put my boots on as fast as my hands would allow. My palms were sweaty, causing me to stumble repeatedly as my laces wouldn't stay knotted. I forced myself to think, to rationalise. I tried to calm my breathing against the adrenaline that was causing my heart and lungs to race. With shaking fingers, I strapped on my knives. The familiar leather and cold metal grounded me.

I turned to leave the cabin, but my gut wrenched, and my hand flew to my neck, feeling for the medallion. It was there, warm and hidden under my shirts. But would it be enough?

Panic now flaring in my gut, I looked at the trove of glittering metal. All of them hung muted, until a flickering light in the middle of the metal horde caught my eye. The same mark as the rune, shining bright like polished silver among dull beaten brass and pewter. The wicked fork engraved in silver. I grabbed it and clipped it quickly around my neck, letting the circle of cold silver fall hidden under my shirt, resting against the other talisman.

Another whistling swoop echoed outside, much louder this time, above the camp. The open sky light clattered menacingly as my wagon and its contents trembled at the creature outside, flying too low. A witch.

The jitters of frightened horses echoed across the camp outside, and the dogs' howling reached new volumes. Bellows and terrified cries of the men and women chorused. I looked about for anything else of use, but my small haven did not hold any weapons, unlike my brother's or Eli's wagons did.

The camp suddenly fell quiet. Only murmurs and whimpers reached me, and I strained to hear sounds above. Then another deafening swoop came, accompanied by an ear-splitting high-pitched screech. Every panel, floorboard and book vibrated. The charms, medallions and coins jingled disturbingly. I quickly supported myself on the wash basin.

My uncle's orders filtered through the sky hatch, over the ricocheting metals above me. Shrieks and cries of the children waking in their beds sent my stomach churning. The women were calling to the men and in the distance, the rasps of old Mutza as she bellowed to my brethren. A loud hissing plunge sounded and almost ducked, even in the safe confines of the caravan.

Black witches hunted humans for blood, spells and dark crafting. But usually witches did not pay any heed to the travellers. We were folk of the in-between, just like them. I kicked myself into action, limbs flying, fuelled by the internal need for Roman and Eli.

After bursting open the door, I took in the chaos unfolding across camp. I locked it shut and ran to the middle of the clan that were gathered around the dying heat of a campfire. All the women had taken shelter, with the children and animals under wagons. The moonlight highlighted wide eyes and worried faces all around. Baja thunderous commands echoed around the field, reverberating into the now silent night.

Baja, Denif, Henris and Zeek were stationed at the centre of camp. Our best men and best fighters. Faces stern, their eyes were trained on the pitch black above, hands uncharacteristically steady. My feet skidded on the cold ground as I reached them, hair whirling about me, unbound. Baja stood stone faced, his oily hair pulled back from his face, his eyes never leaving the sky as I pulled into rank. The gold that decorated his neck and wrists shone in the dying fire light. All charms. All of them for protection. His ebony eyes quickly met mine as he unsheathed a thick skinning dagger, while the other hovered over his sword.

"Steel weapons will do nothing to it. Remember the Man's Isle?" Denif whispered with a tremor.

"Maybe, but they can hurt the bitches, nonetheless," Baja growled, as another shriek darted across the sky.

"There's more than one?" I couldn't help my voice from rising.

"Ay, three of them. But it is only one who keeps diving."

My eyes searched the heavens above me but I couldn't see anything, other than a cloudy night sky and the bright full moon. I couldn't help assessing the men. All a little worse for wear from whiskey, some still exhibiting bruised features and healing cuts from the ambush at the southern village weeks before. My own knuckles still throbbed from the knitted cuts that were healing. But now, nothing moved. Not even Baja and the men huddled together like a blockade. The only movement in the air was our steaming breath, which billowed in wisps and swirls. Hurried snapping and crunches of feet were coming at us from behind and we all whipped round as one to find as Roman and Eli came crashing through the camp towards us. Both were running with determination, faces haunted. They too skidded to a halt and convened amongst us, taking position like two human shields on either side of me.

Roman towered over me, his broad form heavy with muscle, and strength devoured by his furs and coat. His dark hair was tied in a knot at the nape of his neck. Eli was smaller in height than Roman, but still taller than me. His hood down, dark curling strands were plastered around his neck and ears. He only wore a black fleece coat, fitting his arms and chest securely. He must have been high in the trees, not wanting to be weighed down or obstructed by his coats. I gulped, eyeing his dark earthy hair that was partly pulled away from his face, atop his head. His blue and brown eyes looked me over once and then returned to scouring the sky. In his hands, he held his long gnarled decorated staff. He looked fierce standing next to me, making my knees weaken, his stern face with its pale scars highlighted by the moonlight. Roman eyed the sky, breath fogging the air as he carefully removed his crossbow from his back. The distinct clicking of him loading it was followed by others loading theirs around us. Eli looked to me again, his eyes bright in the pale moon and smouldering fire beside us. His thick brows creased for a second, his eyes intently on my own. A silent question. His shoulder nudged me, as his hand grazed against my back. I nodded in answer, pointing my chin up to the depthless night disrupted by a halo of clouds. Eli's eyes reluctantly followed, searching the pockets of the starry sky above. The night was quiet and the sounds of more knives, daggers and swords unsheathing, including my own hunting knife, seemed too loud.

My hackles rose as a black shadow screeched high and out of range. We all flinched, ducking low. I looked to my brother, our eyes meeting, that same dark blue that mirrored the night above. His lips twitched as we both looked to the embers and untouched wood behind us. My lips pursed as I saw the idea bubbling in his mind. I nodded in acknowledgment, turning to Eli. Like me, he knew exactly how my brother's mind worked. I slowly trod around both of my would-be protectors and angled myself in reaching distance of what we needed.

One of the three shadows dived above us tauntingly. The other two circled lazily, not swooping or dividing us. Three, there were definitely three. I noted Eli holding out three fingers, signalling to Roman who stiffened beside me, his furs still clogged with frost from his night time watch. His dark thick brows created shadows over his face as he slowly reached for a stray tree branch in the dying campfire, pulling it from the smouldering remains. His eyes never left the sky as he did so. Steel couldn't fatally hurt a witch, even if you stabbed it through the heart. Iron could, but the only iron we were in possession of was on the tips of a handful of arrows.

Fire, however, could kill a witch.

The main arm of the branch was blackened and cracked with the embers still glowing. Roman began to blow on the branch, trying to tease the embers into flames. A few sparked to life creeping back up the wooden fingers and remaining twigs.

That was enough for me. I grabbed the bottle of Denif's homemade whiskey from his slack fingers. He did not protest as I pulled the cork free with bared teeth and spat it to the frosty ground, before intaking a large mouthful of the fiery liquid for warmth, swallowing until it burnt in my belly. The first gulp seemed to ease my rattling nerves enough to focus. There was an instinctual pull within me towards the sky as one of the lazily hovering shadows high above began to descend, slowly. No form took shape, only swirling darkness. That pull grew stronger within me, pushing my feet a little forward. I took another, larger mouthful, holding it in my mouth and cheeks. The strong alcohol burned my lips and my nose. Roman held the branch above me. Just high enough. It's bark and cracked wood slowly being consumed by fresh flames. I felt the hackles shift and rise again, as another hiss and screech sounded out and a second screeching shadow dove lower over our heads, just as the nearest shadow descending was within reaching distance. That was my cue.

I blew, spraying the whiskey over the tending embers and licking flames. Heat exploded across my face and an eruption of bright burning flames shot out into the space above us. The vast blackness of night was disrupted by the sudden scream of terror and pain. The witch who had descended was now engulfed in a fiery ball, falling fast to the ground.

The witch fell in a flaming heap. Her body writhed, bucking and arching as the remaining snow hissed and billowed steam as she thrashed to and fro. Blue smoke, shimmering in the darkened night, swirled about. It smelt of sickly-sweet herbs and caught thickly in the back of my throat. My nostrils burned and my head spun to the point of light-headedness.

Screams rang out above us. The witch's blackening limbs began to still and the sound of her rattling ribs and gurgling breath seemed stark next to the silence in the clearing. The other two witches were still circling high above, their agonising screams at their fallen sister suddenly quieted. I started forwards but Roman held up a thick arm, blocking me, as he looked at the skies.

"Wait, Rhona, she's..." But he was cut off as two witches landed light-footed in the snow, beside their fallen fellow. The two witches who landed were not what I had expected. The murderous rage that seethed in their eyes made my blood run cold. My heart gave an almighty thud as that tug from within went taught. I stood motionless and frozen as I beheld the beautifully twisted face of the Maiden and the withering glare of the Crone.

Mother be with me.

I felt as though the world had turned. That up had come down and that I was falling into a strange precipice. I wished for the earth beneath my feet to swallow me whole.

Fear ebbed its way up my spine causing every hair on my arms and neck to stand to attention. The men murmured warily in acknowledgment, and Baja sucked in breath through his teeth. I could feel the fear pulsing off everyone as the reality of what I had just done came into sharp focus. I watched in horror, as Baja's fists and knuckles turned white on his dagger. I saw the men beside me form rank, closing in on me as the air filled with the sour tang of terror at the Crone as she roared at the darkness.

Chapter 14

"Who did this?!"

A wave of black matter barrelled into us. I just had time to spin, shielding my head with my hands, but I felt nothing as Eli's form sheltered me from the onslaught. I heard the men cry out as the magic stung, ripping free flesh and smouldering cloth and coats, furs and skin. I gasped, peeking under Eli's arm. Many were on their knees, red faced with small burns across their cheeks and exposed skin as I reeled back, horrified.

I heard Baja shout, "wait, please!"

I turned into Eli, his face strained as some of his face was crisp and burnt from where he had protected me. I grabbed his collar with my knife hand, wiping away some of the darkness that still clutched and burned at his skin. He winced slightly as my light fingers touched some of the sores that were magically beginning to fade. The burns seemed to cool and disappear altogether.

"Please wait, we did not know!" Baja's voice rasped again, pleading with the witches. I braced myself, as did Eli for another battering. But none came for a heartbeat and then another. Cautiously, we turned to face the Maiden and the Crone.

My breath sucked in again, the floor falling away at my feet, seeing who we were beholden to. It was as though every pivotal moment in my life was crashing down upon me, wave upon wave. Like my life was flashing before my very eyes. The Maiden was so young, her skin luminous like the waking moon, with eyes like dying embers. Her sheer gown of darkest blue and unbound long silvery blonde hair floated and whirled in the windless night. The first of the Trinity, a spectacle in her own right of beauty, wrath and violence. I swallowed hard, my airway thickening as I tried and failed to slow my rapid breathing.

This couldn't be.

As my eyes sought the third Trinity, my hands began to shake.

The Crone stood silently regarding her fallen sister, lips moving fast with quiet unspoken words. Such a contrast from the beauty on the other side of the blackened heap in between. The Crone's hair was limp against her sallow face and deep-set age lines stretched across her eyes and mouth, almost deforming her features entirely. Her weathered skin did not fit her tired bone structure, and her back was bent and monstrous. Her dress of muted grey was unmoving on her wilted frame, covering her arms and chest and falling to her gnarled ankles and feet. I swallowed back my bile as my eyes sought the Crone's long and spindly fingers, cracked and darkened with death. They moved with grace, twirling and flourishing in the night air, as though the pains of age had not yet set in those bones. She was a fright to behold and my bowels turned watery.

I felt all the men behind me suck in breath, all the while the Mother, the central pillar of the Trinity, was unmoving in front of me. My heart was cantering, my pulse pounding and palms slick with sweat.

What had I done?

I felt Eli's hand grip my arm, his fingers firm but not painful, as he moved to stand in front of me once again, but I held out my hand to stop him and moved myself out of his way. This was all me. No one else. Yet another blunder to scar and degrade my soul. Another thing to cause me to question my very existence. Lips parted, I gulped down fresh icy air into my lungs.

It was the Mother in a blackened state at my feet. The Maiden, the Mother and the Crone were not to be trifled with. These hallowed beings were myths spoken on the tongues of mortals. Stories of old, of the beings that walked this earth from a time before mere mortals did. But those beings remained. They were hidden in the fabrics between this world and the next. There were those among the humans who saw as we travellers did, and those who saw nothing at all. The last village was evidence of that. But all knew that there was more to these myths and stories told. The Trinity ruled over the children of the Fallen Sisters. The witches, both white and black. Good and evil. Gods on this earth.

The taught thing, swelling within my chest, kept shuffling my feet forward, as though an internal tug was mobilising my stiff limbs. My arms were nearly numb of feeling but an alien warmth grew over my heart as I stepped closer. Looking down, I realised the silver pendant was radiating that warmth, getting hotter the closer I neared these beings. I instinctively pulled out the silver medallions, allowing the warmth to penetrate the flesh and bones of my numb finger. There was a grunt from Eli and I turned back, seeing his mismatched eyes imploring me not to move closer.

"Rhona, what are you doing?" Roman seemed to whine anxiously.

Dazed, I nearly laughed, as that incessant tug kept inching me ever closer. How fitting the medallion Mutza had so adamantly asked me to wear was indeed their sign. The Trinity. If only they had been normal black witches, disgusting beasts that tormented mankind. I silently cursed my unfitting and blurred visions, cursed the teasing gifts that haunt me to the point of frustration. The air was uneasy as the Crone's frosted blue gaze found me. I stilled, forcing my feet to stop moving. The witch's feather grey eyebrows raised up, causing more lines to gather on her ancient forehead. I gulped as her head tilted like a hawk observing its prey, deeming it worth the kill. The Crone and Maiden's attention was solely on me now and not my brethren. Exactly as it should be. Roman's fingers reached for me and brushed my arm, as his clouded breath broke my momentary fixation. Breathing deep, I tried to break the silence.

"Why did you attack us?" My voice halted in my throat at the familiar voice behind me. Mutza. I spun. Eli's eyes were wide as he watched his grandmother hobbling through the men to meet the Trinity. Mutza came beside me, her aged hands resting on her walking stick in front of her, and pale eyes wandering to the stars.

"Attack you? Mortals are still as despicable as they were. You attacked us first." It was the Crone that had replied in a rasping voice that echoed between worlds, as if the witch was on her deathbed or speaking from the grave.

"You lie," I spat, locking eye contact, despite it rattling every nerve within me. "We would not have attacked unprovoked. Your fallen sister is evidence of such." My outstretched hand indicated to the fallen Mother, still unmoving.

The Maiden screeched an unearthly sound, that caused my hairs to stand and my palms to become slick. "Stupid filth, it was I who was diving, not the Mother!"

The Crone's withered lips twitched, and a gruesome sneer shaped her mouth. Her wilted and wrinkled hand outstretched into the night air, fingers black as though stained with tar, clenched into a mighty fist. I froze as the metallic smell of magic embraced me. Smoke formed from her fist and an opaque claw moved before me, coiling and curling until it struck me. I gagged as the unknown force gripped my throat. Vice-like and unyielding. I couldn't breathe. My back arched as I mercilessly tried to draw air down into my burning lungs. The pressure around my windpipe was crushing. Seizing. Causing every muscle and nerve to go rigid like hammered metal or aged stone. My heart was ramming against my rib cage, beating its way free from my agonisingly breathless body. Roman swore as he rushed in a blur of dark fur and leather for the Crone, only to be stopped by an invisible barrier, a wall of nothing but night. The men behind bleated in fear, a flock of frightened sheep cowering to wolves. Baja hissed and bellowed at the stench of their trickery.

"We, the Trinity, lie? Stupid child. We were hunting." As the Crone spoke, her lips revealed brown broken teeth. "But we were not hunting for mere unassuming mortals..."

"Ethereal ones, we aren't mere mortals." My hackles rose and something dripped down my spine, under my shirt, at Mutza's retort. My lungs burned and white lights danced across my eyes. "You and I both know what we are," Mutza spat with venom. The Maiden hissed showing teeth. But Mutza continued brazenly. "Careful sister, she is also not of this world. Just like you three."

Mutza's voice had abruptly cut off the Maiden, and my air waves were once again open and my own. I gasped and spluttered, my throat burning as fresh air clawed down into my lungs, like rats crawling from a drowning cage. Realisation rammed into my mind, awakening me to Mutza's chiming words. I did not know what she could have meant. I had no magic. I couldn't even read runes. I saw the Maiden's pale eyes darken, as they descended from my face and then fell to the spot on my chest where the cold sliver of metal lay. The medallions rested atop my shirt between my breasts. The Maiden hissed quietly, baring more white teeth at the sight of it. The gush of her hiss stung and rang in my ears as she barrelled sheer darkness at me. I cringed, awaiting the impact, but nothing came. The Crone, with blackened fingers, washed away the blow with a sickening twist of her wrist.

"How fortunate to have found another sister," the Crone interrupted, her icy silver eyes watching the Maiden very closely. I stumbled upright, dumbfounded. I moved trying not to cower, chin and lips trembling, like every nerve in my body. My hands found Eli, not my brother, and I held onto him, trying to calm the burning ache and pain in my throat. The Crone's eyes fell on me and then to my chest, seemingly unbothered by me or my medallion. Their symbol. The Maiden's face restored itself to indifference, paused, then her eyes widened slightly, and her brows caused a crease to form on her beautiful youthful face. Shadows flickered like crawling spiders across it.

"A lost sister. Such a shame your heart will not open fully. It's caged, held down, restrained." My tongue felt clogged with ash, choking and leaden and it took everything within me not to crumble. "Such a waste, such a pity," the Maiden finished, the sadness of her words not meeting her calculating eyes. My heart did not beat. Her choice of words hit me like a slap. Bile rose, burning my throat. I clamped my lips harder together.

Dismissing me, the Maiden's eyes travelled to Roman. I felt, rather than heard him draw breath beside me. He was standing once again whole from his charge seconds before. His spine straightened under the witch's gaze, making him taller. A front, even in the presence of such beings.

The Maiden's lovely face widened with a large smile. Her teeth were straight and slightly pointed like rough pearls. "And her sibling's blood sings our songs too! And a male!" She clapped her hands together joyfully but stopped suddenly at the spluttering hiss from the Crone. Creeping a swift glance at my brother and Eli, I saw the fear in their lips and the worry on their brows.

Roman finally found my eyes.

Did you know?

I swallowed, training the bile back down. I had known, of sorts. It was evident in the way our mother had been able to see the past, present and future. Evident in the way voices came to her from the grave and used her voice box as their own. The magic diluted to a single drop of magical blood my mother had claimed and had been gifted with. Small as it may be, but still in our blood, nonetheless. I finally nodded in answer, and in return he gave me a despairing look. Later, I would talk to him about it later.

"Please ethereal ones from the world before, we beg your forgiveness for this grievance. The daughter of this clan was protecting her own, the way we always have against the others of your kind. We beg for your forgiveness. Please do not take her. Do not harm her as retribution." It was Baja, pleading on my behalf, his voice forced in a beseeching manner, like I had never seen. I watched, horrified as he bowed, hands outstretched, submissive. "I will give you anything. Just please know, she will be dealt with by the laws of the travellers for her insolence with this matter. You have the word of the travellers and myself, their king. Just please do not take my niece. I will give you anything."

Tears ran down my face, warm and unrelenting at my uncle now on his knees. My whole body quaked as realisation dawned on me, at the magnitude of my reckless actions. I had killed the Mother. My breath was shallow and my hands gripped Eli's arm harder. I was going to die. The Crone and the Maiden would kill me for such an offence.

Mother be with me.

The remaining Trinity could deem it necessary to slaughter me where I stood, and I didn't blame them. Killing the Mother, the Mother of the Trinity, filled me with bone-chilling fear; my stomach wrenched, and I threw my guts up there and then. I wiped my mouth, feeling the cold embrace of death whispering at my neck. But nothing came. I closed my eyes, holding back the need to bring more of the bile up. When I finally regained some form of strength, I looked up and outrage burned through me, at the sight I beheld. The Maiden and the Crone regarded Baja with mirth. I couldn't take it.

If this was to end, then I wanted it to end on my terms. I wanted everyone to finally know the truth, to be free of this violent dark burden of memory. I lifted my heel to begin my own retribution.

"Your scents are fresh here. Why have you come so far north?"

I froze completely at the Crone's rasp, her cold icy breath clouding the air between us. Pausing with some internal instinct, intrigued. The torment and nerves were only prolonging the suffering. My suffering.

Why am I not dead already?

"To... flee what was in the south," Baja said with dignity. "Too long were we taunted and hunted like cattle."

Both witches' brows crossed, causing creases that marred both their faces. Both looked at the traveller king with predatory intent.

"What was hunting you?" the Maiden whispered, closing her eyes, awaiting the answer. I didn't know if my eyes deceived me, but I thought I saw a flicker at her temple. Her restraint.

I could see my uncle falter in his stance, wariness creeping up his spine at the witches' expressions. "Men from the towns, villagers and farmers who thought we were stealing their crops and killing their livestock. Who call us 'unwanted' because we call the earth our home, instead of bricks and mortar. They'd come into the camp at night, seeking night-time pleasures from our women, asking for fortunes, mystics and magic." Baja stammered over the last word, his teeth chattering with either cold or fear, I could not tell. Tears still fell from my eyes, as I watched. My uncle, my only father figure, bending his knee. To save me. In fear of my life.

The divine creatures before us still stood unmoving. "Others came to hurt us. Murder us. They drove us away," Baja finished, bowing again to the Trinity.

The Crone and the Maiden looked at each other. "It may not have passed this way," the Maiden said to the other. My ear began tingling, and I held my breath not knowing if it was Eli's breath or that otherworldly sense that haunted and taunted me at times.

"Enough of this. What were you hunting?" Mutza's voice croaked, and I jumped, remembering her beside me. Roman grabbed at her arm as she took a step forward towards the Trinity. The blackened pile of dying embers crackled too loudly. She repeated her question. "What were you hunting that brought you down upon this camp?"

The Maiden's voice was venomous as she replied. "So, fearless old woman. And vulnerable. The girl shall be punished for this act of violence on this night. Treacherous fool." She spat on the Mother's body. White light suddenly ignited from the crumbling remains.

"We were hunting a creature. A lycan," the Crone answered. This was truly a horrific night.

A lycan, a creature most fowl. My head whirled, as images and words flashed in my mind. A beast able to shift into a monstrous creature. Part wolf and demon, a hound of terror and darkness. It had not prowled here for more than a thousand years, trapped within the depths of the Fallow. Legend has it that only one such creature was brought about into existence by the Fallen Sister, cursed by blood from Falin and trapped on this Continent, in the heart of the Fallow, by the wards keeping all manner of evil within. I saw Mutza's hands shake as she held onto Eli.

"It seems to have escaped the wards and has been causing havoc in our lands and to the mortals. It savaged a settlement not far from here, men have been taken. The creature has been doing some questionable things." The Crone spoke with strange intent. "The Fallow's inhabitants and others of our world have raised concerns. They called upon us as they have not been able to stop the creature themselves. Even the witches seem to fear it. It's attacking pattern seems to take it back and forth across the Continent." Her eyes found me again. "But this girl…" My stomach dropped and I felt Eli hold me close. "Has robbed us and our kind at the chance to stop it," she announced with anger, through browning chipped teeth. Her watery eyes shone in the dark night, as she looked longingly down at the body, now black and smouldering.

"Please, we did not know. Could not have known," Roman interjected. My brother was now also pleading for my life and the ground beneath me felt like it was moving. I could feel the cold breath of my death lurking once again.

"How far from this path is the town in which it has preyed?" Mutza asked boldly. I heard Eli groan, a plea to his grandmother to stand down.

"Not more than seven miles north," the Crone replied, eyes falling on me. The Mother's remains spluttered and the white light that had begun to seep through the charred, cracked skin glowed steadily brighter. The men behind us all took another step back.

The white light grew until it was blinding, and I shielded my eyes from the glare. There was a sound like lightning ripping limbs from a tree, and the searing light vanished. I was the first to remove my arm from my eyes as a white orb of whirling smoke hovered above the blackened corpse. It floated into the air, swirling like ink in water.

"We move back south. Tonight." Baja was firm with his orders, bowing again to the Crone and the Maiden. The men at the back of the group began to move to the caravans.

"No," the Maiden chided, loud enough to halt them in their tracks. "You will do no such thing." The grim sneer was now back on her face revealing those too white teeth. "A life for a life, payment must be made."

"No!" Roman snarled, throwing his arm protectively in front of me. Eli too, moved me into him, enveloping me entirely in his body. "It was a mistake. Such payment is too harsh for this dealing."

I buried my face in Eli's chest, needing to escape in some form of darkness. Watching my brother and my uncle pleading for my life, fractured the parts of me I had rebuilt over the years. Shattered and fractured the life I had finally begun to live with some semblance of content and I knew my death could be mere seconds away.

The Maiden seethed, as her spittle and clawed hands shook. "Speak to me in such a way again, human, and you will never speak at all," she said with utter venom. The wildness in her eyes made me flinch, my gut twisting. Roman's arm, that had pushed me behind him, now grabbed at his throat. I saw him fall to his knees, his eyes wide and mouth moving, but no sound escaping from his lips. I ran from Eli's embrace, fire now coursing through my veins and muscles as I tried to get to my brother. I fell to my knees beside him, hands clasping his horror-struck face. His face had turned ashen, as his lips began sealing together. The flesh had knit itself into a smooth surface.

"Brother! Brother!" My hands shook as they brushed over his disappearing lips, my stomach churning at the monstrous magic, the fire within me turning molten. Anger burned away the fear. I spun, my hair whirling with me, ready. Not my brother. No other loved one would be harmed because of me.

"I will give you what you ask. My life for hers," I screamed, facing both the bitches in front of me. My outrage and adrenaline now honed into a lethal edge, I stood with my feet grounded to the earth, chest heaving. "Release him and bid my brethren no harm, and you can take my life. I accept my punishment."

I heard Baja rage and scream my name as his men tried to hold him back. I felt, rather than saw, Eli lunge for me. But his fingers did not touch me at the look his grandmother gave.

"Brave girl," the Crone whispered, face thoughtful. My feet leaden, I stepped forward. The Crone's blackened mouth and tongue was vulgar and inky, and twisted unnervingly. "But I have another idea."

The Maiden began to gurgle a chilling screech, but the Crone stopped her with a flick of her wrist. "Quiet!" she snapped, and her claw-like hands twisted and cracked, a glittering mist enveloping her blackened fingers.

The Maiden stopped, frozen and simmering with sheer rage, before she growled, and her face fell into the deepest shadow.

I watched, mesmerised as she inhaled, leashing her temper. Her face smoothed from its seething sculpture and every fibre within me told me to run. But I was a rabbit, caught in the gaze of a wolf.

"The lycan is no longer our responsibility. I pass the burden to you. You will vanquish this being from these lands before more lives are taken. Do this and your life will be spared. Another life will be taken in your place. To settle the balance which has been broken this night." The Crone's voice rang out into the night as clear as a bell.

The Maiden looked upon her sister with disbelief, her delicate fingers shadowed into claws. "You can't be serious!" the Maiden spat, the shock and disbelief mirroring my own. The Crone's blackened hand outstretched, reaching for the swirling orb of light still floating above the Mother's ashen carcass. I watched, pinned to the spot, between other worldly beings who held my life in their hands. The tremors were noticeable now, my entire body shaking in fear. The Maiden's face changed, and my adrenaline muted as a mask of lethal amusement transpired across that deadly, lovely face. Her lips twitched with the faintest smile and it set cold deep into my bones.

"Fail and we will be back. Run, and I will hunt you myself." Her once melodic voice was like sharp, shattered glass, her words tightening something deep in the recesses of my chest. My blood slowed, seeing the promise in her eyes.

"Enough, my sister. It is a greater task than you assume. Even for us." The Crone seemed to smile cruelly, her unspoken promise evident. "Release him and let her journey forth to her new...fate," she finished turning to the billowing orb and cupping her deadened hands around it.

"Until next time, *unwanted* bitch," the Maiden snarled and shot into the night sky in a shimmering stream of darkest smoke.

"You have one month, or we will return to take what is owed to us," the Crone said as disgust transformed her already horrid features. All traces of that cruel smile, gone. She looked to the sky after the Maiden, then turned back to me unexpectedly. "I do not know or understand why this beast of old is here, on this plain. I do not understand the forces at work, for they are not playing by the laws of our magic." Her eyes flashed strangely, and I swore sorrow now filled them as she looked upon the glowing orb in her hands. "Child of in-between, heed my warning. The lycan is as cunning as shadow and deviant like the darkness himself. Silver on its own will not kill it, the way it does to its spawn. Silver, fire and an instrument of death will kill the creature. No blades, no stakes or arrows of wood can rid the earth of its presence. Three and only these three together will do so." She paused her features, that again twisted to that nightmarish sneer as the Maiden screeched high above. "For this night, my warning is done." And she shot into the sky after her sister, leaving a billowing line of ashen smoke in her wake.

Chapter 15

The camp was left in silence at the Trinity's departure. The only sound in my ears was my beating heart and the cold embrace that encased it. It dominated every limb and nerve. My eyes trailed the skies, unfocused and unseeing.

"Rhona," Roman's voice cracked as he reached my side. Strong hands grasped my shoulders and he pulled me to his chest. I inhaled the familiar smell of verbena and rain, the smell of my brother, my family. And just then my lips began to tremble as he held me and said, "we will find the beast and kill it. I promise."

Terror struck me like a blow to the face and I pushed away from him. "No, this is my burden to bear. You cannot come, you will forfeit your own life if you do!" It was almost a sob, but I hastily stopped my betraying eyes from releasing more tears. Biting down on my lip, feeling pain and blood, I focused. My words came out quick and edged with ice. "Brother, you cannot come with me. I forbid you."

"I forbid you to forbid me from this," Roman implored, the sibling authority in his voice trying to outrank my own. His eyes brightened dangerously, and the redness of cold was beginning to flush his nose and cheeks.

Eli marched up beside him. His strange eyes were wary under his shaggy brown hair. He too regarded me with authoritative intent. I saw the moonlight highlight the scar that snaked its way from his throat to the middle of his cheek, touching lightly at the corner of his mouth. I couldn't help but think of how strong he was, after all he had been through. The strength I wish I shared in the moments of desolation and dark whispers, alone in my wagon, when the screams ruptured the peace, and the memories cracked my nearly healing heart.

His fingers moved, signing and creating the sentence I knew was coming, *'in this together'*. His silent nod that followed showed his decision was absolute. It made my stomach flutter, my pulse quickening. I looked at those eyes, staring unabashedly and resolutely along with my brother. Both determined.

I couldn't even comprehend the journey without them, but I knew my heart and soul couldn't bear it. I could feel it's shattered pieces like discarded pottery, barely knitted together over the years like a warped mosaic of pain. Those pieces of my heart and soul were blackened with guilt, shame and a wrath that I kept hidden under the surface. My internal tapestry of the past. **If they came with me and were hurt...** I nearly hurled more bile onto the floor.

I couldn't. I wouldn't let them.

The images that dawned then in my mind ripped and tore gaping holes in my countenance. That cold anchor that had attached to my heart lessened ever so slightly at the thought of leaving them behind. They would be safe, safe and alive.

The rest of our clan started gathering around the dying campfire. The creak of caravan doors opening could be heard as the women looked out, eyes searching the skies as they called to their husbands. A baby's cry echoed eerily throughout our shaken camp. Baja turned to me and our clan's King's fury seemed to ripple against the night.

"You fool! Your life will be in their hands at the end of the month. How could you do such a thing?" His words seemed to rip at my flesh as he spoke.

"Quiet, Baja! It was a witch, nonetheless." All seemed taken aback, even Baja, by the voice that shouted across the embers of the campfire. Mutza was hunched over the edge of the carved camp pit. Her hooded shape glowed in the flickering light. Mutza, the oldest and wisest of our brethren, lowered a shrivelled hand towards the crackling logs. Fire ignited and new flames roared to life at her touch. "She was not to know the Trinity would grace our people with their presence." Mutza's face was illuminated underneath her hood, her hooked nose and wrinkled face glowing in the gold light. Her frosted blind eyes looked at Baja as she said, "it was not for her to know these things. Yet."

Anticipation caused that strange flutter to start in the depth of my stomach. That one word that nearly caused me to convulse. *Yet?* Baja looked to the old woman, as we all did, his eyes wild, chest heaving. My feet moved as though being pulled, step after step, circling the fire. My eyes solely on Mutza, waiting.

"Fate weaves our stories in mysterious ways," the old woman said, her breath visible in the cold air. "Her mother knew this day would come. Just like I did. Chrizta foresaw it on the day she died." Her blind eyes of muted grey, turned to where I now stood, statue-like and barely breathing.

Eli walked past me in a blur towards his grandmother. His wool coat scattered an array of frost as he walked past the reignited fire. He sat, face twisted in disquiet as he beheld his only family. A secret, about my mother, that none of us had known. Mutza clasped his hands and patted them in a comforting manner. My heart ached as Eli looked to me, wide-eyed, mouth aghast at his grandmother's confession. He had not known either and it was with resignation and relief, that I loosened a breath.

"This is the path that was weaved for her, Baja. There is nothing you can do about it. The Great Mother looks down on us all differently." She paused as a grappling cough racked at her chest. Heaving great breaths, the old woman continued. "You have always been a different child," she said, the cough rattling her again and Eli gently stroked her hunched back, easing her through the second fit. "Your ways and ideals are buried deep in your blood, unchanging and irrevocable like the night and the day. This was weaved for you to do. But not alone, young one."

It should only be me, my internal turmoil spoke to me with hounding words. I could feel Roman approach, and tears finally spilled out as I looked upon the roguish smug smile, now spreading across his face.

Insufferable bastard.

I hiccupped, my tears turning into a storm of emotions. Turbulent and raw.

Roman could die.

I turned to Eli, my last salvation and pillar of understanding. He must know the folly in this task.

If you both died, there would be more deaths on my head. My heart.

It was a suicide mission. He must know we couldn't survive this.

Please don't do this.

But when I met his stare so adamantly, I wanted to break.

It would be my fault, all my fault.

The sobs wracking my chest loudly. Roman cradled me then, hushing me into gentle submission. I knew in my heart Roman believed I thought I was going to die at this task alone. That my tears were for my own death. Little did he know they were for his and Eli's, and at the thought of losing another loved one. Because of my own wretched self. After a time, as my tears slowed and my chest heaved its last sob, I saw the clarity in Mutza's words. Felt it, enveloping me in my brother's embrace, in Eli's unspoken promise. I was a fool to think I would have undergone this debt alone.

"What do you mean Chrizta foresaw it?" Baja finally said, still dazed and unmoving. His usually tanned skin was pallid in the golden glow of embers.

Memories long buried started to surface and I closed my eyes. I had always known the old woman was in-between this world and the next, like my mother had been. My mother had predicted things, small things at best. Her gifts were strong, but never had she uttered a prediction to me. My uncle's question seemed to linger in the air with everyone's silence. All that were gathered stood stationary, waiting for the explanation too.

"On the day Chrizta died, she came to me, half mad with rage, and left me with a warning. A warning for Rhona." The cold night seeped into every pore, vein and bone as Mutza's words spilled out across the open space. "The face of three." The old woman's brow wrinkled, as she searched for the memory deep within the aged catacomb of her mind. She stammered, then continued. "Youth will show her no mercy. She must trust in herself, trust in those who shelter her. Time will burden her choices. She must trust in her blood, in the gifts blessed on her. Otherwise all will be lost. Rhona will be lost," Mutza rasped, and the fire spat and crackled as it consumed the last log and branch. I couldn't see anyone breathing, couldn't feel my brother's chest rising and falling as I remained wrapped in his embrace. "Hours later that's when she..." I was numb. Utterly, stupidly numb. I remembered that day. The day of her death nine years ago.

The horror and screams that had ripped from my throat the night our clan had found my mother's burned body. I could still feel my raw throat, the taste of blood on my tongue, as I screamed. It still rang out in my head, as if it was happening again, now. The anger and fear on my mother's face hours before when I had returned to her. When I had returned and had condemned her.

It still haunted my dreams. To the point that most nights I awoke covered in sweat that made my bed shirt cling to me like a second skin. I shut down the thought, closing the door to the hatred and despair clawing at the surface of my skin. Mutza's words tumbled over and over again in my head.

"My mother told you this?" Roman's words were edged in ice, but barely a whisper. I looked up to my brother then, his face cast in shadow and bit my lip. Too long had Roman pondered in frustration over the death of our mother. Too long had his questions been unanswered. But Baja had warned me, pleaded with me, that it was better left unsaid. And over time, I had agreed. Over time my own insecurities had made it impossible to even speak of her death to him. I stepped out of his embrace, fearful my treacherous heart would betray me.

"The morning of her death nine years ago, yes," the old woman proclaimed, bristling. Eli sat stone faced next to his grandmother, looking at his friend and the pain radiating from Roman and from me. "It was a warning, for Rhona and Rhona alone. To be delivered at a time when it would mean something."

I scoffed, my emotions bubbling up to near hysteria. But I soon squashed it back down when the old woman was overcome with another fit coughing and wheezing.

"And you deliver this message from the grave now? My sister's last words? You did not think to tell me, old woman?!" Baja's words ripped into the night, loudly. From the corner of my eye I saw even Roman flinch.

"You were so blinded by her death, your own rage and hate would not have allowed you to cope. You would have wrapped the girl in blankets and coddled her like a baby bird." I watched a nerve flicker in Baja's temple and neck. I clenched my fists as his eyes met mine briefly across the flames.

"That is not true," Baja hissed. My heart ached because only he and I knew it was not true. I was broken when he took us on, as if Roman and I were his own children. I was ripped apart, body and soul, not just because of my mother's death. He had known then and hadn't sheltered me from the truth. He had helped rebuild me, strengthen me. But for my sake he wouldn't tell anyone the reasons why.

Mutza's blind eyes were glazed and her brow wrinkled further. I watched her head tilt as though hearing something we could not. My stomach dropped and I swallowed the hard lump building in my throat.

"Maybe not, but you know not how you would have reacted if I had told you this after her death. So do not talk to me about such things when you know nothing of how the grave speaks to me. You know how words given before death are most sacred." The old woman's face was contracted in a mass of creases, her wrinkled brow furrowed and eyes looking out into the night. "You would not have told the girl or told her too late."

Baja deflated at the accusation. He was lost for words as he looked to me again, and I used what little strength I had left to compose myself. But I knew he saw me clearest of all. His dark brown eyes, framed by even darker brows and lashes, wrinkled and slowly hollowing with age, turned sad as he regarded me. He blinked slowly, closing his eyes from me and our family. He was deciding what action to take. Whether it be for me or for the camp, I did not know. I prayed to the great Mother, it wasn't for my sake. I prayed that he would walk away from me, away from this horror that I had bestowed upon our family, yet again. Although my heart seemed to stop beating as we waited for him to speak, I knew my uncle, like he did me. I heard Roman rustling behind me, but I moved out of his touch, towards Baja. He needed to see me. I dug my nails into my palm, the pain a welcome pressure, as my mind whirled with what to say.

I had to put it right.

He needed to know I no longer needed him, and it was right thing to do to walk away. My feet felt heavy as I walked across the small expanse to my uncle and reaching for his hand, I squeezed it. He had not raised me to be affectionate and foolish, but I knew this was enough.

"Rhona, I can't allow the camp to follow you on this task. It's too dangerous. The children, the women. I...I cannot endanger them for this."

My throat was raw as I spoke. "I do not expect you to. I would never expect you or our brethren to follow me in this." His eyes closed as he nodded in resignation. But I couldn't stop there. "I must leave with haste. But please know this." I lowered my voice for him to hear, and only him. "I thank you, for all you have done for me. I will be eternally grateful for the love and courage you have given me."

He laid his hands on my shoulders and bowed his head. "Don't speak to me as though you will not return, girl," he hushed, aware of all the eyes upon us now. My mouth twisted into a strange smile which I hoped showed fortitude. We shared a look and I felt the sting return to my eyes. I wouldn't cry in front of him. Now was not the time to show any weakness. "I will see you again, Rhona," he breathed and I nodded, allowing his words to fill me and sturdy my spirit. "Pack up the camp; we leave this place tonight," he bellowed and the camp jumped into action. Shouts and calls rang out as every family ran to collect and pack their possessions. Ready to travel back south, and to leave me and this turn of fate behind.

As the camp busied themselves by fire and torchlight, Baja instructed his men to oversee the preparations of their departure. I stood and watched as tents were collapsed and caravans were packed and bolted shut. As fires were doused, the horses were secured to their bridles. I didn't see Baja approach me until he was nearly face to face with me.

"You understand, child, that we cannot follow. You understand my actions up until this point, Rhona, and the choices I have had to make for you? With everything that happened before, with your mother and..." His knowing eyes glazed at his own words and I tensed.

"Of course I do. You have safeguarded me, and your protection and teachings have given me the strength I needed." He placed a hand on my shoulder again and I stilled at the contact. As much as my heart wanted to hold the man, to whom I have known like a father all these years, my lungs couldn't fill with air quick enough as my throat tightened, and I found it hard to breathe. "Do not let the past eat at you, Rhona. Learn from it. Grow from it. Take power from it." I nodded, but fear wrenched my gut as people walked past us, still packing, and readying their departure. "You are stronger than you think, in mind and body. I made sure of that." My lips quaked and he hushed me, like a father would his beloved daughter. I almost lost all sanity as he embraced me, loving and warm. Something he had never done. Since her death. I wrapped my arms around him, feeling the love in his touch. I absorbed it until my weak knees steadied and my eyes no longer burned. I hadn't realised it was something I had been yearning for, for a very long time.

"You may take what resources you need," he said and went to walk away, the cold enveloping me, but he paused before continuing. He looked over his shoulder as he said, "we will travel southeast, past the towns from before. To the coast. To the Opal Cliffs, past the city of Venandi. Do you remember it?"

I nodded, my heart hammering. It was a haven for travellers alike but only during summer.

"Meet us there." Again, a pause as he seemed to stumble over his tongue. "Meet us there, when you have defeated the beast."

Chapter 16

I ran, forcing my legs to move out of their numb state. I heard Roman's voice echoing behind me, calling me back. I couldn't face him now. I leapt up the familiar wooden steps, hurriedly unlocking the door, and shutting it firmly behind me, bolting the door with the brass lock. The familiar smell of rosemary and smoking candles filled my nostrils and I heaved great breaths in and out. All the candles I had lit before had extinguished and the small cabin was smothered by its commonplace shadows. Only the light of the moon above glinted through the partially open sky light. My legs gave way beneath me and I slid down the length of the wooden door, back flush with the faded paint of swirling vines and flowers our mother had painted when we were children. Sickness rolled in my stomach as I thought about what I had done.

The thoughts storming through my mind were merciless and making it hard to think straight. Tears burned my eyes, but I had to focus. Had to think. Clenching my fingers hard against my palms, I focused on the pain. On that settling, centring pain as my nails bit the skin, causing deep indents close to bleeding. I revelled in the pain, allowing the sharpness to focus me. Allowing it to bring about the clarity I needed. The door shuddered with a loud bang and a rasping squeak broke from my throat.

"Rhona, open the door." Roman's shout was muffled from the other side. His fist banged again against the old wood, making the hinges rattle and my body quake with the force. "Rhona, open this door to us, please." His pleads were followed by another pounding fist.

I buried my face in the creases of my jacket. "Go away, Roman. I need to think. I need a minute." My throat only allowed that of a whisper to escape.

"Rhona, please. We need to plan. We need to pack." Romans words were distant through the thick oak. I braced myself as another fist, beat the door, causing it to groan and shudder. The sound of metal scraping and clicking caused the hairs to raise on my arm. Roman was trying the outside lock. He was probably attempting to pick it, a skill set learned from breaking and entering into people's homes as children. Something a distant relative had taught us from another travelling clan, many years ago. Baja had not approved of that particular lesson. But he would not succeed, the locks were hanging tight on the inside of the door.

"For pity's sake, Roman, leave me alone for a minute. Please." I just needed a minute to sort out the tangled mess in my head. To put on the mask, as I always had.

I breathed in deep, the smell of my cabin settling the last of my rattling nerves. Rubbing my eyes with my cool palms, I sighed. There was another pound on the door, which sent my body jolting forward. There was a soft thud as a pile of books fell to the floor, even the ceiling hatch rattled.

"Roman, you will shake this place to the ground and all my possessions within!" I finally shouted, anger searing away the fear and pain. Darkness above, he was strong. I huffed, my lips quivering slightly, and a single tear escaped my eye. My brother was an obnoxious ass. I would have to let the bastard in before he battered my poor home to the ground. Rolling eyes as another of Roman's heavy fists banged against the wood behind me, I huffed again, but my heart jolted as my eyes caught a dark shape above me.

The silhouette was tall and broad, its edges hazily highlighted by the wide open sky light. My breath caught as I assessed the shadow and the entryway above the roof. They had climbed in through the open roof hatch. **Fuck**.

I jolted to my feet, my hand nimbly grabbing the dagger strapped at my thigh. The shadow did not move or breathe. It was a man, but within the depth of the shadow, no features were recognisable. Roman banged on the door at my back yet again, and I heard his distinct laughter rumble from the other side. My heart still did not slow its rapid beat as I realised who stood within the shadow of my home. Eli.

The sound of hinges whining from behind me made me turn to check the door quickly. The look over my shoulder cost me, as Eli moved into my breathing space. His scent filled my cabin, my nose and even me. My achingly taught muscles still did not relax, as my dagger hand lowered. His shadowed strange eyes could now be seen in the dim light. One crisp blue, one warmest brown.

"You do realise now I will forever and always lock that bastard hatch." My words were a quiet hiss.

The frail light reflected in my broken mirror caught the slight smile tugging on his full lips, his scar stretching with the movement. I looked behind him at his worn fedora hat placed on my bundled bed. His shaggy dark hair curled around his ears and neck. The air became thick and heavy as Eli stepped even closer. Only inches lay between us now and I was headily aware that we were almost sharing breath. A stray thought crossed my mind and I had trouble recalling it back within. We were supposed to be this close, or even closer. If I had allowed the betrothal to officially happen. But because of my choices, we never would. That thought cracked open something new and unseen before.

I swallowed, trying to focus and notice other minor things, other than how Eli smelled of mint and Mutza's smoking herbs. Or how the moonlight glimmered on the dewy specks of melted snow on his fur lapels. I tried and failed to bring my attention to anything. Anything, other than what my mind was bringing to light. Roman had stopped his beating of my door and I realised then they had both planned this. The distraction at the door. To stop me from seeing the real trap. I inhaled a long uneven breath, feeling foolish. Feeling pitiful. This wasn't the first crime I had endured.

Another tear escaped my eye as I found the courage to finally look into Eli's eyes. I felt haunted by them. Haunted as they starred in the darkness and shadows. Fear ebbed its way like oil within my stomach, anticipating what he truly saw.

Did he feel pity for me?

Pity for this empty creature I had become. He had never questioned my decision or demanded an answer as to why we were no longer to be wed and partnered in the way our tradition sought. Questions had been bubbling up for some time now. The same questions which had repeated themselves over and over, for the past few weeks.

Had he never truly wanted it?

The way we joked and discussed as children?

The complexity of my thoughts was cut short when Eli inhaled deeply. The sound was loud and stirring, his chest heaving and rising in one slow movement. My mind wandered as his lips moved, and I realised he was trying to speak. But the dimness diminished what words he silently said. The noise, breathy and inaudible. His voice box had been destroyed years ago in a hunting accident, but communication had never been an issue between he, I and Roman. We had created our own language, with our hands. Speaking and reading what Eli was saying in simple gestures and signs created with deft fingers. But now, as he sighed in frustration and winced at this disability, I saw how much this wound still ailed him.

"Eli." His name left my lips without my mind or heart knowing. "I can't lose you or Roman. Not because of this." I had spoken the truth.

Something which was usually twisted by my false mask of confidence and surety. "If you follow me now. If you choose to follow..." But I was cut short. Silenced by the warm calloused hands that now held the base of my neck and my lower back. The air had vanished from the space, from the room and my lungs as Eli held me and rested his brow on my own. He had dipped his head to do so. From the depths of my soul I was alive at his touch, electrified by the gesture he had bestowed upon me. I closed my eyes, as my knees weakened, and my heart cantered feverishly. I tried to plead with him to reconsider but he held me still, hushing me and soothing me in a way I did not know I could be. I then wrapped my arms around his neck, needing to be close to someone again. To be held. His arms encircled me in a vice grip and I only sank deeper into him. Breathing him in.

"Will you bloody open the door now, you insipid witch!" Roman bellowed and fisted the door for good measure.

I started at the sound and was suddenly cold as Eli stepped away from me, the cool night air suddenly biting at my clammy skin. My eyes were still closed as I heard the shrill creak and scrape of my lock and deadbolt unfastening.

As soon as the scrape of metal clicked and detached, Roman came barrelling through the open door, bringing a swift bitter gust with him. It revived me and I gulped down whatever emotion had been building. I spun, feigning rage as Roman stomped into my home. A home which was once his also. His face was plastered with his usual roguish grin as he looked at Eli, wagging his eyebrows insufferably.

"You sly bastards!" I mocked, unable to keep the wry smile from my face as I stalked towards the open ceiling hatch and closed it with a clattering snap. I turned away, feeling my cheeks pulse with heat. My fingers instinctively found my matches, and I began adeptly lighting candles. But even as the flames spluttered to life, they could not replace the warmth and heat that had coiled within my core moments before.

"Well, you didn't open the door. It's your own fault," Roman announced with laughter, as he strode farther into the small caravan. There was barely enough room for three bodies. The candles sizzled and spluttered to life again as I moved about the place, shielding myself from Eli. "And besides, if Eli had not climbed on your roof and entered, which I dare say you did very well..." Roman's voice was filled with admiration at our mute friend. At my betrothed. Mother above, I had to stop thinking like that. We were no longer betrothed! I finally faced both men, face puffy and raised a questioning eyebrow at them. My mask was now back in place, hands on my hips. The room was well lit and I was sorely aware of the pink flush that blotched my neck and exposed chest. But I ignored it, looking baldly to Eli, my eyebrow raising further on my forehead than I thought possible. His features seemed softer in the gold candlelight. I turned, glaring at Roman, my distaste at both of their intrusion palpable.

"What!" Roman asked, fabricating insult. "We, dear sister, would have been waiting all night for you to open the bloody door."

"Well? What should we do?" I muttered, trying to sound bemused.

"I hope I didn't interrupt you two with my brazen banging and thumping?" My skin cooled to ice, and I turned with a scowl at my brother. He was intolerable.

"Yes, you did, you obnoxious swine," I mused, my eyes creasing in the corners in displeasure. He only chuckled, baiting me more. "Can a woman not hold solace in her own home for five minutes?"

"You're barely a woman. Well, you are, but you know what I mean. And no." I rolled my eyes at that as Roman walked about my home, his fingers touching the trinkets and medallions which still hung from the ceiling. I instinctively went for the one now clasped about my neck. The silver was warmed, retaining the heat from my flushed skin. I heard rather than saw our camp still moving with haste to pack.

"You could have at least shut the door behind you, you big lump," I spat, eyeing the open door.

Eli walked to the door and kindly shut it for me. It was bad enough with these two brutes as an audience, let alone my brethren. What on earth did they think of me now? I sighed defeated and sat on my bed, tying the gossamer and shimmering fabrics away. Roman moved a tower of books from a stool and sat down, removing his top layer and hanging it with ease on the hook nailed just above. Eli, I noted, remained standing, his back to the door, eyes only me. He did not remove his coat. Did not make it to sit or find comfort in my space. He did not want to intrude upon my home. My mouth formed a line, and my hand gestured to take a seat at the only other place to sit. Next to me on the bed. But he shook his head. He would not sit on the bed next to me. My stomach seemed to drop ten feet at that.

Roman saw the exchange, his thick eyebrows raised as a twitch flickered in the corner of his mouth.

On cue, my cheeks heated again but I made my mouth take an ill-humoured shape as I asked, "what can we do? If you are both going to follow me in this?" Annoyance tainted my tone. "How are we to hunt a hunter?"

"We travel north, go to the nearby villages, gauge where the attacks have happened and see if that helps with the hunt." Roman looked to Eli, seeking approval at his plan. Eli nodded in agreement.

"It will not be that simple," I sighed, rubbing my face with my hands, cursing at myself. "The Trinity were called upon for a reason. The woodland folk and those from the in-between would not have called on them lightly," I said with finality looking at the stacks of books piled up. Fairy tales, folklore, herbs and medicines. Scriptures of the traveller's history and maps of the stars. I rubbed at my eyes, exhaustion finally setting my muscles stiff.

"What about the runes?" Roman asked, watching me from his stool.

"Runes will not help us in this. Nothing works for me," I groaned, looking at the discarded pouch on the bed, its soft leather, creased and faded. I picked it up, pouring the runes out and cradling them in my hand. Nothing had worked for me. Not properly anyway. I read the signs as and when they came to me, which was rare. As rare as a red moon on summer solstice...

Anger flared in my chest and I bit my lip, fighting the scream I so desperately wanted to let free. The runes in my hand felt like a lead weight. Unnatural and foreign. In frustration and unease, I threw them, my hand shooting the pale stones into the air. They rose, glinting and twisting in the candlelight. Suddenly, as though a finger had run a cold course down my spine, I straightened. My inner compass, abruptly reeling. The necklace around my neck had come free. How, I do not know, but we all watched, as the silver pendant, with its three faced moon, flew from its resting place on my chest. It spun, harmoniously amongst the runes, now falling to the floor. Time seemed to slow as we all got to our feet, all eyes trained on the falling flash of metal as it spiralled to the wooden floor.

There was a chorus of stones and metal spinning against the floor. I stopped short, eyes wide. They all stopped with a *thunk*. I heard Roman gasp. The runes lay as though a meticulous hand had placed them in a neat circle, with the medallion at the centre. The candles flickered and I saw light flash over the beaten and worn silver surface of the three faced moon pendant. I swallowed, my fingers retracting to my palms. My nails biting into my palms for reassurance.

"I would say something's work for you," Roman said, rubbing at his cropped beard. My stomach flipped and I whirled as there was a ratting at the door. Roman moved vigilantly, opening the wooden door a crack to spy the visitor. A spluttering cough sounded through the gap.

"Open the damn door, you three, and let an old woman in," Mutza wheezed as she stumbled over the steps and into the wagon, her gnarled walking stick clicking against the wooden floor. Eli reached his grandmother and sat her cautiously on the stool Roman had vacated. I stood up, utterly bewildered at what was occurring. Never had the old woman entered my domain and within the space of a week, she had visited twice. "Now listen here, Rhona," the old woman tutted and her withered aged lips puckered. "There are no coincidences, child. Did you not hear my words, your mother's words from the grave?"

The old woman's milky eyes darted about the space, her tanned skin gathering in deepest wrinkles at the brow. "Fate weaves paths for us all, my girl, and even you, boy," Mutza spat, her walking stick taping the toe of Eli's boot on instinct. I had noticed how Eli had placed himself beside his grandmother. As blind as the old woman was, I knew she saw more now with her sight gone.

"Are you saying, Mutza, that this is a sign?" I dared, trying hard not to let my voice betray the fear that dwelled from within.

The old woman answered with a sharp nod as both her old claw-like hands finally rested together atop the misshapen wooden cane. "You have to believe, child. You have to believe, for it to make itself known to you," the old woman explained abruptly. "For it to become clear, of course, believe in yourself and the gifts of our people. All three of you." Mutza's mouth puckered again. I saw from the corner of my eye, Roman rolled his eyes. "Even you, Roman," Mutza tutted and I nearly laughed as Roman jumped. "You think your mother was a good seer when she was your age? Ha!" the old woman huffed. "She could barely read leaves in a teacup."

A strange smile formed on Mutza's withered lips as the old woman's eyes glazed at the memory of my mother. "It takes time, girl, and patience. Your gifts are not even budding. Do not doubt them." She blanched as her milky eyes bestowed upon the floor. "Ah. Maybe not so budding as blossoming." She smiled, with cracked and crooked teeth, at me. Unsettled, I rubbed at my chest, at the unfamiliar weight that had settled there and the strange tightness that had been building these past few days. "This has been your path for some time now, girl. Don't run from it," the old woman whispered pointedly.

Roman's voice cracked as he asked, "where do we go from here, Mutza?"

The old woman's slight frame huffed and shuddered. "Well, your plan to go north was the beginning of it, boy," she rasped, shakily. "Take the woodland road and follow the deaths and attacks due north, towards Neath Bridge. I have a feeling what you seek, will find you along the way."

That got all our attention.

"Trust in what I have said. Things aren't what they seem. And this new path before you all is a long one." Mutza raised a shaking hand behind her and grabbed at Eli's coat. She pulled him down, so he now knelt before his grandmother. She cupped his face and I watched as her lips trembled, her unseeing eyes locked on Eli's chest. I clenched my fists and anger boiled within me. At my own reckless, worthless self. I was taking her grandson and her only remaining family, because of a mess I caused. "Do not think of such things," she sputtered, surprising me and I looked to Roman stunned. "This was the path you *all* have to take," she said, still clutching Eli's lapels. That lump in my throat tightened and I wrapped my arms around myself.

Eli looked at me and I failed to keep my lips from quivering as I mouthed 'I'm sorry'.

Mutza patted Eli's chest and turned back to face us. "Remember this, Rhona. All of you. This has been weaved by the fates that loom for some time. I believe what you seek resides in the Fallow." My stomach dropped as the hatch above us rattled with wind. That internal tug seemed to sigh deep within me. I swallowed knowing all too well what lay within the Fallow. I looked to my brother and Eli, who did not seem shocked or the least bit concerned by this.

"That's at least two weeks of travel across the Continent," Roman uttered, his brow still crossed in thought. "We do not have that long. There will be another full moon in twenty-eight days. It could take us just that to reach the Fallow."

"Again, listen to my words. What you seek will find you along the way. But I fear this will not be your only task. More lies ahead of you." And my heart broke as she again clasped at her grandson. Her frail fingers held Eli's cheeks, and stroked stray hairs out of his face. She smiled at him. "My boy. The gods have chosen you for this journey as well. Protect her, at all costs." I started to refuse her request for Eli, but Roman caught my arm, silencing me with a look. "And it is not as it seems. I beg you, remember all is not as it seems."

Eli grunted and nodded in her hands, and his form enveloped her in a fierce hug. I turned away, feeling the burn and ache behind my eyes as new tears threatened to spill.

We would need to pack and secure my home, ready for the journey. I decided there and then that we should only take my wagon, with Balthazar and Ovi, Eli's horse. Sleeping together in here would be fine in rough weather, but I would have to make room. Turning to my brother, I whispered, "we should take my wagon. Baja can take yours with him, and Mutza can have Eli's whilst we are away."

"Agreed." His eyes roamed around the space. "But we will have to clear some of your junk out."

"I also agree," I replied, looking about the small room as well. "I can keep some and keep other possessions in yours for safekeeping."

Together we started quietly deciding what to take and not to take with us. We cleared out the gossamer and unnecessary things, including the chair and majority of my mother's books. I could hear Mutza and Eli speaking in hushed tones as Roman and I busied ourselves preparing to leave. When they were finished saying their goodbyes, I finally turned and approached the old woman.

"Thank you, for the message." A glimmer caught my eye and I saw the medallion still laying undisturbed on the floor. I deftly picked it up and placed it on the chain around my neck, securing it underneath my shirt. Mutza's blind eyes tracked my movements all the way.

"Do not let the past break you. For your future's sake." Her eyes darted to Eli and we both watched him and Roman carry out a crate and trunk from my cabin and into the night, to be stowed in Roman's caravan. "I know why you did not want the marriage to happen with Eli." Panic ebbed its way up my spine and my throat burned. **She knew.** "I feared it would happen after your mother's death. Especially as Eli…" She trailed off, tilting her head again and looking past me.

The panic had mounted, and I couldn't stop myself. "Does Eli know?" My throat strangled out and to my relief Mutza shook her head.

"I look at the woman you have now become because of it. How it has changed you. You are strong in mind, body and soul, Rhona. Do not let the past take that from you." I was dumbfounded, cold with sheer shock and adrenaline. The tears that had threatened to spill earlier, did now. In rivers, down my cheeks. "Hush, child. Your mother told me. She told me why she had to do what she did. Because of what happened to you." A weak moan escaped me and I was frozen. My blood slowed so that everything was dazed about me, but Mutza's words. "I do not blame you. But I understand. He will too, eventually."

My eyes caught sight of Roman and Eli walking back to us, and I rubbed at my face, brushing away the tears hastily and trying to stand taller. The old woman's face changed to sympathy; she knew I had been crying.

The steps to my caravan creaked and Roman and Eli entered the small space, collecting the last of my possessions to store.

"I will leave you all now. But I will pack some things for your travels. Things you will need."

I nodded, afraid my voice would give way to the torment I was engulfed in. I would not let my past define me. I couldn't not now, not in the future. Heaving a breath, I stumbled after the old woman hobbling out of my home. "Mutza." She turned and her face no longer showed pity from before. "Thank you. I mean it. Thank you for telling me."

She smiled at that and nodded, before limping into the night.

I looked out about the camp, surprised at how quickly the area had been packed away. Only one fire blazed now, the flames casting ripples of light across my shadowed people. I swallowed the anger. Swallowed the fear, knowing too well they were all whispering as they packed. Speaking about me and this task. This suicide mission.

Baja walked towards us and I inhaled, willing myself to hold strong. He whistled loudly and two of his men carrying a wooden pallet came trudging through the snow towards us. They lowered the pallet to the ground before the caravan and ran off, jumping onto a moving wagon. My uncle looked at the pallet and the contents within.

"I have set aside food and some provisions for a fortnight. That is all we could spare," he rasped, the moonlight highlighting his weathered face. "There are also three daggers, gunpowder and extra arrows, as well as my crossbow and hunting knife. Samir spared a few coins from his trove for you to purchase more arrows should you need them. If not, use it for more food."

Love filled me and forced out the numbing cold that had wracked me earlier.

"Thank you," Roman offered, eyes wide as he looked at the pallet of goods.

"For everything," I accompanied, and Baja nodded again at me.

He lifted his palm to his head, his fingers touching the centre point of his proud brow and saluted us. It was a farewell to all three of his clan, a respectful salute of goodbye. I bit down on my bottom lip and we three did the same. I could say nothing more as Baja walked away from us to his wife and their cart, his men and escorts on horseback, waiting under the night sky littered with stars.

The wagons and caravans began exiting the shelter of the clearing, one by one, wheels moving over the slush of snow and mud and back out onto the road. Leaving us all alone. I saw Roman's and Eli's caravans being towed by Denif's mules as they made the line and passed us. All eyes were upon us as our clan saluted and left to join the night.

I watched as the lanterns of my people became distant down the road, until the sound of wheels and horses was replaced by silence. The vice-like grip on my heart was suffocating and I was trying my hardest not to break again. I hadn't realised my teeth had been chattering, hadn't realised both men were behind me, until my coat was placed upon my shoulders. I turned to find Roman and Eli looking at me, expectantly. Their faces showed no pity or distrust. How could they not resent me for taking them away from everyone? For getting us into this mess in the first place? I didn't trust my voice enough to speak. I knew it would waver and crack. So I cleared my throat, trying to find something else to do, other than speaking.

"Well, me and Eli were just talking about how boring they had all become," Roman said, his brow cocked in his usual manner. I bit my lip, looking at my boots in the snow. "And besides, we need an adventure."

"One that we will potentially not survive?" I emphasised.

"Those are the best kind. Even if we do not have a map," Roman said matter-of-factly, and the building fear and hysteria made me let loose a laugh. I sobered quickly, breathing in deep. Eli came to stand beside me, silently tapping his temple. I knew he had travelled well. Darkness above, he probably had a map of the Continent memorised. I realised then, that somewhere within the books and journals of my mother and our ancestors, I must have one. I prayed I did. Just in case.

"Don't make me regret this, Roman." I couldn't hide the smile from my lips.

"Oh, I already am, aren't you?" he said sardonically, nudging Eli. I squirmed under Eli's gaze, at the small smile that was on his scarred face.

"North, then."

Chapter 17

It didn't take long to pack my caravan. Eli had even taken the time to fasten our valuables within, so as not to disturb them by the road. Balthazar was attached to the caravan and ready; the other horse we had, Eli's mare Ovi, was saddled and waiting for her master. The dawn was breaking over the tree line, followed by billowing clouds of grey. A storm was on the horizon, it would be upon us within the hour, I could smell it. The clearing was now just mud and patches of scorched earth, but the surrounding trees were still quiet and lifeless, even with nearly all humans gone. That strange feeling crept up my spine as I observed the silent trees. Even with dawn lighting the sky, no birds twittered or sang. No deer danced or rabbits played. It was almost ominous. Such life should have been in abundance here. Wind picked up strands of my hair and blew them across my vision. That wind blew north, and I knew it was one last push to send us on our way.

Roman sat in the driving seat of my wagon and Eli was now mounted on Ovi.

"We'll follow the road north for three days. Do we stop each night?" I asked, already feeling the ache of exhaustion upon me.

"We will ride for a day and a night, taking it in turns to sleep and ride. That way we are always on the road. Making camp wouldn't be the best idea given the circumstances," Roman decided.

I nodded in agreement. "Who will sleep first?" I asked, hoisting myself up to sit beside Roman.

Both Eli and my brother exchanged a look.

"Just because I'm a woman doesn't mean I shouldn't ride during the night," I exclaimed, understanding their shared expression.

Eli smiled, his eyes mischievous. Roman only huffed, climbing back into my cabin from the driver's hatch. "Oh, we know. Now on to our impending doom!" he called as he began undressing to sleep.

My lips tugged as I looked at Eli. "Hush, you imbecile. Now get your beauty sleep, you're looking positively repugnant."

"You wound me," Roman called out and I laughed loudly, the shock and adrenaline of the night's happenings still wreaking havoc on me.

I ushered Balthazar to walk and we began to move onto the road. The lead-like weight in my stomach was resounding, and the laugh and smile that had been on my lips was wiped away. The anchoring weight reminded me of my oncoming fate.

***

Two full days and one night we journeyed, in a storm that did not settle or lessen as we travelled along the rain-soaked, gravel road. The storm was so monstrous I was afraid the clouds would devour and consume the mountains and land, forever lost in a turmoil of grey rain and shattering storms.

Exhausted and shivering, my teeth had chatted in my skull until it was painful. Roman was once again sleeping in my caravan, of which I had just arisen from, and I already regretted leaving the warmth of blankets and dry shelter within. Sleep had taken me quickly when it was my rotation to turn in. My mind had not played tricks on me as my head hit the pillow and I was overcome with sleep instantly. I had not dreamt or stirred throughout my time in the shelter of my home. I awoke dazed but still aching. It was even worse adorning my cold, wet clothes that had not dried in the slightest. When I clambered back out into the seat, Roman grumbled something in irritation which I did not catch. He just climbed back behind me and shut the curtain.

The weather was still dark and oppressive, and already set my mood. Eli, who had already been awake for hours since his stint of sleep, was a short distance ahead riding Ovi. I found I was suddenly annoyed he hadn't turned or even acknowledged me in the few minutes I had been in the driver's seat. Surprised at the awkward feeling that had come over me, I continued to brood and stare at him in the rain. His thick coat and furs were slogged and soaking, and his fedora hat was limp from the downpour. Wondering what had transpired between Eli and my brother, while I had slept, unsettled me. I bit my lip, thinking of possible conversations they had exchanged. Had they been talking about me? Had they talked about this fool's mission they were entrapped in because of me? My thoughts raced as I jolted Balthazar's reign to move forward. As I came up beside Eli, who still looked ahead to the road.

Grinding my teeth, I spat into the rain, "what glorious weather!" No reaction came. Not even a side eye from him. "You know I do believe this is what the weather is like off the continent, in the west. They say it rains so hard that the people now have gills to breathe easily." A slight smirk played at the corner of his mouth. "I do believe it would work in Roman's favour. He would probably use the gills to consume more whiskey and ale. He'd have a tanker at his mouth and one at his neck." I coughed as I inhaled rain from laughing at such an image and was relieved when Eli finally looked at me, a slight smile on his mouth. "Have you eaten?"

He only shook his head in response.

"Let's pray the storm eases soon, so we can light a fire and dry off, brew some tea and eat some dried meat." My stomach grumbled at the thought of hot tea and food. I looked to the clouds above as rain cascaded across my cheeks and eyes. No stars or sky could be seen through the mass of rumbling grey.

We needed to get off the road to rest the horses as well, and to save what ounce of humanity I had left until the rain washed it away and I became insufferable. I huffed as another crack of thunder echoed above. Focusing on the chaotic roaring of rain and wheels trampling over the dirty mush of the road, I tried to quiet my distaste. Steam rolled off both horses' flanks and I leant forward to rub Balthazar. Anything to steal my mind away from the cold causing my hands and legs to ache and turn my mood sourer. Eli had not communicated since my attempt to ease whatever had transpired between him and my brother. He just continued to look ahead, stonelike and offering no attention. Something ached within me and I couldn't bring myself to discover what.

The road ahead was opening up into a valley, and I groaned inwardly. The surrounding trees beside the road would be the only potential shelter, and if we passed them entirely, we wouldn't find dwellings for miles.

Another rumble of thunder erupted above, and I nearly yelped as Eli began to gallop ahead with haste. I strained my eyes, trying to follow him, the rain was too obscuring to see further than a few yards. I knocked on the wood behind me, trying to stir Roman. His snoring had reached its peak of being painful. I halted Balthazar and waited. Hearing another loud snore, I banged my fist harder this time.

"Wake up you bastard!" I called behind and the brute finally began to wake.

He scrambled out, grunting. "What is it?"

"Eli rode ahead, I think he saw something." The reigns cracked in my hands as I gripped them.

"Wait for him to return or signal back."

"What signal? What if he doesn't come back" I fussed, my heartbeat near deafening in my ears.

"A signal would be that he doesn't come back," Roman said quietly, squinting in the rain.

A few minutes later hooves galloped back to us and I readied to have Balthazar bolt, my aching fists tightening on the reigns. Eli and Ovi skidded in a splattering of rain and mud as they came back to us. The mare, huffing from exertion and exhaustion. Eli began signalling and relief flooded me, as I tried to focus ahead. There was a farm no more than a mile away.

As we ventured further in the valley, the farm became a distant smudge ahead. My body aches intensified at the new visage of a dry place to stay and I thanked the Mother.

"Thank Saint Angela and her three breasts!" Roman exclaimed beside me. Scoffing the laugh bubbling up, I tried to imagine the warmth that would soon be seeping into my skin from a fire.

We travelled up the road towards the farm and dismounted at the open gates, rusted and detached. The barn was boarded up with wooden slats and the windows to the farmhouse were broken, ripped fabric curtains were blowing sodden in the storm. It looked abandoned. Roman called out loudly into the rain to see if any life was hiding inside, but nothing stirred. I waited by the caravan and horses as both he and Eli walked the perimeter of the buildings, searching for any instance of life. It was a slight relief when both came back finding none. The farmhouse was a short walk away from the barn, it too had broken glass windows, a luxury by any standards. Curtains and boards blew and creaked in the wind and rain. It looked downright dire in the dying light of day.

"I will check the house just in case," Roman exclaimed as he kicked open the oak door. Eli stayed behind with me, holding Ovi, who huffed and hoofed at the ground. The horse could smell the hay, it seemed, in the barn. It would be a reprieve from the rain, for all of us. And time to dry and warm ourselves out of the storm. Eli watched the house, his eyes darting across its front windows and open door, even with the streams of water that fell off the rim of his hood. I fumbled, abashed, realising I had been staring at him as Roman called out from within.

"All clear," Roman said as he came back through the darkness of the doorway, "looks like it's been abandoned for months." It was a good thing I supposed, to not have to face or pay off the farmer for shelter. "We would be better to stay in the barn though, the house is damp with water and mould. There is no food either, the stores are empty except for old wheat and firewood," he said over the ricocheting rain.

"It will do," I shouted back.

The heavens really had opened and the rain hammered against our cloaks, heavily. Together we all wrestled with the nailed slats, pulling them finally from the barricaded barn. It was thankfully dry and was large enough for my caravan. There were five empty stalls for horses and cattle and mounds of hay were bundled and piled to one side, untouched and miraculously dry. I sent a silent prayer up to the Mother, but my stomach suddenly clenched at the thought of her not being able to hear my thanks. I had killed her. Sickness rolled my gut and I inhaled sharply, trying to steady the oncoming unease.

Tools still hung forgotten on the walls, covered in dusty cobwebs, and limp hessian sacks lay unfilled and unused on a tool station. The smell of dust, earth and musty wheat settled my growing anxiety as I strode around the large space. The farm had not been in use for more than a few months, but why had the people left the farm in the first place? It played upon my mind and spooked me. I could even see that it was not just I who pondered the same, as Roman and Eli looked about the abandoned barn and buildings. Balthazar almost cantered into the stall, as I unhooked him from the steer. I heaved a bundle of hay into his stall and he nudged and nibbled appreciatively.

Eli had done the same for Ovi and then cleared out an empty stall with an old shovel he had found and began laying newer hay to cover the stale smell of animals and muck. An old steel bucket lay in the corner of the barn and we emptied it and began building our fire in it for the night, clearing the area of hay and debris. We opened a barn door, allowing the smoke to leave the enclosed space, so we didn't choke. The weather outside hammered the ground, distorting the grounds and house outside. When the fire in the bucket was roaring and the heat filled the stall in ripples of delicious warmth, Roman shamelessly began removing his clogged furs and leathers until he sat around the new fire, bare-chested and in only his breaches. His boots were removed, and his shirt hung over the wooden dividers.

I debated changing in my caravan but the aches and pains of cold changed my mind quickly. I began removing my furs and cloak, hanging them from an iron nail on a wooden pillar. Roman sat princely next to the fire, his muscled chest and shoulders glowing from the flames. I raised a questioning eyebrow at him, still unsure how much clothing to remove. He only rolled his eyes at me as he outstretched his hands to flames and sighed dramatically. A wet strand of hair fell upon my forehead and eye, and I blew at it frustratingly, losing my footing as I tried to yank my boot. My ill footing caused me to spin on the spot and I had turned enough to see Eli undressing. My gut gave a little spasm as I watched his hands begin the task of removing his own sodden shirt. My throat tightened and he paused halfway through his unbuttoning, suddenly sensing my immediate attention, as his mouth suddenly set in a doubtful line and his eyes darted between Roman and me. I spun, hiding my face, conscious of Roman's smug smile as he lolled in the hay casually in my peripherals. I hissed as I finally pulled the other sodden leather boot from my calf and foot. I began peeling away the woollen coat and shawl, the fibres coarse and wet rubbing uncomfortably against my cold skin. I stopped there, unsure if I could remove any more clothing without embarrassing myself further

"Remove your clothes, woman, before you catch your death of cold," Roman said from behind me and I inhaled slowly through my nose, grinding my teeth. "It's nothing we haven't seen before."

That caused me to falter. Of course, Roman had seen a woman's body before, but had Eli? The thought didn't sit well with me and I scowled at my brother from the side. I peeked at Eli and saw the very same scowl on his own face as he directed daggers at Roman. Fisting my hands, I realised I had no right to feel or question Eli's loyalty. It was not like we were going to get married. I didn't want it and he certainly didn't either. But I couldn't help the strange pressure that built within me at the thought of Eli with another woman. I swallowed down any lingering doubt and began removing my knitted top. I did not face either of them as I undressed to just my shirt and undergarments. My legs now bare and free from my riding breeches, I began hanging my clothes over the side of the stall.

I finally faced the fire, choosing not to look at Roman or Eli as I sat in a bundle of hay, moving my legs to a position which hid some of my modesty. The slick shirt against my breasts couldn't be helped but I chose to ignore them. I began rubbing at my bare legs, trying to encourage the blood flow back into them as the fire's heat slowly crept its embrace over my gooseflesh skin. I looked up quickly to see Eli standing with his back to me.

He was hanging his clothes over the adjacent divider, his broad shoulders and muscles rippling with each movement. The fire light danced off his tanned skin and I found my eyes following the line of his spine down to his narrow hips. Swallowing hard, I tried to look away. But my heart and stomach fluttered like a baby bird and I couldn't shake my gaze. Admittedly, I had not seen him like this since we were children, when he was thin and gangly like my brother had been. I couldn't help but think how times had changed. He turned back to the fire and with a furious blush, I averted my eyes. I hadn't realised

Roman had been sitting watching my every movement, that odious smug look plastered across his face. Silently cursing, I gave him a pointed smile, along with a fowl finger.

Ignoring Roman's aggravating attention, I began trying to untangle and ring out my hair. The wet mass of curls was a sodden disaster, as I painfully separated sections with my fingers. My scalp screamed as I tried to tame the mass. When my fingers finally began winning the battle, I twisted and rang out the water. Streams of droplets fell on the floor, soon evaporating with the fire's heat. I braided it quickly and attempted wrapping it back into a knot, out of the way. But unruly strands escaped and fell limp and damp against my neck and cheeks. Exasperated, I slapped my hands down, done with the burden of hair. My skin prickled as I saw Eli smiling at me over the flames.

Stomach fluttering once again, I swallowed. "It's a mess." I huffed, defeated.

Roman chose that moment to stand and get supplies for a meal. Watching my brother's retreating form rummaging around in my caravan, I began to blush again. It was becoming as easy as breathing, this incessant, unavoidable heat that crept up my neck and face. Eyes darting to Roman, I ground my teeth at his painstakingly long and purposeful movements. Bastard, I thought. A little annoyed and yet positive, thanks to the welcoming embrace of heat, I sighed.

Movement through the flames caught my eye and I saw Eli signalling to me. *'I like your hair.'*

I swallowed, my hand instinctively touching my hair and bun. My teeth grazed my bottom lip as I contemplated what exactly to say. A drop of water fell from the barn roof, sizzling on the flames. The smell of smoke filled my nose. I worked my jaw, but I had nothing to say. So, I just smiled, warmly and truthfully, and was surprised to see a brightness return to Eli's eyes.

"No wonder the old bastard was so gracious gifting us with the food," Roman called out, causing me to start. "There are two loaves of Miriam's bread and some of her spiced squirrel."

Eli's laugh was a ruffle of breath and I smiled even wider at the thought.

"Let's eat what there is and be done with it. Better to have a dry night and horrid food, than a horrible night with, well, horrid food," I said, and we all laughed.

Thankfully there was some goat cheese and salted mix that we gulped down the squirrel meat with. It was not as bad as I expected, but the meat was questionable. Still, my belly was full, and the heat of the fire was lulling my aching limbs into a sensational stupor. The rain outside still hammered on the barn roof above and the dull sound was slowly causing my eyes to become heavy with sleep. Sitting back on a pile of dry straw, my bare legs stretching out, not caring, I sighed appreciatively. My eyes were too heavy now, hypnotised by the dancing flames.

My eyes slowly slopped to Eli, who was sitting opposite me, his own eyes were closed in sleep. His deep-set scar, carved from the base of his throat, past his strong jaw and up to the corner of his full mouth, almost glistened in the fire light. The stubble that grew on his chin and cheeks did not grow where the pale scar tissue was. I watched his deep breathing, my mind thinking of that scar. How it had happened. Despite the threatening scar, he was still handsome. Very handsome, in fact. Which was a strange thing to admit to myself. I held myself, thinking about our situation and the betrothal that should have happened on my eighteenth birthday, nearly three years ago. He had not necessarily renounced the pairing, made for us when we were barely able to walk. However, he had not done anything to hasten it. Well, he had done nothing at all. He had grown distant as he had grown older. Memories flooded me and I recalled the days when we were all inseparable.

Playing bandits, sleeping under the stars, horse riding in the rivers. I had always assumed it was because he had despised being matched to me, that he only saw me as his friend or sister. Losing his voice and the years of growing into a man had hardened his disposition, altering him from the sweet boy I once knew. My mind whirled and spun at the thought. It was absurd. I was spoiled, ruined. I was… I didn't finish the thoughts that began to darken, like the night sky outside. I pinched at the skin on my arms, the quick, sharp pain settling the darkness within. I decided, rather ruthlessly, that even though I would never act upon our betrothal, I could still look at him and at least admire him for the man he had become.

    I couldn't ignore the ache and heaviness of my eyes any longer and I nestled back in the straw, surprisingly comfortable and sluggish with warmth.

Chapter 18

I awoke rested, but my legs were beginning to buzz with cold. The fire was merely dying embers of scorched firewood now. I was however covered by a shawl of thick wool, one that I usually lay with at night inside my caravan. It had been placed over the length of my body. I sat up, puzzled, then felt the shift of fabric up and around my midriff. Mortified at what Eli or Roman may have witnessed caused me to fumble quickly with the fabric of my shirt. I prayed they had not seen the scars which plagued my usually hidden skin. Both Roman and Eli were still sleeping, so I looked up to the rafters of the barn. Dust motes floated in pale rays that filtered through a crack in the wood panelling. After stretching and trying to stir my aching legs and rump into standing, I needed fresh air. Now. I needed to freshen and find a water well or stream. A farm such as this should have one or be near a water source at least.

Thankfully, the barn roof no longer rattled from the onslaught of rain and only the heavy breathing of two men filled my ears as I dressed quietly. My mind kept asking questions of which I did not have the answer to, so I made myself believe Roman must have gathered the shawl to cover me. I reached for my dark riding trousers that hung on a divider beside me. I inwardly sighed, feeling the fabric to be crisp and dry. The tight brown fabric slid over my muscular calves and thighs. I strapped my hunting dagger back to my upper leg, the belt-like buckle fastening securely. The fire was dying out and we needed more logs and kindling. That would be my excuse for venturing out. Opening the barn door, it was like the brisk, sweeping wind was welcoming me. Inhaling sharp cold air as deeply as my lungs would allow, I stilled, existing in the chill of the turning night. The storm had passed and only traces of clouds were far away on the horizon. It was still night, and by the darkness of the sky and the brilliance of the moon, I guessed after midnight. I'd either slept for a few hours or we had slept a day and into the night. I couldn't tell.

The shell of a house caused the hairs to stand on the back of my neck and I hesitated at the open door. The broken windows and weather-ripped drapes hung limp in the hollow holes of windows, like depthless eyes holding ghosts and secrets. The deepest shadow coaxed at my senses, as unease clawed through me. But there was something else as well. That incessant internal tug that stirred deep within me to venture in, anchoring me to choices I had not yet made.

My eyes searched the dark for any movements. No moon or stars flitted through the agape windows. Nothing could be seen, even as my eyes adjusted to the blackness. Stumbling a few paces in, I knocked over a chair. Hissing a rampage of swear words, I stilled as the wood clattered onto the flagstone floor.

My fingertips brushed against the side of a table and then over rough, stone walls. There was a workstation; my fingertips felt the grit, crumbs and webs draped all over it. This had to be a kitchen. The faint smell of dried herbs could be sensed in a room to my left. The aromatic and earthy smell led me further into the dark of the room. A pantry? Continuing forward, trying to find the dry store of firewood, my fingers grasped at something waxen, a thick candle. My free fingers dug deep into the pockets of my military jacket, searching for my flints. Finding them, I quickly pulled out the slim pick and rock, striking. Sparks bloomed and I saw the wick of the candle, so I positioned my hands to strike with accuracy this time. Flint met pick and flame ignited, a splutter of bold orange and yellow, and the smoke curled around my hands and fingers. My eyes tried focusing, to gauge the surroundings through the shadows, and as I turned about the room, the flame light brightened the dead pale face right in front of me.

The shriek that escaped me was strangled as I careened and fell to the floor with a soft thud. Unyielding pain shot up my spine, winding me. The diminished stump of a candle was still clutched desperately in my hand as I held the flame in front of me, hands trembling. The horror of the face leering at me in the darkness became finally clear.

The face, if you could call it that, belonged to no human, dead or alive. It was attached to a body that was not of this world. The strange shape hovered by the nearest wall, cast in the deepest shadow that only could have come from worlds in between. It seemed to be made from shadow and smoke. Its form looked human, frail and brittle with elongated shoulders and arms. Thin and gaunt were its features, like a skeleton not yet done relinquishing the flesh to death. With a start, I looked down to where no feet were visible in the darkness.

It moved closer without footfall and its disfigured framework was grey and transparent, like it was formed by creeping mist on a bleak dawn. Two black holes swarmed where eyes should have been with two skeletal nasal holes just below them. There was no mouth or line of lips. No hair or skin seemed to cover the creature, and in the single flame's glow its domed skull-like head shimmered. It did not move or make a sound, as it hovered. Its thin structure draped in tired grey cloth, that hid nothing of the form underneath. A low whistle, like a bird descending in flight sounded out, the reverberations bouncing off the stone walls and around the phantom-like thing. But the sound came not from the lips the creature possessed. The strange being had created the sound. It was as if the whistling had come from within it. The creature's elongated hand extended towards me, its spindle-like fingers clicking unnaturally.

My ears rang as an internal voice screamed at me to *run*. Bone-like fingers came closer to me, reaching and I crumpled further into a heap on the floor. Never had I seen such a creature and it was horrific to behold. I tried my lungs, readying my voice to scream as loud as I could to wake the others, but those pale grey claws did not reach for me. They had stilled, motionless before me. The claws stayed, the palm up as if in gesture, as though in waiting. Eyes darting between its nightmarish face and hand, I blinked. It did not glide any closer. It just stayed there, waiting. Taking in a gulp of air, I was just about let force the scream that was tightening my throat, when the creature tilted its greyish bone head to the side. It's pitiless eyes, holes of the deepest black, were not monstrous, but peaceful, waiting. It's motion, so animalistic, caused me to pause.

It was looking at me. Really looking. The air still trapped in my chest and lungs, held, and burned as I watched it back, horror struck yet curious. The familiar tingle from my childhood began to creep a slow path up my spine. I released the lungful and observed. There were no weapons, no teeth, or claws to shred flesh. It was almost see through, its body and robes billowing from a windless draft. Its hand was still out, stretched in invitation before me and I saw, what I believe to be its head lower and nod in submission.

Gulping down the fear, allowing oxygen to flow in my body easing the fight that still clutched at my muscles, I bit on my lip. Setting aside the candle, so it stood on the floor, I carefully raised my own hand towards the creature. My scarred fingers shook with uncertainty, as they reached the peak, mere inches from the creature's own, when it made the same whistling sound as before. It was not shrill or painful to hear, it was soft and caressing, like a lark on a winter morning. One long note held again, coaxing and encouraging me. Licking my lips, mouth already dry, I clasped hands with the creatures. It was solid. Cold and ice like to the touch, as though made of stone or granite. Its long bone fingers grasped my wrist and lifted me from the floor with gentle ease. My breast caught in that moment, as an internal chink clanged within me. The unknowing became known, as though a lost memory was trying to resurface, rippling and murky. The kitchen door swung open with a splintering crack of wood and moonlight suddenly shone through the space. Eli barrelled into the room, hunting knife drawn. He halted as he saw the scene before him. Shock shaped his features and then fear, as he beheld the creature and then me. The wraith, if that's what you could call it, had not even flinched.

I stilled, eyes wide and pleading to Eli, mouthing the word "*no*" to him.

The creature made the strange whistling sound again and released me, its skeletal hand moving slowly, hanging once more. The holes in its head, turned their attention on Eli and he stopped his slow countered steps towards me. The thing's head teetered as it surveyed the room, then finally, it turned its eerie attention back to me. Its figure shimmered in the darkness, the parts of the creature that were clear to see, turned watery, the darkness slowly dissolving it. The creature suddenly swooped, its body bowing and arching with the swiftness of no mortal being. It made one last long noted whistle that rang out clear and true to the darkened kitchen, before it dissolved completely into the shadow.

The farmhouse kitchen was left in a state of quiet. Nothing else stirred after the creature's departure and the only sound in my ears was my own staggered gasps. My thoughts tumbled over one another fast. Memories and pictures, flickering and flipping through pages of my mother's books. Eli suddenly, awakening from his shock-stilled state, ran forward, to the stone wall the thing had vanished into. His large hands ran over the stone and brick in assessment. He then turned, facing me, closing the space between us as his eyes searched me for injury. He caught at my wrist, turning it over in his hands for inspection at where the creatures clawed hand had gripped me.

"I'm fine, honestly," I said, quietly dazed. "It did not hurt me, whatever it was."

Eli's gentle fingers finished their scrutiny and his hands then sought out my face, moving it from left to right in the candlelight, searching for any ill or harm. Huffing, I grabbed his own wrist, pulling at his bare arms.

"Eli, I am well. It did not harm me."

His eyes finally met my own and his worry lines softened. His mouth drew into a thin line, and he finally nodded, his assessment complete.

My stomach tightened, as I saw the sight before me. Eli was here, and shirtless. I was touching his bare arms. My hands heated, the palms becoming balmy and warm as though some internal flame coursed through my blood.

I stammered, finding some place to concentrate other than our touching skin. "I went to fetch more wood for the fire. I came in here and… that's when it found me." Words almost choked me.

Had it been real?

It must have been. The image of its strange skeletal face leering in a mist of shadows made me close my eyes and shudder. Its face would haunt my dreams for weeks. Shaking, I wrapped my arms around myself, digging in my fingers into my arms. Pain erupted, this reality proving to be real.

"Do you know what it was?" I asked, trying to hide the relief I felt at his arrival.

Eli cocked his head, indicating a closed doorway in the kitchen wall. The dry store. My brows crossed, confused. He moved away, looking around the dark space. Only a single flame flickered from the floor, where I had discarded it. Eli picked it up and began lighting the remaining wax stumps that were about the room. A dust covered gas lamp hung from the wall by the stone hearth and he lit it quickly, the aged oil sending out a bright yellow glow.

I watched, as Eli paced about, causing dust motes and cobwebs to float about in his wake. Clearing my throat, I realised he was not communicating on purpose.

"Elias, do you know what it was?" I said a second time, aware of his evasiveness, my voice etched in anger.

His eyes found me, and his face twisted in concentration. He stopped and raised his broad shoulders and using his hands, brought them to his throat. His fingers were tightly pinched together as he expanded them in a bursting movement. He then made the same movements in front of his scarred mouth. I understood. A small memory surfacing of our communication as children through hands and fingers.

"A messenger?" I said, stunned.

Eli nodded, searching the space between us. The disturbed dust motes floated erratically from his movements. He then pointed to the furthest corner of the room, cast in unmoving black shadow. My eyes adjusted and took in the corner, veiled in utter black. I knew what he was trying to indicate.

"Shadow?" I whispered, as a shudder rippled through me. Shadow people, or messengers from the other side, were sent by means no one has ever known. Blurred line drawings surfaced from deep within my memory, drawn by my mother's hands with shards of charcoal. I could remember the smudges of ashen black on calf parchment in one of her books. But what was the message? No words were spoken.

If the creature was indeed a shadow messenger, then why did it not deliver a message? Something seemed to lurk in the back of my mind, burrowing and gnawing into a forgotten memory. But as soon as the feeling of the familiar became me, it vanished, leaving me still confused. Eli stared into the darkness of the corner; his profile highlighted by the moon's pale beams that ventured through the open door. His scar was the colour of ashen bone in the faint glow, with his nose straight and brow creased; he was deep in thought. There was a squeak and a shrill clang from an old iron pot hanging on the fire grate, then a rustle of hay and dry wood. I gasped, my voice hiking to a scream. Eli jolted soundlessly and ran to my side, his muscled arms held up in defence and his dagger drawn steadily. Both of us froze as my entire body on edge and my chest panting. It was a mouse running hastily along the far wall. Realisation doused my fear like water to a fire and I laughed, suddenly feeling foolish. I couldn't contain the sound as my laughter rang out, my sides aching and eyes watering, hysteria and fear causing a havoc of emotions. Eli could only smile at me as the relief swept away the edge that had set his features to stone. His scar had creased with it, making his face less baneful. I leaned a hand on him for support as the rolling laugh subsided. When I could control myself again and stood, his smile was gone. His strange eyes bore into mine and then about my face, roaming my details. My cheeks heated and I realised I truly must have looked foolish. He removed my hand from his hard shoulder and a pang of unease stifled my smile. I swallowed as I shied away.

"I'm sorry, I didn't mean to. I know you don't like it, anyone touching you, I mean." My whispered words tumbled out and I could do nothing but look to the wall, rather than to him.

I didn't know if it was hurt or befuddlement that tore at something in my chest. He inhaled and I could hear how deep his lungs drew in breath as he moved closer to me, his brow furrowed and eyes blinking. There was anger in those eyes as they beheld me and I stifled my quiet gasp as he stepped into my space, filling it with him and his scent. Wood smoke, mint, and morning dew. Close enough to share breath, I swallowed again, unable to think of anything but him and my rapid heart. Calloused fingers gripped my slacken hand and placed it firmly back on his bare shoulder. His pupils dilated, the black, overpowering the brown and blue. I tried my mouth, attempting to form words, knowing my face betrayed exactly how I felt, confused and yet riveted. I drew in a shallow breath, drawing my eyes down to where my scarred fingers held his tanned shoulder, coated, and encased by his own scarred fingers.

My breathing wasn't something I could calm as I looked deeply into Eli's eyes, trying to seek out the untold truth that lurked beneath. Rationality evaded me and I presumed he was making a statement. Trying to show that even though I probably repulsed him, he didn't want it to be an issue. His own breathing was ragged as he watched me, his jaw muscles fluttering. My mind spun as a thought dawned like a sun reaching over a dark horizon.

What if he did want me to touch him?

My stomach fell several feet at the thought, my own skin suddenly electrified and erupting with heated shivers. Pursing my lips, I held his gaze waiting for him to crack, waiting to see if this last thought could be true.

But Eli did not move or flinch for that matter. He was still and his eyes, although withholding, were unyielding as they stared back at me. His expression was cold, and anger simmered below its neutral surface. His clenched jaw and guttural breaths told me so. It wasn't want. It was disgust, surely? A pain burst within me, a pain and ache mixed with shame that curdled whatever was in my stomach. Spine straightening, I clenched my teeth at the sudden annoyance now rippling inside me.

He had never been this cold and barren towards me when we were children, when we played and wrestled and hunted. There was always a smile, though marred, that had brightened every time we played. But as we aged and grew out of our childish games, he had grown and changed with it. No more smiles, no more wordless conversations. Just an enigma of straight faces and passing signals. What had changed him so?

A pang of fear pulsed through me at thought of Eli knowing my own kept secret. ***Did he know?***

A cold chill skittered down my spine making me blink at the thought. I prayed to the darkness, prayed that he did not know. I felt my eyes sting, and the numbness return to my soul, as utter fear took me and the darkness of my memory crept ever closer, closing in.

"What aren't you telling me, Elias?" My words were hushed but the demand in them seemed deafening. He didn't even blink and I had to bite on the inside of my cheek, my anger coiling my gut. I snatched my hand back, as though I had been stung, the healing cuts and sores stretched with the strength of my clenched fingers. The pain was welcome.

I watched as the glistening skin on Elias's neck and connecting tissue to his shoulder flickered. The pulse was fast and strong in the moonlight, as if it was thundering through his veins. I looked to his chest, the skin that stretched and smoothed across ribs and muscular pectorals that pounded with each beat.

My teeth sunk into my lower lip, as I watched him. This was not the boy who I had grown with, played with and shared bread with. Something had changed and the unease was building as to why, causing my throat to tighten and the air to thin.

"What do you know, Elias? What do you know?" My voice cracked and broke. My airways ached as my heart galloped in my chest, almost bruising me.

If he knew about what had happened and the truth as to why my mother died... The very thought made my stomach roll.

"Do you know, Elias?" My speech trembled, along with my thin lips.

He couldn't answer, due to what had caused the scars that gnarled and twisted the smooth skin from neck to throat, to mouth. It had been a stag... that had caused such atrocities to his flesh as a young boy. The stag had charged as a young, naïve Elias was caught in his own hunting trap, small fingers unable to loosen the rope and metal in time. The stag had ploughed forward, blundering over its own hooves into his small form. Antlers of sharp bone had torn and shredded the flesh that held his voice box, leaving Elias unable to speak a word ever again. It was a gift from the great Mother that he had survived such devastation. Mutza had raised the mute boy since his own parents were no longer in this life but the next. Like my own mother.

"Eli, why do you toy with me? If you wish to say something, just say it!"

My brother chose that moment to stumble in through the open kitchen door, befuddled with sleep and stretched, yawning loudly. He crossed his arms across his chest, leaning casually on the open door.

"Sneaking off with Eli are we, Rhona?" His features were amused, his tone playful. My fear evaporated along with Roman's smirk as sudden anger boiled and erupted over, burning myself and both Roman and Eli.

"You bastard," I spat, seething like an anointed cat, eyeing both viciously. "You know not of what you speak, Roman, other than shit. I wouldn't," my words were erratic, tumbling over one another like molten iron from a forge. "I couldn't. You know nothing!" I was hissing now.

My lungs filled and I saw the distaste and regret transform Eli's face. Saw his head dip, lips thinning.

"You think this is all a game," I yelled hoarsely, the fury coating my tongue made everything taste venomous in my mouth. My heart ached to look at Eli, to see the disgust. The repulsion. I swallowed hard, pinning, and strapping down the hurt in my own features. "I left to find firewood after something woke me. And a shadow messenger came to me." My voice was quiet, but every word rippled with anger. Roman straightened at my words, wide eyed and worried. From my rage or the shadow messenger I didn't know. "It did not even give me a message at all. It just was there and then not, disappearing as quickly as it had arrived," I gasped down a breath as I started my new verbal battle. "Eli must have awoken and realised I wasn't there. The shadow messenger had presented itself, and it was doing something. Eli came in, saw it and tried to help me!" I yelled.

I was panting while glaring at my idiotic brother. Eli only looked at the floor, quiet and indifferent. I turned my rage into a vicious knife point. Breathing deeply, I tried to calm the rendering of my speech.

As I spoke, my voice was cold and distant. "And besides, I am not the woman for Eli, and nor will I ever be." Roman gulped, eyes darting between me and our friend, as he tried to speak. "Save your words and foolish whims for another day. I have grown tired of you." The cold shell coating me, my armour, hardened even further with my words to Eli. "Do not worry, Eli. I know you well enough to know that I am not the match for you."

Walking to the storeroom, I grabbed the nearest dried logs on the pile and threw one to each man. I grabbed a third, hiding my wince at the sharp bark piercing the skin on my hand. The pain felt good, jolting me. I moulded my features into a bored expression, sighing heavily, and said plainly, "I will keep watch, in case anything else finds us here in the dead of night."

I turned out of the kitchen without a second glance back, glad for the night air that kissed at my heated skin. I ignored the rush of Roman's voice to Eli. I did not care. Did not care if they argued. I was glad to be away from them, even if my lips began to tremble and the hurt, I had felt moments before came crashing in, in waves. The barn was still bathed in a warming glow from the remaining embers and the horses bickered in the stalls. I dumped the log onto the dying fire, coaxing new flames to consume the dried bark and then began tending to the blood that coated my hands, making sure to be rough with myself. I wanted the pain as payment for my outburst. As payment for the way Eli had looked at the way I has spoken of him, of us.

I didn't deserve him.

I never would.

Chapter 19

I didn't quite know when Eli and Roman came back in and sat or fell back to sleep. The murmured rumbles of my brother's quiet words eased until silence finally met my ears. I had been brushing down Balthazar for over an hour, teasing out the knots that had begun to form from the weather and frost. I sourced another apple from our stash of supplies and divided between the two beasts quietly penned in the stables. Both welcomed the late-night snack. When I finally sat back in front of the burning flames, their hypnotic flickers seized my eyes and thoughts, pushing me into a distant place inside myself. The inner voices, after what felt like hours, began rioting against my skull until in my head I was screaming. Mutza had confirmed to knowing the reasons for my mother's death. I saw it when she came to me before we left. She knew why my mother had walked into that village, enraged and ready for blood, and ready to spill and shed it for the revenge of her daughter. I closed my eyes as the image of my mother's feet, blackened and charred, flashed with menace in my head. My fingers found the soft skin under my arm and pinched hard. The sharp pain eradicated the memory quickly and I hissed, stopping the assault and began rubbing at my face. But my mind always played tricks on me. I felt breath on my throat, and the stench of stale ale and pipe smoke filled my nose at times. They always caused me to I flinch, or ricochet from my seat. I found at times, I would have to physically shake myself, to rid them.

My hands rubbed at my face roughly, pulling the skin of my cheeks and eyes with force. A hand gripped the hairs at the base of my skull.

No, no, no, no, no.

A glimmer in a crack of the barn wall caught my eye. The distant sun was rising, brightening the darkness outside and I focused on it, forcing myself to calm and to be still. I looked at the light, in hope that it would burn away those images. My fingers began to tingle, and the numbness of thought began buzzing with life. In the distance, birds sang. I imagined the sun rising within me, shunning away those horrid memories. I breathed deep, my breath quivering as the warmth doused away the lingering threads of pain. It was then I heard it, the low calling whistle. Startled, I looked to both men, dumbfounded to find them still slumbering soundly.

So much for being in this together, I thought.

I stalled, staring at both. Should I wake them, to come with me? But there was a rigidity within me, I couldn't face them yet and explain my emotions from earlier that night. There had been no need for my anger or my outburst. The whole situation had been trivial, and shame pulsed in me at the thought of how I had acted. I rose, waiting to see if an eye would peek open from either Roman or Eli, but neither stirred. The whistle echoed again, and a thought bloomed within me. The messenger had only presented itself to me and me alone.

The barn door creaked as I slipped out in the bitter dawn. The breaking light painted the surrounding area with a pale purple haze. Mist glistened in the neighbouring field and I couldn't tell if it was morning dew of fireflies. This had been a working farm long ago, mostly wheat from the rusted tools and field shears resting against the wall. Weeds were now creeping up the metal and blades. No animals grazed in the fields or walked the yard, there was nothing but eerie silence.

The sky was turning mauve and more clouds lurked far ahead, dark and thick with thunder. An impending chaos in the ghostly tranquillity. I thought of my wagon stationed under the overhanging roof of the barn, wondering if it would be sheltered enough. Leaks had begun to trickle through over the years, and it was slowly aging, the wood and seals now bowed from damp and coarse weather. I looked back to the farmhouse, a shell that was probably once a welcoming home. The broken glass was dark and the stonework dull against the ominous morning mist swallowing the courtyard. There again in the distance, as though coming from within the depths of the house, was the low whistle of the shadow messenger.

I walked to the open doors, gravel crunching under my feet. The room, now in slight shadow, would have been a warm sight after a long day's work some time ago. I imagined the farmer and his wife mulling around, as children ran after chickens, and inviting smells of the evening meal billowed up the chimney. It was nothing of the sort now.

I stepped further into the kitchen, spying another door in the shadow that stretched out into the rest of the house. My footfall was silent on the dust and dirt coated floor as I walked across the room to the door. Opening it, I peered into the gloom of a hallway. There was a single staircase that led to an open landing room. A faint light glowed at the very top, the dawn breaking against the sky. Rays of pale grey shone, and I watched as dust and debris billowed on the morning wind. The sounds of ragged curtains lightly blowing made me pause at the steps. I needed courage, so I clenched my fists as each step groaned under my weight, and I slowly walked up.

It was a large sleeping room at the top of the stairs, wide and open to the elements as the broken window frames allowed all manner of rain, snow and wind in. Four broken beds were crumpled and sodden on the floor, bedding a mess as though the people had left in the middle of the night. Furniture was dotted about the room, blackened and rotting from the onslaught of rain. A hole the size of my head gaped in the ceiling, and broken tiles and wood were left scattered on the floor below.

I walked about the space, taking in the details of the forgotten home. The smell of mildew and must was almost overpowering. Carefully, I moved to the open window; the wooden frames were splintered, glass murky and fractured. I wrapped my arms around myself, the morning chill slowly seeping into me and I physically shivered.

There was but a flickering, a tingle, that then pulsed in my fingers and then the hairs on my neck stood on end as I sensed her in the room before she even dared to speak.

"Daughter of the in-between," the Crone croaked.

I turned from the shattered hole to find her standing across the wooden space. My heart jolted, my body suddenly urging me to run and yet my feet were locked heavy in place with unseen weights.

"I am not here to harm you or reclaim the debt," she crooned, her voice like sand rubbing against my skin. The grim light of morning edged its way across the sodden floor towards the grey veil at her blackened feet. Her features were hazed out by the gauzy fabric that hung over her head, almost obscuring her face and limbs completely in a strange opaque shroud. And yet her dark, hollowed eyes seemed to pierce through the fabric to me. She looked about the place, eyes focusing, seeing beyond the wooden skeleton of the farmhouse. "Yet."

I swallowed hard. "I am doing what you ask of me. I am on my way to repay the debt."

"Good," was her only reply as she walked about the room, and the veil that covered her creased with every step. Her solemn gown underneath rustled around her gnarled ankles.

"What brings you here then?" My voice was strained. I felt cornered, like a rabbit in front of a fox.

The Crone tutted, her wrinkled lips bearing horrid teeth. "Have you received my warning yet?" she mused, her blackened skeletal fingers twisting and twirling at her side, weaving an unseen web with the fibres and strings of magic I could not see.

"I don't know what you mean?" I whispered, watching those fingers work as the colour drained from my face.

"The messenger, child. Did it reach you?"

Clarity hit like a wave on the shore, and I finally forced myself to meet her gaze.

"You sent that thing? You sent the shadow messenger?" She only hissed at me. "Yes, but there was no message given."

My eyes were wide, as she paced before me. Pacing like a cat about to pounce. She tusked and bared her teeth again, stopping her trancelike walk to stand feet from me. The morning light was not kind to her withered skin and sallow face. Her features were ominous in the shroud, making her more harrowing, yet ethereal.

"You are not as brave as I thought," she said and I ground my teeth painfully. She had no idea, but my hands shook with fear and there was no denying I was terrified now, before her. "But you will be. There are darker forces at work here girl, than that of the lycan." She paused, turning away from me to look at the wreck of the room surrounding us. "This is evidence of its work. These people fled their home months ago and have not returned. Fearful of falling prey to the creatures again." Her croaking words were distant as were her grey eyes. My brow furrowed.

Creatures?

"The message was received then. I am limited in how much I can..." She seemed to search for the right words as her forehead wrinkled and her fingers quickened their weaving. "Assist you."

I was roused by that. ***Assist me?***

In what? She had done nothing but threaten my life. Burdening and binding me to a task which would likely kill me.

"I don't understand," I stammered, glaring at her, "why have I been chosen? Why is this all on me?" My body was vibrating now with anger and sheer terror.

The Crone cackled as though she had read every thought that had just entered my head. "Chosen? You are not chosen, silly girl. You are nothing but a pawn. A tool to utilise. That is all. You are nothing more than that."

I choked silently as her face twisted in a mocking sneer. Something in me deflated and crumpled. I was nothing but a tool. A convenience. Nothing but in the right place at the wrong time. I watched as her sneer faded, replaced with a puckered line.

"The woman, the blind one, was right in her direction," she cawed at me and I was once again the centre of her attention. But my mind wandered to Mutza, to the words she had spoken, telling us to ride north. "My patience only goes so far, girl," the Crone spat. "Follow the path further. To where the forest is now as bleak as the sky. Where it is draining all that is ancient and almighty. There will be answers there, I am sure of it. Four days hard ride, and you will be near our territory. At its border there is a large dwelling of both we and them, the humans, and our kind. Your path will become clearer there. But be warned, my assistance will only stretch so far. My hands are tied in these matters."

My hands began to shake.

"Look out for my shadows and be on your guard. My time is up," she said wearily, looking past me to the dawn, "all is not as it seems." She smiled weakly under the grey veil and a ghost of a shiver, clawed its way across my exposed neck. "Even you are not what you seem to be, girl."

Cold encased my skin and for the first time, I began to feel my feet. As one lifted, as though to move towards her, there was a crack, like thunder, and she was gone, devoured by mist and the fabric of the in-between. I spluttered, my breaths heaving as I watched mist begin to seep through the open window. Mind racing, I ran down to the barn. Another warning, another message. But my hurried pace slowed as my thoughts volleyed about in my mind. The Crone had sent the shadow messenger, for what purpose, I was yet to find out. But she had done so with the intent to assist me. Realisation dawned over me and like a balm, her words settled over me, easing the weight that was buried deep in my chest.

Chapter 20

I sat crossed legged beside the fire, which was ablaze with new logs I had retrieved from the pile in the house. I had grabbed the iron kettle from my wagon and my pot of tea leaves infused with herbs, ready to brew and make amends. The dawn had broken fully over the valley as I boiled water sourced from the farms well, and the aromatic smells overwhelmed the hay and musty stalls. Roman stirred first, his mouth stretching and his eyes widening, looking at me. He cleared his throat and sat up, face puckering with the cramping of muscles from an uncomfortable sleep. I chewed on my lower lip, the words I had rehearsed over in my mind poised on the tip of my tongue. Roman rubbed a hand over his face, as his fingers scratching the bristling dark hair protruding from his chin.

"How long have you been awake?" His voice was thick and groggy with sleep.

"All night," I replied, still worrying at my lower lip. "I am sorry for last night. For the short temper," I admitted, my voice as soft as it could be. "You know I didn't mean to be..."

"Such a bitch?" It was a rhetorical question.

I paused, assessing whether he genuinely meant it, or if it was one of his usual jokes. There was no cock of his eyebrow or smirk of his lips and it only made me feel worse. I must have truly been a bitch last night for Roman not to make fun of it. Resigned, I sighed.

"Yes. A bitch. But sometimes, Roman, you say all the wrong things." My eyes found Eli's sleeping form across the fire and Roman's brow crossed as he too looked at our friend questioningly.

"My words upset you?" His tone was quizzical.

"Your face upsets me," I retorted, trying not to smile. Light returned in my brother's eyes and I breathed a small sigh of relief. "No, Roman. Your words did not hurt me. But I think they displeased Eli." My voice was barely a whisper as I watched Eli warily. "He is too honourable to be bound to me. He deserves better. He deserves to have someone, a kind and proper woman, who will love him, and he loves her."

"And you are not a kind and proper woman?"

"Not really." He looked at me suspiciously, but I carried on, unable to deliberate what he must be thinking. "Besides, he does not like me in that way, and you shouldn't tease your friend that way. It's unbecoming. Even for a fiend and rogue such as yourself."

"He's *our* friend," Roman tried interjecting, voice rough. "Why do you dismiss the match, Rhona? You are more than an honourable match for him." My brother's eyes searched mine, and I prayed my face did not falter as I masked it into a bored expression.

"Because he deserves someone..." I did not finish my sentence as Eli began to stir.

I quickly busied myself with the tea and I poured three cups, handing one to each man. I did not dare look at Eli as I felt the heat creep up my cheeks as his fingers graced mine, briefly touching. Both men took the tea and drank. I heard Roman splutter at the hot liquid.

"It's to wake you. It was Mutza's recipe," I offered, finally braving to look at Eli.

He had downed the liquid and was now staring into the flames. I reached for the basket of food that had been gifted to us from the clan, pulling out dried meat, berries, and a few crackers. I poured the rest of the tea into each of our cups, and we ate and drank in silence. Our small breakfast filled the slow empty ache in our stomachs. The silence was demeaning, and I chose to try and make better of the disquiet between us all.

"There is a well to wash in. I found it before dawn this morning, around the back of the barn." Both men nodded, still content in their brooding. Roman was packing away the food supplies and piling up his clothes on his arm, readying to go wash up. Eli had gotten up to tend to his horse in the stall next to Balthazar. Now was my chance. "The shadow messenger wasn't from the other side," I finally said after a time. "It was from the Crone." Both men turned back to me in unison, surprise lighting their faces.

"What?" Roman asked for both of them.

"She sent the messenger. She called me out into the farmhouse. At dawn. She had another message for me." I could feel my heart begin to pound under their assessing gazes. "She means to help us with this journey, it seems." The words felt strange as I spoke them, as though I was voicing a dream.

"What did she say? Did she tell you where we should go? What should we do next?" Roman's words were quick and distraught, as though he was trying to control the annoyance at me with every breath.

"She told me to follow the path Mutza set for us." My voice croaked at the blind woman's name and I saw Eli fidget. I waited as he walked over and sat in between Roman and me, his face serious and intense at the mention of his beloved grandmother. He was still bare chested, his skin warmed pink by the fire. It crackled between us, keeping the morning chill at bay.

Eli's blue and brown eyes were looking intently into mine. He motioned with his hands, about the path northwards, giving a slight grunt. '*She set us on the right path?*'

I nodded at his question. "We must travel north towards where the land is as bleak as the sky, or something like that. There is no question about it. She said it will become clearer after 'four days hard ride'. I'm guessing with the horses and cart, maybe five. Six at most?" My words seemed to expand about the place in front of me. I watched both Eli and Roman absorb the words. "Did I make Mutza's morning brew the way-" I didn't finish as Roman seemed to pounce.

"I am bathing and then we leave," he called behind him, as he strode out the barn door. He was frustrated with me it seemed, for not telling him straight away, or for not waking him, I did not know. I deftly stood and began preparing the horses, needing to occupy my mind on anything but my brother's mood.

In the wake of Roman leaving the barn, I was alone with Eli again. The knowledge caused my spine to straighten and my stomach to flutter, the sensation catching me off guard. Eli was still sitting, drinking his tea and eating his remaining crackers. I watched intently, waiting for him to leave the barn and bathe, but instead I caught his gaze. I cleared my throat quickly.

"I am sorry for how I spoke to you last night. It was uncalled for. Roman knows how to tempt my anger." I tried to smile. "We both know how much of an arse he can be. He offends people for sport, especially his sister." Huffing heavily, I tried to read Eli. It was no use. He was as stonelike and unreadable as ever. "Not only with his mouth but his rutting face as well." I forced a casual smile. Eli's hand was still in mid-air, a cracker inches from his lips as he just looked at me. I couldn't help but squirm and began rubbing the tender skin over my knuckles. I hissed, as the sore cuts and healing skin cracked at my rough fumbling, the healing scab tearing and fresh blood pulsing to the surface.

In one fluid motion, Eli was up in an instant, carrying his old satchel to me from the horse's stall. His hands searched deep within the woven bag Mutza had given him on our departure, the sounds of who knew what rattling as he rummaged. He pulled out a beaten tin pot with a ceramic lid, like the one I stored my beeswax ointment in, the very ointment his grandmother had made for me. Mutza was our clan's healer, prophet, seer, and story keeper. She was a wonder with salve's, balms, tonics and poisons. Healing any itch, boil and wound. I had always wondered if Mutza had taught Eli her trade. I realised it was a sad thing I had never thought to ask him. He sat beside me and unhinged the clay lid, and I was suddenly hit with the smell of rotten eggs and cloves. I nearly gagged at the stench but forced myself to breathe through my mouth, seeing Eli's eyes crease as a small, crooked smile found its place on his scarred face. I watched as he dipped his finger in, spearing out a large amount of the pale yellow cream. He grunted, his lips moving to form the silent word as his head dipped, indicating my hands. Asking my permission. My answering yes was hushed and breathy as I held out both hands for him to see.

The cuts across both sets of knuckles were red and blotchy, bruised in places from misjudged punches. The dark maroon welts of dried blood and healing skin were cracked and tender. They weren't healing very well at all. These wounds originated from the fight weeks ago when the villagers came. They should have healed by now, fresh tissue and skin replacing the scabs and clotted blood. But they were an easy means to settle any chaos within. The pain was something I often relished in, in times of painful and harrowing thoughts, like the memories last night. When I had sat, and watched, mesmerised by the flames, slowly forcing my knuckles into the hard ground, again and again and again. Breaking the skin open, directing that agony from my thoughts to something more tangible.

His eyes found mine, as though understanding entirely but I masked my face into indifference. I was no longer a victim. Not taking his eyes off me he nodded, asking once more for permission. I nodded, clamping my lips firmly together as he cautiously rubbed the yellow cream into each knuckle. The fire that erupted at his touch caused me to inhale sharply, bringing another lungful of the rotten stench with it. Eli held my hands in place while his fingers gently rubbed the cream into the broken, bruised skin.

I could feel my eyes beginning to water as the stinging heat enveloped each wrecked knuckle. My fingers instinctively tightened in Eli's grip as the ointment seeped into every crack and sore. I ground my teeth, dealing with it. After a time, the burning sensation dissipated as quickly as it had come and a cool numbness settled over my hands with welcomed relief.

I sighed at the feeling, and Eli freed my hands from his. I almost moaned as I wriggled my soothed fingers. "Thank you. That feels much better." I smiled at him and tried not to inhale the foul lotion that now coated my skin.

Eli merely nodded and packed the tin of salve away from where it came. He then pulled out fresh clean strips of linen and began to bind my hands. I watched as his fingers wrapped and tied the fabric to my palm and fingers, tightly but in a way, I still had movement. He grunted with a sort of satisfaction and then began to stand and leave. I grabbed his arm. If I didn't say it now, I do not know when a better opportunity would come.

"I mean it, Eli. Thank you. I am sorry for what Roman speculated last night. I know it has never been something you wanted. Being betrothed, I mean."

He didn't move from my touch and grip, and yet he hadn't turned to face me. I didn't know what more to do, other than say what I had planned to say. "I think that's why Baja never made us heel to the obligation." It was a lie, bubbling sourly, but Eli could never truly know why we were never made to wed. "Things were so different when we were children." My voice was quiet as it softened with each word spoken as I watched Eli, still not looking at me. "Know this, though. It is not the life I wanted for you. To be bound to me. I'm a hag, with a death sentence it seems."

I waited for some nod or side smile from Eli, the way he used to when we talked about our betrothal as children. Eli just looked away, to the fire again and the light flickered in his glazed eyes. I saw his chest heave an almighty sigh, his face betraying nothing. I waited, seconds passing before his mouth formed a thin line and I finally let his arm go.

The sound of footfall startled me as Roman strode back into the barn, hair wet and almost black. A shudder of relief rippled through me and for once in my life I was very grateful for his inappropriate entrances.

"Rhona, douse the fire and get the horses ready. I will pack up the supplies and ready the wagon. Eli," Roman said, his eyes darting between him and I, as he tied his wet hair back at the base of his neck. "Eli, you go bathe. We leave soon."

***

We set out on the winter-doused road. The mud and remaining ice caused havoc for both my cart and horses. My cabin seemed to stumble over the long narrow path, away from the dilapidated farmhouse and the Crone's warning and words. No wind tore at us as we travelled, and the balm that had numbed my hands and knuckles lasted until we stopped to water the horses at noon. Without asking, Eli had approached me and placed the tin of salve into my hands, before stalking off to my brother's side. A strange ache began in my chest at that small interaction and I wondered why I felt such a thing.

I had missed Roman and Eli whilst they had travelled away. The nights and days had been long, with only my uncle and his men for company. Conversation had been tight at best with no jokes or games, like we three did. It was always easy with them. I remembered the day they travelled away, remembered begging, and pleading with Baja for me to go with them. But Baja, all powerful and overprotective, deemed it unnecessary for me to assist in the sales and exchanges made between clans and I couldn't argue with our clan king, even if he was blood. I remember the long nights alone in my cabin, sometimes not talking to a soul for hours, even days. It was hard and pieces of me had slowly begun to fracture away without Roman and Eli for company.

Joy blossomed in me at the memory of the day they had returned. I had run at full pelt, as fast as my legs could take me, up the road to their carts. I had lunged at my brother, grappling him in a hug so fierce and consuming. He had known how much I missed him from that hug. Eli had been at the back of the troupe. My heart had danced at his expression. His eyes had lit up from within, to see the camp and his home. To see me. I ran to him and wrapped my arms around him. The weight of him pressing into me, the strength in his arms as he clasped me to him, was stronger than that which Roman had embraced me. His usual indifference to touch, forgotten as he held on to me. I hadn't realised that since that day things had been very different.

We found a small running stream for the horses to drink from, its surface fractured with broken ice that was slowing the flow. It was fresh from the mountain range not two days ahead of us, their faded peaks barely visible against the overcast sky. We rode for two days, stopping late each night to eat stale bread, cheese, nuts and apples from our packs. The bread Miriam had packed had been inedible at best. We saved the dried smoked meats and herbs for a night we could safely camp and laze next to a fire, stewing broth. We slept for only a few hours each night. The horses grazed on the pass way verges, eating as much as they could gain from the cold earth. I coaxed them with apples back to the wagon each time we needed to continue, readying them for another trek.

The mountains were growing steadily closer with each grey morning. But the sky wasn't the only thing that was grey and lifeless about us. The forest to the west of the road, now cresting and overgrowing the path, seemed dead. The road we bore on crept down a small hill and into a shadowy pass of blanched trees. Silence greeted us, as the rustle of wheels and clip clop of horses' feet deafened our ears. I grabbed my cloak, holding it tightly against me as I looked at the deadened trees. The pale lifeless hoard stretched for miles under the shadow of the mountains.

I shuddered at the stillness of this place. Nothing moved in the dull morning mist that caressed the road and bordering tree line. Roman whistled and I pulled Balthazar to a stop. Roman and Eli climbed down from their mounts, bringing about a bucket and filling it with water from skin. The horses drank deeply as we surveyed the landscape ahead.

"This forest was once full of life. A home the Mother herself, treasured," Roman proclaimed as he blocked the wheels of his wagon. "I remember passing here years ago when mother was alive, and you were still wrapped in blankets." My stomach turned to lead at the mention of our mother. Roman was wary as his eyes roved the dead trees. "This is recent. It wasn't that long ago we passed through here," he stated, warily. "It's like a sickness crept through every vein of the forest." I watched as his eyes were again shadowed by his overcasting brows. Memory shone in his eyes as he looked at me. "It was here I saw my first pixie." His face stretched in delight at the forgotten memory as a genuine smile spread across his mouth. Our mouths. I had never known or travelled so close to *this* woodland before. No wonder. Our clan had kept clear of the east just after my mother had died. Was murdered. That sickening clamp gripped my stomach again and I had to physically shake off its clutches.

I walked into the nearby wood, needing to relieve myself, from my stomach or my bladder I couldn't decide. The blistered grass and roots crackled with each of my steps. Roman thankfully brought Balthazar and my cart into a small dip in the trees off the road. The rain had not touched this place as the ground and surroundings glittered with ice. The woods were eerily silent around me, as though the snow had forced all life into a slumber. I looked around at the tall trees, then crouched, looking up and around to distract myself. Like pillars, long and bare, the trees grew closely together. So closely my vision was of only bare trunks and falling shells and leaves. No birds stirred or sang in the bare branches above.

We had been trailing this forest for the past two days, skirting the perimeter, hoping to find open plains and traveller's roads by it, but there was nothing, just this beast of dying woodland and forest as thick and as dense as smoke or shadow.

A prickle of unease ebbed its way up my spine as I redressed. I scanned the woodland floor, searching for tracks of rabbits, foxes and any burrowing animal that would skitter and scuttle. There was nothing. It was completely void of life. The trees stood silently, naked in the harsh winter light, hiding their unseen and unheard occupants well from peering eyes. A familiar touch beckoned me as I remembered the Crone's words. I walked further in amongst the trees, listening hard. I walked deeper still, for what seemed like a minute, before turning to view the tall pins of thin tree trunks closely growing together. I surveyed the path I had trekked, back towards the road and our caravans. They were barely visible through the tangle of branches. Continuing, my foot caught something, making me stumble. My hands shot out, grabbing for a nearby branch to steady myself, but my hand missed or so I thought it did. Falling to a knee, I whirled, turning back to the branch I had known to be there.

The tree had moved. No, not the tree; it's root and extended branch had moved. It had flinched at my touch. I stood, affronted at the sight before me. My breath caught as my cold limbs warmed with the fast thump of my heart. I tried again, outstretching my fingers, to touch the tree trunk and gasped when I viciously received an answering thwack. Dazed, I dared again, hoping my eyes had not deceived me. Thin, spindled branches whipped at my hand yet again and I hissed. The tree had batted away my touch.

I looked dumbfounded at the trees around me. I had been told stories, by Mutza, of beings who guarded the trees and who protected parts of the land from humans. But never once did I imagine them to be the trees themselves…

I tried my voice, about to call for Roman and Eli as I persisted with curious fingers. But before the tree could react, thick fingers closed around my exposed wrist. I held back the scream as his familiar scent hit me. Eli held me back from touching it. A strangled sound came from my throat, either from shock or annoyance. How had he snuck up on me so quietly, without any snapping of twigs or roots underfoot? His answering smirk told me enough. Eli was too good at tracking and sneaking. Too quiet sometimes that I thought even death must envy him. His grip was firm as he shook his head, imploring me not to do it again. Silent in more ways than one, I chided inside.

"What are they?" I asked, looking back to the tree, still and unmoving once more. Wonder filled his eyes as he searched around us, releasing my wrist, his face thoughtful. The phantom feel of his fingers still lingered as I watched him. He stilled, releasing a strained grunt, tilting his head in the direction behind me. His different coloured eyes were bright and round but showed no fear. I quickly looked at his scarred neck and mouth, my lips thinning as my mind replayed his child's voice to me over and over. A heaviness settled itself again in my chest as I tried to imagine what he would sound like, if the accident hadn't happened. One blue and one brown eye shifted back to me. His features changed, shifting strangely as he beheld me. We regarded each other for a moment, and I wondered if he registered the pity on my face. I schooled my features, internally horrified. Eli did not want pity. He made a point of proving he was stronger even with his assumed debilitation. I did not want to be one of those people who looked at him, the way I just had. Ever again. So, I smiled warmly. Friend to friend.

I turned, scanning the trees, feeling Eli's eyes on my back. Deeper into the woodland were pillars of gold, shining brightly. I squinted, focusing enough to see it wasn't gold but day light that filtered through, amongst the grey shadows and decaying forest. I inhaled deeply, as that tenacious pull drew me to explore.

"Does Roman know we are both here?" I asked, eyes fixed on the only streaming light the canopy above seemed to allow. Eli sniffed in answer as his boots deliberately crunched the earth beside me. "Good, he can come running if we need help," I huffed and began walking deeper between the trees, towards the hallowed place. Leaves and twigs crunched underfoot, and branches snagged and pulled at me as I ventured nearer. My hair pulled and I turned, my eyes not betraying me this time. Small and sharp twig-like fingers were wickedly pulling at my dark curls. Their grip was firm, yanking my hair almost from its roots. Cussing, I gently tried pulling them off, trying to tease them into not scalping me. Other branches to my left grasped my collar tightly, and thicker arms of pale splintered wood wrapped around my arms and waist. Scratching small fingers snatched at more of my hair and my woollen shawl. The branches around my waist tightened uncomfortably until I couldn't physically move. The trees held me, stopping me from getting any closer. One whipped my cheekbone, leaving a stinging slash in its wake followed by warmth. The warmth of my blood. I found my voice as panic began to ravage me. "Eli!"

He was close again and moved untouched into my line of sight, assessing all. More twig fingers pulled and gripped at hair, at skin and cloth, halting me completely. I was panting, struggling to free my limbs, my clothes and my hair.

"Why are you free to roam in here but not me?" I asked through gritted teeth, as Eli was indeed untouched by the surrounding trees. Wide eyed, he beheld me, eyes roving over my body, over these incessant woodland captors until those strange eyes of his settled on my hips. My stomach clenched. He then looked over himself, thoughtfully. "Eli, help me…" but before I could finish seething he quickly bent on one knee before me, unbuckling my large hunting knife from my thigh and pulling my blade free from its confines in my right boot.

He threw them in a skidding flash of gleaming metal, away from us onto the forest floor. He stood, eyes frantic as they darted about over the wooden shackles. Slowly those tiny hands and pressing arms began to release me. Wooden fingers and whip-like snares let go of my hair, my clothes, elbows and waist, until I was free.

"I don't understand?" I asked, aware of the sight behind us, where my weapons now lay discarded.

In answer, he opened his coat and held open his hands. He was carrying no steel, no weapons or blades, nothing that could cut or hack down a tree. Nothing that could harm the forest itself. The thought sank in me like a pebble in water. The trees were protecting themselves, protecting whatever lay deep within, from me. From my knives and blades. I chewed on my bottom lip, my stomach flipping a little.

"Thank you," was all I managed as he walked right up to me, not shying away from my quizzical gaze. My back went rigid as his thick thumb gently wiped the blood. Sweet earth and morning dew filled my nose. I could only stare as he subsided.

"I am going to have to come up with another way to say thank you, if you keep rescuing me all the time." My words hit me like a waterfall of heat the moment they escaped my lips. I gulped loudly, wishing the very forest floor would devour me. Eli only watched me, unflinching. His eyes and face betrayed nothing, the only movement the slight flutter across his jaw. He was so close we could almost share breath. My mind kicked in frantically. "Where are your weapons?" My voice was hoarse, strange with the unease at being so close to him.

His eyes shot back to the road, back to where Roman was probably waiting with his staff and cross bow. Understanding tapped me and I sighed heavily.

I rolled my eyes at him. "You could have warned me," I said, sucking on a tooth. Eli's lips twisted with knowing mischief and I slapped his forearm, hard enough to show I meant it. Eli's laugh was quiet and breathy, not a cackle or chuckle like Roman's, but earnest all the same. My heart warmed a little at it, even if I could feel my cheeks were vivid in flush at my inappropriate comment. It was strange, to be so on edge now when we were once so at ease, and to feel my cheeks heat under his imploring stare. Maybe it was age and the fact we should have been married months ago. I had been old enough to be bound to him in marriage for over two years now. But my mother had stated I would not wed until my third year after reaching womanhood. Thankfully that never happened. I had entered womanhood too young and too horrifically. That defeating clang inside of me rang deep within and I had to inhale deeply to steady myself. The memories clawed and scratched in my mind's eye. No darkness, not today. Forcing my mouth from its thin line, I tried to smile. His scent of winter morning and earthen musk battled back the cold that was threatening my inner being. I moved out of his space, feeling the fresh air kiss my heated cheeks and neck. We began moving towards the beams of light, Eli close behind me, steadying my every step.

The shimmering pillars of golden light filtered through the canopy, between the grey bark and mottled wood, onto a settlement of large rocks. The dark slate stone was covered in a carpet of plush green moss. The only green it seemed in this strange brittle wilderness. Eli stepped in their direction, his feet effortlessly cautious over the forest floor, no crunch or cracking to be heard. I followed suit, careful not to touch any of the trees as I went, fearing any more unwelcome contact.

We reached the stones, surrounded by a gathering of taller, broader birch trees. There were three rocks, with roots and depths hidden under the sodden earth and dying leaves. The moss, soft and supple, was untouched by the cold claws of winter. It covered the peaks of the stones almost smothering the dark grey beneath. But the moss could not hide the weathered and worn markings we now saw. They were words in an old ancient tongue, that I could not read or understand. Runes, unlike any I had ever seen.

Crouching, I reached out with timid fingers towards the lichen-covered surface. The thick greenery was lush and damp under my touch. I hadn't realised I had been holding my breath until the burn in my lungs alerted me to it. Nothing had happened when I touched the ancient stones. No trees or enchanted beings stirred or tried to whip my hands away; there was only silence around, disturbed by my own breathing. No flicker of breeze came through the trees or rustled leaves. It was just cold, quiet and damp. I traced the shapes and whirls of the symbols created, grazing pathways in the moss that showed the darkened stone underneath.

These runes were of old magic, I realised, as my fingernails laid fresh pathways over the green. Runes no longer used or seen. On the centre stone, amidst the scrawled aged marking was a dip. The moss was thicker and smothered what lay underneath. My fingernails gripped and scored the carpeted overgrowth and pulled it away from the stone.

My breath caught, as did Eli's. A handprint was carved into the centre of the rock, surrounded and framed by old, inscribed runes. It was no trick of the light. There was a creak of Eli's boots and he was squatting beside me, his thick coat and furs splaying across the forest floor. Even crouching he was taller than me.

"What do you think it could mean?" My voice was barely a whisper as I beheld the stone and the handprint carved into the dark stone. Eli's fingers brushed the excess moss and earth from the surface, cleaning the markings and shapes in the streaming light. I arched around, peering back to the road. I could not see anything. No road or Roman. We were too deep into the woods.

Warm fingers traced mine and my spine instinctually straightened. I turned back to find Eli's hands gently atop my own, moving over my grazed knuckles. My pale olive skin, blemished with fine white scars, looked strange under his golden tanned skin. I forced myself to look into those eyes as they pinned me, and a familiar prickle ebbed its way stronger from my ears to my neck and spine. He was so close; his scent overwhelmed my nose and mouth. But I found myself drinking it in eagerly. My ears hollowed out at the rushing beat of my heart. I couldn't think; all I could do was feel the rush and the surprising thrill. His nose nearly grazed my own and I inhaled his scent deeper into my lungs. A wind rustled and leaves cascaded from the near lifeless canopy and that strange otherworldly tug had my insides quivering. Eli's fingers demanded my hand to move and I yielded to his touch as he pushed my palm into the centre of the stone.

There was a deafening crack and the ground seemed to shudder underfoot. My balance was hindered, and I fell back on my rump. The streams of sunlight misted, billowing almost. Rocks and undergrowth rippled and rattled, and Eli fell on his haunches as the ground continued to shake beneath us. Cussing, I grabbed for him, trying to drag him backwards and away. The air shimmered with a ripple in front of us and golden light shone through the inscribed runes, gleaming bright from within the rock. Vines of glowing light began creeping up from the floor behind. They weaved and grew, snaking and entwining to form an arch way, to the air and forest beyond, like nothing I had ever seen.

My chest was heaving, as was Eli's I realised, my arm still tightly wrapped over his chest. A mess of heavy limbs, we looked, mesmerised. Our breathing was in sync with our galloping hearts. The gateway glittered in the bare broken forest, revealing the vibrant greens and blues of the forest within. It was a gateway to the heart of the forest. My grip tightened instinctively across Eli's chest, my fingers clenching the lapel of his coat as I watched the swirling air. We didn't move as we beheld the forest's true beauty.

The gate had exposed the true woodland in all its splendour, hidden from humans and from unseeing eyes. The air beyond was a haze twinkling with iridescent lights that danced and whizzed about. The forest seemed to breathe again, and an aspen and oak tree creaked. Birds and other beings twittered and sang vivaciously. It was teeming with life.

"Please tell me you are seeing this too," I breathed, my words stirring Eli's hair. He nodded sharply against me. We watched for what felt like minutes. "No one has entered here in a long time," I whispered in awe, looking at the glowing vines of the gateway. My chest heaved at the sight of it. Such a place as this was not found every day and had not been found in centuries, by the looks of it. I thought of Roman's words from earlier:

'Of a forest once thriving with life, akin with old magic'

I then thought of the barren trees, enchanted to protect against axe and blade.

I swallowed.

Roman had said the forest had changed since he remembered. Maybe the heart of the forest was protecting itself like a rib cage and had withered and changed to hide the truth. To make humans not want to come looking... Making people believe it was dying and that a sickness had spread through it, draining it of life.

"Maybe what Roman had heard wasn't true," I said, my voice a soft rush of air, as my knees and thighs began to ache. Eli stilled, listening. "Maybe it wasn't sickness that stripped these trees bare. Maybe it was a way of defence. From us and the humans. To protect it. To protect what lay within the forest. What dwells within," I explained, trying to reason Roman's words. "The trees stopped me from moving on with blades, with steel. Maybe the trees did this to stop people venturing in. Mutza says spirits lived within the trees across the continent. This must be one of them." My body was thrumming, desperate to see what truly lay within.

There was another ripple in the air and the gleaming archway dulled. The golden leaves of light faded away like smoke on a breeze, as quickly as it had appeared. The doorway to the forest was gone. I blinked, the light imprint glowing against my eyelids.

"Go and get Roman."

I could only sit staring whilst Eli ran back through the forest to Roman, my caravan and the horses. A long time passed before I heard the rustle of boots coming up behind me. I hadn't moved. I had stayed on the floor, assessing the shafts of light as leaves and dust danced in their brilliant panes.

"Balthazar?" I asked, not looking round.

"Tied up with the caravan. Hidden off the road. We had to bring them into the trees a hundred yards or more up the tree line from where you came in. They should be safe." Roman's heavy brow was gathered. "Why no weapons?" I looked at Eli; he hadn't been able to communicate to Roman it seemed.

"Because what you said about this place was partly true." Roman stiffened. "These trees are protected."

"How can that be? This wood is dead. Look at it... it's a memory long passed." Roman's eyes darted about the grey trees surrounding us, dull of life and colour.

"Not exactly," I smiled, looking back to the rocks and carved ruins before me. "What did you bring?"

Eli stepped forward, his long wooden staff in hand and a small brown sack tossed over his shoulder. He only nodded at me and I knew he would have grabbed some food and essentials. Just in case. My breathing began to quicken as I stood. I leant forward, pressing my cold palm to the exposed surface of the rock. Golden vines glittered back to life before us all.

"Welcome to the heart of the forest, brother."

Chapter 21

The archway shimmered in Roman's wide eyes, as I stepped through the portal, into the woodland beyond. Roman and Eli's sudden inhalation filled my ears, as well as the roar and call from my blood as I stepped over the threshold and into the other world. My ears popped and I closed my eyes as the ripple of air bristled my hair and clothes. When my foot fell on soft ground and I stilled, eyes tightly shut. My lungs filled with honeysuckle and verbena, the sweet air coating my nostrils and tongue. It was warm, as though the spring and summer were unending, the balmy air delicately pressing against my exposed neck and hands. I opened my eyes.

I realised that the ripple and gateway had not been deceiving us, as my eyes roved over the thrumming wood.

Creaking oaks, ancient and wise, sighed in the sweet breeze, their substantial trunks as wide as they were tall. Strange lilac leaves open and closing from the oak tree's thick arms and branches, shivered. Towering ash trees were covered with luminous leaves of blue and green, a mirage of swaying sapphires and emeralds. Moss, thick and heavy, enveloped and carpeted the forest floor. Other plants, strange and alien, gasped open, and large yellow and mustard pods were spitting minute purple and pink creatures, which floated up and up. The canopy above allowed streams of glowing light to filter through, distorted only by the flowing cascade of pink cherry blossoms that waltzed to the sounds of the forest. Birds and bugs peeped and hummed in a chorus. Rabbits and deer darted in between the trees, unafraid and uncaring of the human now in their midst. I could hear the babble of water from a stream nearby and my heart filled with sheer wonderment at all that I beheld. Iridescent lights flew across my path, the distinct shimmer of multicoloured wings visible as some stopped in front of me, whizzing and whirling, before skittering off in streams of multicoloured light. Fairies. The forest sighed again as Eli and Roman flanked me either side. Eyes twinkled from within the folds of trees, watching us. I stepped further in, turning in a circle to view all, taking in as much as I possibly could. I could feel my eyes burning with joy. Never had I ever seen so much life, so much unimaginable beauty and magic. As a child, stories were told, as old as the wind, about places hidden and concealed. Of places outside of the Fallow in the human lands, still connected to a world from long ago. Never have I dreamed of such a place on this continent. A tear strayed a path down my cheek and my smile widened, as I looked back at both men. My heart thumping as they too looked with unashamed emotion.

My smile dropped from my face, like thundering rain, as the gate closed behind them, golden vines and leaves vanishing into the purple haze and air. I stumbled, as panic caused my throat to dry. Eli and Roman both spun to see the light dampening into nothing, as the gate disappeared. Roman gasped, his voice strained, trying to formulate a curse. I hushed him, panic easing as I beheld some small salvation. The same rocks and stones, a mirror image of the ones on our side. Handprint untouched and covered in green.

"You can leave the way you came," said a voice behind us.

It was an ancient tone, like leaves and rocks tumbling over one another for a thousand years. A voice of depth and belonging, carried to us on that mystic breeze. My breath caught as my spine went ramrod straight and I felt, rather than saw, both Eli and Roman tense beside me at the new speaker. As the oaks creaked and stretched behind us, I turned slowly on light feet. My heart leapt, stomach flipping as though I had fallen from a great height at the creature awaiting us.

A stag stood in the middle of the small clearing, highlighted and glowing in the flowing light. My mouth went dry, eyes widening, devouring the sight before me. The stag was immense, larger than any male beast I had ever trailed or hunted. His fur was a thick gleaming russet with antlers spiralling up towards the heavens. I gasped. His antlers were a tangle of creeping bones, beautiful and dangerous, sharp and stunning, harsh but glorious, emblazoned with vines and flowers like living badges, growing alongside the mighty beast. His dark eyes glittered as he watched us, hoof stomping on the mossy ground. The very air danced and shimmered about him.

"Hunters have not ventured here in a long time. Have not found our haven for nearly a century." The voice rippled through the clearing, strange and echoing. Prickles erupted across my arms and back, adrenaline and awe igniting my blood. I licked my lips.

"We mean you no harm. We carry no weapons." My voice reverberated back across the trees and the cherry blossoms spun placidly around each of my words. I took a step closer, daring to show my empty palms, upturned and clammy.

"You are hunters, but…" The pause was tangible in the sweet violet air. My lungs froze, breath waiting as it continued. "…for no creature that dwells within here. This haven." The voice had a sharp and unyielding edge, as its prying words hit its mark. It knew we were hunting the lycan. My lungs released, my anxious breath stirring more blossoms and spirits. My eyes darted to my brother in recognition as the stag's horned head tilted, observing me. Observing us.

"Your words are true. We are hunters, of sorts, but we mean you and all here no harm." The very forest dulled to a diluted buzz. Barely any sound could be heard, as it waited with bated breath on my answers.

"We hunt for another creature." The quiet was thick and suffocating. "A creature who has escaped the Fallow and is causing death and destruction in its wake."

"It is not the only creature who is doing this," the voice sighed, the sound like rustling leaves and aged creaking branches, as the through the forest itself spoke. Not the stag, I realised. I watched tentatively, eyes roving the shadowy places in between the trees. The stag stomped its hoof again and golden sparks erupted from the mossy floor, bringing my focus quickly back to him. "It has been some time since any in the forest ventured past the protective border, into the human lands. Tell me, what do you hope to find in here?"

Again, the forest, the trees and creatures held their breath. My lips moved, trying to form words. This was the judgment call. One that could play in our favour or not at all. Eli stepped into my line of vision, his form merely a shadow to my right. He moved forward, hands open, palms up as my own were. Submissive. I could see his wide eyes as he beheld the creature and my stomach lurched as the memory ripped through me. Eli, a young boy, throat ravaged from a stag. From being in the wrong place at the wrong time. A ball grew in my own throat making it hard to swallow. I staggered to reach for him. The sudden need to sooth away that memory, forced me to stretch to try and touch him. My lips formed his name and to my surprise he began to bend on one knee, inclining his head, bowing. He was bowing low to the stag and the forest beyond.

I looked about, searching for words to appease this creature and the occupants of the forest. And as though the Mother herself had whispered the words into my ear, my answer transpired. I looked to Roman, my eyes pleading with him to follow suit. We both bowed on one knee. Heads down.

"We seek hope. Hope and knowledge to help us on our task. A task set by the Crone herself, to me. My brethren follow as aid, to help me against the dangers we know lay ahead of us." The last words whooshed out of my body. That anchor and chain deep within me went taught with apprehension, wrapped tightly around my heart and soul, weighing me down to the task and journey at hand. I bit my bottom lip, praying these words would ring true. "I am to hunt a lycan. For a life debt. For a crime I did not think was possible." I didn't know if what we said here would help us, but I had to try. "I do not know how to find it. How to hunt and kill it... I do not know if it can even be killed. Please, can you help us?"

Eli stood at my words; his acknowledgment done. I began to stand, finding his fingers firm yet gentle on my wrist, as he assisted me standing. I swallowed. Eli's eyes crinkled in the corners, as I looked at him and that heaviness in me soothed. The weight, lifting slightly, as his lip twitched in the corner. A small, proud smile.

Time seemed to stand still, unmoving as the stag assessed me further. My fingers, I realised, were too warm, and woven into Eli's. I didn't flinch, nor did I worry at this brief intimacy. His fingers were my only anchor at that moment.

"Follow him," the voice rasped across the clearing, it's tone and strange symphony raising the hairs on my nape. But I realised, I wasn't afraid as the stag turned, head still watching us, beckoning us to follow.

***

My hand was still in Eli's, our fingers in vice-like grip as we followed the stag deep into the forest, my fingers entwined in his, thick and tanned. My palms grew clammy at this closeness, as I worried what he must think. Did he feel the need to lead me? Lead me as a brother perhaps, like Roman would when we were children. But we weren't children and my cheeks heated at the thought that he was holding my hand, not out of brotherly care, but because he wanted to. I didn't let myself delve too deep into those types of notions. Those feelings would bring about another fear that always threatened to open up the past. Could it all have changed?

"I have never seen such a place." Roman's voice was quietly strained as we walked after the stag. "Mother had described places like this, but none have been seen for an age." I bit my lip, as he cleared his throat.

"Are you getting emotional, brother?" I teased, lifting my brows at him. The mischief elated me as he looked at me, sheepishly. "Do you need a handkerchief?" I giggled, smiling even more broadly when I heard Eli scoff. Roman only nudged me with a fur covered shoulder, pushing his untamed hair back into a knot at the nape of his neck.

"Do you need me to hold your hand too or are you happy with Eli doing it?" he retorted, his grin that of a wolf as he sauntered past me. My brows gathered furiously at the backhanded comment. I swallowed but felt Eli's fingers only tighten around my own. I ground my teeth at Roman, wishing I had something to launch at the back of his head.

We followed for a long time, an abundance of colour growing fast and gaily from the earth beneath our feet. The stag led us deeper and further than any had dared for a long time. My head swam with the beauty of our surroundings, as we walked. My mind catalogued every colour, plant, tree and being that we passed. My fingers tightened instinctively every now and then, feeling the skin of another in my own hand, to ensure all I was seeing was real. Eli's hand never once tried to rid me of my grip, and I was quietly grateful.

The colours started to fade with each passing step as we followed the stag further into the wood, as though only patches of life still thrived in pockets. My eyes were no longer enraptured by vivacity, as I became aware of the change. A clearing suddenly opened ahead, in an array of white light, blinding and stark. My feet slowed, heaviness settling over me as we beheld what lay in the centre of the clearing.

A monstrous carcass of pallid wood stretched up from the centre, a tree so ancient and overbearing that it dwarfed all living trees surrounding it. Its branches were a mass of milky arms, twisting and growing around it and to the sky above. A millennium had thickened its branches, growing them stronger and broader than any oak, elm or yew I had ever seen.

No leaves grew or flourished from this historic growth. That's what I noticed first, the lack of life again. The pale bark was bleached of colour, as though a raging thirst ravaged the mighty tree. It's trunk, as wide as a castle turret, was gnarled and at its centre, embedded deep, was a knife. It was pierced into the core of the tree, into its heart. I beheld the dark metal, my throat becoming thick and tight as I observed the polished volcanic glass. My hands became clammy as my eyes studied the steel handle, that have been crafted, twisted and hammered around that dark blade. Coppery brown bled from the wound. The dried gore had run in long streaks down the whitewashed bark and body of the tree.

I couldn't take my eyes off it, and I could feel the unease and loathing build within me. I had seen a knife like that before, long ago. My stomach flipped as I nearly hurled my guts up, but the voice that fell upon my ears stopped me.

"The heart of the forest has been desecrated," said the otherworldly voice. But it was still not the stag who spoke to us. The burnished beast walked to the reposed tree, his majestic antlers an array of opulence against the stark lifeless form. Something moved behind him in the shadows. My blood began to thrum, instinctively alert. My legs automatically moved into a defensive stance, back straightening. Eli's broad form swiftly moved to stand in front of me. Sweeping robes of dirty midnight rustled into the light and before us, there now stood a withered man. His skin was as shrivelled and blanched as the tree beside him.

"The heart of the forest, this living vessel of life, has been killed." The old man, if you could call him that, looked upon the dead limbs with dark watery eyes.

I froze. Completely still. There were twisting horns that protruded from his forehead. Moss and scales grew from the cloak that encompassed his body. It was like the forest was growing on him.

He came further into the clearing, towards us. "By a dark blade, a cursed one. So strong it has poisoned the surrounding forest." His voice was an echo, aged and lulling, as though his was the voice of the forest itself. The old man swayed; his legs strained as he held himself steady with shaking arms on a staff of sleek wood. He looked to his companion, the beautiful stag who had led us to this very spot. "It is time, old friend," he said to the stag and there was a pause in the world as man and beast looked at each other. The stag was there instantly, the old man's frail hands clasping around a lowered antler to steady himself. The ground around them that was once plush and green, now dead and washed of colour.

"Who are you?" Roman's voice was hoarse as his eyes darted about the clearing, assessing.

"Someone who cares," the old man replied exhaustedly, still holding onto the stag's antlers as it led him to a surfaced root.

The dead root suddenly groaned and moved, arching to meet the old man's rump from the ashen earth. The shock must have been apparent on my face as his old features creased into a small smile. My eyes shot to Roman and the look we exchanged was nothing but cautious.

Magic?

Roman only nodded, his heavy brow gathered, face curious. Eli stepped back, his body shielding me entirely. I huffed and dodged around him.

"We mean you no harm. On my life, I swear it. We chanced upon you, upon this," I said looking about the wondrous place. "Can you help us?" I asked, treading carefully towards the hermit.

His midnight robes were filthy, and his long grey hair was a mess of matted tendrils and locks. His thin hands and wrists were inked in aged blue-black ink, like tattooed shackles etched deep within his pores. His papery skin, so ashen and stretched over his frame and skull, seemed translucent in the light. A jolt went through me and I stopped short in front of him, at seeing his eyes. Wholly black, no whites or hazel or blue or green. All black from duct to crease.

"Do not fear me, girl. I am not the monster you seek, or one you should worry yourself with." His voice was a rasp, but clearer now. Not distorted like the echoes that previously greeted us.

"You're a thern?" The question was out before I had time to process it. "A real thern of the forest?" The awe raised my voice and widened my eyes, and I was answered by that soft smile again. A thern, a creature whispered about in legends. A protector of the woodland, and of all magical life that relied on the flora and fauna to survive.

"That I am, and alas, the last." His sigh rattled his chest and the stag lowered itself to the ground, lying next to the herder, protecting him from us.

"The last?" Roman's voice was careful. "How can you be the last? The legends we have been told stated that there were seven of you on this continent." Roman's voice was suddenly urgent, the worry transforming his face. Hearing my brother's words changed the lucid curiosity within me, churning it into something else entirely. But I didn't understand. I racked my memory for a story, verbal or written about the seven therns but I couldn't bring anything forward. I did not know what Roman spoke of or recognise that calculated look he shared with Eli.

"Your stories were true, boy. There were seven of us, but now I am the last, here before you."

"What is going on, Roman? What does this mean?" My voice ebbed away, the frustration thickening each word.

Roman began to speak but the thern cut him off. "We therns were the guardians. We have been for a thousand years." The stag's soft muzzle nudged at the robed knee beside him, affectionately. "We protect the living beings in each of our dwellings, monster and creature alike. We keep the magic alive in a world where magic was banished. After the ascension, we were left. Seven to protect the seven gates, so humans remained safe and unaware. To foster the life within."

"I don't understand?"

The thern continued, dazed. "We weren't the only ones regarded to hold the balance of these continents and the isles that surround them. There were others like us, in charge of overseeing the order of things." His chest gave another rattling sigh, his black eyes penetrating mine. "I believe you have already encountered some of them." My heart began to pummel against the fibres that held it in my chest. The Trinity. "But no more. I am the last of the therns. My brothers are dead." He rested his forehead on that of the stag, both eyes closed in resignation at his words. I swallowed hard, unable to comprehend what was happening.

"But I don't understand? Is this why so many creatures have been seen? Why are so many passing the binding that once kept them?" My voice felt as frail as the therns in front of me.

"The therns protect the seven hearts and gates of the realm, Rhona. The veil between this one and the others. Without the therns, the realms remain open, unguarded, and unchecked. All manner of creature could be roaming the land." I saw his gulp as the realisation of his words hit him.

"So, the Fallow thern, he too is dead?" Roman's cheeks leached of colour as he spoke, and I knew suddenly why all of this was important.

The Fallow was where the darkest and most dreaded creatures dwelled. If the gatekeepers there were dead, who knew what manner of evil could leak its way across the continent. Eli shuffled beside me and I caught his eye. He too was pale as he rubbed his stubble, eyes closing.

"But why are the others dead? Why has this happened?" I asked.

"I am one of the keepers of the Fallow," the old creature said, his voice and breath rattling against his ribs.

"But the Fallow is another three to four days of hard riding," I voiced, perplexed.

"The Fallow is all of this land, this continent. The woods are merely the entryways into the realm of the Fallow. I have been waiting for you."

I couldn't speak and neither could Roman. We could both only take in what was being said.

"I am the last, because of the Fallow. My brothers were guardians and herders of the other doorways into the mortal world. I felt them all die - slaughtered. By what creature, I do not know. But all of them, their realms and the very heart of each was desecrated like this." His withered hand rose and pointed to the blade at the centre of the tree. "I was not here when this happened, but I felt it, like a shard of glass had sliced an artery. It was instant, the curse. The forest began to succumb to the poison, to the decayed position that you saw before you entered the protected realm. It has been sucking all life from within. For what, I can only fear and imagine," he gasped, black eyes wild.

Instinct overcame me and I ran to him, dropping to my knees before him. I held his thin hands through an almighty gasp. "What creatures could have done this?"

"One who wants to disrupt the balance of this world." His words were coated in blood and my heart strained at the sight of red smeared across his teeth. I heard Eli before I felt him, his form kneeling beside me. Warmth enveloped my back, chasing away the cruel cold that crept its way over my skin. "I have been waiting for you. The unwanted in nature and name." I froze, as did Eli. The stag lowered its head, resting it tentatively on the therns knee. That strange warmth erupted within me. My fingers began to prickle in the familiar way, and I tried to steady my breathing. "It has been some time."

"How long has it been like this?" Roman asked, his voice raw behind me. He too had moved closer. I understood why he asked. The creatures we hunted had been scarce for months. The people in the towns and villages we had visited had been fidgety, whispering of horrors and unfortunate events.

"Months," he replied, gasping down a shallow breath. "I gave as much of my life as I could, to protect as much as it would allow without killing me. I tried…" He stammered, his black pools of eyes were glassy, unseeing as he looked about the place; at the gargantuan trees that grew fiercely in every colour, to the birds and beasts that my eyes couldn't see, to the small pockets enclosed and cautioned, allowing the remnants of this magical place to thrive. I could feel his pain, at the words he spoke. He was the reason this forest was still partly protected, and still alive. "I was told you would come. I waited. For you all." My hand found a knee, Eli's, and I gripped it, steadying myself. "You have come to know what you need for your quest. It all links into one path."

"The Crone, set us on this path. She set me on this quest to seek the lycan, and to repay a life debt." My voice was quiet.

The familiar thrum in my blood erupted over me. I listened to it. Eli shifted behind me and Roman came even closer to the thern, resting on the ground next to the stag. The old creature smiled again, blood coating his teeth.

"With every death there is birth. Remember that." Bile coated my tongue at the therns laboured words. "I do not have much more, but I know now what I must do." His frail fingers grasped my wrist. "Once I do this, all boundaries and barriers will be gone. The Fallow and its creatures will be able to roam the world, free."

"That can't be." My voice was tinged with the sting of tears.

"What can we do to help you?" Roman asked, his voice quiet.

"You are already doing it," the thern wheezed, fresh blood coating his tongue and teeth. "I have saved just enough to help you. To see you through to the end."

My heart and stomach dropped, the implication in his words was deafening. The world we knew would not be the same. Creatures would roam and hunt. Evil creatures spawned from a dark dawn a millennia ago. Fear coated my tongue and acid crept its way up from my stomach. This mission, this task and this life debt, was now even more complicated than I could have ever foresaw.

"I believe you will find what you are looking for with these," he wheezed, fingers digging into the skin on my wrist. His fingernails were embedded into my skin and I gasped at the pain. My free hand shot up, grabbing and clawing at his hands strangling my own. With swiftness, he grabbed my free hand, grappling with it. Eli and Romans flew up, gripping and trying to unhook the therns claws from my wrists. It's eyes of bottomless darkness penetrated my own and I was frozen.

"These are the keys to this place and the others. This sanctuary can only be entered by those without weapons, those without malice in their hearts for the creatures within. That is why you entered this place. These keys allow the bearer entry to all of the seven gates, across and into the depths of the Fallow." Light began to erupt from his palms and searing hot agony pulsed up my arms. The scream on my lips was horse as my voice failed me.

"These gifts are for you. Ask of the Fallow and it shall provide."

The pain engulfed me, like fire was burning my hands, my wrists and arms. White hot flame from that of the sun and the moon. My sight pulsed, my eyes unseeing what was happening around me. I could hear

Eli and Roman still battling to rid me of the therns vice grip. The pain rippling up my arms was unending. In my stark vision, my mother's horrified face blazoned to life. Her muted screams echoed in the distance as she burned at the stake, the skin bubbling and blistering as flame consumed her.

And then it was gone, and the air whooshed from up from within and underneath me. I flew on a phantom wind, high in the air. I landed in a heap on the mossy floor, the impact muffled and soft. It was moments, maybe even hours before my eyes, now streaming with tears blinking. Distorted faces swam in my vision. I couldn't move or speak, with the ringing in my ears, shocking me into submission. My whole body ached from the onslaught of fire. Sounds in the distance became clearer, as though I was swimming up from the depths of a watery place. I was being shaken, and my name, though strange, was being called by the two forms, blurred and dark.

Chapter 22

Clarity finally came to me and all that was wrong was made right. I heaved a breath deep into my lungs as both Eli and Roman's distressed faces became clear. My name on their lips came crashing into my ears as the dullness subsided and I was returned to this place and time. I blinked, the light searing my dry eyes.

"By the darkness, Rhona!" Roman cried as he pulled me up, my body still limp.

I coughed and spluttered, feeling the ache from my ribs at being thrown so far. Eli's hands encased my cheeks, and his eyes roved my face, searchingly. I nodded, still shaking with coughs and aches.

"I will be fine." My voice was a wheeze. My ribs barked as I inhaled, and my fingers felt strange as I fisted my hands. Realisation dawned on me, and I whirled to look back at the thern. On shaking legs, I stood, too quickly, and my vision blackened at the edges. But I forced my legs to move. The stag was still kneeling next to the thern, its head bowed, eyes closed.

"Don't go near that thing, Rhona," Roman hissed behind me. But I hushed him, finally nearing the old creature.

"What did you do to me?" My voice still felt distant in my ears. The therns skin had turned ashen. His breathing was more laboured, slowing with each inhale and exhale. I looked over his pale, limp form. He was dying. "Things are not what they seem." His words rattled about in my head, their familiarity pulsing as my body's normality came slowly back. "I am sorry to have bestowed such a thing, but it was the only way."

The stag's breath rippled the dead grass and white blossoms around him. I could only observe as a slow, mournful whine left the creatures snout. The therns chest rose in another gurgle, his eyes unseeing, face peaceful. I felt and saw the final breath. The breath he let go of rippled passed me, passed Roman and Eli and across the forest and woodland. Silence fell and my skin prickled. The colours around us muted. The large pale tree, with no leaves or plumage quivered, unnaturally. The ground quaked underfoot and I could hear Roman and Eli's exhalation of fright. A cracking sounded out, as though roots were ripped from the ground, and a rock shattered from the mountains and water crashed on land. This forest reverberated and quaked with that last life breath, the magic and barrier evidently gone. The stag raised its head, along with its towering horns with the vines that encircled them. A cry was called, something that shook me to my very core. The large beast moaned and disintegrated into a thousand butterflies that flew and fluttered away on the breeze. Leaving us alone with lifeless thern. The last thern was dead. The last guardian of the magical realms. Gone. And now the whole forest knew it.

***

The gate opened and we fell back into our world, my eyes slowly adjusted to the bleached colours once again. The floor under my feet was cold, unlike the soft moss that carpeted the hidden heart. The air in my lungs felt thicker and burned as my breath suddenly swirled ahead. I hadn't realised how warm it had been moments before, until a wind picked at my hair and exposed my neck to its icy bite. I stumbled, dazed and shivering.

Roman was behind me rustling, as he began rubbing the arms of his coat for heat. Eli, however, just stood, spellbound at the gate we had just come through. The stone, now dull and dark. The moss was less vibrant than it had seemed before. Everything around us was grey and lifeless once again. Instinctively, I moved toward him, my hand reaching out until it rested on his shoulder. His warmth seeped into my skin and gave me a strange comfort. I looked up from where my hand rested to find Eli watching me intently. Eyes locking, I realised he was eager to talk. To communicate.

'Was it real?' he signed to me, eyes round and full of shock and wonder. I nodded, wholly aware it was madness now, our present circumstances. As I looked at my scarred skin under Eli's tanned fingers, a thrill went through me. His hand engulfed my own, his broad fingers pressing mine closer. It took me a moment or two before I saw it. There, peeking through a torn piece of my shirt sleeve, was a band of deep blue. I gasped loudly, quickly pulling up the sleeve of my coat, revealing my arm now blemished and marked by seven bands of bluish ink. I rubbed at my skin and found the ink to be deep within, bold and unmoving. I had been marked. The seven rings seemed as though they had been there for years and not minutes, just as the therns wrists had been. Seven keys to seven gates. Eli's callused fingers shifted my sleeve on my other arm, revealing matching bands. I moved my hands, observing the tattoo in the dim light under the forest canopy.

"You've been marked by the thern and forest, Rhona?" A question or a reflection, I did not know. "You now hold all the keys?" Roman's voice was gruff as he wandered over, observing my wrists decorated by the unusual ink. I swallowed seeing the worry lining his eyes. I felt it then. Like a tonic, dissolving into my bloodstream. The dizziness and fatigue that had plagued me moments before, was ebbing. The muscles in my legs felt strong as did my arms. The pain in my rib was ceasing to a dull ache, which was manageable. The cold air in my lungs was awakening, the air on my skin, electrifying.

"I don't understand what's happening. This is all maddening." I whispered, aware every sense was currently in chaos. The cold wind rippled the trees, causing the deadened foliage to cascade around us like ash. My chest tightened and it took everything within me to stop my hands from shaking. Roman paced the small space ahead, muttering to himself, whilst I tried to focus on anything but the chill creeping up my spine. I watched Roman's footfall, dizzyingly.

"By the Mother, Roman, cease your pacing." I began to rub at my temples, my mind a mess of whirring unanswered questions. Roman huffed, crossing his arms, but continued his stomping and droning. I hissed, glaring at him. I heard an oomph and had to stifle a laugh, as a root protruded from the earth, catching his foot. Roman stumbled and spun, catching himself in time to avoid falling face first. He whirled at us, eyes wild. How convenient, I thought. Eli caught my attention to the side, his brows were thickly furrowed, looking about the floor sharply. I ignored him, smirking like a cat. But my smirk was soon wiped from my face. The tattoos caught my attention again and my heartbeat sped again as I beheld them. The ink seemed bright, as though moonlight was shimmering through the dark blue ink. But I noticed it was diminishing. I turned away so the others couldn't see, fixated on the skin. I tried to recall what my skin looked like before. It couldn't be.

"We need to get back to the road," Roman said, interrupting my curious thoughts. Eli looked up at that, circling around. I knew that he was trying to navigate the way back to the road, and it seemed with great difficulty. The trees grew closely together, arms and branches all tangled and twisted. There was no way we would find the road before nightfall. I tried looking through the woven canopy above, wishing for some way back to the warmth of my cart and poor Balthazar. How long had we been in that place? Surely no more than an hour? But the cast of shadow on the ground and through the tree told me differently. It was early morning when we ventured here, and now it looked like dusk was only minutes away.

Eli moved into my line of vision, looking past me, towards something. My neck muscles tightened at the look on his face. I turned, my lungs inhaling the cold air sharply. The tall narrow trees were banking, stretching their pale trunks into a visible parting. The grey limbs twisted and knitted into a protective pathway that curved through the thickest parts of the forest.

"By the Mother..." breathed Roman in disbelief. A slim but distinctive trail was now laid ahead of us. My heart began to hammer, as every fibre within me came alive. I was overcome with an urge to follow the path, to see our horses and the road. The bands on my wrist warmed in confidence, and confirmation. "If this is what we think it is, we have to follow it. Back to Balthazar and Ovi," Roman said with suspicion, although his eyes portrayed something different. I looked to the pathway and felt my foot pick up its step, ready to tread ahead.

"Do you think this means the forest wants to help us?" The words came out more confidently than I recognised, but I held steady on that surety embodying me.

"Not us, Rhona." My brother's words were the awakening I needed. "You," he finished, showing his tanned, unmarked wrists. Panic rose within me, as Eli did the same. Their skin was unmarked by tattoos or bands or keys.

"But why me and not either of you?" I asked, my voice breaking. It hadn't occurred to me that the thern would only give one of us the keys.

Roman looked solemn as he again eyed the tattoos. "It's all been directed at you, Rhona. Not us."

I gulped loudly, feeling my throat constrict. I couldn't stop the shaking. I turned back to Eli, breathing deeply to clear my head and settle my rattling nerves. I was relieved to see no fear shone in his eyes, no worry or doubt clouded that one blue and one brown eye. Just trust. My world shifted at that look and acknowledgment. I was suddenly irrevocably glad he was here with me and I closed my eyes, filling my lungs slowly again and began to follow the path. For several minutes, we walked in silence as the last few hours played out in my mind. The thern, the knife piercing the heart of the tree, all seven realms now open and unguarded by beings older than I could even comprehend. Again, and again each part spun in my head. The Trinity, the lycan. The realisation of what was happening made my stomach drop and the ground quake under the soles of my boots. So much so I didn't hear the crashing of trees uprooting before it was too late.

Chapter 23

Eli's hand wrapped around my waist and pulled me back as branches crashed and sprayed across the pathway. I hit the solid earth hard, the wind ripping out of me, as Eli's heavy form covered me from the battering of bits of tree and earth. The roar that followed sent a cold unending fear clawing through me. The ground shook and trembled as the Knarrock troll ravaged through the quiet forest towards us, uprooting trees and showering mud and debris across the ground. Eli grunted in pain at an impact to his back, the muscles in his neck and shoulders quivering as the full blow was absorbed by him. He was still trying to protect me. Anger swelled through me, not at his protection, but at the unnerving need to suddenly protect *him*. I ventured a look through the gap between Eli's body and my own. The horned creature roared again, saliva and earth raining down. Its rock-like hands thundered against the earth again as it bellowed another ferocious growl.

This couldn't be it. This couldn't be our end.

Dread coated my tongue and took away my voice as I tried and failed to scream as the Knarrock troll battered the ground again, feet from us. My mind raced. Eli, my Eli, if I could call him that, was sheltering me. Out of responsibility or something other than brother-like affection.

My wrists warmed unexpectedly, and I knew then it was not from the places our skin and bodies touched. His face was distraught as he looked down at me, horror widening his beautiful eyes. He was baring his teeth against the pain or fear. His lips and nose were so close to my own that we shared ragged breath. I looked at my wrists, at the bands of ink still exposed. My chest was a symphony of wild heartbeats, but I knew in my bones what I had to do.

Urgency made me bold as I leant even closer, the illusive heat around my hands and wrists chasing away the cold fear as I pressed my lips to his.

It was instinctual. Resolute. I needed to feel them against my own, if this was my last moment on earth. My lips were firm and coarse against his mouth and a fire lit up my heart at the sensation of him against me. I felt him still as I suddenly pulled away, and as I glared back at the troll, I began to free myself under Eli's weight. The shock of my kiss held him still as I released myself from his shelter. Everything seemed to slow as I stood on shaking legs, all around me a riot of devastation. I heard my name being called from afar as I moved.

I screamed in answer to the Knarrock's fresh raging roar, holding my arms out to stop it. The bands on my wrist blazed with heat as they began glowing bright blue and the creature reared, another deafening growl rippling from its jagged mouth of rock and bone teeth. It's boulder-like arms beat the ground again in defiance, but its eyes, black and beady, looked right into my own, challenging me.

I stepped forward, shouting with all the power my voice allowed. "Stop!"

The creature reared, spluttering, but settled on its knuckles in front of me, affronted. I heard the shallow breathing of Roman and Eli behind me, just as the creature did, as its black eyes darted behind me. I moved impulsively, shielding them.

"No! These are my people. You will not harm them!"

My blood was like lightning in my veins. This glaring glow at my wrists pulsed at my words, bringing the Knarrock's attention back to me. Its jagged mouth parted in answer, but a wolf-like whine escaped, low and unnerving. No roar. Its eyes looked to my wrists, the blue light reflecting in the beads of onyx as they rested back on my face.

"Go home," I demanded, mustering some authority.

The stone-like scales transformed in understanding and its features and its eyes shone with intelligence. I kept my arms and wrists aloft and uncovered, the brightness of the bands fading back to the inky blue. My legs were shaking, as though every nerve and muscle were lucid and not compliant. My stomach was knotted so much that I didn't know if at any moment I would hurl my guts onto the floor. But I kept my ground and a straight back and glare, as this inner tuition was telling me too. The creature huffed in resignation, its face moulding in recognition as I continued my glare, taking in every detail. The Knarrock's horns of bone like twisted oak trees were spiralled feet above its already towering form. It must have been twenty feet tall. My mouth went dry, my stomach twisting in terror. Its broad mountain-like chest heaved and as it turned to leave, it stopped, bowing back with a submissive huff of hot breath. Those dark eyes caught mine one last time before, it left the way it came.

I watched as its mountainous body disappeared into the sea of pale trees, my heart cantering and a sheen of sweat coating me from head to toe. I felt lightheaded and my vision seemed to blur around the edges. My fingers numbly touched my chest, and I held the medallion, the silver disk slick in my palm. My breath was the only thing I could feel or hear for some time. Someone moaned behind me and it immediately washed away the oncoming haze. I whirled, stomach dropping at seeing blood pooling through Eli's coat from his ribs. A shard of wood penetrated through the fabric, slowly darkening from the blood seeping through. I ran to him, skidding and falling to my knees. Fear and anguish radiated through me, silencing the chorus of erratic heartbeats. The sight of Eli hurt, wounded, sent an unending ripple within me. Deafening and hollow.

"Eli? Eli, look at me?"

His eyes found mine, solidly. I saw the muscles strain in his neck as he clenched his teeth, his hand reaching for the shard protruding.

"No, don't pull it out until we have the means to wrap and stop the flow of blood." My voice was unseasoned to this desperation. "Can you breathe?" I asked, looking at the wound. The wood that was protruding seemed shallow, but I could not be sure. Roman was fumbling beside me, his speech and words incoherent.

Eli nodded in response and I sighed, relief and anxiety flooding me. "I don't think it has pierced your lung, thank the Mother." And the Crone, my inner thoughts said. "But we need to get you back to the wagon. I have some of Mutza's salves and bandages there to dress it. Can you stand?"

Eli nodded and I wrapped his arm around my shoulder, trying to take his weight on my own. I gripped at his fingers, now coated in blood, and squeezed letting him know I was there. Now and always.

Roman carefully reached under his other arm and lifted him, not touching the injury as we supported Eli down the path.

When we finally reached the road again, I ran ahead, leaving Roman to support Eli. I grappled with the salve and bandages and when they caught up, I worked quickly to remove the shard and bind Eli's wound. Thankfully, it was shallow, but it needed cauterising to staunch the blood flow. I cleaned and wrapped what I could, and we ventured further up the road seeking shelter in the trees for the caravan and ponies. Nightfall was upon us and within minutes the trees answered our silent need for shelter. A tunnel of branches took us off the road and into a copse of trees, quiet and undisturbed. It was a clearing big enough for my caravan and both horses. The tunnel disappeared into thicket and forest the moment we entered the small refuge, the shadows growing thick and fast to protect us from view. I didn't know if it was the inner calling and prayer I was demanding upon the universe or simple luck, but I was grateful, nonetheless.

Safely within our surroundings, Roman lit a fire. I searched for something metal, wide enough to burn the open wound but found only a copper ladle. Eli thankfully nodded when I presented it, a little embarrassed. I began heating the metal in the open flames, watching the copper slowly begin to glow. Roman busily prepared fresh bandages from an old, washed bed shirt, whilst I was left with the task of removing Eli's coat and shirt. My stomach tightened at the thought.

"You need to do it," I said as I stirred the flames around the ladle.

"Why so bashful now, Rhona?" Roman's voice was laced with quiet mischief, given the current situation. "Anyone would assume you'd jump at the chance, after that kiss." My spine locked and I ground my teeth, my face turning crimson.

"What of it?" I asked, mortified.

I couldn't deny the sudden need to be close to Eli. The knot in my chest winding tighter at the thought of him being harmed couldn't be ignored. I knew in my heart, whatever this was, it wasn't the love for a brother or friend. It pierced me deeper. But even if Eli did feel the same, I wouldn't allow him to be tied to me. But it was my brother's next words that stalled me into silence.

"Don't break his heart, Rhona."

There was genuine concern that resonated in his voice. I stumbled to find my words but before I could probe him further, he moved away from me and over to his best friend. I gazed with glazed eyes at the roaring flames, stunned.

Could Eli feel the same for me?

The thought caused my hands to shake and nerves to tingle. Surely not? Why would he feel that way about me? Those words clanged throughout me like a ringing bell and my heart sank at the thought; the reasoning as to why he would feel obliged to be kind to me and to have allowed me to have kissed him. I'm supposed to be his betrothed. He must feel morally bound to me. My heart continued to sink into the deepest, darkest rivet of me, shying away from any light or hope.

"I need help removing his clothes," Roman called, making my stomach flip, catapulting me into the now.

I rolled my eyes, turning to find both men sharing a stubborn look. I swallowed, fisting my hands. I had seen Eli shirtless before. But that was before our kiss. The kiss I had unabashedly planted on him, before I knew what had been building within me. I sighed, knowing my brother would make me do this, for sport or some self-gratification.

Sweat beaded on Eli's brow and I mopped it away gently, not daring to look at him or my brother. I knelt in front of Eli, my back to the fire and glowing metal. I began to unbutton Eli's shirt, my fingers guiltily lumbering as more skin was revealed. With my blade, I began to carefully cut away the fabric that had dried with blood against his skin. I inhaled, steading my mind and hands as I cautiously peeled the ruined shirt from his ribs. He did not flinch under my touch as I mopped away blood and prepared the wound with sage water.

"Ready?"

It was a rhetorical question, as I picked up the glowing ladle handle with Eli's ruined shirt. Roman grasped at Eli's arms, spreading them, giving me clear access to the gape of open flesh.

My eyes found Eli's. "Look at me." He did so without question, causing my blood to heat. I rested my knee as gently as I could into the centre of his chest, pinning him. My breath hitched at the contact.

Eli abruptly shook off Roman's grip on his uninjured side and a thrill went through me as his arm wrapped itself around the inside of my leg, holding it in place, his grip firm and steady. His one blue and brown eye pinning me, like I pinned him now. I held his gaze and before I let my thoughts spiral, I gritted my teeth and pushed the searing metal into the seeping gash, hearing and smelling his skin sizzle. I pushed harder with my knee as he jolted, gasping. His eyes never left my own. I held the ladle there for another few seconds and then pulled it away quickly before his skin stuck to it. I dropped it quickly, the heat burning my own hand through the thin fabric. A quiet, gurgled cry left Eli's ravaged throat. Sweat beaded his brow as every muscle and scar on his neck and face strained. After letting the air get to the burnt skin, I grabbed the salve and began quickly working to ease the pain. Delirium was coming over him from the pain and I had to work quickly. Eli's breathing was short and shallow as I pulled him over me, his arms touching my thighs and hips, his chin nestled against the crook of my neck, heavy and limp, whilst I wrapped the knotted bandage around his chest. His breath played havoc with the hairs on my nape, as his head rested wearily on my shoulder.

I finished wrapping the bandage, carefully knotting it firmly to his front. Resting him back down, I reached blindly for my flask of water and proceeded to carefully pour it into Eli's mouth, watching as some poured out and over his scarred chin and neck. His scars never bothered me. I never thought they took away from his quiet beauty. Eli's eyes were unfocused, and I went quickly to brew a sleeping draft for him.

I watched him over the fire, his sweat slick skin glistening in the flames golden light. I watched how his muscled chest and ribs inhaled deeply. I looked back to the tea bubbling away in the pot and when I ventured my gaze again to Eli, I found my brother looking at me, bemused.

"Why did you not want the marriage, Rhona?"

I didn't need this now. This was not the time or place to discuss such things. Annoyance gripped me, but I flexed rigid fingers, gaining some feeling back.

"I know you; I know your heart. You do feel for Eli, don't you?" His words weren't hushed, and I goggled at his audacity. My heart was hammering as I cursed loudly. Eli was right there. In hearing distance. My entire face burned, and I cursed again even louder.

"Roman! Stop it, please just stop it," I pleaded, my voice strained as I looked at my betrothed, fearful of what he would make of Roman's words.

"He's out of it," Roman said simply, his face sombre and hands clasped in waiting.

I hissed and looked at Eli. It was true his eyelids were heavy and unfocused, yet it did nothing to suppress my anxious mind and fidgeting hands.

"Why do you ask me such forward things?" I spat, feeling the burn in my eyes as I watched Eli's eyes roll and his breathing hitch.

"Because I know you love him of sorts." Roman rubbed a rough hand over his shorn beard. He crossed his arms. My stomach tightened at our mother's dark eyes, his eyes, looking back at me, searching. "You say it's because you aren't deserving of him. Which is ridiculous. I don't understand you, haven't understood this entire arrangement," he huffed, frustrated but I couldn't bring myself to look at him. My mirror. My brother. Who knew me so well and yet so little. My heart fractured.

"Do you not realise? Fuck, Rhona, do you not know anything?" He looked to his friend. No, our friend, who was practically unconscious. His voice softened, his face sad, as he continued to look at Eli. "I just do not know why you do not have him. Why you haven't..." Roman's words were cut short and he physically shook himself. "We need to rest. All of us."

He said no more to me after that, choosing to sleep under the canopy of trees next to the fire, watching Eli. I had dribbled what I could of the sleeping draft into Eli's mouth, carefully working his mouth, so he swallowed and took it down without choking. I worried about him being warm all night, exposed outside, and even considered hauling him into my cabin. But I couldn't move him. Not yet.

After that, I climbed the steps of my caravan, my body and mind physically and mentally exhausted. The last few days events had caught up with me in a manner which caused me to slump and fall into a dark, dreamless sleep as soon as I laid down on my bed.

Chapter 24

I awoke groggy and aching, with my body contorted in an uncomfortable position and smothered by the blankets of my bed. Knocking rattled on the door, stirring me further.

"Rhona, Eli needs his wounds redressed and another draft boiled." It was Roman's voice and with sleep-filled lids, I rolled my eyes.

I stretched, yawning loudly. "I'm coming."

I rose, my limbs and muscles barking in protest. Roman didn't have a clue about drafts or herbalism. He had never shown interest when Mutza and my mother had tried to teach us as children. The only other person who knew how to create a sedative tea and clean a wound, was the one who needed it. Eli had always made a point of attending his grandmother's lessons and leaving Roman to whine. I had always admired that about Eli. He knew things, had learned things, others would deem unnecessary for a man.

Even as we had grown and Roman had begun gallivanting off to hunt with our uncle, Eli still attended his grandmother's teachings. Though they weren't as regular as they once had been when we were children. I searched about the place; I had removed my jacket in the night, and I was now standing in clothes that were three days old. The smell of stale clothing and body odour assaulted me, and I winced. I would wash after tending to Eli. I grabbed some mugwort, chamomile, willow bark and valerian from the tins and pots Mutza had given to us, knowing exactly what was needed for a dreamless, painless rest. I had concocted many teas myself over the years when the nightmares were too vivid and the memories too real. I passed my cracked and fractured mirror. I glimpsed the mess and mound of matted dark hair atop my head. But I didn't care. Eli needed me.

When my door cracked open, light streamed through the pale, lifeless canopy. We were still safe and not visible from the road. A small haven. My feet trod down my steps, the wood creaking with the damp and cold. I huffed, looking about the small encampment. I froze mid-turn, seeing Eli's and Roman's wide-eyed expression. Their looks of shock and amusement were followed by Roman's loud cackle. My hackles rose in answer.

I looked down at myself in the reflection of my only window. Clothes dishevelled, my shirt askew. My hands reached up, finding the mass of hair flopping in a heap to the side. I looked a mess.

"Oh, fuck off. I chose to tend to Eli, rather than myself." Though as I said the words aloud, my bladder ached, and I needed to relieve myself soon. Eli's eyes followed me as I walked the small distance closer and was grateful to find only appreciation in his eyes and an exhausted smile. He looked pale and his skin was dewy from sweat. I prayed a fever wouldn't set in.

I knelt beside the new fire Roman must have created; the logs were fresh and not yet devoured. My brow creased and I scanned the trees, fearful of what or who he had hacked down for new kindling.

"What tree did you butcher for a new fire?" My voice was gritty and grainy with sleep.

"None," Roman said, and I gawked. "That, dear sister, has been burning all night."

"You're joking? How?" But I knew and looked to my wrists in answer. The skin was smooth, with a few stark whisks of scars, but I looked past those to the blueish bands that were dull. Something tapped at my memory and I remembered a warmth last night.

"Were you worried we would get cold?"

I threw the tin screw pot at Roman, and it hit him with a devilishly satisfying clunk on his cheek bone, stunning his smug face into shock. Eli huffed his approval and I smiled like a cat at him. Roman handed me back the pot carefully, looking about the trees, warily. If what these bands represented meant I could ask things of this forest and the creatures in it. Roman knew he had better behave. Satisfaction empowered me at the thought and the smile stayed on my face for a while.

"I only mean. If you did think that, then it happened." His tone was quizzical, face thoughtful. "As in, if you did think it, Rhona, then that magic, those things on your wrist, kept the fire burning all night."

I looked at *those things*, he was referring too. Trying to remember my train of thoughts last night.

"Well?" Roman asked, mouth pursed and eyes alight.

"I might have," I whispered, busying myself with a fresh pot. The water within was not enough for a fresh draft for Eli. I looked at the trees. There must be water nearby, somewhere. "We need some more water. I don't have enough for the tea, let alone the day." I stood, turning, assessing the direction of the sun above.

"I haven't ventured past this clearing, in case I got lost," Roman admitted. To be fair, I didn't blame him. We had only found this safe space through the magic. The strange magic now connected with me. My throat constricted just thinking about it.

"I will see if there is water nearby. We need to restock anyway." Setting aside the iron kettle, I trod back to my cabin, ready to get my coat.

"Erm... Rhona," Roman's voice blurted out at a strange octave behind me. I held my next step. Instinct told me to be cautious, and yet

I knew before I turned at what I would find. A tree was banking, stretching unnaturally over into the clearing. Its pale branches began to twist and spiral together until they arched into the clearing, all knotting and weaving in a unanimous point. I watched, utterly mesmerised. In my heart, I knew what would come next.

Small droplets of water began drizzling up from the ground, up the distorted bent trunk. It trailed up the spine of the tree, over the limbs, until the water snaked and streamed down the arching pointed branches. Water fell, dribbling and dripping into a pool on the dry, cold floor. I stood there momentarily, taking it all in. Roman was right. The bastard was *right*.

I ran to it, grabbing the iron kettle, skidding on my knees in front of it. As soon as I placed the open pot underneath the water flow, it ruptured, pouring more freely. Roman scoffed behind me, spluttering obscenities. I paid him no head. I couldn't gather myself quick enough to even admit he had been right. The pot was filling quickly. I sent a silent prayer of thanks up to the Mother, the Crone, the Maiden, and anyone that was listening.

"Roman, fill the skins with water and a few flasks. There may not be water for a few days." I still hadn't turned to face him.

"I should not worry, Rhona. Travelling with you, is finally having its advantages."

I smiled, but continued concentrating on filling the kettle, setting an image in my mind, then waiting.

There was a whipping crack, followed by Roman's howl. The laughter that rose from me was freeing and loud. I fell back on my back, my ribs aching from the onslaught of cackles and snorts that came from me.

"You bitch!" Roman howled and I finally turned to see him hopping, clasping his arse.

I was still snickering and sniffling when the pot was full and as I walked back to the fire. I placed the kettle over the blaze and then finally turned to Eli. He looked at me in a way I had never seen. There was a smile on his lips, proud and opulent. His eyes, those eyes of two colours were bold as he watched me. I smiled coyly, pushing back the grabble of hair behind my ears.

He began to sign. *'He deserved it'*. My smile only grew wider.

After I had finished cleaning Eli's wound with fresh shirt bandages, I gave him a cup of the tea I had brewed. He was out cold in a matter of moments. I didn't realise I had been sat watching him for some time until Roman's dark form moved in my peripherals and came to sit beside me.

"I'm worried, Rhona." His voice was hushed. "For you."

His words set my teeth on edge. But it was time to look at him. Talk to him. Sibling to sibling.

"This is a great gift." His voice was contemplative, eyes observing the bands of ink peeking through the torn fabric at my wrist. "But, at what cost?" My brow creased and I began rubbing my hands, causing the healing skin on my knuckles to sting, the pain my anchor. I hadn't thought of what Roman had stated, or of what these keys would or could do. I hadn't even considered whether it was a blessing or a burden. Memories began to flood me, stories our mother told of the legend of the therns. I wracked my brain for any element of importance, any sign or murmur of these keys. But there were none. It was a gift, something so unbelievable, I couldn't deny it. But Roman was right, at what cost? To me, to my health or to my mind.

I was yet to find out.

I sat trying to understand what new path fate had weaved for me. My mind exhausted itself until only me, within me, remained. I sat feeling the heat from the fire, the ever-burning logs, never dissolving from the flames. The sky above was beginning to turn, the hues of pink and purple streaking high above. The trees were solemnly present, watchful and hearing. I had never truly come to realise the magic in this world until that exact moment. It was an awakening.

The time passed in my quiet solace, and the same percussion of foul screams and blistered skin played in my mind. It was a phantom parade, repeated over and over again in my head. I needed to bathe and rid myself of this dirt that coated me like a second skin. I went to my cabin, with the fresh water the forest, these keys, had provided. I washed vigorously. The small bar of withered soap lathering and cleansing me until my face and body were clean. In a small trunk, next to my bed, I found clean shirt and riding trousers. I dressed in them quickly, finally tying my hair on top of my head in a knot.

When I returned to sit by the fire with Roman and Eli, the forest around us was silent, more so than it had been hours earlier. I watched the flames as I began boiling another draft of tea. I hadn't realised Roman had been speaking until a chill began to claw its way up my spine. The strange claws mused their way steadily up my back and over the skin on my arms until they brought me back to the present, and I was faced with Roman and his eyes searching through the trees. There was a dull sound on the horizon, unmistakably horses. As I began to focus, my eyes clearing and senses coming back to life, it was confirmed, the distant thundering of hooves down the road. It grew louder, echoing throughout the trees, and rumbled through our haven of a clearing. Men cried out in the distance and a horn sounded out, disturbing the silence throughout the forest and woodland.

It was now too dark to see through the trees and even the night sky above. The trees around were protecting us so thoroughly that we needed more light. I stood, listening. They, whoever they were, were a mile up the road. I searched the space, my eyes finding the frosted lamp that still hung unused on my caravan. But as if on cue, my palms warmed and my wrists began to heat as small glowing fireflies weaved through the darkest of shadow towards us. They swarmed and then settled on a phantom breeze, suspended around me, glowing pale yellow and green, highlighting the small expanse about my body. I had no time to gasp as the rider's horns bellowed in the night again and the tattoos pulsed on my flesh in answer to the unspoken call.

"Stay here, keep Eli safe." A preternatural instinct was taking over me, filling me. "Take Eli to my caravan and rest him on my bed. Give him the draft I've just boiled." My voice was stark, yet confident in the dying light. It felt unfamiliar, but this time I realised I was choosing the words in which I spoke. "It will allow him to sleep longer than his unconscious mind will." I moved, running to my caravan, and grabbing my discarded hunting knife. I strapped it tightly to my thigh, the trees around me began rustling restlessly.

"No, Rhona, what are you doing? You can't go alone. You don't know who they are, what they could do?" Roman's words sent violent fingernails of ice to my very core and a memory began to resurface, haunting and horrific. But I inhaled deeply, clenching my fists against such a blight. The warmth from the rings set in ink on my skin settled my nerves. I knew if I lifted the sleeves of my shirt, I would find a blue effervescent light. "Rhona, that horn is the call of a hunting party," Roman hissed, now kneeling beside Eli, looking back and forth between us two.

"I don't intend to do anything, brother, but observe. Something you are formidably good at." I smiled at him, my face feeling foreign and not my own. This strength, this guiding and knowing sense of self, was not me. It couldn't be. But I followed it, allowing it to lead me.

"Do as I say, Roman, or I'll set the forest on you," I said, trying to bring some humour, but inside my own head it was a different matter. I repeated over and over the therns last words to me. His whispered croak, circling in my mind as I felt the forest move with me. *The forest will provide.'* I walked to the edge of the small clearing, turning back to my brother, who sat dumbfounded. It was time to fully test these rings.

"I will be careful." I looked finally at Eli, the worry straining on my face, the truth betraying my heart and said to Roman rather coldly, "look after him, you fool." And I walked into the trees and beyond, suddenly consumed by darkness.

I replayed the therns words over and over again as I moved into the thickest area of black and shadow. The fireflies suddenly followed and began to accompany me, glowing softly, showing the pale skeletal trunks and branches ahead of me. "I am in need of a path, silent and unnoticeable, back to the road." My words were barely a whispered breath, my first conscious ask of the forest.

The trees surrounding me answered. Roots cracked and shifted. Branches retracted and closed in. The forest floor grew soft under my feet. I looked down, my heart hammering as the fireflies illuminated a trail of soft moss under me and ahead. I exhaled in awe and the trees about me sighed.

Wonder filled me, and it was strange, feeling a delight so uncommon. Something I had not felt truly since my mother had… I shook myself. I could not go there now. I absorbed the feeling, breathing it in deep and it swelled, filling me down to my bones.

Could this truly be a gift?

I realised that for the first time in a long time I felt almost whole. I felt unfractured and strong. All I knew was that I would have to test this in the future. I walked along the soft earthy path, keenly aware that my feet made no sound. Pride surged through me at the forest and its willingness to help. I heard the horn call out again and I quickened my pace, the fireflies swirling and twisting ahead, lighting my path.

Chapter 25

As I trod lightly down the path, the road was becoming more visible ahead. The waning moon glowed pale and I could see light, like illuminated ghosts, filtering through the canopy. I slowed my steps, mentally asking these marvellous little living lights that flurried and flowed about me to soften their glow. The fireflies did so, as I crept closer to the opening. It was elating and yet my mind was troubled, as dark and unnatural thoughts sparked at what I could ask of the forest. I bit the inside of my cheek and the sharp tang of blood coating my tongue flushed them away. A horse huffed breathlessly, down the road. They would be passing soon; they were mere seconds away. I quickly gathered myself, and my silent request to stop the light of the fireflies happened immediately, like a flame doused in water. I could still feel them flurrying around me, waiting for another silent command. I prayed they had vanished in time, so no eyes had been drawn to me and my hiding place.

Hooves thundered against stone and earth, and I braced myself. I saw the first rider gallop ahead, going north. The same direction we were headed. Then another and then another, until I counted twelve. They were followed by a wagon, it's dark bulking shape, shifting and manoeuvring fast over the road.

I peeked out, my head passing the limbs that sheltered me, trying to get a better look. I trailed my eyes across their murky shapes. A horn blew boldly on the road behind my line of sight, the sound vibrating across my bones. I jumped out of my skin and fell, toppling over myself into the road. Horse hooves were immediately halted and then proceeded to parade around me. ***Fuck.***

There was a screech followed by a scatter of flint and stones, as the rest of the horses and the carriage skidded to a stop up ahead. Heart racing, I flew up, blood pumping to every muscle as my legs forced me into a careful stance. The lone rider at my back began circling me. I couldn't see the rider, as they paced about me on a steed as dark and towering as Balthazar. The moonlight only showed glimpses of their features. They wore a black scarf or sheath that covered everything but their eyes. I noticed the haughty stance in their seat and the silver buckle of their sleek riding boots. Both the horse and leather boots alone bared great money. My pulse was deafening in my ears as I swivelled, following the rider. It was too dark in the shadows, as he paraded around me, to discern any other things of note.

The fireflies swirled out of the forest, surrounding me, their simple green and blue lights bobbing in a circle. The rider hissed and the horse reared, huffing and spluttering. Creaking began as trees and branches ripped and cracked behind me. I whirled as my stomach dropped at the thought of what manner of creature I may have summoned. Roman and Eli came crashing through the shadows, wide eyed and armed to the teeth. I nearly gasped in relief. Roman and Eli jumped into the road, assessing me. I could decipher a gleam of Roman's blade, and Eli's arm holding his staff aloft and ready. I didn't miss the knowing look Roman directed at me in the light of the fireflies. I knew what he was thinking.

So much for observing.

I ground my teeth at that look.

They came to stand beside me, their hulking shapes grazing against either of my shoulders. I heard Eli's ragged deep intakes of breath, as his lungs worked. My thoughts shot to the pain he must be feeling from running to me. Anger flared but I steeled it, reaching out my hand and grabbing his. I was returned by his reassuring grip, which he quickly released, leaving the faint touch of his shaking fingers. More horses had begun galloping towards us from where they had halted up the road. The rider had ceased their circling and finally removed the sheath that covered their face. It was a man. But none like I had ever seen. His hip and leg gathered over his saddle and stirrups. He landed lightly on the ground, removing his gloves, finger by finger. The fireflies were still billowing about me and from their glow, they highlighted the white of his silken hair, the straight nose and his pale silver eyes.

"What in the darkness are three *unwanted* doing this far north?" His voice was gruff with cold, eyes calculating. His unnerving eyes shifted over each of us with the keenness of a hawk. I tried my voice, as Eli's hand suddenly crept across my middle, moving to stand in front of me. Shielding me. This was one occasion that I was grateful for such overbearing protectiveness.

"We could say the same, for you, *friend*." Roman's voice had a bitter edge to it. I observed the man in front of us, if I could call him a man. There was a scattering of shadows as some of his men halted behind him. His eyes were trained on the fireflies dancing about, their luminescent glow shining in his eyes. My mind sped into action, willing them to disappear. They flew off, away from me and back into the darkness of the forest. I watched his silver eyes trail them until they were consumed by the shadows.

"Are you a witch?" There was no threat in the rider's voice, but curiosity, edged with something else.

Eli's hand gripped my hip, slowly pushing me behind him further. My skin prickled as his fingers touched exposed skin on my abdomen. I found my voice then; it took all the strength in me not to allow it to be wobbly and betray my true emotion.

"I am not. I can assure you." Those eyes, as pale as the moon, homed in on me. "We are travelling north and found a haven in this woodland for the night." It wasn't a lie. Yet wasn't the sole truth either.

The stranger's eyes creased and patrolled me, and both the men beside me shuffled their stances. My chest constricted as his eyes locked with my own again. I couldn't blink, couldn't look away. I set my jaw, daring him to push further. The waning moon highlighted a flicker of muscle in his temple. No one said anything for what felt like a minute, as every nerve sharpened and went on high alert. This man was not someone who we could walk away from. Every instinct within me screamed it. Even as his eyes left my own and my lung whooshed with a deep infill of breath.

"Where is your troupe?" That voice was grainy on my skin, as his horse nuzzled him. I watched the beast, so much like Balthazar who was back within the secrecy of the forest behind us.

"They are heading east." It was Roman who answered. "Away from the disturbance in the north and foul villagers in the south." I straightened, my palms beginning to slick with sweat at his inclination. His lie. Our family was travelling west again, to Opal Bay, where they could potentially stay a while, undisturbed.

"Then what are you three doing so far from your clan?" There was no distaste or hate in his voice, unlike we had encountered many times.

"Does it matter?" I asked, irritated. He was beginning to grind on my very soul. But as his eyes shot back to me, with their cold metallic sheen. There was humour there.

"It matters to me, as the lands further on this road are my own."

Interesting.

That pinned me. I didn't realise the land in the north belonged to anyone. Could he be a lord or governor of the lands beyond? The stranger looked behind him, to his men gathered and armed. I hadn't realised bows and swords had been drawn, until an arrow quivered. Some of his men were still stationed around the carriage up the road, the moon shining eerily over their shapes. The stranger whistled, low and long. It was like the ground had begun shaking under my very feet, and as though lightning had struck me, down to my very core. I had heard that whistle before. That low, sharp string of gathered lips. The Cone's messenger.

My breath crept up on me, cold in my lungs as I breathed deep, not allowing the shock to show on my face. This was the sign, I realised. The message the Crone had bade me back at the farm. It reverberated throughout me, causing shivers to caress my skin.

"What land is yours to the north?" I asked.

He looked insulted that I had no knowledge of who he was or his land. "Neath Briar," he retorted through gritted teeth.

"Then it is you whom we seek." My voice sounded bold, compared to the tremor of my hands. "We have followed this road north, to seek out that which is ravaging *your* lands."

"What is this?" There was no spite or presumption in the stranger's voice. "Who are you?" More men were coming down the road towards us.

"No one. Only three travellers, who know of what beast ails you and your lands." Roman's voice was tight, but he was refusing to give away our intentions. I was grateful for it. Especially when he could be such an arse.

"You seek the lycan?" The stranger's voice was still edged with humour, an untold joke that set my teeth on edge. But his face did brighten a fraction, eyes becoming less cold.

Eli's fingers dug into the softness of my stomach, their heat searing me. The skin on my arms warmed in answer. I couldn't tell if it was the keys, tattooed there, or my own body reacting. That lightning erupted within, filling me with a static that I couldn't ignore. I stepped forward, away from those searing fingertips and his body that engulfed my senses, until I came to stand again in front of the man, letting this wave of courage ride over me.

Years ago, I would have quivered under the scrutiny of a man like him. Years ago, I would have cowered, screamed or fled, scared and overcome with shame. But my voice was steady, my body strong. My mind fractured but capable. I didn't know if it was the power that was radiating from these keys, hidden by my military jacket, or the sheer hysteria that was making me so brazen, but I went with it. I embodied it, until the child that once shied and scurried away, was locked tightly in the vault of my memories. I had vowed never to be that child again, and now was not the time to crack or splinter. I held my chin high, feigning this bold being wearing my skin.

"My name is Rhona. This is Eli and Roman. What do we call you?"

Interest shone then in the stranger's eyes. Intellect and intrigue. His smile was wolfish as he grasped the reins of his horse. "You may call me Finian." Those sharp eyes and that smile took my breath away, his teeth glimmering white in the feeble moonlight. "Lord of the Neath Briar Estate."

The name registered, my mental map locating the large province attached to that of the Fallow and its surrounding borders. An awareness settled over me and the Crones words echoed in my mind. I smiled, forcing all the cunning and confidence in that false flash of teeth.

"Nice to meet you, Lord Finian."

"The pleasure is all mine, Rhona." He pronounced my name so intrinsically, that the hairs on my nape stood to attention, as did every nerve and sense.

Roman, cleared his throat and I heard Eli staff finally landed with a thud on the earth. "Now that the niceties are over with. Can I ask, why you, Lord Farrian-" Roman began.

"-Finian."

"Apologies." Roman rubbed at his face, the epitome of arrogance. "Lord Finian, why are you so far away from home?"

I strived to keep the complicit mask on my face; as always, Roman did not disappoint, with his careless and provocative manners finally rippling to the surface. I tried not to roll my eyes. I couldn't disregard the tension that radiated from Eli now behind me. Or that of Roman, though he did a good show of displaying the very opposite.

The wolfish grin returned on Finian's face, looking my brother dead in the eye. He looked behind him and there was an unspoken message relayed. His men finally started to lower their weapons and chorus of clicks and shifts sounded out as crossbows and swords were placed away in safety.

"Me and my men are returning home, from a hunt, which you are now holding us from achieving." There was a challenge in his tone, something I know Eli and Roman had not missed.

I ruffled myself, knowing all too well, Roman had likely ground against his authority. We were common folk and for one of us to address a Lord in such a way wasn't unheard of, but not done by simple villagers and city folk. But we were neither of those. We made our own rules and had no masters.

"Do you intend to ride all night back to your lands, or were you intending to rest and begin again in the morning?" I asked, wondering whether Finian would deem himself too high on the class scale to answer me.

"We have been travelling for three days. But our intentions were to secure a place for the night," he said matter-of-factly as his eyes bore into mine, my skin flushing at that gaze. His roguish smile was a mirror reflection of the one Roman wore at times. Roman cleared his throat behind me, the sound grating and bothersome. I continued to smile at the lord, until the enormity of my words clanged through me like a bell.

"What I meant was," I started, my voice stumbling as I tried to correct any indecent meaning that could have been read, "we know of a shelter within this woodland. We have travelled ourselves to reach the north. To help you rid your lands of the lycan."

My skin and cheeks were flushed under lord Finian's scrutiny. I clenched my fists, trying to bring some level of determination to my being. We needed to follow him. We needed access to his lands, so we could freely hunt the creature. If what Mutza and the Crone had said were true, the creature was returning there, near to the Fallow.

"Me and my men wish not to invade your…" There was a pause as the lord gripped for words. "Dwelling."

He looked ahead to the road again, to the large dark carriage. I followed his gaze. The moon's phosphorous rays highlighted that there were no windows. I strained my eyes, catching the glimpse of locks on an entry way at the back. It was a prison cell. A cage on wheels. My breath caught, remembering a carriage of the same size and shape at the Tavern at Hantonway Bridge. Thoughts raced in my head and I looked to my brother, imploring him for some civility.

"We would welcome a Lord to make camp with us." Roman's eyes never left mine, the teasing question there evident.

"You truly wish to help us?" Lord Finian had stepped forwards, his eyes searching. He was looking for a lie, which in truth was not there. We were here to help him but for our own reasons and business. Something I would not tell this lord, *yet*. I realised then, that I felt trust towards him. This he was indeed a man which we could trust and commune within this death challenge. The world shifted, as though it had slowed to this very moment.

"Then I thank you for your hospitality." Finian's hand reached out and grasped my own, shaking it. He did so to Roman and Eli. The tension in all of us, gone.

Chapter 26

After we had shaken hands with Lord Finian, he and his men looked expectantly along the road to see where we had made camp. A rider trotted up ahead, presumably relaying the message to the other men still stationed up by the carriage. I wondered then if there was anyone, or anything, in there. There was no sign of life, only the formidable straight walls and locked door. The sharp angles and dark, black wood were too similar to that we saw at the tavern. Could it be the very same carriage we had seen back in Hantonway? From my point of view, I could see no window or bars for eyes and hands to peek through. I kept glancing at it as it trailed along the road towards us, trying to glimpse life within.

"I must say, when Rhona fell out on the road, I thought we were about to encounter a witch," Finian spoke behind me, as we waded up the road, meeting the men and carriage half way.

"She's a witch at times."

That got my guard up. Surely my brother wouldn't be that stupid?

"How long have you been on the road?" Finian asked.

There was a pause and I heard Roman gruffly clear his throat. "He's a mute, he cannot speak." I turned at that, seeing Roman's hand on Eli's shoulder. Eli's face was set in that stone-like manner as always. His eyes surveying the Lord.

"My apologies," Finian replied empathetically, nodding to Eli.

"Rhona is my sister." Roman gestured to me and all I could do was shape my mouth into some form between a smile and a grimace, my sole focus still on Eli. Sweat had beaded on his forehead. I watched the lapels of his jacket rise and fall with his chest. He was in pain and knowing Roman, hadn't been fed enough of the pain relief.

"Let's get back to camp and I can fix everyone something to eat," I pronounced, loudly. Eli's gaze found my own, knowing from my glare that my direction was not about food, but to see to him and his wound. He needed to rest, and I would probably need to redress it, thanks to his sprint through the trees.

"Is it just yourselves? Or do you have others with you?"

It wasn't Finian, but a man climbing down from his horse, his copper beard and dark blue eyes glinting. I looked at him, seeing the distrust lined in his brow and mouth.

"It's just us. We have two horses and my caravan in the woods." My stomach tightened but I held myself firm. The man looked along the road, seeing no pathway into the trees. None big enough for a cart. I swallowed, realising my error.

The man's voice started to rise in warning. "Finian," he started.

I rallied my thoughts, feeling the warmth creep over my skin at the silent command of my wrist markings.

Show an entry way into our camp, so hidden that eyes couldn't easily detect it at night, I thought.

I felt the skitter of magic crawl over my wrists in answer, just as I passed a creaking tree. The path that appeared was barely visible, shrouded in the deepest shadow, but wide enough for a cart and many horses.

I heaved a great silent breath, relaxing at the sight of it. It was hard to see and detect from the road. I walked towards it, branches and tree arms covering the main entrance. I thanked the forest again, my words inaudible and under my breath, turning finally with a small smile on my face. Finian's man looked dumbfounded, but there was still suspicion in his eyes as he trounced over, inspecting the darkened path.

"This is what we found," I countered, trying to sound genuine. "We followed the trail and it opened into a small clearing. Our horses and caravan are there." I pointed down the corridor of twigs and dead branches. The forest looked just as bleak and bare.

Finian clapped a hand on the back of his man, a smile gathering on his mouth.

"See, Lucius. Lead us to camp then, Rhona."

The way he said my name made my stomach clench, but I found myself smiling at the stranger and his men as I led them down the path to Balthazar and my home.

***

The clearing had doubled in size when we arrived. Our horse and my caravan, to the west of it. The fire was still roaring its welcoming warmth under a sky dusted with stars. Appreciative sounds rang out from the men as I walked up to Balthazar and stroked his velvet nose, feeling the eyes of Finian upon me. The kettle was now steaming on the flames and I quickly grabbed it, before it spluttered more water.

"Tea?" I directed to Finian.

He nodded in answer, surveying the little crevice of quiet in the woods. Roman stomped over to me, pretending to help me.

"What the bloody hell are you playing at, Rhona?" His voice was a hushed whisper, barely a caress of breath, but there was no denying the alarm in his tone. I looked back, noting Eli taking a seat on his bed roll. Finian and his red-headed man seated themselves next to him. The firelight turned the Lord's hair a pale gold. Turning back, I saw Roman's face was a mix of fury and fear.

"His whistle. It's the same sound the messenger delivered to me," I breathed back quickly. Roman's eyes widened and he looked behind me then in understanding. His eyes met mine and I nodded, mouthing '*trust me*'.

The large dark cart rolled into the clearing. The wood panelling was painted black and its wheels of iron and wood whined as it rolled over the uneven ground. The firelight glimmered over the smooth surface of the doors and several padlocks and bolts, sealing whatever it was inside.

My palms became clammy just looking at the monstrous thing. I wondered if the locks on the outside were the only thing keeping whoever or whatever it was inside. Could there be runes or wards over it as well? Two men stationed themselves away from the troupe, next to the prison and trees. It was far away from us, to not draw any unwanted questions I realised. I looked pointedly to Roman and then to Eli. They hadn't missed the strangeness of it all, too. No sounds could be heard from within, but the wooden walls, for all we knew, were so thick and overbearing it dulled any noise. I brewed black tea for the men sitting around the campfire, noting the other four who stood stationed by the entrance out of the clearing and back down the path. Their horses were tied to nearby trees and huffed and grunted under the canopy of dead limbs and branches.

"We only have three mugs, I'm afraid." I was suddenly aware of our lack of utensils.

"Not to worry, we have our own." Finian smiled at me as he leaned back, reaching into a dark pack he had strapped to his person. After the tea was brewed, I carefully poured it into each cup waiting. Finally sitting myself, I refilled the kettle and started mixing the herbs for Eli. The jars and pots were still beside the fire from before. Something skittered over my skin as I looked up from my work. All the men were eyeing the brew with trepidation and none were drinking. I looked to Roman puzzled.

"They probably think we've poisoned it." His voice carried an edge of distaste. I looked at my own cup, untouched, and quickly picked it up, drinking the dark tea. Roman followed suit, as did Eli. Hot tea spilled over my lips and I wiped the remnants away after a short gasp. The hot liquid settled my haunches as I looked at these odious men.

"It's just tea," I said, looking each of them directly in the eye.

Finian looked about with a fervid grin plastered across his face. There was an exchange of looks between them all, the moonlight showing the whites of their eyes. A hollow laugh escaped my lips. Finian raised his cup, his eyes trained on my face. I could only sit there, allowing that cool gaze to flicker over my exposed skin. I kept myself rigid, smoothing my features to graceful nonchalance even though all instincts dared me to bare my teeth at him. The man, Lucius, took a swig first. Then others around him followed. I held my breath, my body suddenly tense for some unexplained reason.

"It's not poison," Lucius coughed, "but it tastes like shit." There was a murmur of laughter from the men and Finian. Shock must have shown on my face, as Roman's raucous laughter bellowed next to me.

"I agree with you there, my friend," he spat, between his guffaws. I didn't know whether to be amused or pissed off. Even as Eli smiled weakly, so I slapped his knee, affronted.

"It's fine, Rhona. Thank you. We've not had a hot meal or drink for a few nights now," Finian declared and raised his cup in gratitude to me. I said nothing and returned my attention to preparing the herbs. As the night grew darker and the temperature dropped near freezing, the men talked between themselves, all huddled closely to the fire. Plumes of breath wafted in the air around us from the cold and my arse and legs were near numb with it. Eli graciously extended his blanket to me, and I snuggled in a little closer, the exchange warming me.

As talk and tongues eased, we began to learn their names. Lucius, it seemed, was Finian's steward and his right-hand man. We were introduced to Brennan, an older man in Finian's party, hair as grey as the snow peaked mountain tops and a beard to rival any man. He was a doctor. Each name and occupation I catalogued, and the information began to support my suspicions that there was someone being withheld in that cart. Then Rion and Daven, brothers and huntsmen of sorts. They spoke little and watched the camp and surrounding with keen scrutiny, feebly sipping their tea. The two men stationed and guarding the cart were Caleb and John. Both were said to be skilled with a crossbow, and again huntsmen. The four protecting the entrance to our small copse of trees did not share their names, only glares. The youngest of the party was Rufus, Lucius's son. He had been graced with the same fiery hair and brow as his father. He was jittery and spoke very little, as his eyes constantly darted back to the prison cart.

"Can I ask?" The polite chatter had died and Finian's words rang out. "How did you know my lands were under siege?"

Roman glared in my direction, but I ignored him, trusting my gut. "The Trinity," was my only reply.

Brows gathered on the men and Lucius scoffed; Finian only watched us, thoughtfully.

"It is true. We and our brethren had a," Roman's eyes fell upon me as he spoke, pity and careful consideration lining his mouth, "let's just say, Rhona here had a run in with the Mother and the Crone."

"You met the Maiden, the Mother and the Crone?" Rufus fretted, fear edging his words as his voice broke. He must have only been fifteen years old. His voice and sparse stubble gave him away.

"Aye, and it wasn't a pleasant encounter," Roman replied, still eyeing me.

Finian took another long drag of his tea, draining the mug.

"What did they say to you? Did they mention the Fall-" Rufus began speaking in a rush of words and trembling lips.

"Hush boy!" his father bellowed, and my stomach flipped at a secret, so blatantly being withheld. There was a pause as the logs crackled and snapped in the flames.

"I'm making a decision." Finian's voice was quiet, as his face paled.

"My Lord," Lucius began, alarmed, but Finian held up a silencing hand. His silvery eyes locked with mine across the fire.

"I'm making a decision to trust my gut here." My own gut tightened in response, at his choice of words. As they had been my own earlier, in my head. I braced myself, fidgeting only slightly to relax the tightness in my legs. "If what you say is the truth, and the Trinity sent you north to find my lands, to seek out the lycan..." The party of men straightened at their Lord's words. "Then tell me why you were tasked with this challenge. Tell me why they haven't answered our calls and prayers to assist us." His eyes shone with quiet fury. "Why have they sent a traveller girl and her comrades?"

My ears were roaring in the silence that followed. As Roman cleared his throat, about to speak, I straightened my spine, extending a hand to stop him. This, I realised, was not his story to tell. The logs continued to be devoured as I gathered myself under the pressing gaze of Finian and his men.

"I have been sent, as a life debt." I let the enormity of my words sink in before I continued. "The Trinity were south of here, and we assumed they were witches attacking our camp. I attacked back." I heaved a great breath. "I burned and killed the Mother." My voice rasped each word slowly, as what felt like a precipice opened underneath me. Relaying what had happened, forming the words and speaking of it, sent the reality crashing down upon me. My throat tightened and my nerves ratcheted against my skin.

"That can't be, they..." Rufus had begun to speak and Finian hissed at the boy, silencing him with those cold grey eyes.

"The Maiden wanted my head for the crime I committed." I almost laughed as hysteria bubbled up at the thought of the death that had nearly become me. "She was determined to take my life, as payment for what I had just done. The murder I had committed." My words were sour as the memory curdled my stomach.

Was I a murderer? For defending my people?

I inhaled sharply, not allowing myself to venture down that path and train of thought. Not now anyway. "But it was the Crone who decided against it. She, by some miracle, gave me this fool's task instead, as punishment. A life for a life. I must take the life of the lycan, or the remaining Trinity will take my own."

There. I had said it. It had been spoken into existence. The reality of my words beat against my heart and through my lungs. The understanding felt confining, suffocating almost. The pulse of my blood was like a phantom death toll in my ears and I swallowed against the trembling that wanted to overcome me. Finian's features didn't even blanch as I told my tale. His eyes were still cold and calculating as he watched me. His face did not betray his thoughts or feelings, staying stern and unmoving. And I was like a rabbit caught in a snare. After a time, his eyes fell away and I slumped, released by the weight and questions that they had held.

"And you two?" Lucius asked, not looking at Roman and Eli, but watching his son.

"Well, we couldn't let Rhona here have all the fun," Roman replied, swigging from a bottle of mead he had pulled out of his pack.

I rolled my eyes. Only he would joke in such a situation. We shared a withering look and I gestured for him to share the mead with me. He obliged, understanding my needs. I wanted the numbness. I craved the peace that came from drinking.

"So, you believe you murdered the Mother?" Finian's question was flat and lifeless, but it stirred the air around me. My head titled, as I finally and willingly looked at the Lord. His eyes shone in the light of the flames. His high cheekbones and narrow nose were unusually pert for a man. It gave him an unearthly look. His ice white hair shimmered and fell across his forehead above his matching brows, both pale and thick, that arched at my assessment. I answered his question truthfully, allowing every essence of it to show in my face. I had killed the Mother. I had watched her burn and whither in front of us. Watched how the Maiden had seethed and raged, as the need for death coursed through her like an endless waterfall. Saw the hate and wrath burn in her gaze as she looked at me, needing the satisfaction of death.

"I am not a liar, Lord Finian." My stomach jolted, my voice mirroring his flat tone. Memories paraded around those same words from a childlike voice. "I blew whiskey-soaked fire at her and watched as she burned to ash before me." I swallowed. The mead did nothing to numb this reality, so I continued to swig.

"I believe you," Finian finally admitted, after what felt like too long a time of staring into the roaring flames.

Winds from the north blew and began disturbing the trees. I shivered, skulking under the blanket further. My leg grazed Eli's and he didn't flinch, but I saw his eyes dart to me quickly. I shared what was left of the loaf of bread and dried meat we had in our packs with Finian and his men and was surprised by the ensemble of gratified moans. When the men were fed, I signed to Eli to lift his shirt. He was overdue for a redressing. I gathered fresh cloth to bandage his wounds and grabbed the herbs I had stored in my wagon. When I returned Eli was shirtless and Finian, Brennan and Rufus were gathered around him. Walking closer, I heard Roman telling the tale of the troll and how Eli acquired such a battering. I stopped short, remembering Brennan had mentioned he was a doctor. The older man, hearing my footfall, turned to me.

"This is good work, Rhona. It needs cleaning, as the burn has stretched open. But he will be fine." I bowed my head in appreciation, thankful for the confirmation that Eli would be well. "What do you have there?" Brennan asked, his hand reaching to a pair of wire rimmed spectacles, as he eyed the jars and cloth bags in my hands.

"Yarrow, rosemary and valerian. To paste on the wound with goat fat. I've also brewed him tea, to ease the pain," I said honestly, the older man's eyes creased, and he wrinkled his nose.

"No, not rosemary," he said, shaking his head. "Do you have any dried lavender?" My chin dipped as my brow creased.

"Lavender?" I asked.

"Yes, it's good for burns and is that of an infection killer. You'd do well to replace the rosemary with lavender to dress his wound." There was no snobbery, and his tone wasn't patronising as he turned, assessing the wound again. I nodded, bewildered, to his back, dropping the herbs before them all and heading back to my cabin. Doctors were expensive commodities to have in a village or town. We travelling folk had our own methods of healing. I had never ventured to seek out the council and help of a doctor. Even when *it* happened and Baja had tried to force me to go to see one, to assess what injury had happened on my small child's body. But I had refused, coldly and impertinently. I found the lavender and returned to them all, still gathered in quiet conversation around Eli. Roman was waffling on, his tale spinning and weaving. From Eli's expression beside him, he was put out at being the centre of attention. I began to work, under the scrutiny and instruction of Brennan. It ruffled my feathers and caused prickles to roam up my back to be under his watchful gaze, but I did everything he instructed, aware of Finian's eyes upon me the entire time.

"That's it. You're doing very well," Brennan commended.

"It's not the first wound I've healed," I said with some whisper of venom.

He had no idea how many wounds I had healed. How many scars external and internal, littered my body, like miniature trophies. He was unaware of the night-time raids, the stones being thrown. He was unaware of the assaults from the past, some more harrowing than I would care to comment on. They were all mine. Scars, traumas, memories. But I gritted my teeth, trying not to disrupt the slowly knitted fabric of friendship we were building on this night. We needed Finian. We needed access to his lands.

When the bonds were tied, my eyes finally fell upon Eli. The relief that shone in his eyes, from the redressing and herbs, gave me peace and I unclenched my jaw. He signed me *'thanks'* and I couldn't help it as my fingers pushed back his dark hair from his sweat soaked brow.

"Rest," was all I managed as my fingers returned and I tried to hide the tremor.

We sat about after that, continuing our talking. Finian had informed us about his lands and the two villages within his estate. My pulse had raced as he spoke of his people. The lycan had ransacked half of a village, slaying many. All had to be burned on a pile, to stop any form of transformation. He spoke sincerely of his people and families under his care, and how he had commanded them to gather on his estate, under his father's protection. I couldn't comprehend how big his estate must be to house so many people. As he spoke, the edge of awareness and distrust slowly faded away. However, I couldn't deny that my eyes wandered back to the prison wagon every now and then.

Brennan pulled out two sea glass bottles full of amber liquid, swirling them with delight shining in a toothy grin. "I think this calls for a special drink, ya think, laddie?" The older man had a thick accent and I realised with a smile that you couldn't see his lips, only his teeth, under the coarse, curling hair of his beard.

"Yes, I think it is." Finian shared a smile with the man and then the rest of his party. "Will you three partake? It's a small thanks for sharing your meal with us."

A bottle was passed to Roman and he took it sceptically. He pulled the cork out with his teeth and smelled deeply. "This is real whiskey," Roman said, eyes bright.

"Of course," Finian replied, his expression incredulous.

I forced myself to lighten the mood, since I hadn't spoken more than a few words. Not since my omission of bloody murder. "The whiskey we brew could be used to embalm a corpse. It is darker and tastes like the fires from hell."

"That sounds like my kind of drink!" Brennan bellowed and a stir of laughter erupted again.

Roman finally swigged from the frosted bottle and sighed. The look of euphoria eased the crease in his brow and mouth. We could very rarely afford whiskey, well not the real kind anyway. Roman took another appreciative gulp, smacking his lips loudly. He passed it to Eli, who to my surprise, declined it. I was passed the bottle, the weight of the glass causing my fingers to grip it harder. I smiled at my brother, at the satisfied smile that was now plastered across his face as he lounged next to the fire.

I took a mouthful, expecting the whiskey to burn my tongue, but it was pleasant and smooth. I took another gulp, feeling that warm sensation erupt deep in my belly. I leaned over, passing the bottle back to Finian, who took it and saluted me. His bright eyes followed me as he tilted his back. My mouth dried as the muscles in his neck stretched, the base of his throat shadowed. He chugged three of four mouthfuls before handing it back to Brennan. There was something to this man, which my instinct paused at. As though every now and then my awareness was cloaked and blinded. I felt at ease and then I didn't. I could not put my finger on it, but my blood thrummed, the instinctual pull and twist of my gut, not letting me be assured.

Could I truly trust this man, whose eyes were as blanched as cold steel? Whose hair was as white as a man thrice his age?

Yet here I was, sharing a drink with him. Following a being's warning. A being who ideally wants me killed.

But did she?

Questions ran circles in my mind, the fraying threads of our conversation, the warning, the messenger. Nothing made sense. This journey, the creatures, these keys now marking my skin. My fingers idly picked the cracked drying skin around my short nails, my ears straining to hear what whispered conversations were being had. But there were none.

The bottles ran out quickly with so many men, but the small amount I had had made me feel comforted and at ease. The liquid warm and lucid, circulating in my blood made my thoughts less chaotic. My eyes wandered back to the prison and courage took over my tongue.

"So, what or who is in that carriage?"

The murmur or talk stopped immediately.

Chapter 27

No one had dared move or breathe, my question still being chewed and swallowed. I observed them all around us. Their eyes darted, and there was a quiet cough and clearing of a man's throat. Leather creaked as some men changed their seated positions. I had struck a nerve, something they hadn't wanted us to invoke. An owl hooted faintly in the distance, the first animal sound I heard for days. That was the only sign I needed.

"I wondered when you were going to ask that," Finian mused, as he churned the logs in the fire with a rogue branch. His silver eyes shone white against the flames. All the men continued to be silent as they waited, their bodies tight, muscles clenched. No weapons had been raised, but I sensed fingers on triggers and bracing on the shafts of arrows, palms finding hilts and slowly relieving steel from sheaths. "I think it's only right that we be as truthful as you." I felt Eli straighten next to me, his own hands carefully sliding across the blanket to his staff. "We have a witch in there."

All our eyes shot to their dark towering carriage and my blood chilled. I heard Roman cough, his hand wiping his chin. His broad form straightened; jaw clenched. "It is why we are so far south. We hoped we would find some, to assist us with ridding our lands of the lycan."

"And I take it, she desisted from your offer, hence the prison on wheels?" Roman asked, a single dark brow raised as he watched Finian closely, his crossbow now resting atop his bent knee. The steel arrowhead gleamed with menace.

"Yes and no. She is not a prisoner. We have no intention of harming her. But we need her, need her kind to help with the beast."

I leaned forward, trying to gauge the authenticity of his words. Was he bluffing? But when I looked at his small army of men, huntsmen, soldiers, and a doctor, it was clear.

"So there were no witches in your own lands who could have helped?" I asked, afraid of the answer. Lucius fidgeted next to Finian, a silent plea on his lips as he looked at his master.

"There were no others. They have all fled," Finian replied, eyes trained on the fire, mouth set in a straight line.

I persisted, needing to know whether the knowing twinges of my gut were right. The whiskey in my blood loosened my tongue further. "And was this because you ran them out of your lands, or they left of their own free will?"

"The latter. The lycan has been plaguing us and wreaking havoc for a month or more. We only realised the extent of the atrocities ten days ago, when we started to search our own lands. We found only bloodshed and devastation." Finian's face contorted at that, his mouth twisting. There was pain in that gesture, pain and anger that creased his perfect face. His eyes turned glassy as he looked at me, hollow and haunted. I could see no lie there. I could not imagine the horrors he and his men must have seen, as an array of memories caused my gut to wrench. They were all solemn around the fire, victims to their own haunting memories.

I couldn't stop myself, as I asked, "is she a white or black witch?" The idea that a black witch was in that contraption made the whiskey churn in my gut and the sweet lull evaporate into sharp awareness. My impulses rallied. The fight or flight building in me. If it were a black witch in there, imitating a white, we were all in deep shit.

"It's a white witch," Lucius bristled, a sneer marring his auburn-bearded mouth.

"If *she's* not a prisoner, then why is *she* in that contraption?" Roman dared, clearing his throat, eyeing the red-headed man.

None of the men said anything as they all shot glances left and right to their comrades. Finian levelled a stare at Roman, both men challenging each other. Roman, to his credit, didn't back down from the Lord's gaze. In fact, it had seemed to liven him, Finian's imperious manner rising in competition with Roman's dark arrogance.

"I agree. If she isn't a threat, and if you wish her to help you, then she should not be in there. She should be here, with us, sharing the fire's warmth." My voice was hollow as I too stared down Finian. My hands rubbed together, the only sign of my unease. He released a sigh so heavy and shrouded in doubt, that it stopped me short.

Finian looked at me, face uncertain. "Let her out," Finian ordered in a rasp. I shot to my feet, as did Eli. The men stirred and weapons began clicking in place. The huntsmen guarding the wagon looked to their Lord, hesitating. "Open the goddamn door!" he bellowed in answer and for the first time, I witnessed the Lord, his tone and way he held himself in front of his subjects. The locks to the doors were swiftly unlocked, keys and bolts scraping and clunking in the silent night.

I held my breath, as the door creaked open, the dark hinges squawking in protest in the sudden biting cold. Darkness and shadow were all that could be seen in the moonlight. Nothing moved or stirred from within. From my angle, the inner of the carriage looked completely empty, save for a whisper of smoke and mist creeping out into the moonlit night. One of Finian's men moved forward to peer into the cavern of dark wood. I felt my body strain, neck arching to try and see.

A body flew out, jumping over the man's head and shoulders, running into the night. The men rallied and there was a clamber of shouts as they began to chase her. The moonlight shone on her dark skin, the colour of rich earth, as the skin over her exposed arms and legs shimmered. Her hair was shorn to her scalp. Dark and tightly curled. The threadbare tunic she wore was sodden and ripped, as her legs were pumping at great speed towards the tunnel out of the clearing. Lucius cursed loudly, all of them sprinting with effort to reach her before she escaped.

My thoughts rallied and the forest answered. The trees began to move, swaying and groaning, as limbs and roots lifted and moved. A tangle of arms and branches knitted together. The entryway was gone. Devoured entirely, all surrounding trees shifted and moved in tight formation to prevent her escaping through a crack of slip in trunks.

"Rhona!" Roman bellowed, eyes wide, face glowing in a blue light. At the sound of my name, Finian and Lucius whirled, their own faces mirroring the shock on my brother's face. My hands and arms were tingling, the blue hue of iridescent light glimmered brightly through the tattered fabric of my shirt. It was too late, as the witch skidded on the mulched, sodden ground, spinning around to look for another route of escape. There was none. She changed direction, beginning to run towards me, only to stop abruptly at the sight of me and my now glowing arms and hands. Her silver eyes locked with my own.

The warmth that radiated and pulsed under my skin, from the keys, subsided and the light vanished entirely as my pulse hastened. Eli sharply tried to bundle me behind him, his staff raised in defence. Roman moved to shield me, his crossbow arrow weaving from Finian, Lucius and the witch, who was now stalking slowly towards us.

"You *are* a witch!" Lucius spat, his eyes trained on my wrists. A nerve in his jaw flickered as he bared his teeth. Wind ripped through the trees, causing me to shudder.

"No, she is not." The witch, who was now only feet from us, stood unabashed in her dishevelled tunic. Her voice resonated with a rich accent. I could not place it. Her smooth skin, so dark and stark against the pale dirty shift, was beautiful. I couldn't stop my eyes from roving over her, from her cropped black hair, to her high cheekbones and full lips. My eyes stopped venturing when I finally caught her own. Silver. Cadaverous and unnerving. Just like the tales spoke of. Some witches glamoured their eyes, to hide their true nature from normal folk, but this witch did not. Her lips twisted into a sneer as she growled, "she is something else."

Time seemed to slow at that moment, the world moving at an unnatural pace as I watched the menace unfold in front of me. Lucius primed himself and set off, hurtling towards us, sword drawn, as did three others of Finian's men, rage and fear rippling over their faces. Eli stepped ahead, back shifting, his staff raised further ready to defend. The witch turned, just in time to see Rion and Daven run close enough to knock her to the ground. She jumped to the side, her face and torso landing on the earth first. Roman's hand roughly pushed at my gut, forcing me back, as he yelled for me to run.

"Stop." It wasn't a shout, but a command. Every man paused. "No one is to touch her." Finian's eyes sharpened, his pupils contracting, as he stared me down. Fear and mistrust shaped his features into something wicked and otherworldly. The world shifted again, time forming back to its rapid pace. The noises and sounds that had dulled were now high in my ears.

"I am not a witch!" I shouted, my voice echoing across the clearing. "I swear." Finian's nose wrinkled as his lip raised, flashing teeth. "I can explain."

"That magic is not that of a witch, my Lord. It is not the magic that flows through my blood or my sisters." The witch's voice was a rumble of sullen chords. Her nostrils flared, as she inhaled sharply. Did my ears just deceive me? I sharpened my gaze.

My Lord?

My skin prickled as I finally saw this troupe for what they truly were. "Her bloodline is faint, from a great grandmother perhaps. But such power would not come from a diluted lineage."

"She's not your captee, but your accomplice?" I barked, completely tricked. The words tasted ashen. We had been played as fools. "What is this? Who are you all, really?"

"We are of no consequence to you. But you, I have never seen power such as yours. Not in a human." The witch's silver eyes shone bright against dark lids. My stomach dropped in aching realisation. Finian's eyes were the same silver. The very same glimmer and metallic iris. I swallowed, chest now heaving. We were in a trap. This plan, this urge to follow them, had been a trick. Was it from the Crone? As a quick and effortless way to gain retribution for the murder of the Mother?

"No consequence? And yet here you all are, weapons raised at us?" Roman snarled, his crossbow still moving across the party slowly closing in.

"My Lord, there is rope and the iron shackles in the carriage," Lucius urged, as he took a step closer.

"Take another step and this arrow goes through your fucking skull," Roman retaliated, shifting the aim of his weapon. Eli growled in response.

"Enough," I hissed and the trees around us rattled their branches. "Lord Finian, if that's really your name, I would suggest you ask your men to lower their weapons. Or you will all see exactly what I can do." The threat in my voice was palpable and the trees shuddered again in answer. The strange and now familiar sensation built in my palms, pulsing up my wrists in answer. "Move," I whispered to Eli and Roman, pushing past them. My illuminated hands outstretched and open. The men gasped, as swords and bows creaked, now aiming at me. Finian, raised a hand, halting his men. A cool breeze grazed my cheek, the forest quivering around us at the steel drawn.

"Finian, we have not lied to you. We have travelled all this way to help you." I found his eyes, those same witch eyes as the woman stood before me, watching every flicker of muscle and movement of my mouth and hands.

"Help yourself more-like," Lucius spat on the ground.

"Here." I raised my hands, wiping the air. Trails of illuminated mist followed in their wake from the cold night creeping in. The blockade of trees at the entrance, untangled and unfurled. Roots again crashed and dived into the ground as the entryway shifted, back into view. The witch whirled, hissing words in another language. Finian stumbled, his mouth agape as he turned to see the tunnel and pathway back to the road. "Whether you like it or not. We need each other."

There was a ping of a bow string and a glint of metal streaked at great speed towards my chest.

Chapter 28

I heard Eli grunt behind me, saw his hand swerve my side, fingers painfully outstretched, trying to move me. But I was immovable as the arrow flew. Finian roared at his men, his face stricken as he watched it. In that second, I wasn't afraid. The heat and light at my wrists, blared to an unbelievable roar of fiery blue light. There was a bellowing groan and earth rumbled as trees ripped from roots, clashing in my ears. There was a shadow that passed over me, the flash of a great tree, uprooting and falling. It fell in front of me, the ground shaking underfoot as it thudded and bounced. Leaves and wood shattered around me. The arrow buried deep into the heart of the mottled trunk. The feathered tip vibrated, teasingly, as the forest moaned all around us. The glare from my skin vanished, and the heat that had been near painful was receding, leaving only my hammering heart. My palms were slick, hands shaking as I looked at the tree at my feet. I hadn't acknowledged Roman's form clashing with one of Finian's huntsmen. Finian roared again as he, Lucius and Brennan tried to pull Roman off the man. Fists met skin, the sounds of gushing breath, as a gut was punched hard. Eli made a run towards my brother, but I grabbed his lapel. He stopped instantly. His eyes whipped to me, assessing me. His chest heaved, face white.

"Stop. Now." My voice was dark as I commanded the men before me, eyes still on Eli. They all obeyed. Finian faced me again, mouth aghast, eyes wary. "Do you not see? I am not the one trying to hurt or deceive you. Let go of my brother."

They did. Roman huffed and pushed them away forcefully. He squared up to the man, who had fired, fury and wrath morphing his face from handsome to terrible.

"Try that again and I will gut you and make you swallow it," he seethed, teeth bared. Blood ran from a cut on his brow.

There was a silent exchange between Finian and Lucius. A calculation of threat.

"I will tell you all, Finian, if you and your men promise no harm will come to us. I need you. Need access to your lands. I can help stop the lycan." My voice shook as I grounded my heels, straightening and trying to tame the unrelenting shakes across my body.

"Asta, come here. All will be forgiven," Finian fretted, his eyes now on the witch still near me.

I was about to speak again, forcing them to see our side, when the winds shifted again. Hairs pulled from my braid, snaking in front of my eyes. The trees groaned again in answer. The branches rustled a chorus, as a bone chilling sound erupted into the night. It rebounded across the clearing, seeping through the trees to the east of us.

"What the fuck was that?" Roman spat blood, eyes unnaturally wide as he looked about.

It echoed again, louder this time and the wind that had picked up, its cold breath clawing across my exposed neck and hands.

"Father?" Rufus spluttered, terror morphing his adolescent face.

"Quiet boy!" Lucius hissed, his own wary eyes darting about the shadowed wood surrounding us.

"Asta, get behind us. Lucius, Rion, Daven, check the road. Brennan help Rufus. We're leaving," Finian commanded, eyeing the fire. I caught his thinking and the flames extinguished immediately. All of us now in total darkness, with only the moon's frail light, illuminating our murky shapes.

"We need her, my Lord," the witch, Asta, whispered a hiss back. "You know as well as I do, if those things find us, we are all dead."

"What is it?" Roman's voice was edged with quiet panic, as the moonlight caught his wide eyes scanning the tree line around us.

"It's one of the turned. The lycan's spawn," Asta whispered. Her round eyes searched above to the moon.

"Turned?" I asked, my own voice a gush of fear.

"Creatures the lycan has bitten. Men and women who turn into a form of a beast at night," the witch replied, turning in a circle. "I can ward this place. Maybe banish our scents on a wind south. But I fear it will be too late."

"Do it and make haste," Finian commanded. His white hair flashed, and silver eyes darted to me across the clearing. "Rhona, if you do wish to help us, do something."

I turned to the tree, their towering forms swaying. Asta behind me knelt on the cold earth, her hands flat to the ground, her face raised to the moon. Words echoed across the space, words in a language I did not know. Within seconds, the smell of the sodden earth, the oak and damp forest was gone from my nose. The winds pulsed, blowing southward, away from us and the camp. She was casting a spell to remove our scents.

"Girl, if you can shelter us, cover the tunnel again. Make it so the creature cannot enter here," she said with urgency. Her words numbed the oncoming terror that threatened to take away my sanity. I nodded, finally spinning to the trees again, palms outstretched, mind racing.

Shelter us and make it so no creature can enter this place.

Hide us, please, I thought.

I repeated the words over and over in my head. The bands heated in answer, the light shimmering across my skin. It bloomed, near blinding me.

There was another rumble and woodland grew, sprouting new life from the sodden earth. The limbs and trunks grew in a mass of arms and branches, knotting together, weaving across the tunnel and all around us. They grew in height, twisting and braiding high above the canopy, creating a cage that stretched to cover the moon. There was another roar and wood splintered in the distance. The sounds chilled me to the bone, but I persisted, clenching my jaw, the words in my head reaching a scream. I could have been screaming, for my lips and throat raged with the words in my head. The beast boomed a blood-curdling sound, as a dark shadow careened through the trees ahead of me. Long, clawed limbs tore the earth in gigantic strides. Its mottled fur was the colour of ash over, that flickered and swathed over great muscles. Eyes of glowing blue, rimmed with red, grew larger as the creature charged towards me. The roots of the trees curled and slithered forward, gaining ground.

I truly was screaming now, as the keys coursing static agony up my arms and across my chest. The beast was feet from me, it's teeth jagged and drooling, twitching at my nearness. Its fur didn't cover all its body, peeling skin clung to its shoulders and back, I noticed, as it bounded closer to the clearing, as a mass of teeth and razor-like claws jumped forth. I had never seen such a creature, and as pure horror ruptured my sanity, every nerve trembled, the gaps between the trees finally grew smaller as they pressed tighter together, until a resounding hush met my ears. There was nothing as a barricade of oak and elm completely sheltered us in darkness and shadow. Without acknowledging the thought, the fireflies rallied around me, filling the coveting cove of weaved wood in sparking green light. No sounds of crashing or howling could be heard. The pulse in my ears was deafening, my vision whirling as though I had drunk too much whiskey. Cold air breathed on my wrists as the light from the keys dwindled and sparked out. Shimmers of unfocused spots danced across my eyes. My knees gave way, muscles trembling, unable to stand anymore.

The skin of my back barked as cold crashed through me. My bones shook and ached as my body hit the floor. Shadows passed over me. The familiar scent of dried blood and morning mist filled my nose. My neck lifted under a warm press of skin. Everything sounded distant and hollow as I tried to focus on the stars shooting across the sky, through dark hands clawing at the eternal blackness above.

***

I awoke to my head pounding and body distraught. Pulling my papery tongue from the roof of my mouth, I gasped, needing water. The muscles of my arms strained as I tried to lift myself from the uncomfortable place I had fallen. A shadow moved before me, but it formed and materialised in ways that no human could. My eyelids flickered, trying to focus, but it was no use. Exhaustion soaked me, darkening my sight and I succumbed to another wave of sleep. After a time, my awareness began creeping back, the world around me becoming coherent and physical. I could hear wheels rolling over stony ground and the creak and rock of familiar wood. I opened my eyes, my lashes fluttering against golden light that seared. It moved over me, but it was not that of the day or night. It flickered and rippled across warped, stained wood. My body jolted involuntarily, and I became aware we were moving along a road. The safe space around me, my cabin, came into sharp focus. Rosemary and herbs caressed my nose, but another scent was close, too familiar. Metallic and fresh, like the first breath of a crisp winter's morning. My eyes sought out the silver and gold medallions clanging above me, watching them sway to and fro.

I stirred further, finding hands resting on either side of my shoulders. Their nails were embedded with dirt, with small scars visible over their rough surface. The golden skin glowed in the candlelight. The sound of breath heaving and releasing in quiet slumber enveloped my ears. Something was uncomfortable. A lump was digging into my spine. A wedged foot or leg perhaps? But I knew those hands and that scent. My mind settled, knowing it to be Eli. I was in my bed, and Eli was laying behind me, sitting upright, his body supporting my limp form.

A strong flush coursed up my neck and face, realising the intimacy in such a thing. We had never been this close. But it didn't feel strange or abnormal, to my surprise. It felt peaceful. From where my head was resting on his chest, he was sleeping deeply, and my own body was falling and rising with each inhale.

"How are you feeling?"

I cringed, the small moment of content evaporating. Eli jumped, suddenly awake and receptive. He shifted forwards promptly and leaned over me. Stretching my neck, I found his blue and brown eyes assessing me. Both were darkened with fatigue. It was not he who had spoken. I moved my body slowly, peeling my back and neck up, away from his warmth. My cheeks blazed again as I sourced the voice that had come from the shadows of my small home.

Asta sat on the floor across from us, the dark skin of her long legs shimmering from the candles lit about the space, as she rested against the darkened door. The medallions glittered, sending shafts and streaks of gold across the wooden walls and I could only acknowledge her, as my hand reached for my throat.

It felt like I was swallowing glass.

A water skin was passed to me and with shaking fingers, I unplugged the cork and drank deeply, the water within soothing and cooling the harshness of my throat.

"That was great magic you performed back there," Asta offered, her pale eyes creasing as a perfectly defined brow raised within the shadows. I leant forward, further away from Eli's cocoon of heat. I continued to drink, watching her. Her short, cropped hair was darker than my own, but it was sparse in places. From clippers or shears perhaps, it was cut sharply and hurriedly. Her full lips were pursed as she waited. For me to drink more or answer her, I didn't know. I took another long gulp, draining much of the skin pouch, and drowning the fiery burn of my mouth and throat. "Your brother said you were *gifted* with that magic. Is that true?"

I eyed her warily, swallowing the last mouthful of cold, clear water. A tentative hand stroked my spine then, trying to soothe me. Eli. I let the touch, his touch, radiate through me. His comfort and presence brought me back into each fibre of myself.

"What has Roman told you?" It hurt to speak, and I winced at the pain.

"Not much. Only before we came upon you, you..." her sterling eyes pierced me, "had *acquired* that power."

Clearing my throat brought on another sear of pain.

"Is there more water?" I croaked, feeling the hollow at the base of my throat. She handed me a jug and I downed it, appreciating every lick of cold that plummeted into my belly.

"Your body is tired. The magic you used was great and cost you a lot." Her eyes narrowed on me. "You created magic I have not seen for many years. No mortal could carry such power. Your body is not built or made to wield it." I waited, my aching muscles tense under her scrutiny as she spoke. Eli made a shallow noise behind me and I turned to him. His face was open, eyes watchful. There was no fear or distrust there as his hands moved, to communicate. *'We can trust her, Rhona.'*

Air filled deep into my lungs and I turned back, not doubting him. "My brother is right. But gifted is not the word I would use." Asta's head cocked to the side, her eyes sharpening. There was an otherworldly hue to her dark brown skin and her eyes glimmered strangely in the flickering flames.

"We came across a boundary within the forest, near where you found us. A gateway revealed itself." I guzzled down the last of the water, my gaze never leaving her. She was barely breathing. I gasped, the skin and track of my throat finally manageable. "There was a thern. One of the tree hearts…a dark blade had stabbed it and…" I couldn't bring myself to finish the words. Swallowing what felt like ash and grit, my breath shuddered in my lungs.

"One of the Sisters has been stabbed?" Her voice was no more than a whisper. I didn't grasp her meaning for a second.

Sisters?

"Then it is what I have feared." Her eyes pulled away; her face obscured as it fell into darkness. The witch in front of me seemed to crumple. At what, I did not know or understand. "The thern, did it say anything else?" her voice rasped.

"What do you mean by Sisters?" My question was unanswered for a time, as Asta held her head in her hands. I noticed then, whilst in her silence, the chain of glittering silver around her ankle. Her feet were bare and she was still only wearing the dirty linen shift. Her skin was prickled, her bare feet covered in dirt and blistered from winter. I reached out. My brow gathered at seeing her, truly seeing her.

Opening the wooden trunk next to my bed, I pulled out an old woven shawl and a pair of dark grey riding trousers. I would find some old boots or shoes for her later. The chill from outside was seeping in the cracks of the skylight above and I could only imagine how cold I would have been in such little clothing. She looked up as I handed them over, my small offering of peace.

"Thank you," was all she said, but gratitude warmed her cold eyes as he wrapped the shawl about herself and spun on her rump to fully face us. "If what you say is true, Rhona, then what will come is something of nightmares. That tree, which the thern was guarding, I can only assume was one of the Sisters. One of the Fallen, bound in tree form. And if the thern guarding her gave you his keys, it is because the other guardians have been slain as well."

I recounted the therns words back in the forest. How a blade had pierced all the heart trees. How the other thern and the others were murdered. I swallowed down the bile rising from my stomach. An irritation at my wrists caught my attention and I scratched the skin under my sleeve.

"May I?" she asked.

I obliged, pushing up the sleeves of my shirt to where the dark blue bands were stark against my olive skin. The scars at my wrists and forearms were like ghosts against a dark streak of night and Asta leaned forward, her hands hovering but not touching my skin as I rotated my wrists. She sat back on her haunches, looking alarmed and I straightened.

"That gateway you passed through took you to the Fallow. To one of the Sisters realms."

Panic began to set in. What she was saying did not make sense as we had been miles from the Fallow, but she shifted closer at our expressions.

"This land, all of it, is the Fallow. A land of magic. Humans took over and built their cities, claiming this land thousands of years ago, when magic was first trapped and warded. But this land, this continent, *is* the Fallow. I believe you happened upon one of the seven gateways, and one that very few know of. The gateways are to the outer realms, where the guardians and trees create the border and wards that keep the beings shunned and imprisoned within the heart of the Fallow." Asta's voice became laced with fear, her hands animating her words. "Do you not see, Rhona?" She looked at me imploringly. "Surely you know the tales of old as well as I do. Your clan, your travelling family, like many, will have had a storyteller or soothsayer." Mutza's face swam into my mind and I felt Eli fidget behind me. His body, still inexplicable close to my own. When Asta found no inclined acknowledgement she huffed, infuriated.

"Those trees are *the* Sisters. They are the gatekeepers and wards that keep the Fallen One and her spawn contained. If they have been slain, desecrated even, the creatures who have been contained and trapped within the Fallow are now free. They can now pass over into the human territories. There is no manner of hell they will not unleash, in vengeance for their mother." The name of who she spoke rang clearly in my mind. Armelle.

Movement caught my attention and Eli had begun signing to me. "He says, *'they are only legends, stories.'*" Eli's face was cast in shadow, but his eyes were alight from within. I gulped, bleakness becoming me.

"Legends, yes. But explain to me how you came across a Knarrock troll. Explain why a lycan is loose and free from the Fallow. Explain how witches, both black and white, have fled the north. Fled their homes."

I couldn't explain it. Couldn't bring myself to even comprehend the seriousness of what had occurred. My lip quivered, trying to devour the scream I wanted to let loose.

"But the Trinity?" My voice wavered, knowing exactly what her answer would be.

"Are not intact. Their power is weak now the Mother is no more. And besides, they are not gatekeepers. They take court over the witches and they will have some power over those things. We are descendants of Falin after all. The beasts that stalk and prowl within the Fallow cannot be ruled by witches."

The bile rising was acidic and burned anew at the back of my throat. My heart hammered in my chest, that otherworldly tug pulling at a rib over my heart.

"The Crone visited me, after she set me on this life debt. She told me there were darker forces at work. She spoke of other creatures, but she did not speak any more of them."

"You spoke with the Crone?" Asta's tone was desperate, and she scrambled forward, eyes so large I could see the whites around her steel irises. "So, she is aware," Asta confirmed, her teeth gritted, when I nodded. She sat back finally, arms resting on bent knees. "There is much you need to learn, Rhona." I wrinkled my nose at what she spoke of, annoyed at her premature assessment of me.

"I have a question for you," I said through bared teeth, my anger simmering to the surface now. "Are you a white witch and what part do you have to play in Finian's game?" I moved away from Eli, sitting up fully, feeling the life returning to my limbs.

"That is two. But...I am a white witch. My mother, however, was a black witch. And Finian isn't playing games. He is trying to save his people," the witch revealed, leaning her head against the door. "He is a good man."

"He is a child of a witch as well, isn't he?" My question was out before I could stop myself. Asta only eyed me from her slumped seat. Confirming my assessment.

"I will make a deal with you, Rhona." She said my name like a curse. "I will teach you what you need to know about basic magic. To help you wield and manage the *gifts* that have been bestowed upon you. I ask only this." I waited, feeling ambushed in my own skin, my own home. "That next time the Crone visits you, I will be there with you."

My mouth opened, as I considered her terms.

"It is time I spoke to my grandmother." She said the latter with venom and the world shifted underneath me.

Asta was the granddaughter of the Crone.

Chapter 29

After Asta's declaration, we had been stunned into silence, that silence had turned promptly into another bout of sleep, which my mind and body desperately welcomed again. The much-needed rest was dreamless; a solace of darkness and tranquillity that my mind couldn't rupture or ruin with screams. When I awoke, I was in my bed again, bundled and wrapped from head to toe in wool and fleece. Eli was no longer with me and my skin yearned for his closeness, a feeling of emptiness replacing the comfort. Rubbing my face roughly, I thought such feelings were futile. I couldn't understand this sudden urge. I had never experienced it before they had returned from their travels with the other clan. But I was certain of one thing; whatever this feeling was, could cause harm to Eli and myself.

Wrestling with the bedding, I mused, thinking about him in my bed and the heat of his skin, flush with my own. Warmth bloomed deep within me and I stifled it quickly, turning my thoughts to more menial things. Sighing, I rolled over finding a fresh jug of water and some stale biscuits on a pile of disjointed books. From the stacking of the biscuits, it had been Eli who had left them for me. I smiled at that.

Stomach rumbling, I sat up, devouring the aged baked goods greedily. A solitary candle flickered beside me, all the others now extinguished, but daylight filtered in from the hatch above. I blinked at the flicker of pale, grey sky passing overhead, wondering how long I had been sleeping. The sound of someone's inhalation made my eyes fly, searching my cabin.

Asta was still perched up against the door, stooped and sleeping awkwardly. Her head tossed this way and that as the wagon stumbled over the uneven road. How she was sleeping in such a manner I would never know. I whispered her name, but my throat was still tight, causing a serpentine hiss to escape my lips. She jolted, careening upward onto unsteady feet, eye blazing and teeth bared.

"It was only me!" I heaved, scrambling back into the safety of blankets and throws. "I was going to ask you if you wanted to..." The foolishness of my words stopped me short, as I beheld the panting witch before me. Her eyes were severe, wrath shining from within and whatever calm collected nature I had witnessed before had been replaced by a creature of nightmares. "You looked cold, and uncomfortable," I almost squeaked, swallowing back my fear. "Do you want to get in with me?"

There I said it. I had asked a witch to join me in bed. I held my breath, watching the witch as her eyes gained focus, the harshness melting with recognition. Her lips moved to cover her teeth as her head cocked, looking at me with predatory focus. She blinked, still panting. I patted the cover, although my face was anything but welcoming. She walked cautiously over to the edge of the bed. My lungs released and I slowly peeled away a blanket, shifting myself over.

"Do you wish to bed me, Rhona?" she asked, eyeing me.

I hiccupped a throaty laugh that caused me to wince. "Never," I spluttered, and watched her sit on the furthest reach of my bed. Her face was unreadable as she looked over the entanglement of covers. "Get in, it's freezing," I commanded groggily, with some authority. I paused, debating whether I was losing my mind. But the witch obeyed, sliding under, guardedly.

Her arms and legs were shivering with cold and I forced myself to get up, swinging my still aching legs and body round to the floor. Standing, I waddled over to my trunk, riffling through the clothes I had collected over the years. I found what I was looking for. A knitted jumper of soft grey wool. The hem and neckline was unravelling in places, but we could fix that.

"Here," I threw the jumper to her and she deftly caught it in one hand. I looked to the door, to where she had been sitting. The trousers I had gifted remained neatly folded in a pile on the floor. "Put it on, and those trousers," I encouraged, walking over and grabbing them before going back to the bed. She looked at me curiously, as though I had grown two heads. "Do witches not wear borrowed clothes?" I questioned, sliding back under the warmth. I felt rigid, keenly aware we lay mere inches from each other. If only Baja could see me now.

"My clothes are fine," Asta retorted acidly, eyeing me from the side. She couldn't hide her tremors, as she gripped the woollen covering closer.

"Are all witches this proud?" I asked, raising a brow, finally daring to look at her.

"I am not proud. It is..." her lips quivered, words failing her. "I have rarely received kindness." She looked away, jaw flickering. Something in my chest shifted as I beheld her.

"I understand," I ventured softly. "We have rarely had kindness bestowed upon us, as travellers."

Her grey quartz eyes found me then, their burrowed lines releasing. Clearing her throat, she carefully pulled the jumper over her head, sliding her bare arms from under the shawl and into the sleeves.

"You can keep them," I offered, looking away as she dressed. The wagon bumped over something large and we vaulted forward. "Who the fuck is driving my home?" I spat, pushing hair from my face, praying the wheels would stand such an onslaught.

"Rufus, I believe," she replied quietly, a small smile tugging at her lips.

I sat admiring the dim daylight passing over the hatch, wondering why Rufus was driving and not Roman or Eli. From the corner of my sight, I saw Asta's hands stroking the wool, her fingers tenderly following the weave of knit. I swallowed a lump in my throat, my thoughts a jumble of assumptions I didn't want to voice. But then the clearing came crashing back to me and Asta running for her life, when Finian and his men released her from the prison box. Finian's words to her before everything went into madness and chaos were *'all will be forgiven'*.

"Are you a prisoner of Finian's?" I asked, eyeing her.

She didn't stop her hands or fingers as they continued to stroke the soft fibres of wool. "Yes and no. It is a long story." Her words were barely audible, and I wondered if it was because my home possibly had an entourage of riders around it listening. "I wronged his father and as retribution he wanted my head." My head jolted back, my eyes wide. "Finian stepped in and asked for leniency. I was ordered to help gather witches instead. Trap them. Bring them back to his land, to try and help fight."

I wanted so desperately to ask what it was she had done, how she had wronged the imperious man outside, but now was not the best time. There would be another time. "Finian's father sounds delightful."

"He's spiteful and hateful of my kind." Her eyes darted to mine and she looked away cautiously.

"Is your home in Finian's lands?" I tried probing, the witch beside me reticent.

"My mother originated from an island to the south. I was born in a village within Terra Knox, but that has not been my home for some time."

"And your mother?" I inquired, trying to gauge the woman now in my bed.

"She is not worth mentioning." Her answer was spoken with such challenge and surety, I was sure it *was* worth mentioning. Curiosity got the better of me, her unconscionable challenge spurring me on.

"Roman and I, we no longer have a mother. She died."

Asta's eyes slid away from the sleeve she had been admiring. Her nostrils flared and brow crinkled. "How?" Her response was direct, my plan working.

"She was murdered. Burned at the stake. The people that did it thought she was a black witch. She had…" I swallowed, my throat pressing against my spine, "harmed a nobleman."

My stomach proceeded to drop several feet, the memory crashing into me, over and over. My teeth clenched, jaw straining, whilst my mind wrestled with the screams within. I looked at the small cowering child in my mind. Me. I was screaming at her, screaming at her to leave me. Leave and rid me of these memories.

"I am sorry for your loss and for her suffering." I watched her hands writhe on top of the covers, seeing her rich dusky skin house an array of small golden scars. Just like my own. "There is witch blood within you, but it is very weak. Was I right earlier?"

She had been right, earlier in the clearing. Our bloodline was mixed with that of witches, but from a hundred years ago.

"Yes, on my mother's side." Several moments passed with only the sound of the wagon wheels and crumbling road. Every now and then we heard the distant sounds of murmured words from the men riding outside.

"My mother was a black witch. Evil incarnate. Hateful and cruel." I hadn't been prepared for her to say that. Asta's deep accented voice continued. "My twin is her daughter in blood and mind. Both are gifted with blood magic."

My plan had worked, and yet, I hadn't expected such truth to be so easily given. I sat, stumped, unable to process such a mother, or a sister, especially when the memories that I had of my mother were adoring. It had been a childhood filled with love, laughter and singing, until the day she died. I tried to clear my throat, my palms becoming heated, as the darkest memories of my childhood began to hound and beat against their restraints. But her last statement sent a barrel of questions upon my lips.

"Blood magic?"

"Yes." Her dark eyes glanced at me warily, her lips thin. "That is the type of magic they wield."

"I don't understand. I believed there to only be black and white witches, you know, good and bad," I dared to ask, brow quizzical. I had never heard of such things. Mutza had only ever told stories of the dark and the light, the good and the bad. We had no knowledge of *types* of magic. The thought stirred something in me, a state of fretfulness I hadn't considered.

"There are. But this knowledge is not necessarily shared with mortals." Again, her eyes darted to me, shielding her thoughts entirely. "I will be chastised if I tell you, but I am already in a predicament with my own people. Hunting witches with humans is enough to burn any witch for treason." She rubbed her umber skin with long, elegant fingers. "I am what we call a weaver. I use the fabric of the world to weave and create spells, plucking the threads of creation and binding them to my needs."

I sat perplexed, my mouth open indignantly.

"My mother and sister have blood magic. They need the life force within blood to create and manipulate magic to their will. They either sacrifice their own blood to achieve their need, or other living things. The cost and price of such magic is deadly."

The hairs on my skin puckered and stood to attention. I watched the witch beside me squirm at the details she was confessing, the struggle evident. She moved her mouth, trying to form words, but none came. They were not something I should know. This information, these facts, were disturbing. Disturbing and sacred. But she continued. "There are other types of magic, two other divisions which we witch's, both black and white can be blessed with. Matter magic and alchemy magic."

I swallowed, waiting.

"Matter magic uses the organic matter which all things in creation are built from. Witches who possess this magic can manipulate and conceive for their desire and purpose. But when matter magic is used, the source of that creation or spell will be forever changed, and never revert back to its true form."

My knuckles were white as I gripped the fleece covering. Words failed me.

"Alchemy magic is the use of herbs and potions. The creation and production, with science, to conceive and affect things. It can be used for good and bad. Healing and destruction. Witches who are blessed with such magic can create a sleeping draft for a gracefully peaceful and instant death or one which will infect the receiver with hours, days even, of agony and torment before their final gurgling breath." Her words quickened, her tone rough. "Many white witches are born with this ability, this source of power. However, black and white can be born with any of the breeds of magic, but they must follow the three pillars of the craft." Asta wiped at her top lip. I could only watch and listen. "Productive, protection and destruction. White witches are blessed with productivity and protection in their blood. Whereas black witches are glorified with protection and destruction."

"And the Trinity?" My voice was barely a murmur.

"Convey all three of the pillars. The Crone is a Weaver like myself; I inherited my grandmother's gifts. The Trinity is the court in which we must abide. Black and white. The ascension dictates the ruling for the next hundred years. I'm sure you have heard of this?" she revealed, her dark eyes wide in the candlelight.

We knew of the ascension, of when a witch was selected to take the place of the Maiden. The Maiden would then ascend to the Mother and the Mother to the Crone. It was the unwritten ruling over their race since the time after Falin.

"But your mother was a black witch? So, shouldn't you be one too?" My question seemed to echo about the space, my voice finally found.

"I chose a different path. And I am glad for it," she confessed, wrapping her arms about her as she leant back, jaw set and eye distant.

I watched her, seeing the calmness return to her still frame, the crease smoothing between her dark brows. What she had just told me was something that could never be undone. Passing the knowledge would come with a price. It felt abrasive in my mind. The very thought of such different means to wield magic made my hands clammy. But I was glad she had sought to tell me.

I looked to the witch beside me, at the scars on her warm ebony skin, the shift covering her torso underneath the jumper I had given her. She was a weaver, which was still something my mind couldn't quite grasp or comprehend. But if she weaved the threads of the tapestry of life, like she said, she would be a very valuable ally.

Some of the tension had left my body at the thought and I, too, laid back. "Can I ask why?" I whispered.

"Excuse me?" Her voice held an edge.

"What made you choose the path of a white witch? I thought you were either born into dark magic or light."

"No, it is not as easy as that. Upbringing and parentage determine it, mostly. Usually black witches birth more black witches. Witches with white magic, birth white witches. It is not always the case though. I was an anomaly. An unwanted child, shunned and despised since I could walk and talk."

I let the severity of this information sink into me, wondering how she had survived with a mother like that. I realised then, with some level of alarm, her words from earlier. Her grandmother. The Crone. I wet my lips, judging when would be best to bring that matter up, but Asta wasn't finished.

"She tried to change me. To make me more like her and my sister. But my path was already set deep within my purpose, my blood, my instinct. She could do nothing to persuade me otherwise," she shuddered, her eyes glazed as she watched the medallions. "I ran away when I was six and ten years."

I whistled, a usual facade between myself and Roman. I hadn't meant to do it, but it was becoming easier to converse with her. Even if she was a witch.

"How long ago was that?" I ventured, watching her closely. She looked about my age, although her eyes and mouth held cunning in them, unseen in youth.

"Four and fifty years."

I bolted upright at that, rushing to face her, the astonishment, plain as day on my face. "How?" I accused, in awe.

"It is the life of a witch. It's in our blood, in our magic. We live long lives. The ascended, like my grandmother, live thrice the lifetime of normal witches. The Crone is nearly two hundred and fifty years old." Her shoulders raised in a slanted shrug and a small proud smile shone on her lips.

"You're seventy years of age?" I couldn't stop my eyes from widening, my brows from raising.

"I am, but in human years I am that of three and twenty years old."

I scoffed at that. She was older than me in many ways, form, physique, wisdom, but she looked not much older than I.

"How old are you?" she asked, rolling her head to watch me.

"Nearly one and twenty years."

"And your brother and the...mute one?" As soon as she referred to Eli, my muscles crystallised, back straightening sharply as venom coursed through me. My nose flared and I couldn't control the ice that coated my tongue.

"His name is Elias. He is my friend." I tried to calm the blaze of anger, the urge to protect, as I gripped the woollen throw, knuckles near white. "You will do well, to refer to him by his name-"

"I did not know it. Hence why I asked," Asta interrupted, "so that viper tongue can go back behind your teeth." Her silver eyes dulled to a dark pewter as they beheld me.

I doused the fiery rage, wrestling the urge to retaliate. Maybe she hadn't known his name, either way, I needed to reign in my emotions. My ferociousness gave me pause for thought.

"I apologise. He is a good man. He deserves to be addressed by his name," I replied, taming the frost on my tongue.

"I take it you two are...?" Her question was suspended in the air, tangible and pulsing.

"We are what?" My pulse quickened, mouth becoming dry. Eli and I were nothing. Nothing but friends. The lie in my head felt foul on my tongue, so I didn't voice it. But the kiss replayed in my mind's eyes and the phantom brush of his lips upon mine caused me to fidget.

Asta's eyes wrinkled, her pupils shrinking as the ghost of a smirk shaped her mouth. "I see."

"You do not see!" I exclaimed, hands beating the covers.

"What I see is a woman who is *hiding* her heart."

Her fervid smile of white teeth against her full lips, caused me to shrink back, ashamed. Her features only grew more mischievous. At that moment, I was reminded of Roman and his wicked ways. Rolling my eyes, I grabbed the jug of water and began drinking, unable to form a retort.

A throating laugh rolled up from her chest as she lay there, surveying sharp nails. "Have you bedded Eli at least?"

I coughed an array of swear words, water shooting out my mouth. "That is personal!"

"Well, have you?" Her eyes were bright.

"No, I have not." I couldn't hide the grim expression that clouded my face.

"But you have-"

"That is none of your business," I panted, still trying to clear my throat and my airways from water and potential choking. When it finally subsided, I turned to her, my face betraying me entirely.

In the past, I had had a sexual relationship, a brief and bland one. Something I had forced myself to do whilst Eli and Roman were away. Malik was a farmer's hand from the southern village. He had been gruff but kind, needing the release as much as I had. It had been the education I needed to rid me of my incessant self-loathing.

I had been careful, brewing a contraceptive tea every morning and drinking it before Baja or anyone became aware. For three weeks, we had bundled together in arms, mouths, and teeth, aggressively relieving an itch which had come about in my older years. I hadn't realised such a thing could be pleasurable. My own need being to rid me of the fear, rid me of the weakness which had shaped me and my childhood. This misgiving was frowned upon within traveller communities, our virginity sacred, but I had not been sacred for many years. I could feel the shadows forming within me, feelings that pulled deep into chaos and memory looming. Thankfully, Asta cleared her throat, bringing me back to the harsh reality and the witch in my bed.

"How old are *Elias*," she said his name with a purr, "and your brother?"

I eyed her, abashed. "Roman is four and twenty years." I gulped, feeling the heat flush building over my nose and cheek bones. "Eli is the same."

Malik had been my age at the time. Lean yet muscular with a tangle of long brown hair. Asta's chuckle was rambunctious as she smiled knowingly at me, inches across the bed. I heaved a breath through my nose, ignoring her laughter. I had thought about Eli. About what it would have been like if our paths had stayed attuned and we had married young. He would have been my first and my only if the ways of traveller held sway over our lives. Cunning ignited within me and I knew what would silence her.

"So, you and Finian? Are you? Is that the wrong you speak of?" Her snickers stopped abruptly.

"We are nothing. I am being forced to help. I was the only witch in the region of his land who stayed and did not flee." Finally, another worthwhile confession. I turned on my side, resting my head on my hands, hopelessly trying to stop them from twitching. This is what we needed to know. What I needed to know. "Why?"

"You ask a lot of questions, Rhona."

"As do you," I snapped back.

She made an agitated sound, squirming under the covers, moving her head from side to side, stretching. I caught a glimpse of a scar within her dark hair, from her ear to the centre of her skull. She noticed, her hand shooting her to pat at the area.

"My mother gave it to me. When I left."

I hissed loudly, unable to take my gaze away from it. "I am sorry," was all I managed as I pushed a stray tendril of hair off of my face. "Is she still alive?"

"Unfortunately, yes," she paused, licking her lips, "my sister is alive also. I have not seen her for more than twenty years." She was thoughtful as her fingers idly stroked the wool of her jumper again. "We witches know such things. Can sense them."

Another tendril of hair fell upon my forehead, obscuring my sight. I sat up, reaching for my comb. I began furiously detangling the mess of knots and curls, trying and failing to tame them into submission.

"What is that?" Asta rasped, eyeing it watchfully.

"A comb," I replied, showing it to her.

The alabaster shaft and carving glinted in the pale daylight. She cautiously sat up, hands braced behind her as she surveyed me returning to combing. My hand stilled, mid tangle. I pulled the teeth away, slowly passing it to her. My mind whirled, wondering if she knew it was my mother, if she could tell what it was and what it was made from. Her slender fingers took it from me gingerly.

"This was made from...death." Her voice was near inaudible, causing me to swallow loudly. She did know. "It has power and great pain within."

Asta's eyes ignited, as though the silver was swirling in a grey furnace. I had noticed that her eyes changed at the strike of an emotion or mood. A jolt shot down my neck and I stretched it, feigning indifference. I couldn't disclose the truth that this was my daily reminder that the death of my mother was on my hands.

"It is the bone of my mother," I offered, weakly. "When a member of our family dies, our ritual is to burn their body on a pyre. Never bury. We are travellers, our ashes are scattered to the wind, so even at rest we can follow the north wind, and the spirits of our ancestors. However, a piece of us stays with our people, travelling along the road with them. I inherited this. After we found my mother..." a piercing scream echoed in my ears and I paled, the memory still as vivid as though it were yesterday. "When we found her, she had already been burned, but not in the way we would have honoured her with. My uncle carved this for me. Roman inherited my mother's ring and I inherited the comb." I couldn't keep the manner of distaste that shaped my mouth as I said it.

Asta only watched me with preternatural stillness. I could feel her eyes searching every flicker and scatter of my gaze. Feel her assess my uneven breath. I rolled onto my back again. Unable to control the urge to spill everything about me to this witch. To this woman. Something deep in me stirred, as the incessant tug on my rib began.

"Eli is my betrothed."

She blanched and it was her turn to roll towards me, her hand propping up her head, brow raised waiting.

"It is a long story, but we were betrothed as children and we never took our vows." The words tasted bitter and I had to shut my eyes against the darkness beginning to swell again.

"You do not need to tell me anymore. I can hear your heartbeat from here."

My lids ripped open at that. Pity lined her dark shimmering skin and even in the dull candlelight she looked luminous and otherworldly. "You know nothing," I spat with acid, my teeth grinding painfully.

"I can see enough to know you are not whole."

Her words shook me. My fingers grazing the soft skin above my wrist, my nails digging in deeply. A wave of pain grew as my nails bit, tearing the flesh of my arm, until it snuffed out the growing agitation, as my mind homed in on that agonising relief.

Warm fingers encompassed mine, pulling my nails away carefully. I hadn't realised I had shut my eyes tight against the world, until I found Asta's face, grave and grievous.

"I do not expect you to tell me. But I see enough to know your past, your history, is still alive in you."

I could see the whites of her eyes as her fingers still held my own, stopping them from resuming the affliction. I could not break her eye contact, even as my eyes began to sting and the haze of tears nearly blurred my vision. A single tear strayed, falling down my cheek. I wiped it away swiftly, pulling my hand out of her own. She knew nothing.

"I am still fatigued," was all I managed as I rolled away from her feigning sleep. I could feel her eyes piercing the skin of my neck and spine for a time, until another blissful sleep did take me.

Chapter 30

When I finally awoke it was to the sounds of whispering. My cabin door creaked and moaned, the hinges needing oil. I was distinctly aware someone had exited my small home, as a brisk breeze nipped at my face, and the sound of footfall faded. I peeked an eye open and found Roman's great hulking form, standing over me, his shadow dark in the near twilight. I jumped, scrambling to sit up right.

"Roman, you complete arse!"

"You are alive, then," he scolded, eyes ominous, brow creased.

"Yes, of course," I snarled, pushing back the mess of dark curls on my face. I noticed Asta was no longer in my bed.

"*You* scared the hell out of us back there. You've been asleep for nearly two days," he accused, rubbing his stubbled chin. "I mean for the Mother's sake, you used magic, Rhona. And from what Asta's has been telling me, great magic. Like that of a witch."

I paused, holding my tongue. I was not a witch. It was the keys, these bands on my wrists that were magic, not me. I chewed on my lip, unable to tamper down my temper at being woken so abruptly.

"Well?" Roman growled, eyeing me pointedly.

"Well, what? You know as well as I do, I am no witch." I chucked the blankets off of me with force, spinning myself to stand and get moving. My legs felt stronger, my muscles no longer fatigued, and my mind was clear. I had needed that rest more so than I would have cared to admit.

"You do not get it do you? Magic has a cost. That stunt you pulled back there could have cost you, your life," he stammered, and my temper was washed away by his audible fear. I swallowed, looking away. "Just do me one favour?"

I rolled my eyes, biting my inner cheek.

"Learn what you can from Asta. There are other elements to this now which we must take into consideration."

I blanched, remembering the witch in my bed and the conversations we had had. I would have to speak to her again and learn from her. Her bargain rang clear in my ears. As payment for Asta teaching me, I had to give her an audience with the Crone, her grandmother. My stomach gurgled and I smacked my lips, feigning boredom at Roman's request. As always, he saw right through me.

"We are on Finian's land now. It won't be long until we reach his estate, so wash yourself because you stink."

Roman hurried out the door, his face alight with mischievous swagger. His words hit me, and it took me a second to react before I launched myself across the bed, ready to kick his vain arse to the road. Panting and seething at my shuddering door, I turned, seeing my reflection for the first time. In the fractures of my mirror I looked unusually pale. The circles under my eyes were darker, my cheekbones sallow and shadowed. My hair was a ratted mess, half up half down due to sleep.

I bathed thoroughly, the icy water waking every slumbering nerve back to life. I managed to wash my hair and braided it tightly back. It did nothing to take away from the haunted face looking back at me from the mirror. I dressed quickly in a clean tunic, wrapping a woollen shawl tightly around my neck and shoulders. Water remained in my jug and I drank deeply before opening my cabin door. It was turning twilight, the sky slowly darkening to a glimmering mauve. The light breeze held a chilly bite, but no snow littered the road or neighbouring fields. Four of Finian's riders were trailing my wagon, and I realised two of were Rion and Daven, Finian's huntsman. My stomach twisted as I observed their exhausted horses walking slowly.

Had they not made camp whilst I was out cold?

I frowned; their horses confirmed such. I had the unhindered feeling they were stationed behind me to make sure I didn't run away or escape.

I stood on my cabin steps, closing the cabin door behind me, feeling the air cool the flush on my skin. A man, with his face covered by a black scarf, leant over to his fellow rider. Prickles erupted up my spine as the two exchanged muffled words. Deep within me, a roaring began, and my anger flared anew. I swung my leg, grabbing the rigging of my wagon and hoisted myself up onto the roof. My arms quivered but I wouldn't let that show. Aware the entire time of Rion's, Daven's and the others' eyes on my back. The road was smooth enough that I walked along the roof easily, my footfall light and unwavering. Finian's white hair was luminous in the dying daylight, of which highlighted his night black attire and broad shoulders, something I hadn't taken a note of before. He was surrounded by his other men, all riding ahead cautiously on the quiet track. In the midst of them, I saw Eli riding Ovi, whilst Roman rode an unknown horse. Asta was riding beside him, and they were talking hushedly to each other. Even Eli was taking part in his small way, nodding, and signing to Roman. As I watched, jealousy strangled me as Eli bestowed upon Asta a wide smile. It was a smile he rarely shared nowadays, and I ground my jaw, fisting my hands.

No one had noticed I had returned from the dead yet and was out of my wagon. I was surprised Rion and Daven had not yet called ahead or alerted anyone. I looked down, noting the sheen on Balthazar's rump and the tired arch of his neck. Angered flared again. Rufus was indeed riding in the driver's seat of my wagon, his fists near white, clenching Balthazar's reins. I whistled below, earning me a startle from Rufus who looked up aghast. All the others turned in their saddles to gape at me. I revelled in their curious and dumbstruck expressions, but I could only bring myself to glare at them all individually.

"Move over," I hissed at the young boy in my seat.

He shuffled over, his freckled face pale. I leapt off the roof, landing the six feet below onto the driver's seat. My legs and feet were stealthy and supple as I settled, unruffled at the sudden jolting impact. I sat down with a heavy thunk, bringing my foot up to rest on top of the footboard, whilst I snatched the reins from Rufus. Roman and Eli shared a sidelong look and my fist tightened around the leather.

Finian however looked curious, as he trotted over to walk beside me.

"Good morning, Rhona, or should I say good evening?" he smirked, his light eyes assessing. "How are you feeling?"

I finally deemed it reasonable to look at the Lord, throwing every gust of my current distrust in a single look.

"I don't know what your plan was back there. Or what bargain you struck with Asta, but you've not told us the truth." Energy flowed through me with every word.

"Well, well, you've awoken well," he taunted, still smirking. "I've informed your brother and Eli of what happened."

"Well, you will need to inform me also," I spat.

"Fair is fair, I suppose." I huffed at that, waiting for him to continue. When he didn't, I pulled on Balthazar's rein's, halting my beast. Finian's men continued to walk around us, all eyeing their Lord, who watched me, intrigued. "I'm sure Asta has told you enough," he rebuked, his eyes trailing the witch ahead.

"Asta didn't tell me anything." This gave him pause and he rubbed his neck.

"Asta, is in debt to me. Very much in the same way you are to the Trinity." I swallowed, my eyes finding the witch and her grave stare. "I offered her a task as payment and punishment, if you will, for it. She was supposed to help us incur and acquire the services of more white witches. But alas, none showed themselves to us. From what we have heard, they are in hiding or have travelled south. She ran away from us in the clearing because your magic, the very smell and taste of it, scared her. She thought we were in the presence of a black witch. That is why she ran."

What Asta had confessed last night was true, of sorts, but not the running part... We hadn't even ventured to that topic of conversation, although I had desperately wanted to.

"Have you forgiven her? Pardoned her?" I asked, looking at the woman, now back in quiet conversation with my brother. Eli had turned in his saddle, watching us, his cheeks pink with cold. He looked better, his palette back to its warm golden glow. I clucked Balthazar on to walk again and Finian followed beside me.

"I have, although it is not my pardon she needs." He ran his fingers through his hair, pushing it back from his eyes. I pursed my lips, cocking my eyebrow. He was still not telling me the whole truth it seemed.

"How am I supposed to trust you and tell you about this magic, if you cannot do the same to me?"

"I guess we'll just have to learn to trust each other then, won't we?" That roguish smirk returned to his lips as his head tilted, regarding me. Warmth radiated into the very core of me, his smile only growing more wide and profound as if he knew. I inhaled quickly through my nose, rolling my eyes.

"Do you think you can kill the lycan?" he asked, voice hushed.

"I have to," I replied, staring ahead at the road. I really did. Otherwise my fate, my future, would be in jeopardy. "Do you think we can?" I asked, finally freeing myself from within.

"I believe in you. More so than I did a few days ago. And especially with those markings on your wrist," he revealed, face serious. "Especially since they were given to you from the last thern still breathing."

I closed my eyes, silently calling my brother every name under the sun. "So Roman has told you?" I questioned. My brother was insufferable.

"Yes and no. He told me that those *keys*, if you can call them that, allow you to ask things of the forest. And it obeys. He said those markings are the reason you could do such things and you are not a white or black witch, which I believe. However," his devilish smirk returned, and I saw a flash of white teeth, "tell me, Rhona, are those markings anywhere else on your body?"

I scoffed a laugh, stunned. A sudden heat pooled in the core of me. I bit my lip, afraid to reply. It turned out the Lord did have a sense of humour, too similar it seemed to that of my brother. There was an uncomfortable hiccup beside me and I turned, realising poor Rufus was still sitting next to me, blushing and wide eyed. The poor lad looked utterly stuck. I tried to swallow the knot in my throat as I turned on Finian, humiliated. He only shrugged, his smile broadening.

"How far are we from Neath Briar and the estate anyway?" I said, trying to change the topic of conversation and rid myself of the heat now flushing my cheeks.

"We are on my land. We should be on the estate by midnight," he replied, eyeing the turning sky. The waning moon was nearly visible on the horizon and the sky was free of clouds. The fields either side of the road were dusted with a lavender hue as the sun began its final descent below the mountain range ahead. The sky was smudged with mauve and pink, and the winter wind blew lazily. I watched his smile fade as he said, "then the real work begins."

Finian's words were tinged with apprehension as his gaze wandered towards those immense mountains far ahead. They were barely visible, shrouded in mist and the sun's dying light. But even looking upon the Fallow Mountains from where I sat, many, many miles away from it, I could sense the palpitations and pressure of raw magic.

***

Finian had been right; we arrived on the borders to his estate near midnight. The waning moon was at its peak in the star-littered sky, the midnight mist nearly soaking our coats and clothes. Flaming torches could be seen as we rode down the estate's road, towards a barricade of high walls, wooden spikes and an enormous iron gate. Finian had continued to ride beside me on his horse, Lameer, he told me. As we were approaching the gate, he whistled ahead. That same low, long note that gave me chills. It was returned by a harmony whistle, distant from the barricades of the gate and high walls. I searched the darkness, trying to gauge the height and length of the wall.

His estate had to have been great, to have stone walls taller than four men. I craned my neck as we reached the iron gate, the metal dark and dangerous, trying to see the shadowed guards walking atop the barricade. Finian and his men rode ahead, right up the gate. I halted Balthazar, noting all the men and women stationed atop the walls. The torchlight glinted spears and arrowheads. There were longbows and crossbows drawn and ready. Extensive wooden stakes, sharpened to deathly points, protruded from the earth at the base of the walls. Great ballistae were manoeuvring and being directed at us.

"This place is a fucking fortress," Roman cautioned and I flinched, unaware that he had come up be beside me.

"Aye, it is now." Rufus, who had been sleeping up until now, had awoken groggily. He stretched, a small smile on his mouth. "Home," he croaked, jumping from my passenger seat to run to his father and the others at the gate.

Eli walked Ovi towards us, his eyes never leaving the guards and their weapons. Something clawed at my skin as I beheld it all. The vastness of the wall and the height of it.

Fucking fortress was right.

Ovi gave a grumbled whinny, which Balthazar returned. Both horses were exhausted and in need of a good meal and groom. I reached over and rubbed Balthazar's flank, soothingly, trying to give my mind something else to wander to.

"Any minute, boy, and I'll have you settled," I said softly, feeling his quivering. "I know, I know."

"This is bad," Roman said under his breath, eyeing Eli. That got my attention as I saw their exchanged look.

"What?"

"This place is a fortress, built to keep things out and people in."

"So?" I hissed, not grasping what he was insinuating.

"Rhona, the weapons, the ballistae. You wouldn't have all this here, these people, these guards, these huntsmen, if it was just a lycan." There was an edge to his voice and my stomach dropped in understanding.

This place was a garrison, a stronghold. A battlefield. My breath stumbled as I looked past the towering walls to the faint outline of the mountains in the distance. I swallowed.

"Is that..." I started.

"The Fallow," Roman finished, his face pale.

The Fallow Mountains were in two or three days reach. We were so close to the Fallow, the area of stories and legends we had heard as children. Our clan had never ventured this close. We had only ever journeyed far around it. We knew what lurked and what was held captive within. The Fallow was a pressing silhouette on the horizon, which felt unsettlingly close now with the wards down. My empty stomach bubbled with bile and I swallowed the fear creeping up the back of my throat. We had walked into the beast's lair. Ahead, Finian and the others exchanged words with the guards high above, and then creaking began and the same whistle called out along the wall.

"The Crone wanted us to come here," I muttered, leaning over to rest my arms on my knees, releasing the reins. "That whistle was the same as the one from the Shadow Messenger."

"It cannot be. Surely the Messenger gave you something else? A bird's call maybe?" Roman said and I could hear the doubt in his voice.

"No, Roman. This is the place we need to be."

"But surely the Crone would have said, go to Neath Briar, if that was truly her plan for you?" The cynicism made my skin crawl and all I could do was rub at my bitter cheeks and tired eyes.

"She can only give me so much. She said so herself," I replied, overcome and deflated. I inhaled a deep breath, filling my lungs, trying to settle the building unrest and unease. I looked at Eli, finding him thoughtful. Roman began to speak again but Eli whacked him with the back of his hand, stopping him abruptly. He began signing in the darkness.

'Nothing is as it seems. Grandmother.'

My heart swelled and a small spark of surety ignited within me. Roman looked at Eli with resignation.

"Thank you, Eli." My thanks was guttural and nearly edged with tears. But thankfully none spilled as I sniffed, feigning calm confidence. The gates groaned and heavy metal hinges whined as the iron door opened slowly. It did not open fully, stopping just enough to allow one cart to pass through at a time. Finian and his men were a blur of shadows ahead as they rallied and began making their way through.

There was a glimmer of auburn hair and Rufus came running towards us.

"Come, come," he wheezed, staggering up to sit in my passenger seat. "We must get in quickly," he said, reaching for the fallen reins. I held my hand up, stopping him.

"What else lurks on your land boy?" Roman asked rather menacingly.

The boy paled, his freckles stark in the waning moonlight. "Finian and his father will explain." His voice broke, careening high.

I picked up the reins and we all passed under the shadow of the gate.

There was a thunderous boom and the ground shook as the gate shut behind us. Murmurs of conversation could be heard ahead and as we passed the wall; we could see Neath Briar Estate alight with flaming torches and glittering candles. We continued until the sight before me made me halt Balthazar again. Eli and Roman, to their credit, had the same reaction as I, as we beheld the estate and all occupancy.

As many as fifty tents were erected everywhere on the vast grounds, far away from the walls and close to the imposing house. Bonfires blazed about the tents, with people and families huddled together around them. At first glance, it could have been perceived as an army camp, but upon closer inspection you could see and hear desperation of the people dwelling here. Washing lines protruded from one tent to another. A large well near a towering oak tree had a queue of people waiting their turn to gather water. Men and women patrolled the encampment and the lower walls surrounding the place, with great dogs walking with them on leashes, smelling the ground and air. The stately house was lit from within, its many windows bright with moving candles and silhouettes of its occupants. From its size, it looked like it could house a hundred people.

I stood slowly on my driver's seat, craning my neck to get a better look. There were so many people, all gathered here in one place. In the far distance, from what I could see behind the estate house, blackness loomed. Mighty trees darkened the horizon and far beyond that, the Fallow Mountain dominated the skyline.

"It's something. isn't it?" Rufus's voice broke again as he looked upon the mass of communing bodies.

I blew out a staggering breath, looking down at him. It was as if all the unwanted across the continent had accumulated here. But they were not like us, not like Roman, Eli and me. They were not unwanted. These were townspeople and village people who used to dwell on the Neath Briar lands. So many had chosen to stay and to be here. I was astounded. My gut wrenched as I saw many women wandering about, their numbers greater than that of the men here.

"Where are all the men?" I asked Rufus, scanning the tents.

"Many have died defending this place. Or have been taken and made into the turned," he said, his voice sorrowful as he too watched a young mother, belly swollen with child, hefting a full pale of water with a small babe on her hip. "But you're here now!" he rejoiced, and I hushed him angrily, as a few eyes turned in our direction. Hooves galloped towards us and Lucius came into view. Rufus cowered at the sight of him, his joyful smile falling immediately.

"Rhona, Roman and Eli, leave your mounts. Rufus will take your horses to the stables to water and feed them." I saw the boy diminish further. "You're to stay in the house as guests."

From the tone and glare on the man's face there was no fighting this, but I tried anyway. Conscious of all the curious eyes now upon us, peeking over tents and makeshift homes from wagons and farm carts.

"But my cart is more than suitable for us."

"It is at the Lord's request that you stay in the house. Two families were made to vacate their rooms for *you*."

He said the last word with such venom, I could only imagine what he was thinking. Unwanted. Scum. They were some of the scathing insults I saw simmering in his blue eyes.

"That is not necessary, besides my home..." I began.

"It is not up for discussion. Rufus will take your *home* to a secure location, at the back of the main house, by the kitchens," Lucius spat with finality. I could only blink as he turned abruptly and rode off back to the house.

"Well, that's that then," I confessed, biting my lip.

"He can be that way at times," Rufus muttered, watching his retreating father.

"What? Like a bastard?" Roman gibed, coming down from his horse.

Eli followed suit, patting Ovi. Both men tied their horse's reins to the double bar of my wagon. Realising there was no way to get out of this, I climbed down. Hands grasped my hips, and I turned, finding Eli behind me, steadying my descent. His broad hands fell away from my waist as soon as my feet touched the frosted grassy earth, and he stepped out of my space. Sudden heat bloomed across my chest and abdomen, and I straightened, turning away. The skin under my coat was still tingling, the phantom handprints still caressing me.

"Look after my horse, Rufus, or you'll have me to answer to," I threatened with a wicked smile. The boy swallowed and nodded hastily, loosening the reins and flicking the steed to walk. Balthazar obeyed, and Ovi and the other beasts followed.

Chapter 31

Stale smoke filled my lungs as we walked through the camp towards the estate home. Chickens ran between tents, unable to roost with all these bodies jammed together. Farm carts and wagons that were idly stationed and unused were being chopped for firewood or piled high as barricades on the wall.

The wide gravel path, leading up to the marble steps of the house, was dishevelled. The lawns were gouged, and the shrubbery was unkempt and overgrown. It was the grandest house I had ever seen, and yet it was not. The giant oak doors were wide open, with men and women walking in and out into the night, traipsing mud, and all manner of muck across the threshold. Torches of gold flame and ivory candles illuminated the entryway on cast iron chandeliers. The black and white marble floors of the foyer were chipped and badly scuffed; the usual grand ornamentation glimpsed in such places, was covered with dust sheets or removed entirely, the ghostly reminders of paintings that once hung could be seen on the ivory floral wallpaper. I felt pity for Finian. So much wealth to be lost or sold. The enormous staircase, with people milling about upon the three levels, gave me pause. I had never seen such beautiful marble. I imagined ladies in fine dresses walking down them, with balls, parties and music taking place long, long ago. I touched my hand to my chest, my eyes bringing to life this now tired house. Several doorways led into other grand rooms and from what I could peek, all of them were occupied. The smell of baked bread wafted through a door to my right and my stomach grumbled dramatically. I turned on the spot, marvelling at it all, marvelling at the hundreds of people living here.

"He wasn't kidding when he said he had taken in the neighbouring village folk, " Roman breathed, dark brows gathered as he readjusted his crossbow. Unbelievably, there was a tone of admiration in his voice.

Many footsteps echoed on the marble, coming towards us, and we turned to see Finian and an entourage of men behind him. Finian previously had seemed collected and dominant but around these men, as he walked to meet us, tension radiated from his face and his shoulders. I watched his throat contract and gulp.

"This, Father, is Rhona, and her brethren, Roman and Elias." Finian's introduction echoed off the walls and floors and for a heartbeat, every soul in the ground floor rooms quieted. I swallowed, meeting the gaze of Finian and then his father. "This is my father, Lord August Briar."

The man before us was nothing like his son. Finian, with his icy hair and pale silvery eyes, could have been crafted from the rock of the moon, pale and ethereal. And yet the man in front of me could have been cast from its shadow. Finian's father had night black hair, streaked with peppery strands of grey and eyes of mahogany. Grey stubble covered his chin and the slash of healing skin across his lip and nose hardened his already harsh features. He looked older than Baja, but his eyes shone with youthful clarity, loaded and suspicious. His once elegant tunic looked aged and frayed in places, the stitching loose and faded. I waited as those mahogany eyes inspected us. The Lord's lip twitched with dissatisfaction and I ground my teeth, knowing exactly what to expect from a man such as he. The creak of boots beside me told me Roman felt the same. His fists were clenching around the leather strap across his chest.

"Is this *really* all you have to show for it, boy?" the man turned, sneering at his son. "Not a single witch worth their magic, other than that useless thing out there. And these three meagre peasants," Lord August seethed, spraying spit.

I lifted my chin, unflinching. Hate rooted deep within me, burning me with fiery disdain. Men like this would never scare me again.

"Do you take me for a fool?" Lord August's face turned savage, his complexion purple as a vein trembled in his temple and neck. He rounded on Finian and, to my disbelief, I saw a shadow of the person who was in the woods, commanding his men. Finian paled at his father's taunts. His eyes were glazed and unseeing, allowing every whip of word to strike. "I sent you out there with fifteen of my best men and you only returned with twelve, because you allowed three to run off, " he raged, and a crack echoed across the marble, making me flinch. Red bloomed across Finian's shocked face. The man had struck his son. I attempted to move, but a hand caught me, holding me still. I looked down to see Roman's vice-like grip, holding me to the spot. He struck his son so openly and with such vehemence.

Fuck him and his kind.

I couldn't help it as I stepped forward out of my brother's grip, shoulders back and sneering.

"Lord Briar, allow me to advise you, we have been sent…" I began.

"Do not speak to me, woman," Lord August bellowed, his saliva hitting my face. Again, I did not flinch as every muscle and nerve went taught and sharp. Controlling the rage riding me was becoming difficult. I saw the muscles flickering in Finian's jaw, those silver eyes turning to ice as they rose from the floor to me.

"My Lord, I have seen this traveller woman's magic. We were lucky to find her." It was Lucius who had spoken. The red-headed man looked warily at me. "She is gifted. Magic uncommon to a common witch."

"Poppycock!" Lord August spat again, turning now on Lucius.

The anger was near boiling in my blood and I turned on the old bastard.

"I'd be more than happy to give you a personal demonstration of my gifts, you vicious old shit." My breath was hot and burning as it came out in strained gasps.

"Rhona," Roman grunted, grabbing me again.

"How dare you? I could have you hanged for such an insult, you bitch," said the Lord, his own voice rippling with vehemence.

"Father, you will do no such thing. The magic she wields is powerful, but she is not a witch." Finian had stepped in, voice raised.

"I will hear none of it. You've let me down for the last time, Finian. *I* will go and bring back the type of witches we need, and not some conjurer of tarots and tricks." The older man whirled and began shouting names of men, rallying them. "Lucius, get Solomon and Davis. Tell Tariq to bring my horse around to the front and tell the cooks to prepare enough food for fourteen men. We're going hunting."

"Shall I prepare my horse to join you, my Lord?" Lucius asked, his eyes down. All the while his son, Rufus, eyed the old Lord fearfully behind him.

"No. You have disappointed me as much as Finian. I do not require you for this, Lucius." And with that, Lord August began charging away, commanding, and bellowing to the council of men in his wake. Lucius walked away in the other direction, eyes dark, with Rufus tailing behind with his head down. Finian was left in our presence, the skin on his cheek glowing angry in the torchlight. The commotion of people around me blurred to a dull buzz and I couldn't help the pity that began stirring as I looked at him. Asta had been right. His father was a monster.

"My father is," Finian began, unable to meet any of our gaze.

"A prick?" Roman jumped in.

"A bastard?" I interjected.

Eli began signing with his hands. *'A son of a bitch?'*

I snickered silently, seeing the smug look on his scarred face. Eli's eyes caught mine and he winked. My lips burned, the memory of our kiss still lingering there. I inhaled, mentally shaking myself as Finian ran his hands through his hair, lips pursed.

"Yes to all, including whatever Elias said." He exhaled, rubbing his neck.

"We've dealt with worse." I reached out, touching his arm. The silver in his eyes ignited at the gesture, and a flutter began in the depths of my stomach.

"May I show you to your rooms?" He cleared his throat. "They're on the third floor, in my wing."

I shuffled on the spot, my feet restless as the manor suddenly felt overbearing. I heard Roman inhale deeply beside me.

"We are happy to stay outside with the others," Roman replied.

I knew exactly what he was getting at. With the poor folk. It was true, we would be better suited outside. We never stayed or slept inside stone walls for more than a night. We preferred to be outside, sleeping in our tents or caravans. It was the way of the traveller. We owned no property or land. We were merely guests, free to roam and observe, never devour and possess.

"Besides, we have our own arrangements," I said, raising a brow.

"Please, stay the night here. Bathe, rest, eat. And in the morning if you feel more suited to your usual dwellings, then you are free to return to them," Finian nearly stammered. The man was completely shaken. "Just please, allow me to repay the kindness you bestowed upon us in the woods?"

He finally looked me in the eye. A man trying to regain control. Instinct wouldn't allow me to budge or simper. But I knew, deep within me, I needed to tamper down that resolve. He wasn't a villain, and I wasn't a child anymore. I sighed heavily, turning to Roman. His dark eyebrows were high on his forehead, lips puckered. I knew what he was thinking as the very same thoughts were circling in my own head.

A bath would be nice.

"A bath and food would be welcome," I replied, feeling the grim coating of mud on my skin.

"Show us to our rooms then, Finian." Roman swept his hand before him, in a courtly gesture, wagging his eyebrows.

Unbelievable.

***

Roman and Eli were shown to a room which housed two beds and had an adjoining washroom. It had been vigorously cleaned and fresh bedding was tucked in neatly. No straw and no fleece. My skin prickled in anticipation at such a treat and my mind wandered at the delight of sleeping in an actual bed.

But as Finian gestured around the room, I clocked the two beds again. I bit my lip, wondering exactly where I was to sleep. We were to be separate and something within me tensed. A fire blazed in a grate opposite both their beds, the orange and yellow dancing across the dark wood walls. Finian left the room, and our eyes were still trailing the four walls when we noticed he was halfway along the corridor.

My stomach dropped several feet when I realised Finian had secured a room solely for me. We followed further down the corridor of Finian's wing, the boys trailing behind, counting the doors between us. A whoosh of breath left me when Finian opened the door. Instantly, my spine went rigid and my fingers twitched.

A large bed adorned with velvet hangings sat at the centre of the room. A large lead window with patterned curtains occupied the adjacent wall and another fire blazed in a grate with a large white marble surround. The colours were muted but warm. Dark and comfortable. Red, rouge and burnt orange. Earthy and rich. I gulped, taking in the mahogany wood walls and russet furnishings. Soot had collected around the walls, showing the ghostly shapes of past paintings and pictures that had once hung, like the entryway of the manor. Many thoughts crossed my mind at once. **Maybe they had to sell their luxuries to afford the upkeep of such a manor? Or to feed the villagers that now called the estate their home?** That thought gave me pause as I watched Finian inspect the room. His fingers glided over the dressing table and bed linen, his nostrils flaring. My room hosted more luxury items than Roman and Eli's, and I could feel their eyes behind me scan the four corners of the room.

"There is a washroom behind the door to the left of the bed and a dressing room to the right," Finian went on, opening the doors to the rooms beyond.

Oil lanterns had been lit in each, giving me a glimpse of a tiled room with a copper tub that glistened in the washroom. I stayed in the doorway, assessing every detail. It was larger than my caravan, so much so, my skin prickled and my body was suddenly stiff.

"The maids have changed the sheets and removed the other beds. Everything has been cleaned and I've ordered food to be brought up to you. Baths will be drawn shortly when more water has been boiled."

I swallowed, still stuck and unmoving, until Roman shoved me in the room. My feet acted quickly to stop me falling on my face, as I spun hissing at him.

"Will it do?" Finian asked, eyeing my stricken face. I changed it quickly, smiling at him.

"Yes," I swallowed, eyes wide. "I've never stayed in such a grand room before." It was the truth, I had never stayed in such a room; nor had I ever stayed in a room by myself, other than my wagon. The walls seemed too vast, too open, compared to my small home on wheels. I swallowed again, assuring my smile met my eyes. "Thank you. It really is wonderful."

Finian's eyes brightened and a smile returned to his handsome face. I shiver crept up my spine and I stiffened. "I'll send Asta up with some fresh clothes and see where your meals are. My room is two doors down. Knock if you need anything." His eyes flashed and his smile crept to the right of his face. I could do nothing but blink. And with that Finian left, passing both Roman and Eli who still stood in my doorway.

Roman and Eli's eyes were tracing the room and its only occupant. Me. Hands on my hips, I cleared my throat, disturbing them. Eli's mouth twisted as he trudged in, checking the window. All the locks and fastenings are secured. He then walked into the washroom, returning to the main room a minute later. Roman followed suit, choosing to check the dressing room. I followed him, keen to see what the hell a dressing room was. I gasped, barrelling past Roman into the square suite, seeing another dressing table, with a mirror. Four large wardrobes in dark mahogany stood on either wall, with a plush velvet chair the colour of red wine. The carpet was threadbare, the patterns worn and unrecognisable. It was beautiful. There was a creak behind me, and I heard Roman whistle. I spun, grabbing a wardrobe door and seeing an array of colourful garments and dresses within. I opened my mouth to speak, my words evading me at seeing the feminine frills and bouquets of lace. My stomach curdled at the obstinate fabrics.

"I think Finian likes you," Roman whispered, brow arched.

"What?"

"This room has been locked for a long time. You can smell it. But he's given this room to you and unlocked this door, with all these fancy dresses." His tone was grating, and I fisted my hands.

"Maybe the maids unlocked it by accident," I retorted. He made it his mission in life to vex me. My tongue was about to become sharp and I ground my teeth. It was a ridiculous notion, but I couldn't deny the smell of the room. The musty smell, clearly indicating the stale fabrics had been left hanging for a long time. This had been a woman's room a long time ago and they had loved this room. The carpet evidence of that.

I jumped as Roman's lips were suddenly by my ear whispering. "Then why have all the silver brushes and scent jars been polished?"

I jostled, turning to see the sparkling silver laid carefully on the dressing table. My jaw dropped. His chuckle vibrated the air behind me and I had no words. Hinges squeaked again as Eli pushed open the door, his eyes roaming the room and seeing my face. I closed my mouth quickly, as his dark brows gathered, and a strange look passed over his face.

"Right, both of you get out. I need to bathe," I demanded, pushing Roman with force from the room.

"Of course, my *Lady*-"

"Get the fuck out, you beast!" I bellowed, slamming the door in Roman's self-righteous face.

Chapter 32

Hot water and soap were delivered to my room by the maids. They came in hauling the steaming buckets, and took them into the private bathing chamber, and I waited, bouncing on my toes, for them to finally leave before diving into the copper bathtub. Every muscle soaked up the delicious heat as I scrubbed away the dirt and muck smeared across my skin and in my hair. As I lazed in the suds and murky water, the door to the chamber burst open and I screamed, jumping from the tub. A small mousy laundry girl was frozen to the door, eye wide and mouth aghast. She squeaked and grabbed my clothes before running away. The door to the bedchamber shut with a bang and I waited, hyperventilating. When I gathered that no one else would disturb me, I finished washing as quickly as possible.

Once clean, I ended up ransacking the closet for a shirt or nightdress, naked. As soon as the plain cotton shift grazed my naked thighs, there was another knock at the door with a delivery of baked bread and a small shred of roasted meat with vegetables, carried in on a tray by a broad woman with a scowl.

"Thank you," I stammered, watching the woman and her floured apron place the tray on the small table in the window. "I'm sorry, a young girl came in and grabbed my clothes whilst I was-"

"Yes, they are being cleaned and mended," she answered abruptly, the scowl still twisting her pudgy face. She barged past me and out of the door with a huff.

My hollow stomach growled and gurgled, and I ran to the food, quickly forgetting the rude woman. It lasted less than a breath as I shovelled it down greedily, burning my tongue. Once sated with food, I rummaged around the draws and cabinets in the room. There were no books or beautiful things displayed on the walls in the main bedchamber and the old smoke marks on the walls, where pictures had once hung, were the only reminders that this was once a fine room. That and the gathered heavy silk curtains around the four-poster bed. The dressing room, however, was another story.

Another knock rattled the door and I hurried to it, opening it with a small smile on my face. The bath and food had worked wonders on my mood but the comfort I was feeling shattered, when yet another stranger stood at the door, my old clothes in hand.

Where was Asta? Perhaps Finian had assigned her another task or duty.

"Your clothes, Miss," the woman said, shoving them to me.

I barely had time to mutter a thanks when she was already marching up the hall to the staircase. I looked down; these were not the dirty clothes collected earlier. These were from my trunk in my caravan and my stomach flipped and unease skittered over my skin.

People must have gone into my cabin.

My thoughts whirred fast at what they would have seen or touched. My books, my bed, my mother's collections of emblem saints, medallions and trinkets that hung from the ceiling. The herbs gathered and pinned on the walls. My home, my possessions. It was no wonder for the hostility. The wary looks. I was *unwanted* after all. Our ways of living were strange to them.

I unfolded the neat pile, noticing new stitching on some of the well-worn shirts and trousers. I forced my legs into a pair of riding pants, feeling the fabric stick to my too-warm skin. I placed my boots, knives, and coat over a chair beside my bed, ready should I need to vacate quickly. With my hands on my hips, I surveyed the room again. I would return to my cabin tomorrow, too where I belonged. The decision settled in me, like a pebble falling through water. *I didn't belong here.*

I proceeded to pull the sheets away from where they were tucked and creased neatly. The soft bedding wrinkled in my hand and I was reluctant to get in. It was such a difference from the fleece and hand-woven blankets that lined my straw filled bed.

There was a soft knock and then a click and I spun, seeing the door open. Finian stood in the doorway, bathed and clean, his white hair wet and slick back. He wore a black shirt and trousers and as my eyes followed the line of his body, I realised his feet were bare.

"Are you settled?" His voice was quiet as his hand closed the door behind him.

My skin prickled, the fire suddenly too warm on my exposed arms and chest. My hands dropped the bedding that had been clutched in them and I straightened, aware of my heartbeat pulsing in my ears. My damp hair tickled my forearms as it hung limp and the cotton shift abruptly felt itchy. I couldn't speak. The words I wanted to say, stale on my tongue.

What was he doing here?

"You look better." There was an all too familiar glint in his eyes as he beheld me, and I was too aware of how my body was swiftly reacting. "I took the liberty of overseeing your clothes and personal effects delivered from your home to you." Relief must have shone on my face. He continued, "I made sure only your clothes were touched, and I have someone guarding your possessions out in the camp."

I felt hot, my blood thrumming, as his eyes lazily moved up and down the length of me, stopping short at the thin fabric barely covering the shape of my breasts. I didn't know if it was fear or if it was defiance that quickly equipped my tongue.

"Do Lord's not know how to knock?" I said, glaring at him. "What can I help you with, Finian?" My rasp was steel edged.

"Not a damn thing." His eyes finally rose to meet my own, their silver hollow dark. "I just wanted to see if you were being accommodated well. That you were being looked after."

"I can look after myself," I snapped back.

"Oh, I believe you. I just wanted to see something."

He began walking towards me and each of his steps caused the floorboards to creak and groan. I didn't dare move. I felt, rather than saw, his eyes do another sweep of me. A sweep of my body, now cleaned and unobscured by layers of shirts, coats and shawls. My breath felt cold as I inhaled through my teeth, and he stood in front of me, us mere inches apart.

Cedar and something sweet filled my nose, and I saw the glisten of water still on his neck and temple. His pupils dilated; the pale shimmer of pewter being devoured entirely by black.

"Is there anything you need from *me*, Rhona?" he asked, and I felt his words brush my face. **He was so close.**

Like a well within me, my stomach churned and every hair on my body felt electrified. An ache began to build, and a molten need began coursing through me. It had been a while since I had scratched that itch. A while since I had learned of the pleasures a woman can feel in the arms of a man. Rather than…

A cold sliver clawed down my spine and I swallowed, my lungs feeling strained. Finian's head tilted as he watched me intently. Heat flushed my cheeks when I realised, he understood too well what my body was betraying. What my nipples were now standing at attention for.

"If you need anything, Rhona, I am only two doors down to the left." His breath caressed my face again as he took another look, his eyes flaring at the peaks under the shift, and left my room.

He left me reeling and hyper aware of what churned and burned between my legs.

***

The bed had been comfortable, too comfortable, and I had careened into a dark, dreamless sleep which felt endless. The usual recurring nightmares and screams did not pay me heed that night. It had been a blessing. But it had ended, rather harshly, by aggravated knocking on my door. I rose out of bed, hearing Roman cussing behind the wood. I had locked the door upon Finian leaving last night, cursing myself for losing face and not asking the questions that I had wanted to ask since we had arrived.

The door swung open to reveal Roman and Eli stood there, fully dressed and cleaned from head to toe. It was possibly the cleanest I had seen them for some time.

"What's happening?" I yawned, stretching my arms behind me. A cold water sensation crashed over me. I was standing in a bed shirt, my trousers discarded in the night. I quickly covered my body with the door.

"Nothing. But Finian wants to see us in the hall," Roman said, looking away.

"What, why?"

"I don't know. To plan? Get dressed, we'll be out here waiting," he fussed, turning his back. Eli looked to him and then to me and I saw the flicker of worry leave his eyes.

"Give me five minutes," I yawned again, slamming the door.

I was dressed and ready in five minutes, after a rush of fumbled laces, splashing water over my face and cleaning my teeth with the powdered mint left in the bathing chamber. When I strapped the last dagger to my thigh, Roman barged in. I nearly laughed. Five minutes was a feat.

"Ready?" he asked, as his eyes roving over the room and the bedding. **What in the mother was he looking for?**

"Yes," I drawled, my brow gathered at his insistence. He was already grating on me this morning.

"Good, now let's get food and see what His Majesty fucking wants."

Roman and Eli were already walking down the hall when I closed my door, prowling to the main staircase and armed to the teeth. They must have woken early and gone to my caravan. When we entered the dining area, families were already seated and eating their breakfast on large, long benches. The hall was a chorus of chatting, and the smells of eggs and cured meats wafted across to us as we slowly walked through the archway. The chatter died instantaneously.

"Well, this is bloody awkward," Roman breathed.

Every eye was turned to us, cutlery paused mid-air as all in the dining hall beheld the travellers. Something sharpened in me and wanted to bite and snap at all who gawked. Too long had we endured this. Too long had we been perceived with such prejudice. I was sick of it and of them. Hate burned in me, boiling my blood.

"Fuck them," I spat, loudly, and walked into the hall, feeling my spine straighten and their oily scorn smother me like a new armour. I did not heed to these people. I had done nothing but exist.

The silence ended with a murmur of whispers as I made my way to the high table. Finian sat at its centre, his white hair glowing in the streams of morning light coming through the windows behind. His metallic eyes trailed my every step towards him.

He was accompanied by Lucius and Rufus, as well as Rion and Daven. They must have been ordered to stay behind as well. No one spoke as I approached them and Finian turned to the empty chair beside him, his eyes inviting me to sit. Roman and Eli took the seats next to me, and platefuls of eggs and grilled goat's meat were placed in front of us. Lucius and the others continued their quiet discussion, so low that my ears strained to hear. They spoke about the lord leaving and the men he had chosen to accompany him.

"Did you sleep well?" Finian asked, leaning in close to me, whilst my mouth was full. I chewed slowly, designing an appropriate answer. Roman, thankfully, saved me from having to confess I had slept well enough that the thought of returning to my caravan this evening wouldn't be as agreeable.

"Yes, thank you. Although some small urchin came in the night and grabbed our clothes and ran," Roman accused, around a mouthful of meat.

I stifled my laugh, finding his thick brows creased in mocking severity. Finian had expected me to answer by the look on his face, but he nodded and returned to eating his own breakfast. I looked up over a spoonful of egg, finding eyes watching us. But not just me, I realised. But also, Finian. I watched a couple of elderly men staring, their twisted, whispered words focused on Finian.

Could it be that he is not liked on his own father's estate?

I remembered his father's cruel and cold welcome, hearing the backhand across the face. The question bubbled up and I turned to Finian.

"Your mother was a witch, was she not?"

He froze, his jaw muscle flickering. He lowered his fork and turned to me, his look icy.

"Yes." I waited for him to continue, noting the shadow under his eyes. Roman and Eli had stilled beside me, their eating too quiet for such men. "She was a black witch and a fiend. You saw how my father treated me; it's because of her."

"Why?" I whispered, feeling the lump form in my throat.

"Because she swindled my father into marriage. Played him a fool in the marriage bed and used his lands, so near the Fallow. When I was born and my father saw the eyes I bore, a witch's eyes, he knew. He beheaded her and spent my childhood years battering and berating his only son for being of mixed blood."

I paused, my breakfast curdling in my stomach.

"I know this sounds cruel, but why did he not remarry and bear more children?" Roman asked, rather casually.

"My mother cursed him before he took her head. Believe me he tried. Took four wives after her and all could not bear him children. So, he was stuck with me."

"And do you have power?" I croaked, interested now I understood the man beside me was half a *black* witch. Even if the thought rattled me.

"Males cannot inherit the magical gene. It is only the females. I only inherited the eyes and the hair. And unlike my mother, who glamoured hers to hide her true identity, for me it's a constant reminder of the bitch who pushed me into the world."

It was like blow after blow. Another tale of an unhappy childhood; first Asta and now Finian.

Maybe I wasn't alone in my torment.

Chapter 33

After breakfast, Finian showed us to the stables where I spied Balthazar eating his weight in oats. The morning was grey and bleak, the sky threatening fresh snowfall. There was no wind however, only the hurried clouds gathering and moving to the peak of the mountain in the distance, the Fallow Mountain itself.

Finian continued to show us the estate and in the daylight, I was once again in awe at how many people were living on the grounds. Tents littered the considerable courtyard at the front of the estate, but the back of the estate was no man's land and heavy patrols were underway. The north of the residence and gardens bordered the Fallow, with the ghostly forest grazing the farthest border and wall. There were acres of land, but the wall had been built to contain those who dwelled here as safely and securely as possible. We walked the lower perimeter of the wall and I was grateful for the shawl I wrapped about myself. The air was too chilled and biting, even without the wind. The men and women patrolling the border and top of the walls watched vigilantly as we walked by. Some eyed us with suspicion, while others nodded or bowed to Finian as he approached.

The wall of stone and wood was unending, wrapping around the manor house and holding. Lookouts towered every hundred feet, all positioned to watch and observe a certain area of the Fallow. Between the lookouts, deadly ballistae were stationed, armed and ready to let loose bolts the size of two men.

"We've been unfortunate to suffer ten attacks this month by the turned," I heard Finian explaining to Roman and Eli. Both my brethren were still armed, eyes watchful as they followed the Lord.

I knew them too well; both being huntsmen, they were mapping the terrain and getting to know the size and space of the forest beyond. I was no huntsman, but even I could see the lapse in the fortress. There was only one escape. The main gate. I swallowed down the building doubt and restlessness. I was second guessing everything, yet again, and a small part of me felt hopeless. Agitation became me, remembering the Crone's cryptic words and manner of *help*. When we climbed the steps up onto the wall, my breath shook as we finally beheld the Fallow beyond.

The forest itself was endless. The trees and flora were growing and thriving in a bittersweet symphony of colour, unlike the winter-dusted world on the outskirts. The Fallow stretched both west and east, expanding past the walls until the eye could not make out detail and the blur of clouds met the blur of brush. The Fallow Mountain sat centre, rising up in a great mound of ebony stone. The jagged rupture of rock was strange to look at and my blood chilled seeing it obscure the pale, clouded sky.

"They come at night usually. I heard from my father's men that there was another raid of seven beasts whilst I was away." Finian's voice sounded distant as they walked ahead.

My feet felt like they were laden with lead and I stopped, feeling that incessant internal tug. The skin on my wrists and arms tightened. The bands of ink darkened skin became a storm of sensation all of a sudden. I looked out over the wall, watching the gargantuan trees on the other side, their shapes and sprawling branches reaching above the wall and to the heavens. I contracted my fingers, my hands feeling heavy. With my fingertips buzzing, I lifted my palm before me, recognising that dull heat as it worked through the bands and the keys, feeling the magic stirring. The trees ahead groaned in answer, moving and swaying on a non-existent breeze. I moved my hand from left to right watching the wave of bristling branches creak and move. The keys on my forearms and wrists recognized them. I could feel it, something heavy and suffocating within.

Tanned fingers touched my elbow and I jumped, allowing my arm to fall. Eli was beside me, his eyes searching for my own. The ghost of the feeling before evaporated, its heaviness lifted as I looked into his blue and brown eyes. I felt his fingers skim my own, the touch sending a wave of emotion ricocheting through me. But it was swallowed whole by the oily thing buried deep in the bands of my wrist, that thrive and called out to be unhinged and freed. The static from the magic built in my veins, the power longing to be connected back to the source.

"I can feel it," I said, looking back out at the Fallow. "It's like the keys know something isn't right within. The balance is shot or something."

Roman and Finian had walked back to us, both looking guarded. I couldn't stomach those looks. The pity and suspicion. An idea burned within me and I was startled at how quickly it took shape. Inhaling, I set my jaw. I was not something to pity, not ever again.

"Where is your weakest point in the wall?" I demanded, needed to release the itch building in my skin. The magic was clawing to get out and do something. What I had in mind would be a small reprieve.

Finian walked us to a break in the wall, the rubble and stones laying beaten and jagged on the ground. Some of the men on the watchtower nearest were leaning over the barriers, alert. Two ballistae creaked and swung to face the section where I was now standing, looking into the depths of the Fallow.

"What are you doing, Rhona?" Roman's voice was hoarse behind me.

"Shut up." I needed to think. The rising need within me was dizzying.

I parted my feet, needing to steady myself further and inhaled deeply, filling my lungs with the cold frigid air that gave me the clarity I needed. The idea became clearer in my mind.

There was an uncertain moment when my silent task was met with silence itself. I breathed in deep again, reinforcing the image in my mind. There was a shudder and the ground underfoot rumbled. The tree canopy ruffled, and branches snapped and cracked in the Fallow. The tree nearest us moved, roots rupturing and sinking. Vines grew and trailed up over the wall, growing fast and thick. I heard gasps behind me and the ballistae charges shift. The vines grew tall, their spiny and thorned limbs creeping like serpents, devouring the broken rock and rubble until the wall strengthened into a barricade of razor thorns and stakes. A whoosh of breath escaped me and the exhaustion hit me. My muscles and mind ached from it but I kept my feet and heels planted, balancing myself inside and out. A whistle rang out behind me and I knew it was Roman before I even turned.

All three men were wide-eyed in dismay and my ego ignited inside my chest.

"Any other weak points?" I directed at Finian, whose brows were high, and mouth was puckered as he surveyed the monstrous growth. More guards had gathered on the walls watching me, fear and reverence plain on their faces.

Finian shook his head, burying his hands deep into his pockets. "Remind me never to piss you off."

"Noted," I retorted and began walking to find my caravan, needing some herbal tea.

**

Thankfully, none of the men followed me as I trudged about the encampment, searching for my caravan. I found it around the back of the stables, guarded and untouched. I needed to smell my home and feel the familiar wrap of memories and wood. I unlocked the bolts and entered my darkened space, ignoring the men shuffling outside who had been assigned to watch over it. Walking the short steps to the side and finding the flint, I lit candles quickly. The usually warm room was cool and bitter in the shadows. A hiss sounded from behind me and I spun, affronted.

The Crone stood motionless in my home, glowing ethereally in the small array of candle flames dancing about on books. I fell back on the bed, aghast. She was so close and in my home! The veil covering her withered head fell, revealing her aged and lined face. Her mottled grey skin and puckered mouth twisted as she regarded the walls, the furniture and me in a heap on the bed. Her withered lips exposing her rotting teeth.

"This was your mother's wagon?" her voice rasped, the very essence of it hollow and clawing.

Her blackened fingertips flicked and grasped at the air, the joints clicking unnaturally. The flames of my candles grew and became blazing, causing the room to brighten. My chest was heaving, pulse racing. What, in all that was dark, was she doing here?

"Her scent lingers here. A mix of you and your brother." She turned on the spot and I noticed her exposed, gnarled feet hovering from the wooden floor. "You made it then. To this place." The Crone's hiss was barely audible as she turned back to me and I was at the mercy of her full attention.

"Yes, this was my mother's cabin and yes, we're here, aren't we?" My lips formed the words and stumbled feebly.

"You have surprised me," she clucked, her pale eyes boring into my own. I shivered, unable to move. "There is something else afoot here girl. Something I have been unable to see clearly."

My mind raced and Asta's face spun in my vision. "I met your granddaughter, Asta." The words were out before I could stop them.

"Yes," she paused, her lips near snarling, "How is the blood of my blood?"

"She's here in this camp." The Crone's eyes flashed at my reply. "She wishes to speak with you."

"I have no time for her now-"

"-Why? Because she is a white witch?" I snapped, the adrenaline sharpening my tongue. I found my legs then and stood on unsteady feet.

"I have no issue with the blood of my blood choosing the side of the light," the Crone objected, her eyes shining with fury.

"Then let me fetch her, I will make haste." I tried to move but the witch before me raised a withered hand. I froze, immobile.

"I do not have time, I have been gone for too long as it is." Her words were jarred and exhausted. I watched her drooping brow gather, causing more lines and wrinkles to cluster. She sagged, her feet slowly expanding and spreading on the floor. "I *am* a black witch. I was chosen by the council nearly three hundred years ago as a maiden to fulfil the duty of the Trinity. As the witches, both black and white before me. We grow with time and with time we learn. But this is not something I would have ever thought possible."

I was released, the blood buzzing and pumping loudly in my ears as every nerve and limb could finally move freely. I began to protest but the Crone glared at me.

"The Fallow is compromised. The Fallen Sister's desecrated. The Fallow wards are holding on by a mere thread. And they will not stand for long. The power of the Trinity is dwindling, the very foundations punctured."

My hands began to shake.

Because of me, her unspoken words directed.

"I see you, girl. See your past, see your present. I know what happened to you as a child. Know what still haunts you and creeps in your mind when you least expect it."

I swallowed, suddenly cold. The blackness swirled in my mind, the toxic grip of pain and memory threatening to beat me down once again. Bile rose in my stomach as the Crone stared me down.

"Your past is entwining with your future, Rhona. You'd do well to strengthen yourself both mentally and physically to finally slay the demons of your memory."

Sweat beaded on my brow and I could feel the hot breath on my neck of laboured lungs. I could smell the stink of him filling my nose, sickeningly. The hairs on my scalp stung, the tormenting reminder of my hair clasped painfully in his fist whilst my child's body was held down. The bile was in my throat, rising to burn my tongue.

"I know what he did to you."

Her words were ablaze in my head, my ears not wholly hearing her. The darkness rumbled inside of me. The wrath and hate and agony grinding down to my bones. My hands were shaking uncontrollably, and tears burned in my eyes, threatening to spill. The breath in my lungs felt poisonous and heavy as I gasped back a sob.

"Control it. Own your fury and pain. Shape it, sharpen it and wield it. Become the vengeful creature you only deem to become in your dreams."

What the Crone was saying to me was something I would never have imagined. The thing I had tempered down all these years welcomed her advice. The wrathful creature within me, smashed against the cage I had created. Keen to be free. To release itself on the world. But I couldn't. I couldn't turn into that person. There would be no coming back. I would be consumed. Eternally.

"You will face him again. You will face your monster. Your past and future have now been weaved together, wound tightly and sewn with agony and wrath. My magic will only last for a few days, and then the hell contained over the wall will break free."

Cold, from the deepest night and darkest shadow, slithered in my veins. The echoes in my mind chorused together in a harrowing song. I shuddered, the Crone's words washing over me. I would see him again. See the bastard who broke me, who used my childlike body and discarded it like rotten meat and who killed my mother because of it.

Revenge beat in my chest. The tide of it was like a roaring blaze. Burning. Raging. Absolving the cold and ridding me of it. Turbulent and raving. Fused and violent. I clenched my fists, dragging air into my lungs through clenched teeth. The Crone cackled, the laugh cawing and grating against my fevered skin. I closed my eyes, barricading the onslaught that was on the precipice of ravaging me whole.

"That's right, taper it. Use it. You'll need it in the days to come," she snarled, and I growled back, opening my eyes. The darkness seeped back into the crevices from where they came. The memories locked themselves back down under a canopy of rage. The lock to my cabin door rattled and cold air blew in as it opened and daylight filtered in. The candles extinguished in a breathy hiss sending wisps of smoke swirling to the open door. The Crone turned and, with a thundering crack, vanished.

"Grandmother!" Asta bellowed. The witch stood, door still in hand, appalled. "You said you would tell me the next time you met with her," she yelled. I heaved, the fury still coursing in my blood. Asta's eyes widened as she looked at me, really looked at me. "What did she say to you?" Her voice was quiet as she quickly shut the door, encasing us in shadow. I fell back on the bed, the straw and rumpled covers uncomfortable on my tight skin. Asta flicked her wrist and a golden thread of sheer light danced into existence. She muttered something and the flames ignited once more.

"I don't want to talk about it," I warned, unable to look at her.

"Tell me, please," she pleaded and I finally raised my eyes to meet her.

"My past is coming back to haunt me," was all I could manage, as the bile rose finally and filled my mouth. I ran to the basin and emptied my stomach. Cool hands gently pulled my fallen hair away from my face. "Water, please," I grunted, spitting the remnants from my mouth and tongue. Asta handed me the pitcher of stale water beside my bed and I swilled it in my mouth.

"This past of yours, is the reason your mother is in the afterlife?" she asked, her voice barely a whisper.

I nodded, wiping my face.

"And the reason for the pain in your eyes?"

Tears burned and, at last, fell, the weight of everything falling on me anew. "Yes," was all I managed.

"Tell me?" Asta croaked, and for the first time in my life, I told my story.

Chapter 34

Asta stayed with me whilst I told my story. She comforted me and helped me when bile rose again, the acid blistering my throat. I was compelled to tell her all of it, every dark facet of my past and every broken and beaten part of me which had never healed. The pieces of me, fractured and defective, were there to see. Through my sobs and anguished words, Asta listened. I didn't want any pity. What was done was done and yet she calmed me. Her silver eyes glazed and stared distantly on occasion, when words failed me, but I knew from the line on her mouth and her delicate touch that she was there with me. She was there, reliving my story, reliving every memory, as I spoke my truth. We talked for hours in the shadows of my home, undisturbed, until my eyes couldn't cry anymore, my teeth chattering had subsided, and my breathing had regulated.

"Your secret is safe with me," she announced as I finally stretched, my legs no longer quivering.

I nodded, feeling her eyes upon me as I fussed over my puffy eyes in the cracked mirror of my basin. Shadows had darkened the blue and I recognised the wraith staring back at me. I *was* broken. But I had conquered something in those moments before. I had done something I had never dreamed of. Touching my fingers to my lips, I tasted tears, the salty trails now crystalised on my cheeks. I looked hollow; my haunted memories were mapped across my face. I closed my eyes, sealing off the void and the depths of which one day would consume me and when I opened my eyes at the cracked mirror, the wraith looking back at me had gone. My mask, though subtle, was now in place again.

I realised then I had not offered Asta the same promise. When she told me about the pillars of the craft, or the types of magic both black and white witches wield, I had only absorbed the information. I had done nothing to offer security. Internally, I chastised myself.

"Did you tell the Crone, my grandmother, about the keys?" she asked, her silver eyes distant.

"No, I didn't get the opportunity," I answered, my throat raw.

"Good, that will be for the best," she said, thinking aloud.

"Why?"

"Because she is still bound to the court. The Trinity. If she is helping you, it is without their knowledge." This information stumped me and I opened my mouth. "Now is not the time to ask. We will speak of this later," she said, face cast in shadow. It dawned on me then, that she was wearing the clothes I had given her. Something small swelled in my heart as I looked at her.

"Are you well?" It was the only question I could ask, without confirming my suspicions.

"Yes, Lord August ordered me to enchant weapons last night before they left. It was late when I finished and I didn't want to call on your rooms," she trailed off, her demeanour changing entirely.

"It is fine, Finian had some women bring me clothes. I just wanted to see if you were well."

"I will be, when this is all over," she replied, looking at the door.

"Asta..." She turned back to me, her face cautious. "What did you do to warrant being brought into all of this? To be commanded and used?"

"It is complicated." Her words were sharp, but I didn't miss the fear in her eyes as she said them. "I will tell you soon. But now we must find Finian. He requested you."

"Requested?" I scoffed, amused.

A smile shaped her full lips, the glimmering skin on her umber cheeks smoothing. "I'll take you to him," she smirked, but the pain still lingered in her eyes.

***

We found Finian and the others training, practising with his sword with different opponents. Many men who were not on duty or patrolling were utilising the time by training as well. Across the training ground, I spied Roman and Eli watching Finian's every move, both men contemplating his tactics and education, it seemed. It was no wonder, Finian was shirtless and battling two men with his sword and shield in hand.

"I heard about your altercation with the wall," Asta mused, from my right.

We walked to the edge, the men near us, moving away. I huffed a small drop of pride swelling in my chest.

"So did everyone else apparently," I said, raising a brow.

"That would be because of me," she reassured. "They stay away from me."

Her eyes darkened, the rich lull of her voice becoming pointed. I watched her closely as she surveyed the fighting. I saw the scars across her scalp and neck. She had been in her own battles and had her own story, and yet she hadn't crumpled and complained like a broken child. She was standing tall and strong, not allowing the glances and whispers to batter her down. I swallowed, turning back to the men and the clashing of metal. Roman caught my gaze and motioned to Eli. His eyes locked on me across the fray and my skin prickled at his intensity.

"Where the fuck have you been?" Roman asked, causing the men and women training nearby to turn and look.

"With Asta," I retorted, eyeing the witch beside me. Roman and Eli didn't need to know about the Crone's visit. Not this one anyway.

"Hello, again," she retorted at my brother and I smiled. Eli nodded to her respectfully but then his eyes moved back and over me.

"What have you two been up to?" I observed the men training, my eyes finding Finian now battling four men all at once and with ease. Sweat glistened on his pale skin and more muscles than I could count rippled over his back and arms as he wielded his long sword, effortlessly. His white hair was slicked back, his entire aura absorbed in the fight. The men he was sparring with, whooshed and wheezed with each battering they took from him. The straw and leather padding they wore masked the true impact of such jabs and slices. He twisted and spun, his sword arm high above him as he kicked out with his leg, sending a man onto his back, whilst turning his torso to block an attack from behind. Raising his shield, he pushed back on an oncoming blow before spinning low and raising his sword to hit not one, but three opponents, all at once. Roman whistled low beside me, his own eyes trained on Finian.

"He is a skilled fighter," I declared, unable to remove my focus from him.

"The best," Asta offered, watching intently. "It is his witch's blood. It strengthens and intensifies his will. Everything." The awe in Asta's voice was far from adoring. There was an edge to it.

A gong rang out and more men entered the ring, all armoured and protected. Swords, axes and other weapons were drawn, circling Finian now. My breath caught. There were now fifteen fighters about to bear down on the lord. I stilled, watching in anticipation. Finian danced on the spot, his feet moving back and forth swiftly as he extended his arms, stretching his muscles and neck. Those bright eyes of his darted across the people gathered, assessing all. Then he moved, taking one by one down as they dove, ducked and ran for him. The clash and clang of metal was deafening, but he never faltered. His sword arced and dove in the air, shining in the winter light, until only one person stood, the rest rolling on the floor or crawling away. I watched Finian feint left as his opponent moved and skidded, realising his mistake. Finian swords landed softly at the neck of the man still standing and a look of triumph erupted on his face, morphing it into something else entirely. My lungs burned and I inhaled, needing air.

I watched, captivated, as his hand pushed his damp hair away from his brow. Roman cleared his throat at such a display and when I peered around at Eli, I saw a distinct roll of his eyes. I bit my lip at that. Finian spied me across the training ground then and whistled at Rufus, who I realised was on the side lines. The young boy ran over to his Lord, carrying a skin of water and a cloth. Finian downed the drink and poured it over his head and face, wiping it away, before handing it back to Rufus and walking over to us. Asta fidgeted beside me uneasily as his wide steps brought him closer to me.

"There you are. Thank you, Asta," Finian huffed, breathless. She nodded and bowed her head slightly. It set my teeth on edge.

"Tired, Finian?" Roman goaded, inspecting the shirtless man before me. Finian to his credit rose to the occasion, a brow raising in question.

"Do you both fight?" he asked. The man had just beaten down nearly fifteen men, he was not in the mood to be trifled with. A lucid thought crept in my mind as I watched a bead of sweat trickle down from his temple to the muscles in his neck.

Roman only puckered his mouth. "A little." But his eyes had darkened, the challenge rippling in them. The heat building cooled and now I rolled my eyes.

"Join us, unless sword fighting is not your forte?" Finian taunted, looking at me.

"Boxing, actually," Roman spat on the ground, crossing his bulging arms. Even in his coat and furs, he was well formed. I looked at my brother, the giant pain in my arse, tongue sucking at my teeth.

"Fighting men, indeed." Finian's silver eyes creased, calculating.

"Gentleman please, contain yourselves," I snapped, noting the locked glare they were both partaking in. "Finian, you summoned me?" I hissed.

"Summoned you?" Roman questioned and I saw Eli's brow gather, his face becoming stern.

"Yes, summoned," I tusked, turning back to Finian, hands on my hips. The Lord looked suddenly trapped by my accusation.

"I merely wanted to say thank you. For the wall. And to invite you to have dinner with me this eve, in my chamber," he replied in earnest.

I blinked and swallowed down the guilt that flashed in me. My hands fell from my hips as I glared quickly back at my brother. "Thank you." My hands fretted with a toggle on my coat. "We *all* accept. What time should Asta and I be ready for?"

Finian and Asta started, and I could feel Asta's sterling eyes boring into my skull as I continued to watch Finian form his answer. There was the briefest flicker of surprise on his face, which he quickly replaced with smooth surety. A smile played on the corner of his mouth as he looked at me and my skin heated immediately.

"Be ready for eight. Dinner will be served sharply."

***

Asta came back to the room I was staying in. I sighed, walking through the dim hallway and through the door, seeing the bed made and fresh logs near the fire. The bedroom was opulent and warm, and I realised it was becoming more and more inviting, unlike my currently unused caravan. Asta licked her lips, staying on the threshold.

"What is it?" I asked, turning to see her scanning the room.

"This was his mother's room," she breathed, finally looking at me. She took the step over the threshold, walking into the middle of the wooden floor. A thought popped up and I quickly acted.

"Where do you stay?"

Asta answered swiftly, unchecked. "With a..." she paused, the words rolling around her mouth, "friend."

A secret plagued her eyes as she looked at me, but I didn't press her for it. There was a great part of me that trusted the witch in my room, a strange unknown part that felt attuned to her. It bewildered me to give my trust so easily when for so long I was a locked vault, unable to converse or commit to anyone outside my small circle of family and friends.

"You're more than welcome to stay with me here. I'm sure we can get another bed. There's plenty of room." I spread my arms for emphasis. But Asta only looked at me warily. I waited for her to say something, but the reluctance still lined her mouth. "You don't have to tell me or stay for that matter. I just wanted to make sure you are safe here. That the same respects get paid to you as they have been me."

She nodded, slowly looking about the room again. She seemed distant in thought, the contemplation on her face visible and changing.

"You will see tonight, I suppose. I will knock for you before eight and we can arrive together as a party." Her voice was meek as she turned to leave, carefully glancing back at me, before closing the door.

***

Fresh hot water was brought to my room soon after, and the bath and soaps beckoned me. I smiled as politely as I could at the women who had delivered it, keenly aware of their snide looks and tempered mouths. I bathed myself, washing my hair and scalp, allowing the hot water to rid me of the tidal wave of emotions from the day. The water in the tub was still clear and frothy as I soaked, compared to the murky concoction of mud, tears and blood from hard travel yesterday, but I finally felt thoroughly clean. My soapy hand reached up to push back the wet hair on my forehead and my fingertips grazed across the missing hair on my brow. The small scar that split one brow entirely in two. I pulled my hand away, admiring the crinkled ridges of my fingers. I had never been able to wash so well as an adult. My bathing habits happened in streams and rivers. The only hot water for washing was boiled in an iron kettle and cast into my basin in my cabin for a wash. I couldn't get used to this, to the feel of the hot water. The night sky outside my window called to me. The stars softly glinted as they began their nightly parade in the sky above.

I sighed, deeming it time to vacate the water before all my limbs were as pruned and wrinkly as my hands. The cotton cloths piled next to the copper tub mopped my body quickly, drying me from head to toe. I leant forwards, gathering my damp hair on top of my head and twisted it into a knot, away from my face and neck. The shift I had found the night before had been folded on the bed, by hands that were not mine. I wrestled it on and walked to the dressing room, opening the door and peering in nervously. The brushes and combs on the dressing table enticed me and I walked in about to pick one up, when a quiet knock sounded on the door. Opening it, I found Finian in the hall, his face cast in shadow.

"May I come in?" he asked gently. My skin heated, my bare legs a buzz with goose bumps.

"It is your home. Of course." My voice was strained, revealing my agitation. I turned, walking back and around the bed, needing some space between us this time. If Roman or even Eli saw, they would lose their shit. A pang of nervousness contracted my stomach at the thought of Eli knowing, let alone knowing this was the second time Finian had entered my room.

The door clicked hushedly and Finian stood there, dressed in a black dress tunic and trousers. I looked at the fabric, the hems and cuffs of his sleeve stitched with an emerald thread that glistened in the firelight. His white hair was pushed back, revealing his proud nose and high cheekbones.

"I had hoped to be having dinner with only *you* this evening." I swallowed, feeling entirely exposed. His silver eyes were molten once more as he beheld me, nearly naked, save for the cotton shift. "But I had to extend the invitation to Asta, your brother and Elias as well."

"How unfortunate for you," I dared, my hands clasping the fabric lower against my thighs.

"It is." His eyes danced as he considered me. "You intrigue me, Rhona."

I didn't know if that was a compliment or a criticism, but my body betrayed me nonetheless. The flush that had threatened to rupture, coursed over my cheeks and neck. The heat built and skittered down into the core of my belly. Finian moved closer to the bed, walking to the foot of it. My eyes stalked him as he moved, aware of the closing distance between us.

Finian wiped the corner of his mouth, before placing his hands into deep pockets. "I think you are a witch of sorts," he breathed. He was closing the distance, the air about me becoming heavy and thick, until he stood before me, towering above. I had to lift my head to meet his gaze again and I tried desperately to quiet my heartbeat as it pounded in my chest. The room had become overly warm as the smell of him filled my nose. Cedar and something sweet like cinnamon. I unhinged my jaw, swallowing the lump down deep.

"Why do you think I'm a witch?" My voice was not my own. Looking down, I saw the buttons of the shift were open and I grabbed them, holding them closed at my chest.

"Because I can't stop thinking about you." My eyes shot up to his, to the roguish smirk playing on his mouth.

I inhaled, needing air. "You don't know me," I breathed, my heartbeat now as loud as a drum in my ears. The fire growing in my belly ignited between my legs. The influx of need pulsed dangerously. How long had it been, since I had been close to a man? Since I had released the pent-up energy, the anxiety, the fear? With him standing before me, it felt like an age. An age of longing.

Finian lifted a hand out of his pocket, his nose flaring as he read the flicker of my eyelids. His fingers grazed my cheek and I gasped, the throb between my legs unrelenting. I could if I wanted to. I could give in and take this man and allow myself the release my body so frightfully craved. I hesitated, my mind and body a conflict and battlefield all of its own.

I raised my hand to strike him across the face, my elbow strained for the impact. I jolted, my bones singing as his hand whipped up and grabbed my wrist, stunning me. He was so fast. Unnaturally fast. Asta's voice rang in the back of my head, *'half black witch'* and I swallowed loudly. A sultry chuckle escaped from his mouth and I couldn't tear my eyes away from his lips, or at the flash of his teeth. His thumb casually skimmed across the pulse at the base of my wrist, the vein betraying the rapid rush of my blood. His thumbnail grazed the lines and inked bars that decorated the skin on my arms and disappeared under the cuff of the shift. I sucked in breath through my teeth, the feel of him enraging something wicked within me. The heat from his touch was near searing and I stilled, trying to ground myself. He tilted his head like a predator, bringing his lips down to the exposed skin below my palm.

"Do not touch me, without my permission," I exhaled, gulping down air to cool the fire in my blood.

Finian's smirk only grew devious against my skin, his bright eyes glowing with fervent hunger. "Why? You may like it." he quipped, his words tickling the flesh at my pulse and he released me. Phantom lips were still brushing against my skin as I lowered my hand. My mouth opened and closed. "Looking forward to our dinner, Rhona."

He swaggered to the door, the sheer dominance of him radiating across the room. My heart was still pounding, along with the contemptuous creature between my legs. The dull ache was now rising and clouding my judgement.

"Feel free to borrow whatever gown you would like for dinner this evening. Whatever you choose, you'll be a feast for the eyes."

I scoffed, abashed and breathless.

The door closed behind him as he exited, and my eyes widened in shock. **The lech.**

I gathered myself, from the daze of his outright carnality. I walked to the dressing room, his words still spinning in my mind. Thoughts rallied of him touching me, of his lips upon my skin and his hands in my hair. Something moved in the corner of my eye and I started, seeing my own reflection. My cheeks were flushed, and my skin looked fevered. My fingers traced my lips as I imagined what it would be like to allow Finian to do all that his burning eyes promised.

Mother above.

I spun, turning to the silken and satin dresses hanging in the wardrobes. The thought was already blooming in my mind as I surveyed the fabrics and frills. The wicked creature, Finian had spurred to life, smiled as I shut the wardrobe doors loudly.

There was no way I was wearing a fucking dress.

Chapter 35

Asta had knocked on my door fifteen minutes before eight o'clock, and I had pulled her into the room instantly. She spun, dazed, as I quickly closed the door. She wore a simple black woven dress, with long flowing sleeves and a square neckline. Her cheekbones and rounded ears were dusted with the faintest gold. It made her skin glow, and I knew that all who looked upon her now would know she was a witch. She looked exquisite.

"You look beautiful," I stammered, awed by the sight of her.

Her dark skin glistened and her cropped hair was smoothed to her scalp. A dark brow raised as she surveyed me from head to toe. I walked back into the dressing room and she followed as I grabbed my belt from the dressing table and fastened it around my waist, my sheathed jagger attached firmly at my hip.

I had chosen to wear my riding trousers and the only clean blouse I currently owned. It just so happened to be embroidered and floral, which frustrated me. My leather basque was sitting underneath my breasts, was fastened tight by laces at the front. It was the only formal piece I owned, worn at celebrations and weddings. Usually the women of my brethren would wear flowing skirts and entwine their hair with flowers on such occasions, but I had neither. I looked presentable, and pretty, even. My curls were brushed and fell in waves neatly down my back for once.

"Finian did tell you that you could borrow any of these dresses, did he not?" Asta spluttered, emphasising the closed wardrobes.

"Yes, but I'm not going to wear a dress just for him," I spat, pulling on one of my boots. I heard rather than saw Asta huff a laugh. "He said you probably wouldn't wear one," she said, her hand on her chin. That got my back up.

"You've spoken to him?" I asked, invested.

"Yes, about ten minutes ago. He said to see if you were ready." Her smile was superior. "He also said, `you'd probably not attend this evening in one of the dresses he offered, out of spite.'"

I stood, aghast, but closed my mouth quickly, composing my face. Her brows reached new heights as she bit her lip. Amusement danced off her and I was relieved to see her high spirits, even if it was at my expense. There was another knock at my door and I rolled my eyes. Asta thankfully went to answer it as I battled on the other boot. Roman and Eli entered the room, both clean shaven and beards primed and smooth. Roman's ebony hair was tied back and shining at the nape of his neck and Eli's was swept back, his curls tamed around his ears and jaw. His unusual eyes were luminous as he beheld me. When I pulled my eyes away a punch of horror blazed through me as I noticed what both were wearing.

Roman wore a cream tunic over a navy dress shirt, embroidered with silver. The square fitted shoulders cut his broad chest in a way that drew the eye across his chest and down to his narrow waist. Eli wore a deep navy, velvet tunic, the gold buttons undone, revealing the black shirt underneath. The cut and design of the tunic, the very same as Roman's, revealing the well-formed torso underneath. The dark blue velvet made his sun-kissed skin gleam and his blue eye brighten. His pale scars were visible over the collar of the shift, and up his jaw but I found myself breathless looking at him. Reality hit suddenly and I couldn't help but gape at them both, and the clothes they both wore. They were not clothes that they owned.

"Where did you get those from?" I complained, throwing my hands up.

"Finian and Lucius gave them to us, for dinner this eve," Roman retorted, moving his arms and the muscles trapped in the fabric. "Why are you wearing that?" he asked, cocking his head.

"Because Finian told her to wear a dress-" Asta started, trying to conceal her laugh.

"It's a long story," I interrupted, glaring at the witch, as I tied the final laces on my boot together. I stood, smoothing myself down, suddenly feeling extremely underdressed. "Besides I don't own any dresses-"

Roman and Asta began to speak at once, pointing to the dresses behind me.

"I do not *own* any dresses and I am not about to borrow one of his dead mother's so he can parade me about," I snapped, flustered. I bent over, pretending to contend with the other boot, but I raised my gaze, finding Eli. My words had barrelled about the room, their unspoken meaning evident. Eli stood behind Roman, his jaw clenched, face stony. I returned my attention to reknitting the laces but didn't miss the feel of his gaze trailing my body.

"I'd only parade you around a little." Finian's voice was clear as he entered the room.

I froze, my hands dropping the knot. I looked up, finding Finian strutting into my room, still wearing the same black tunic as before, his eyes dancing wickedly. I swore animatedly in my head, my cheeks flushing at being caught.

Roman's head snapped back and forth between the two of us. "She's ready," he said, motioning to me with a thumb. "And we're famished," Roman announced, stalking past Finian and out into the hall.

Eli's eyes connected to mine and for a moment, anger flashed in them. My stomach fell at that look and I was too aware of the tight corset, cinching my waist. Eli turned towards the door, his mouth set in its usual stubborn line. As he reached Finian, he slowed. It dawned on me then that both of them were the same height and stature, one dark and one light. Eli's tanned skin and dark hair were vibrant against the dark velvet of his tunic. I couldn't see his face as he shared a look with the Lord before he followed Roman out into the hall. Finian's pale brows rose as he contemplated that look, but they quickly fell, his attention returning to me and Asta.

"Dinner is served, ladies."

***

Finian's chamber had been readied for a small banquet. A long table, with eight chairs, was stationed in a large sitting room, and a roaring fire was already ablaze in the large, white stone hearth. Maroon velvet drapes hung at three points across the far wall, indicating large windows behind. Books were stacked on the walls near the fireplace, the variety of spines creating a mirage of colour. Relief flooded me as I saw three of the seats already in use, although it was short lived when I recognised the russet hair of Lucius sat at one end. Rufus, the young boy with the same flaming hair as his father, sat to his right. The other person sat next to Rufus I did not know. They shared the same auburn hair as Rufus and Lucius, but it was short and cropped to the scalp. He was young, with a smooth round face and the same cool blue eyes.

Finian followed us into his suite and made the introductions. I nodded to Lucius blandly, but smiled at Rufus, who grinned back at me.

"This," Finian paused, taking in the stern look of Lucius's face, "is Jax. Lucius' other child."

The one called Jax stood from his seat and raised a broad hand to shake. I took it timidly, smiling at the young man. His pale blue eyes were feathered with long red lashes and he had the same mattering of freckles that his brother Rufus had. Jax nodded to me after we shook hands and his eyes found Asta behind me. I saw his pupils' contract at the sight of her and suddenly our conversation from earlier made sense.

"Jax, this is Rhona, Roman, her brother, and Elias, their friend." Finian was polite in his introductions, even with the assaulted glare brazenly displayed on Lucius' face. "Asta, you know."

Finian indicated for us to sit and I aimed for the chair in the middle of the table, but a hard hand rested on my back and my head snapped, finding Finian guiding me to the chair to his right. I looked up at him, to the wolfish grin cutting his mouth. He pulled out the chair and I sat down slowly, watching him take the seat at the head of the table next to me. Wood scraped vehemently to my other side and Eli sat down beside me, a lethal calm emanating off of him. I steeled myself, feigning indifference at the two men poised at my left and right. Closing my eyes, I plastered a serene smile on my lips and began unfolding the napkin on my plate. There was a smash of a fist on the tabletop, causing plates and goblets to titter and wobble. All heads whipped to the end of the table, towards Lucius.

"Let's cut the shit, Finian. This is my *daughter,* and *her* name is Jacqueline," Lucius fumed, eyes seething at the young man known as Jax.

"Father!" Jax exclaimed, his face reddening to a bright crimson.

"Well, you are! This facade is ridiculous. You are a woman, not a man! Your name is Jacqueline," he spat, wine spraying.

"Lucius, enough," Finian demanded, his voice low and deadly.

"It is an insult, my Lord. To me and my father before me. And to my very own mother who Jacqueline was named after," Lucius yelled, his lips stained with claret. Rufus flinched beside his father as his eyes darted back and forth. "I will not pretend. I cannot. It is not natural."

I watched the young person known as Jax, cower and lower their head ashamed. I directed my sight across from Jax to Asta, who looked distraught, the nerve in her temple flickering. Stunned, I inspected the reality unravelling before me. I was no one to judge or to be prejudiced against such things and I wouldn't let the anger and opinions of one man dictate my own. I looked at Jax, to his smooth skin and wide eyes.

Jax *had* been Jacqueline, maybe as a child, but now they were Jax. They were no longer the child they once were, no longer the person their parents had wanted them to be, but who they themselves wanted to be. I looked upon the young man before me, remembering my own past self, left behind and discarded because I had grown, because I had become who I needed to be for myself. I saw the look of adoration and pain flash across Asta's face in the following silence, and saw the anger surge for her friend, the person who meant something to her, being spurned and ridiculed, for merely being who they truly were. Anger even swelled within me in that moment and I could smell and sense the magic about to erupt from Asta, as if the Fallow beyond could feel the magic a breadth away, enticing the keys at my wrists to react. I cut in, the building tension becoming suffocating.

"It is nice to make your acquaintance, Jax," I plastered a genuine smile as I spoke to the young man, ignoring his father who stared at me aghast from the end of the table. More silence followed and Jax did not return my smile, as his eyes cut sharply to his father, his freckles darkening against his paling skin. So, I continued, "Finian, you've tempted us all here with a feast this evening, but I must ask, will there be desert?"

Roman choked on his wine, but I ignored him, even as Finian's eyes glittered at me, ready to diffuse the room.

"I've asked for a berry cobbler to be delivered for dessert. The chef is renowned for it and it seemed fitting on such special occasions as this." Finian raised his goblet towards me. "To new friends and allies."

We all toasted, eager to appease the previous topic of conversation and eat. My stomach growled when roasted pheasant and stewed vegetables were brought into the chamber, along with cheeses and chutneys displayed with fruits and fresh bread on wooden boards. My mouth was near salivating as we began to dig in and the conversation turned mutual and polite, although Lucius spoke no more to anyone and disregarded any comments or questions directed at him. Rufus, on the other hand, spoke enough for all of us.

I was full to the brim when I finally set my knife and fork down, resting back on my chair, I watched the people around me finishing their meals. Roman was still devouring a bird's leg, one of four on his plate and I bit down on my bottom lip, hiding the smile at the sight of such a beast. Asta's gold dusted ears glinted in the firelight and I saw a brief look she shared with Jax across the table. I knew at that moment, what they were to each other. I would respectfully wait however, for her to tell me so I could grant her the same grace and promise that she had offered me. Eli was signing with my brother beside me, his plate empty, wine untouched. I felt the closeness of him before I saw Finian lean into me.

"I could have more dessert brought to your chamber later this evening," he whispered, his words barely audible.

The dull ache from earlier, began coursing up my inner thighs and I sucked a tooth, sensing Eli stiffen beside me.

"You'd like that, wouldn't you?" I quietly retorted, not looking at him. I engaged my hands with folding my napkin.

"You have no idea." His quiet chuckle was breathy and unnerving. I couldn't deny the rising heat in my blood, or deny the need building within me.

"Are you always this flirtatious with guests?"

"Only the ones that save my life," he mused, resting his head on his hand. I turned to look at him. "And there was me thinking that minor detail was overlooked."

"That could never be overlooked. You could never be overlooked."

I swallowed, his words eddying in my head. Like lightning the question came into view, the one I had been meaning to ask since our encounter with his delightful father. "I do have a question for you, Finian." I saw the light dance in his eyes and his mouth cocked in an impertinent manner. "Why has your father not called for aid from the other cities and towns across the Continent? Why not ask for help from the Crown? Your King and Queen?"

Sobriety transformed his face and I watched him chew on his answer.

"We used to have forces sent to watch and guard the wall. Other territories would send guards, soldiers, and huntsmen. But no more." I waited, the sudden tension within me building again. "For the past month, no one has come to assist us. My father has written and sent sentries and messengers across the Continent, but none have answered. None have come to our aid. They have forgotten us, or something else is at work here," he finished, his eyes distant.

That was not the first time I had heard those words and felt the ramifications of them. Something was at work here. The seven hearts stabbed, the seven therns murdered. The wards of the Fallow falling. Magic folk both dark and light roaming the land. Someone wanted chaos. Someone wanted the humans focused on the havoc the creatures would ensue across the land. But for what reason? What, other than beasts and creatures, could be within the Fallow? I chewed on my cheek, feeling the pain sharpen my mind as I stewed over the thoughts dipping in and out of my focus.

I looked down the table, apprehension curving my spine. Asta was in conversation quietly with Rufus and Jax, Rufus was grinning with gappy teeth as Jax scooped peas onto a spoon and catapulted them towards his brother.

"It's why she was due to die, you know," Finian whispered and my eyes shot back to him. "Asta, I mean. She helped Jacqueline become Jax. Not through magic, but through trust and building his confidence. They were friends for some time before they were lovers." His metallic eyes dipped to my mouth as he said it and consciously, I licked my lips. "Asta showed Jax how to bind his breasts and cut his hair. Lucius found them one day and demanded my father stone the witch for cursing his daughter."

I turned back to Asta, whose glittering eyes were solely on Jax across the table. They shared glances, brief and subtle, but what they shared was evident enough. There was love there, real and ardent love. A lump caught in my throat as I watched them. They shared smiles but not touches, both afraid of the man glaring from the end of the table. They spoke little to each other, but mainly through and with Rufus, which the young boy was unbeknownst to, admiring the attention.

"Love is love, no matter whose eyes," I voiced, my throat tight. "Asta told me you saw to it that she didn't lose her head for it." Turning back to Finian and finding I was the sole attention of his gaze. The muscle in his jaw flickered and the apple of his throat bobbed.

"Yes. The loss of life over something like that would have been too cruel. Even for my father and he has a history of killing witches for spite."

"And you? Would you kill a witch?" I asked, wanting to end the conversation.

"Only if she tried to kill me first."

That was all I needed to hear as I picked up my goblet and drank the wine deeply.

***

When the dinner had finished, I made my excuses not to stay for more wine. Roman had cordially agreed, to my surprise. Eli, however, was still stone-faced, and agreed to stay with him. My eyes creased as I left them to discuss the past attacks, and how and when the lycan and its spawn hunted. Lucius had left straight after dinner, slamming the door in his wake. Both Asta and Jax had visibly relaxed as soon as the lock finished shuddering and the hinges silenced. They both walked Rufus back to his room, no doubt taking the opportunity to spend time together without the watchful gaze of Jax's prejudiced father. I said a brief goodnight to them both and watched them walk side by side down the hall, admiring the way the light from the lanterns created a halo around them.

Back within my room, I unfastened the basque, relishing in the feel and the release of my ribs. Throwing it on a chair, I sighed and walked around the room, pacing, my skin feeling too tight and my mind restless.

I needed fresh air.

I opened the curtains to find the lead windows sealed tightly shut. The dark night outside was peaceful, and it called to me and to the traveller within.

I exited my room, closing the door quietly behind me, not wanting to alert Finian or my brother of my wanderings. When I got to the base of the staircase, the hall and occupied rooms were still buzzing with activity. People were amid swapping shifts and readying themselves for a night's watch on the wall or perimeter and I walked unchecked and unhindered out the door and into the courtyard, my legs taking me to the back of the estate, to the stables.

Gas lanterns lit the outside of the barns and pens, and the horses inside were feeding and drowsy. I wandered in, spying Balthazar in a stall at the end. There was a welding and farriers' station at the back, with work benches and fresh bales of hay and no one was around to stop me as I grasped a few handfuls of fresh hay and doted on my beast. His ears flipped backwards and forwards as I brought the treat. My small apology for not seeing him today. His velvet lips nipped the straw from my open palms, and I breathed a sigh of relief. The sweet and pungent smell of the animals calmed me, with the cold night kissing away the tackiness of my too-warm skin. I needed to breathe, to think. Away from those silver eyes of Finian. I rested my forehead against a beam, the wood rough against my skin, trying to ground myself.

Too many emotions had ransacked me today, exhausting me completely. I needed to think, not to feel. To understand and decipher the Crone's words of warning but Balthazar nudged my head and I smiled, rubbing his nose, scratching him the way he liked.

There was a scuff of boots at the doorway to the barn and I turned, finding Eli in the doorway, his eyes shadowed. That internal tug pulled at my rib and I could do nothing but clench my fists as I watched him in the entryway, and the night air began billowing curls around his ears and nape. The deep blue tunic he had worn at dinner was now gone, leaving only the black shirt, open at the collar. He stepped closer, moving into the barn, and my heartbeat quickened. I couldn't make out his mood, the light in the stables was too dim to distinguish him, but something in the stance of his walk made my stomach tighten. My breath sharpened when he did finally reach me, with his forehead stern and his eyes intense and binding, as he considered me. I tried to lick my lips, but my mouth was suddenly dry.

"Did you not enjoy Roman and Finian's company?" It was barely a rasp, so I swallowed, trying to clear my throat.

The muscles in Eli's neck flickered as he breathed and though the scars on his neck and jaw were barely visible, I knew they were there as my mind wondered about his personal badges of survival, of life.

He shook his head somewhat and I heard his chest take a deep breath in. My foot moved away from the door to Balthazar's pen and I instinctively walked to Eli, needing to see him more clearly, but my foot landed awkwardly, and I fell. Strong hands grabbed at my waist, stopping me from hitting the floor, as he pulled me up and into him, and my feet found the floor again and my heels ground firmly down.

His hands lingered as I snapped my head up. He smelled of fresh picked rosemary and morning mist, the coax of it still prevalent on his skin. My fingers dug into the black cotton on his forearms, my nails biting the fabric as I held him back. My eyes roamed across his chest, finding the smooth skin at the base of his throat, which met and melted into the silvery skin. The colours were beautiful, and my fingertips itched to touch his scars.

I inhaled, filling my lungs with his smell, needing it, wanting it. I felt his breath on my cheekbone as his nose skimmed my temple and I closed my eyes, briefly allowing the feel of him to spread throughout me, to ingrain it into my bones and blood. I wanted to hold his quiet stillness, to hold it and trap it, allowing it to strengthen me. He had always had that effect on me, even as children. I didn't want to move, or breakaway just yet, afraid of what I might find when I met him, face to face.

Rough and calloused fingers found the tip of my chin and my blood roared in my ears as he titled my face up to his. There was a deep line indented between his thick dark brows as he looked at me with such intensity, that I had to open my mouth for more air. The barn was too quiet, like a void of silence had enveloped us and only us. I could hear my heart beating so hard against my bones that I was afraid it would bruise. I wondered if Eli could hear its frenzied rhythm as I was trapped in his slowly blinking gaze. He was always so unreadable, so distant. But now as I looked into his eyes, I knew resolutely what shone deep within them and I trembled. I'd never seen him look this way before. Never seen his eyes drive and burrow into my soul, the way they were doing right then. Wild. Unending.

The swell of knots tightened in my belly, the fire slowly reheating my flushed skin as he held me and the air between us became taught and crackling as my skin seemed to tighten over my bones.

There was a sheen and burn to his skin, as though he too were inexplicably susceptible to the rising wave beginning to ride me. All I could do and all I could think of doing was getting closer. Our noses grazed each other, my body was still flush against his as heat slivered down further between my legs.

His familiarity felt sure in the lamp light and I closed my eyes, allowing it to soothe me. When I opened my eyes, his pupils contracted and then dilated, and a muscle twitched in his jaw. On instinct I raised my hand, placing it where the tremor had been.

"Eli…" I begin to say, my voice breathy, my throat and mouth starved of aid. Without warning his lips crashed into mine and his body engulfed me, as his stumbling lips became fevered and unrelenting. I stilled, as every nerve caused me to go rigid.

But he pulled away quickly, as my body tensed and I blinked, trying to regain control over the shock. My mind, a rampant riddle of questions, steadily caught up.

He had kissed me.

Clarity crashed over me and a volley of intense want erupted across every nerve, and the heat that had pooled in my belly ignited to an inferno as I launched myself at him. My hands grabbed either side of his face, the feel of his stubble rough against my hands as I pulled his lips down onto my own again.

Suddenly, his arms wrapped around my waist in a vice-like grip, pulling my body flush to his, that I could feel our hearts beating as one. Opening my mouth, he rumbled, low and carnal as I allowed him in, and our tongues danced and consumed one another. Gasping for air, I separated us, only for his hand to reach up and encase my neck, whilst his thumb possessively toyed with the pulse at the stretch of my throat.

His other fingers grappled with the hair at my nape, pulling tightly, exposing my throat to him as his mouth and teeth began licking and nipping at my collar bone. I gulped at the fevered thrill coursing across my skin, at his lips burning me, leaving me yearning. My hands surged up into his hair and I grasped his curls, forcing his mouth to meet mine again, needing the taste of him on my tongue, and like wine, it blazed in my blood. I moaned in submission when his tongue swept in again, claiming me.

We stumbled back and his back hit the far wall of the stable, with him taking the brunt of both of our colliding bodies. My back arched as his lips moved to my jaw again and another breathy moan escaped my lips. His guttural growl vibrated across my collarbone and down the crease of my breasts. He manoeuvred us, until my back was flush with the wall, and he towered over me. We parted, our eyes ablaze as we devoured each other heatedly. Our breathing was laboured, and my hands were itching to touch him more.

I had never felt such a feeling before. Such unrelenting need.

My lips felt bruised and wet, the taste of him compelling me further that I kissed him again, claiming his mouth with another stroke of my tongue across his bottom lip. Every hair on my body stood to attention as his hands brushed over my waist and hips, his fingers occasionally digging into the fabric of my shirt, releasing it from where it was captured in the waist of my trousers. I shuddered, as my whimper escaped, and his teeth grazed my jawline. I could hear words passing over my lips and I realised I was rasping his name, coaxingly. The heat raging at the core of me was escalating to a point where my sense of control was being overruled entirely. I wanted this. I needed this. Release. Escapism. I knew if it went any further it would be trouble.

It would be irreversible.

But my heart overruled my head and I continued, holding Eli's body as close as I could. I raised my leg to wrap around his waist, my back still pinned to the wall, supported. His hands gripped my thigh, holding it, exposing the covered bundled centre point of me. I could feel him, feel the hardness of him, as it pressed tightly against his trousers, restricted. I ground myself against him, against it, knowing exactly what the ache building needed. His mouth withdrew and I opened my fluttering eyes and found his eyes suddenly watchful of me. He was assessing me, his hand lowering my leg to the ground before finally resting it on my cheek. He brushed his nose against mine longingly, his eyes never leaving my own. There was a darkness I had never seen in them as his nostrils flared, his chest rising and falling.

He didn't make any more moves, respectfully trying to calm the fervent lust raging inside of him, I realised. I was nearly mewling against him, needing more of him, not caring about his respect, or my own. Needing to taste him and feel him. Needing him inside me. Thoughts were racing in his mind, I could tell, as his eyes darted across my face, trying to read every detail. His fingers grasping the soft spot of my neck, his fingertips locating my pulse, holding me still, possessive and hungry. It was intoxicating.

I couldn't understand why he was holding back, why we weren't already doing what I wanted to do? But I knew then, as a waterfall of understanding crashed upon me. It was Eli and he was waiting for my consent. Waiting for my confirmation. I rubbed my nose against his chin, sighing heavily as his familiar scent filled my nose, my lungs, and my head.

I knew in that moment I couldn't lie to myself anymore.

"I want this, Eli. I want you," I whispered, reading the flutter of his pulse and the set of his jaw.

His eyes flooded with shock, but changed quickly, eclipsing. His pupils dilated, until the colours I had come to love were near black with lust. Triumph flashed briefly as his mouth surged against mine once again and he groaned. He didn't hold back then as his hands deftly removed his shirt. My own hands stumbled over the toggles and leather laces. I finally freed myself, exposing my chest and breasts, the torchlight flickering over my skin. Pale green and brown bruising dusted my ribs, the bones now mended, as he stood back, taking in the sight of me. I breathed heavily, the prospect of my immediate future causing me to tremble. I swallowed, my throat tightening along with the bundle of nerves between my legs at the way his eyes devoured my flesh, my breasts and my face. It was a funny thing to behold, to see the want and lust riding Eli and myself. Thoughts rode me, wondering if the reasons for Eli becoming distant all this time, was because of this. Because he wanted me, the way I wanted him. I hadn't realised until he had come back, returned with Roman from their travels and he no longer looked like a friend. But something else entirely.

He stepped closer, dropping to his knees before me, whilst his hands pinned my hips against the cold wood, the panelling biting against my spine. His stubbled jaw rubbed against the soft skin at my navel, his nose tracing the line of my stomach and hip bones. Rough fingers reached up to trace my breast, followed by a palm, caressing it, causing my nipples to peak. I arched my back, revelling. His lips trailed down my left hip bone, leaving me weak as his nose dove in-between my legs. His lips and teeth nipped above the pinnacle of my sex, the fabric of my riding trousers suddenly suffocating and uncooperative. His hands left their tenuous teasing of my breast and began unbuttoning. His fingers moved with slow satisfaction as he looked up at me. His eyes were so dark, they were almost black, the warm brown and blue engulfed. I was held captive in that gaze, even as his hands pulled the fabric away from my arse and thighs, until it was ruched around my ankles. His fingers deftly unfastened one of my boots, whipping it off and sliding the tight fabric gathered at my ankle away, freeing one leg entirely.

I was breathing harder now, my heart hammering like a war drum within me. Every possible nerve and sense focused on the fact Eli was between my legs. The core of me ached and pulsed uncomfortably. His palm slowly rode up my thigh, over my navel until it reached my chest again. His hands, a hunter and fighter's callused hands, crept languidly over my breast, leaving me reeling for more.

The ache in my belly and in my bones was tormenting, the need for him wholly primal. I was slick and wet; the want was overriding every physical and mental barrier I had ever constructed. I didn't know what he would do, or what to expect, until his mouth found the lips of my sex and his tongue licked between the crease, down to the very core of me. I rocked, my pelvis bowing, as my back arched, and a loud whimper escaped me.

His hand pinned my hips, the other holding firm on my rump as his tongue continued to taste me, gliding, and concentrating on the bundle of nerves, over and over again. I cried out, as wave upon wave of shattering life flowed over me. He lifted my free leg, tossing it over his shoulder, opening me wide for him. My hands gripped his head, fingers tightly clamping on fistfuls of hair, pushing him further into me. He growled again as another simpering moan bellowed out of me. Every nerve, every sense, was building, raging in me to a cataclysmic symphony of need. There was a cliff which I was reaching as my skin electrified and the small beacon between my legs pulsed. I was nearly reaching it, about to fall over the cliff as it built higher still, my moans becoming pleasurable screams of his name. I was reaching the pinnacle, something I had never experienced before. My previous episodes of sex barely pleasurable or delivering me to such ecstasy. Suddenly the force that had built ricocheted and every nerve went taught as the explosion impacted me. The world blazed as shimmering lights scattered across my vision. My body shook at the impact. He continued to lick, coaxing out further tremors and moans from me as I descended to earth. My hands were still clamped, and my hips dipped as my legs shook, I couldn't take it anymore.

He removed his mouth, standing and gripping my limp heaving body to his, he lifted me around the corner to the farrier's work benches. My arse touched the bench as his lips were upon my mouth again. I tasted myself, tasted my ecstasy on his tongue, and it sent me over the edge and my eyes rolled back as his fingertips skimmed their way up to my throat. He pulled away, his thumb resting on my pulse in that dominating way as he looked down upon me, lustful and bleary eyed. He kissed me again, but it was soft and unhurried. His lips were moulded to my own with supine gentleness.

When the haze began to fade, I was ready, wanting to go further, needing all of him. My hands smoothed down from his jaw, gliding softly over the jagged scars to his chest, moving to his trousers. My trembling fingers began unbuttoning but his strong hands caught mine and halted me. He shook his head, a small smirk playing at the corner of his mouth.

"Why not?" I asked, my voice barely recognisable.

Eli signed, his hands communicating to me *'not here'*.

I raised a curved brow, but he kissed me again and I caught his bottom lip with my teeth and tugged. I wanted him, wanted him inside me, but he shook his head again. Carefully, he raised my calf and slipped my foot through the leg of my trousers, pushing the fabric gently and mindfully over the muscles of my leg. Defeat slowly ebbed its way into me and my cheeks flushed, a little ashamed at my screams and mewls. I jumped down, pulling my trousers up over shaking legs. Eli grabbed my blouse from where I had discarded it and handed it back to me, the pulse of his neck still distinct and the bulge of his trousers catching my eyes. Dressing in my shirt, I pulled it over my head. He was always putting my needs first. My heart warmed and that internal tug twitched. Bracing my hands behind me, I jumped back up onto the bench.

"Eli," I hushed, and his eyes were molten as he looked at me, fully dressed. I reached for him and he came to me, standing between my legs, jaw tense. I wasn't about to be defeated, needing to know and feel him and his own need for myself. "You're not getting away so easily," I teased over his lips as I caught his face and kissed him deeply.

He pulled my hips closer to him and I reached down the space between us. My hand gripped at the large ripple of fabric straining between his legs and stroked down. I watched Eli's eyes shutter as he inhaled sharply through clenched teeth. I was rewarded by his fingers digging into my hips, his cock at the mercy of my hand. There was no room for air between us as we rocked together, my hand moving up and down the fabric, creating friction. Keeping my eyes open, I watched enthralled and empowered as Eli's eyes became wide as my pace hastened, building momentum. His arm locked around my spine, holding me tighter still but I continued. His mouth opened, only air escaping, as I revelled in the sudden pump and throb of him as he released under my hand's movement. His torso shook until I slowed my hand and his hitched breath whooshed out of him entirely. Resting his brow against my own, he closed his eyes, basking in the subsiding feelings.

When his eyes finally opened, he kissed the tip of my nose, the warmth of his breath soothing my cheeks. The crisp night air flitted through the slats of the barn and I realised that sweat coated us both. His arm pulled me off the bench and I slid down his body, until my feet, one booted one not, touched the hay covered floor.

We were still close as we parted. Stepping only breadths apart as we retrieved my discarded boot and Eli helped me put it on. I watched his rough fingers meticulously string up the laces. A curl was plastered to his brow, the shimmer of the strands beckoning me. Timidly I smoothed it away, pushing it back into the other waves. I gulped, watching him as his eyes flicked up to me occasionally.

Would it have been like this? If we had gone through with our betrothal?

The thought stirred something in me as he finished up tying the knot and helped me stand. I could say nothing as his eyes roved my face, assessing for any flicker of doubt. I could tell from the way the crease was prominent on his brow and the way his jaw clenched.

"No regrets, Eli," I whispered, bringing my hand to sooth away the tight muscles of his jaw.

His mouth twitched and a small smile graced his handsome face as his eyes illuminated as he beheld me. He began signing to me and I looked down at the one word he was communicating, *'never'*.

***

We walked back to my room, side by side, our fingertips skimming each other every now and then. My legs were still strained as I walked up the flights of stairs to our landing and hall. The lanterns were now lit fully, and every doorway could be seen in the looming night. My footfall slowed as we approached my door, feeling Eli behind, towering over me.

Would he come into my rooms?

The thought galvanized me. We *had* just started something. This was *something*. My throat grew tight as I peeked behind me, my door handle now in grasping distance. A child crying within the house echoed from above and the hairs on my neck stood to attention. I felt suddenly cold, the heat and rosiness to our passion doused completely. The childlike cries deep in my mind were mirroring that of the child in the distance. My creeping darkness, my shame, crept and slithered across my skin. Screams penetrated the ache of lust and replaced them with clawing guilt. My hand shook as I took the brass door handle, knuckle unnaturally white as I unlocked and opened the door. My lungs shook and a ragged breath escaped. This was not supposed to happen. The memories began their usual taunt, making my skin crawl and stomach turn. My mind brought back the smell of vile breath and my thighs felt rough hands. The flesh memories caused me to nearly cry out.

Eli's hand lightly touched my shoulder and I jumped, my body rigid and somewhere else. I couldn't turn, couldn't move my feet as his brow rested against the back of my head. The shadow of him felt overbearing, my shadows dispelling everything from me. He sighed as his strong hands encircled my waist. My door was still open, my feet unmoving at the threshold. There was a shift of fabric at my waist and I forced down the lump in my throat, slowly moving my head to see what it was.

Eli's hands were signing to me. My eyes burned, tears beginning to prickle as I watched his long, agile fingers speak to me. *'You need your sleep. I will leave you.'*

Every muscle was locked as the fear creeped in. My sanity and present self were expelled to the back of my mind, screaming and beating against the body frozen by the memories that took hold. I felt Eli pull away, his final breath, deep and long. Still I couldn't move. Hot tears spilled, tears for Eli and tears for myself. From the corner of my eye I saw him retreating, head down, cast in deepest shadow. I heard the sharp click and shut of a door and the silent sob escaped in a sour gurgle as my body unlocked and I flew into my room, to the awaiting bed and let the tidal wave of self-loathing and disgrace ride me. I was that child once again, balling and whimpering into the night alone.

Chapter 36

Hammering suddenly appeared in the recesses of my dreams. The pounding and chorus of voices became louder and near deafening as I rolled and tried to shield myself in the cotton covers of the bed. Wood banged and shuddered. I began to drift up from the depths of past faces, until a bleary eye peaked open. The door to my room burst open, crashing against plaster and stone. I scrambled, the faces fading from my vision as Roman charged into the room, accompanied by Eli.

"Get dressed, they're under attack!" My brother's bellow shook the sleep from me.

I heard it then, clear as day; a strange bell was being struck somewhere in the grounds. People were screaming, and the corridor outside appeared to be filled with women and children moving in haste. I forced my legs to stand, not caring about being in nothing but a night shirt. The sounds and wide eyes of my brother and Eli shocked me like icy water. I ran to the changing room, donning my trousers, shirt and coat. I weaved the laces of my boots hurriedly, stumbling over the rivets of metal needed to secure the leather. Grabbing my hunting knife, I strapped it to my thigh. I then slipped my dagger in the calf of my boot and turned to see my brother watching me, eyes guarded.

He bore several hunting knives, a sword, his crossbow and shaft of arrows. Eli had his own crossbow, strapped to his back, his sharp, curved cutlass sheathed at his waist and his long staff in his right hand.

Both men were fully dressed and armed to the teeth, brows dusted with sweat and eyes keenly searching the window and night beyond.

"Those two won't do. These are beasts, remember!" Roman scolded, eyeing my meagre weapons.

Eli stepped forward, unfastening his cutlass. The curved blade was longer than my forearm and sharpened to perfection. It was attached to an old belt, which he circled around my waist. I felt him tense in my space and my stomach dropped, acid burning my throat. His fingers made quick work of the buckle as he notched the brass. I traced his hair and nose with my eyes as he worked on me, my hands eager to reach out and let him know I was well now. That I would be better one day. That it hadn't been him, that had made me turn into a shell in the hallway. That it hadn't been what we'd done, but something else.

Men shouting across the grounds rumbled through the thin, paned glass of my room. Something whipped and cracked outside, and we all ran to the window. A ballista had been cranked and released. The air split and sang as the bolt soared into the night towards the Fallow.

"We need to move now! We need to find Finian," Roman said, turning and running out the door.

I had no time to digest how Eli hadn't touched me, how his finger had worked swiftly to fasten the belt without a hint of contact. Not even a look. I followed, with Eli at my back, and we ran down the corridor towards the flurry of screaming and crying families running into the house from the grounds. The clock in the hall clanged two in the morning and I saw Rufus standing on a plinth, directing the frantic families into the rooms and up the stairs. To hide in the safety of the house.

Men and women, some in makeshift armour, were sprinting with swords and long bows to the wall. Bonfires were coming to life across the sleepy, misted expanse of the estate. The flames roared and chased away the night, highlighting the length of the manor and land. In the distance, I heard the distinct voice of Finian, commanding his men that were stationed on top of the wall. Logs were loaded and fires lit in caged burners across the high stone barricade, the light dancing against the dark sphere above us. I stopped, my breath caught at the sight of the starless sky above, the clouds billowing above promising storms and wretched weather.

"Rhona!" My name being called, made me spin. Asta was running towards me, her eyes frantic.

"Asta, is everyone inside safe?"

"Nearly," she huffed. "I need to seal the door. Roman, Eli - Finian needs you on the wall. Rhona, come with me," she commanded as her hand grabbed at my wrist, pulling me to follow her.

"No, Rhona stays with us," Roman snarled, lunging for me.

"She has magic, like me. She can help me with the shields and use the forest. I will protect her." Asta was panting, as her fingers dug painfully into my palm. Roman's teeth snapped together.

"I'll be safe, Roman. I'll find you both soon," I said, turning to follow Asta.

Eli stepped forward then, his hand reaching to catch my fingers and I stopped, twisting to see his eyes pleading with me. My lungs burned, as though airless at that look and I shook Asta off, walking the distance back to Eli and grabbed his face with both hands. I kissed him, our mouths crashing once again. His arms encircled me, the muscles crushing me to him. It felt like the world had slowed and the havoc surrounding us had eased into nothingness in that second. We parted quickly and I rested my brow against his, showing no fear as I gazed into his worried eyes.

"I will be safe," I whispered and turned, running with Asta back to the entryway of the estate house, aware of Roman's wide-eyed, shocked face. My thigh muscles barked as my legs worked forward. The crowd was thinning, and a group of armed guards were shuffling around the doors, waiting for the last stragglers to pass over the threshold, into the safety of the house.

"Do I want to know?" Asta asked, her eyes scanning the fleeing people. She was still wearing her black dress, her skin dusted with the faintest gold.

"Now is not the time," I hissed, watching the last family barrel through the doorway. The guards began hauling the large oak doors shut. Everything groaned as the hefty wood closed together with a shudder and the bulky locking bar slid into place. The guards stumbled back, as Asta moved closer to the studded, arched entrance.

There was a roar and a scream at the back of the estate and the guards around us began drawing their swords, the shrill and scrape of metal jarring my teeth. I did the same, unleashing Eli's cutlass from his curved leather sheath and the cold weight of it in my hands felt strange and yet comforting. Something crashed in the distance behind the house as we heard the volley of another bolt being fired. Screams sounded out from within the estate and I flinched. Men called out across the ground and then Finian's bellowing voice echoed over to us from the wall.

"Asta, what are you-" My words caught in my throat as the witch before me twisted to face me. It was not the woman I had come to know these past few days. Her eyes were wholly white, the silver iris and glow gone. Her umber skin glistened in the night and her lips moved so fast I couldn't make out what language she was speaking, as a cruel smile played on her mouth at seeing the horror on my face.

Her arms swirled in the air as her body ducked and writhed. Her spine stretched and straightened as her arms came down in an arc above her head, her lips still moving rapidly. My fingernails caught the wrap of the hilt of the cutlass, as I gripped the weapon tighter in my hand, fixated by the woman before me.

"Move behind me, Rhona," she rasped, her resonant voice now edged with power.

I watched as her elegant fingers snapped and struck at the air, pulling to life gold and silver threads. The unearthly cords glistened in the night above her, fading into the canopy of cloud as her hands worked and weaved. The strands began entwining into an intricate display of light and a pattern began building, wider and higher as her fingers snatched and caught more and more luminous ribbons from the nothingness of night sky. I watched, stunned and in awe, as the air began to crackle and sear with her magic.

Her voice rose and her words became a deafening hum, unintelligible and not of this world. She placed a foot behind her, arching her back at the creation growing and then, with a whipping snap of her wrist, she sent the lustrous weave hurtling towards the closed oak doors.

The scream about to escape me died in my throat and I heard the guards behind me gasp and sputter as the pattern scorched the doors, the smell of singed wood filling the air.

"Test it!" Asta roared, gasping. Her voice had returned to its usual husky manner and I was glad for it. Her skin and cheeks were glistening with sweat and her metallic eyes had restored themselves, the ghostly white now gone. A guard beside me drew his bow, the string creaking and let an arrow fly. There was a blaring burst of noise as the arrow hit a glittering wall, bouncing off the wood unmarked.

It was a barrier.

I choked, completely impressed at the magic, even if it terrified me.

"You, there, gather more men and protect the entryway. You three, follow me and Rhona to the wall!" Asta ordered and again I was in awe of her, as she charged through the guards and gathered fighters. The witch commanded meagre men like a queen. I smiled wickedly and followed her. "You can tell me about what I just witnessed later," she mused to me as I reached her side.

"As long as your eyes don't do that thing again," I warned, but the smile was still on my lips.

We ran to the rampart, the crescendo of roars and guttural howls beyond the wall made my skin turn cold as we did. I had fought but never against creatures. Never beasts. Adrenaline pumped through me, my heart cantering at full speed as we made our way through the armed men and women to the wall.

"How many turned?" Asta called above, reaching a rickety wooden ladder leading up onto the barricade.

"We believe nine. Possibly more. And other creatures." The voice was familiar, and I tried to place it as my hands slipped on the wooden steps I was climbing.

Strong hands gripped underneath my armpits and hauled me up. It was Jax. He steadied me on the wall and turned to help Asta up. I noted the wicked-looking axe strapped across his agile back and a long sword strapped to his waist. It dawned on me then that Jax was strong. That he had fought and trained. Trained and pursued who he was supposed to be. I smiled weakly at him, as a lump formed in my throat, at the thought of what I had been doing all this time, whilst this person had struggled and fought to become who he was born to be. To become Jax.

"What others?" Asta heaved, as she ripped the fabric of her skirt, freeing her legs for better mobility.

"A skineth and wood spector," Jax replied, eyes wary. They shared a knowing look as Jax reached behind him to the axe on his back and unclipped it. His hands and knuckles cracked around the belly of the handle.

My blood ran cold as I readjusted the cutlass in my hands, the handle biting into the flesh of my palm. Asta and Jax showed such strength, such composure, as they looked at each other and I wondered if they felt the same pitiful fear that was within me.

"Where's Finian?" I asked as another bolt ripped through the air nearest us.

Jax pointed in the distance, to the adjacent wall, and I saw Finian and his men, arrows cocked, following an unseen creature on the other side of the wall. My heart sank as I squinted, seeing Eli and Roman's forms in the night, crossbows searching for prey.

"Do you know how to use that?" Jax asked, eyeing the sword in my hands. The red head was pale in the firelight, his stark, blue eyes wide.

"She doesn't need to," Asta affirmed as she cast a glance over the lip of the wall. Her hands then gripped my upper arms, her face fierce. "Rhona, you need to ask the Fallow for help."

"But I don't know how. It incapacitated me last time. I don't know what I need to do." I sounded weak, feeble, and it turned my stomach.

"You do know. Remember what I told you, about our magic. There is always a price. Always. It will eat away at your own strength if you do not take from something else." Her eyes were insistent.

I remembered our conversation. Remembered her telling me about the pillars of magic, about the need and use of magic and what it takes from the wielder. Blood magic for blood. Matter for matter. I never asked what weaving took from her. Or about the world in which she picked and plucked the threads. My eyes roved over her; she was flawless and strong. Her magic used great power, the shield at the entryway was evidence of that. But what did she draw from?

"Rhona?" She shook me, bringing me back from the depths of thought.

"Yes, I will try."

"Good."

There was a scrape of talons against stone and blood curdling snarl ripped through the air near to us. A turned began clawing its way up the wall a hundred yards from us. I could see it clearly now, the monster. It wasn't a wolf or a man, but something deformed and in-between. It was nearly hairless, its torso and long limbs grey and muscled. Its face was riveted, jowls and snout snarling. The air sang with thirty arrows shot from the other men and women stationed on the wall and they hit their mark. The creature howled and wheezed, its claws sparking against the stone. Acid rose in my throat as I watched the creature writhe in pain. Black seeped from the beast's maw, its human-like brown eyes growing dark as its bloodied body, spotted with so many arrows, fell forty feet to the forest flow below. I followed its fall, craning my neck and saw it transform back to man. The body was consumed by the shadow of the forest.

A scream sounded behind us and I spun, fear gripping me. In the darkness something jumped, a dark body flew high over the wall. It landed beside the blazing fire, the flames illuminating the protruding bones and leathery, meshed hide of the skineth. Its long, bone claws hung to its unnaturally bent knees as it prowled the ground. Fighters and guards were running towards it. The skineth's gaping mouth hosted rotten fangs, and its pointed ears rose like horns atop its domed head. Finian spied the creature and began shooting down the ladder and steps to the ground below.

I watched in horror as the creature easily disembowelled two men, its sword-like nails cutting through flesh as the men charged. Asta beside me gasped, her eyes blazing at the sight of the beast. Men cried out to our left as another turned crawled up and breached the wall. The fanged creature slunk over the stone, arrows flying and skimming its scaly skin. Jax ran forwards, axe drawn and arching high above his head. Several arrows shot through the air, one skimming the flaying fabric of Jax's shirt, as he brought the axe down upon the creature's shoulder.

The beast whined, head and jaws snapping at Jax as he moved with the beast out of reach. Through clenched teeth, Asta began spitting an array of words, pulling and plucking red wefts from the air around her.

More arrows flew, hitting and sinking deep into the flesh and fur of the creature. Blood oozed from the wounds but Jax still skirted, unable to dislodge the axe from where it was embedded in bone. The creature wasn't going down.

I heard Asta gush and hiss, and her hands ripped the air in front of her. The red ribbons of glistening thread spun like a knife, cutting through the air towards the beast. The creature's head was torn off its shoulders, falling to the ground, acrid blood gushing and spraying. She spun around to face me then, blood spatter on her face and eyes glowing white.

"Do something!" she screamed.

My mouth moved, unable to form words as she gave me a wretched look. They moved away from me, up the wall to where the archers and fighters were making their way down to the fray of the fighting. The skineth was circling a group of guards, Finian at the centre. Its horrific claws tore up the ground in which they dug and scraped.

I looked ahead, to the wall opposite. Roman and Eli were battling as I rotated, and my stomach dropped, fear and wrath igniting my blood. It was the awakening I needed as another bellowing roar sounded below me. Facing the forest and Fallow beyond, I ripped up the sleeves of my coat, exposing my arms and wrists to the icy night. The keys began to gleam ominously as my mind battled with what to ask. This gift was something I needed to learn and understand, but I played to my strengths and to what I already knew.

Lights began to spark and ignite across the shadowed forest beyond and suddenly thousands of fireflies, fire nymphs and luna moths soared out of the forest and into the night. They surged and splayed across the sky, lighting the ground below in a watery pale light, bettering the vision of the fighters and people battling the creatures penetrating the walls and grounds. I saw six turned clawing their way across the grounds and the skineth mauling the guards surrounding it.

I swung around, running as fast as I could along the wall. My legs moved under me, pushing and fighting to be faster. The keys grew warm at my wrists as a rippling wind coaxed and moved me further. I jumped and twisted, moving along the wall around fighters and archers still defending against the creatures lurking below. There were so many. More than nine. More than twenty. The chorus of howls billowed up the stone and across the night sky. Running past Asta and Jax, I swerved them, their calls and shouts trailing behind me.

I headed towards the wall, where the forest had crept and rebuilt the stone, and soon stumbled, my feet landing awkwardly. I fell forwards but pulled my body in tight and rolled. The landing bruised my spine and neck, but I forced every bit of strength into the muscles of my legs as I whipped back up and pushed forward and onwards. Now was not the time for weakness and I wasn't weak, not with these keys, not with this gift.

I was nearing the vines and roots, which I had moulded to the wall to fix the weakened break. The glittering forest folk highlighted the pathway above me. The blues, whites and greens were dazzling and ethereal. A ladder was perched before the drop, near the newly grown barricade, and I clambered down it, falling the last six steps to the cold ground below. There weren't many fighters here, the majority still battling the skineth, in the centre of the grounds. Ropes had been slung and harpooned over the monstrous creature. Its dead victims littered the floor around it, their blood black and glistening under the dark sky. Eli was running towards Finian and his men whilst Roman held up a man, both of them hobbling towards the Lord.

I rounded on the forest; on the growth I had conjured the day previous. The bands of dark magic at my wrists bloomed to life and the blue light seeped from my skin, and like a great wave of splintered wood and ivy vines, the forest answered my call. It swept up and over the wall, seeking out and creeping across the slaughtered to the beasts lurking, striking them down, ensnaring them.

I heard Asta scream my name and saw her running full pelt atop the wall. One of the turned had crept over near me, it's dark mottled skin, splattered with unknown blood. Gold shining eyes homed in on me as it prowled closer, shredding the ground under long paws and claws.

Come to me, I beckoned in my mind, the pulse of magic heating my blood. The keys blazed as the turned lunged. Vines whipped and struck, ensnaring the creature, gripping its legs and hide. It whimpered, its jaw gnashing at the air in front of me, causing my hair to ripple. There was a crippling crack as the creeping arms writhed around the beast, engulfing it and snapping its spine. The vines closed about its body and pulled it through the barricade of roots and foliage, into the forest beyond. As it was devoured by the leaves and darkness, I saw its distended paw transform into a limp fist. These creatures were human, could potentially be human again. The thought rotted some of the anger in me, replacing it with pity.

A roar echoed behind me, as my bedraggled hair was blown around me by some mighty breath. Asta screamed my name again in the distance, and the sound churned my stomach, my blood pumping to the warning bell. I twisted to the left in time to escape the groping branched arm, hammering down to the ground. Spinning on an uneven footing, I beheld my attacker. The wood spector stood before me. I gasped, mouth wide at the mythical being, unable to take my eyes off it.

It was a Fallow being, a creature of legend, made from wood but animated and alive. Its bark skin and long limbs steered towards me again, as its dark black eyes narrowed. It swung its trunk like arms, towering over me, ready to strike downwards.

The keys flared and I raised my arms, readying the flora and vines to pull me out of the way. But the being stopped, mid strike. Its arm was up and black eyes bright, as the blue glare of the keys shimmered across its face. Its husk of a mouth moved, and a whirring groan escaped as it beheld the keys, beheld me. Its arm lowered, face registering. Stunned, I watched the creature, watched its dappled and cragged face change in understanding. It was like the Knarrock troll. Heart hammering my mind finally caught up.

"Help the people against the skineth, now." I pointed my finger, my voice rough and raw from my screaming command.

The creature bowed its head, the joints and limbs creaking like that of an ancient ash tree. It whirled, and began charging into the fight, the ground shaking with every great step. I ran to follow, needing to protect the creature under my charge, feeling it through the keys, like a second consciousness. We ran towards the skineth and the men struggling to contain the ferocious creature. I neared the foul beast, seeing its talons cutting and shearing the ropes and nets being thrown.

Roman and Eli were there, defending blow after blow of the skineth's claws, with Finian and his men beside them. The skineth screeched a blood-chilling yowl as a sword finally pierced its hide.

A roar rumbled ominously in the night, deeper and darker than the creatures about us. It was followed by a chorus of pitiful moans and howls from the turned, making my blood run cold in understanding. The lycan.

"Roman, move!" I yelled, my voice hoarse as I barrelled into Finian and Daven, forcing both men out the way of the wood spector as it charged. Its arms reached and dove for the skineth. Roman spun, eyes wide and dodged it in time. The wood spector's bark-covered arms made contact, embedding, and gripping the foul creature by the chest. Its arms extended and grew in length, forcing the creature out of the fray and high above us. The skineth squirmed and snapped, shrieking.

"Do not touch the wood spector," I bellowed, eyeing the men and their weapons about us. "It is our ally."

Men stumbled back, gasping and clutching at wounds. Roman was gaping from the ground, eyeing the captured beast dangling above the wood spector. The creature of timber and bark faced me, in waiting.

"Take it *far* away from here!" I commanded through gritted teeth.

The spector obeyed, walking the monster, thrashing high above, over the wall and into the depths of the forest beyond. There was another deafening howl in the night, and I flinched, the sound louder and closer than before. The Crone's words echoed in my mind, turning my blood icy.

"Where the fuck is it?" Roman spat blood on the ground beside me and I whirled, looking for Eli. I couldn't see him in the fray, couldn't see his form or eyes searching for us. Panic sickened my stomach and made my mouth go dry. I looked up to the sky above, at the glittering array of lights. Clenching my teeth, the sheer terror morphing me into something else. I raised my arms, the command in my mind. The lights blazed brighter, glaring down and lighting the ground all around us. Finian shielded his eyes as he staggered towards me. His arm was bleeding and there was a gash atop his brow, which wept down his face. His eyes searched the mass of fighters.

"Where is Lucius?" he asked, frantically.

"My Lord," Lucius' voice was a spluttering rasp from the floor.

My hand whipped up to my mouth at the bloodied sight of his chest, ripped open. The cavity and bones of his ribs glistened under the bright pale light above. Finian ran and skidded, landing on bent knees next to his man. Blood pulsed and oozed in a puddle around him. My stomach was in my throat, ready to overcome my mouth as I began to move towards the man, pale and panting gurgled breaths.

Finian gripped Lucius' hand, their fingers clasped tightly as the lights above dimmed. Exhaustion was overcoming me and every muscle seemed to scream with fatigue. I stumbled, my legs trudging over the blood-soaked floor. We were near the wall of flora and fauna I had conjured, and I knew what I needed to do.

I turned to my brother, my voice weak. "Find Eli, I need to…" But I didn't continue as I saw him, saw Eli's staff flashing high in an arc in the distance. He was accompanied by two other guards, all fighting a turned. "Roman, go to him," I fretted, my throat aching.

My knees gave way, and I planted my hand into the blood-soaked earth. Roman was running towards Eli as I heaved a great breath, letting it fill the depth of my lungs with tainted air.

There was always a price, as Asta said. Always a need for payment in energy, blood or matter. But this wasn't witch magic. This was something different. My nails dug deep into the earth and I closed my eyes. I pulled what I needed from the Fallow. The keys glowed stark against my skin, the blue hues shimmering brightly as a pulse of life forked and veined towards me. Veins of essence from the heart of the Fallow.

"What the fuck?" men behind me murmured.

I heard the outcries and the shallow gasps of Lucius as he took his last breaths. But I focused, shutting out the onslaught of noise and pain, closing off the emotion and exhaustion, something I had come to do on instinct over the years. White glowing seams and vessels erupted across the gore covered floor. The frigidity within me melted, as my legs and arms felt full and empowered. My mind fixated and sharpened, the dullness that had descended was obliterated, as every sense was overwrought with life once more. My lungs filled with the crisp night air and my tongue tasted the blood and festering bodies around me. Releasing the ground, I closed my eyes as the bands of blue light diminished.

"Rhona! Please, please heal him."

It was Finian, his voice anguished. My legs lifted me up as though weightless. I spun on nimble toes and went the short distance to him, my mind already readying myself. My knees knelt in Lucius' blood, still warm on the frosted earth. I looked upon the man, at his white cheeks and lips. His mouth was smeared with his blood and his eyes searched the heavens and lights above, glassy and not in this world.

"I can try, Finian," I whispered, unable to take my eyes from the gaping wound.

I did what I thought I knew to do, my mind and thoughts asking the same of the Fallow. I dug my fingers into the earth again, clawing the cold and blood under my fingernails. I rested my other hand over Lucius's chest, feeling the lifeless heart beneath no longer beating.

My lips trembled. "Finian, I don't think-"

"Just try, please! He was like a father to me." His bereft words clung to me as I tried to pull the energy from the Fallow, aware there was no heart to animate, no mind to reconnect. The light had completely faded from Lucius' blue eyes and my chest heaved back the sob that wanted to escape. I tried nonetheless, picturing the white veins, pulsing life towards me and into Lucius.

But nothing happened. The Fallow did not answer, did not obey. I kept trying, my voice aching as I whined, calling upon anyone who would listen above and around me, until I was screaming. Screaming for the forest to obey. But still nothing happened.

"Finian, I'm sorry." The words were hoarse on my tongue and teeth, my throat tight and stricken. Finian sniffed, his forehead pressed against the man dead in front of us and I saw his shoulders shudder as a silent sob rocked him.

I heard the earth tear and shudder beneath me. Heard the hollers and terrified shouts of the men and women around us as more turned grappled over the walls, landing as men and women. Their beast forms vanished, leaving only the humans remaining, barely clothed and bearing down on us. Their war cries deafened my ears as I scrambled back, my gut clenching. I needed my brother and Eli. My eyes searched the crowd, the fleeing and injured blundering and running away. Familiar eyes locked upon me in the blur of movement, as Roman and Eli came running towards us, bloodied and armed. Relief washed over me, my eyes watering at the sight of them safe and unharmed.

Another bloodcurdling roar bellowed as more screams rang out into the night. There was a sound like stone being cleaved in two, like blades against flint and we all whirled at the new creature who descended over the far wall.

Footsteps sounded behind me as I looked at the beast in horror. The lycan had come. It was here. This creature before us was more like a wolf than its spawn. Its long pale fur stuck out on its haunches and in divots down its spine. Its long arms and legs pounded the ground with formidable claws, and it had a tail which whipped to and fro. Lamp-like eyes darted about the place, one decorated with a grey slash of scarring, as its white lips rippled and snarled, exposing slate-like teeth. Something twisted in the depth of me at the lycan's eyes.

"Mother above," Roman exhaled.

Nothing in my life had prepared me for such a thing. A creature of nightmares.

Its spawn began writhing around it, their joints and limbs changing and elongating back into those unnatural beasts like before. Every thought eddied from my head as I looked upon the lycan, completely frozen. Its eyes, those yellow eyes, haunted and grasped at something in the back of my memory. I bit down on my trembling lip.

"What do we do?" Asta's plea rang out somewhere behind me and I turned in a haze, finding myself surrounded by my friends and the people I had come to know these past few days.

"We fight," Finian spat, crimson-stained teeth bared. He was vibrating with wrath, glaring at the creature. His fists tightened on the hilt of his sword, his knuckles, taught and bloody. I heard Daven and Rion do the same, heard the familiar locking and clicks of their crossbows, ready to shoot. I saw Roman unsheathe another blade, as Eli stamped the cane of his staff deep into the ground. My heart shuttered, hands going numb, as Roman lifted his fist to his mouth, his bearded lips kissing the silver ring on his finger. Our mother's ring.

"We won't survive, there are too many!" It was Daven, straining his bow string and nocking another arrow, eyes trained on the lycan.

"Asta, what do we do?" I whispered, eyes burning.

"Pray to my grandmother, pray we survive this," she croaked back. Jax was beside her, axe raised and face streaked with dried blood. I saw Asta's silver eyes meet the bright blue of Jax's and the longing in that stare they shared. The longing for a future which was now uncertain, the things I had merely glimpsed, now diminishing. Her metallic eyes locked with my own and I couldn't stop the stray tear that fell. I nodded to the witch, bringing my fingers up in a salute worthy of any friend and of the woman who was owed so much more than what this world had dealt her so far. She blinked and bowed her head lightly to me. Her elegant dark fingers began plucking golden threads from the nothingness about us, the air sizzling and sparking with magic. Anger erupted within me, anger for all who were around me. Hate and anger for the cards we had been dealt, for the time we had all been fighting. For life, for love and acceptance. My eyes darted from all of them. From Roman, to Eli. My eyes strayed and connected with Eli's longer than my heart could take and I had to break away, blinking away the haze of tears that threatened to burn and blur my eyes. The fire of emotions turned vicious in my veins. I felt the wrath with new unadulterated passion. I had dragged my brother and Eli into this. They had come, out of a need to protect me. I had stolen their futures from them. The way I had stolen my mother's future, long ago. The thoughts burned and scorched deep within me, turning what was once soft to stone, what was once sweet to acid. We all deserved so much more.

Warmth flushed at the bones on my chest, as my breaths heaved furiously. Silver caught my eye, shining in a flash under my shirt, from the sky of hazy beings.

My fingers stumbled, as I quickly sheathed Eli's cutlass and grappled for the chain around my neck, remembering what Mutza had told me. I enclosed my fist around it, calling the Crone and the Maiden, the entities who had gotten me and my family into this mess. They had done nothing but play games with cryptic words and death sentences and had done nothing but allow the Fallow to fall and these creatures to create chaos.

I allied every spiteful thought in my head, every curse of rage and frustration, beckoning them to help and aid us. I called for them to do something, anything, even if it meant the inevitable.

Yellow eyes locked upon me and the keys etched into my skin glowed again. The flush and flow of fever building in my fingertips was creeping all the way to my elbows. In the depths of my skull, I was screaming.

The turned all began to attack, lunging forward at the remaining people standing and defending. The lycan still held my gaze as terror slithered its way up my spine, but I ground my teeth, digging my heels into the earth, my fists clenched, as a scream echoed from my throat. A turned jumped above us and Rion and Daven shot arrows, whilst Finian's blade sliced its under belly. Red rain showered down, hot and putrid. I heard Eli grunt as another turned snapped, teeth gouging the wood of his staff held in its mottled jaw. Vines rushed and showered debris around us as they hurtled up into the sky, like tentacles of thorns and bracken. My mind whirled, knowing exactly what pain I wanted to inflict. The vines descended, hurtling down to the ground, aiming for the creature focused on *my* Eli. I captured the beast and a roar ripped from Roman as he brought his sword down on the creature's neck, severing its head from its shoulders, gore spraying everywhere. I did not take heed of the men falling around us, turning back into the mortals they once were, now dead. Asta's fingertips began to glow, the threads gathered, creating a golden cage of light which she aimed at the stalking lycan, coming towards us. I inhaled sharply, urging the vines to rip and gauge the new beast, as the glittering confine hurtled towards it. The creature dodged, jumping over the vines and razor thorns that were snatching to ensnare it. It dodged the magic barricade and prison, which trapped two other turned. The lycan continued to prowl towards us, its spawn rallying more viciously with every strike. Heaving a great breath, I tasted blood in my mouth; blood from the magic and from my teeth gnashing together in credence.

 I slammed my fist to the ground, the idea coming instinctively. The very earth opened and cracked, the wintered surface gouged apart. Roots snaked and snatched from the depths of the crevice of mud and stone. The flora snares tackled the turned left and right. Grim satisfaction blossomed in me at seeing the magic break the creatures. My vision blurred under the frothy glow from above, but my heart stopped when Asta gasped and Jax shouted out. A turned had tackled Asta to the maroon-spattered floor, its talons dredged up the earth about her in a shower of mud and grit, as she held it back with all her might. My heart stopped as its grey, fleshy maw aimed for her exposed throat and I ran, screaming, for her. I unsheathed the cutlass and brought it down atop the thing, with every ounce of strength I possessed in my arms and chest. The blade sliced deep and cleanly through the beast's exposed neck, and hot blood spurted over me, baptising me in death. I relished the feel of it, as that cold creature within me came closer to the surface with each passing minute. I unhooked my blade and drove it into another beast, not caring how and why.

 There was a crack like thunder that ripped through clouds, and the Crone appeared in the midst of the carnage, followed by the Maiden.

Chapter 37

"Grandmother, help us!" Asta screamed at the Crone.

The Crone's veil vanished in a wisp of black smoke and her blackened gnarled fingers began weaving in the night. Turned, fell, and crumpled around us as black glittering threads whipped out. Shadows zipped and zoomed from her fingers as she worked. I saw the Maiden bare her teeth, taking in the chaos about her, eyes wide and manic.

A thin-limbed turned rushed towards Finian, who had his back turned as he battled another beast with Rion. Both men were dealing deadly blows, but Finian hadn't begun to react to the creature nearing him, its claws extended, mouth ready to devour. I ran, bending low, my nail tearing up the earth to my side as the keys flared to life again with a blinding glow. The ground rumbled as the turned galloped into a sinkhole, the earth and snowy moss consuming it whole. I heard a shriek so shrill and penetrating that I winced; the Maiden had screamed frantically. I spun, eyes squinting trying to gauge what else was happening. I saw the entity, the Maiden, glaring at me, eyes rapacious on the magical binds illuminated on my skin. More turned began attacking, narrowing in on us.

I got to Finian as another beast lunged and forced him to the ground and rolled us out the way of its thrashing teeth. Finian's blade shot past me, burying deep into the chest of it, as it fell atop us. More blood and acrid liquid spilled upon my back as I let loose a frenzied scream through gritted teeth. My knees barked as I forced myself up, eyes skimming all around us. The Crone was weaving spell after spell, with Asta next to her, my friend's eyes wholly white. Both witches conjured wefts and threads to combat the turned that were moving in. There must have been fifty, all controlled and amenable to the great creature prowling just out of reach. The lycan was snapping its jowls, its eyes darting to something I could not see.

Now was my chance to try and end it, to try and stop what had started. I wrestled with the cutlass, my instrument of death. The keys flared to life as fire coursed through my veins.

A hand grabbed me, spinning me round forcefully. Silver eyes searched mine, as his equally silver hair brushed my forehead as his breath soaked my stained skin.

"You can't kill that thing alone!" he growled. His cut and bloodied face was swelling. I tried shaking him off, but his grip held firm, eyes insistent.

"Let me go, Finian!"

But his eyes went round, the black pupil shrinking. My body reacted, the knowing tug from within propelling me. Time slowed as my heartbeat pulsed in my ears. I spun, seeing the world in crystal clarity. I saw the swords arc and slash, and the hairless turned lurching and pouncing on the remaining men and women fighting with us. My brother and Eli were fighting back to back with Jax, every blow they delivered, laboured. Asta and the Crone's magic surged like a wave across the creature barrelling forward. Then the lycan leapt high into the air, towards me. Its yellow eyes were focused on my face, as the lights above shone every detail across the glossy lens of its gaze.

My mother's soft voice called to me, as Finian's hands failed to push me free from the death that awaited. She called to me, called my name so softly, like a waking whisper. I swallowed, closing my eyes.

The air whooshed out of my lungs as my ribs cracked. The force of the hit shook me to my very core. I fell, the weight of the creature falling to the frosted ground, splattered with drying blood.

His scent hit me before my eyes opened, and terror so earth-shattering rocked me as I saw Eli protecting me. He had run and pushed me out of the way, I realised, as the lycan's teeth and jaw locked into his exposed back and shoulder.

I screamed as Eli's blood gushed. He held me firm, protecting me from the beast assaulting him. Eli's name ripped from my lips as he gurgled and groaned, his face in shocked agony. Something split the night, the sound ripping the air like a whip striking. The lycan fell as a bolt from a ballista, pierced its pale side, splitting its fur and breaking its ribs. The creature let loose a high-pitched whine, as its yellow eyes searched the grounds, and its legs collapsed and faltered underneath its hulking form.

Its gaze locked on someone in the distance, a person in shadow. A pale hand stretched and pointed to the Fallow and the lycan moaned once more, cowering. It bolted away, it's spawn and children cowering before they retreated back into the darkness from which they came.

Dazed, I watched the last of the creatures vault the walls until the sound of Eli's strangled gasps brought me back to the here and now. I screamed his name, my lips trembling as I tried to gently move and lower him to the ground. The fabric of his coat was hacked and shredded. Blood and flesh covered it and I saw the bone of his shoulder blade peeking through as I assessed his wounds with bleary eyes.

He was too pale, the blood pooling behind him like a dark halo about his head. Tears burned and fell uncontrollably, as I feebly smoothed and mopped the curls away from his brow. Roman skidded towards us, my brother frantic as he took in the blood merging in the dark.

Not like this, please not like this.

I gasped and spluttered, my breaths strangled as I leant down to kiss him, to kiss the lips that were nearly white and as cold as the frost on the first winter's morning. His brown and blue eyes, those beautiful eyes, were locked onto me.

"Rhona, move!" Asta commanded behind me.

I tried to move away, but my arms and legs disobeyed. Asta forced me out the way and I saw with a flash of fear, her eyes were still white, the silver iris' eaten away by magic. Her fingers shimmered and her lips began summoning tiny threads of white from the air about us.

"What are you doing, child?" The rasp sounded too close. I pulled my eyes away from Eli, and from Asta threading another knot and weft of white light. The Crone stood a short distance away, her grey sodden robes billowing.

"Trying to save him," Asta spat, her fingers still plucking new threads. It felt like my lungs were locked as I silently battled for breath. He couldn't die like this.

"There is no point. He has been bitten. He will become one of them. A turned," the Crone said, her withered and hideous face sneering.

"He must live. It is better for him to return as a creature, than not to return at all," the witch, my friend, seethed, as her tapestry glowed brighter. I watched, unable to blink or breathe as the white threads lowered and sank over Eli's chest, vanishing deep into the heart of him. "The bleeding should stop, allowing the change to happen. Allowing him to live." I didn't know if Asta was speaking to me or herself.

I couldn't comprehend what she was saying or what was happening as I knelt back down next to Eli, resting my hand against his cheek. My fingers numbly caressed his skin, shaping the brown curls I had wanted to touch so much around his ears as the chaos that had ensued us moments before dulled and I could only focus on the roar in my ears. I heard the others around me faintly over the thrum of my heart and heard the exhaustion and rage mould their voices. But I could do nothing but be with Eli.

"Where the fuck were you? We needed you. Needed your help earlier than when you bloody deemed it necessary to come!" Roman snarled and I flinched. I had never heard such anger in his voice.

"We arrived when we were called," the Crone rasped.

"Rhona summoned them. I don't think she knew she had the-" Asta tried to speak but Roman cut her off again.

"What do you mean?"

"The charm, she used it to call them," Asta confirmed, voice edged with ice.

"What charm? You know what, forget it. Will Eli live? Will he live?!"

"For now. But he will be under the control and dominance of the lycan," the Crone wheezed. "I see Rhona has been bestowed with something she should not have."

"The keys to the Fallow." This speaker was shrill, and her voice felt like claws against my mind, bringing my focus back from my blood tainted fingers and to the people and entities now gathered. The Maiden was also here.

"Ah, sister. There *you* are," the Crone said and felt the air shift and crackle. "You have done enough here. Follow the lycan and its issue. Trail them-"

"But the keys," the Maiden panted.

"I will deal with them," the Crone ordered, voice rumbling.

"Why does she have them?" the Maiden demanded, and I felt the echo of her power across the expanse and the shift in energy as she spoke to the Crone.

"I do not know. The thern must have bestowed them upon her,"

"Yes, and thank the Mother it did," Finian croaked and I heard him spit on the floor. Silence briefly followed as I lifted Eli's hand to my lips. His fingers were slack, there was no pressure. No grip. Finian mumbled something and I heard the muted conversation with Jax about Lucius. Another blow and death. I couldn't imagine the pain. Didn't want to relive and revisit it. To lose your father - I shivered, thinking of Jax and poor Rufus.

"She is not worthy of such gifts... isn't even worthy to wield them," the Maiden sneered, and my focus changed. "They will kill her. Slowly. You know this." I heard the purr in her voice, but I did not care. I moved my hand over Eli's mouth, feeling for his breath. It was too slow.

There was a crackling snap which resounded across the broken estate and the Maiden shrieked into the night, flying high above into the darkening cloud. My fingers continued to stroke the pathway down from Eli's temple to his cheek. His eyes were now closed, his breathing too quiet and shallow for me to bear. I leant forwards, resting my ear to his chest, praying to the mother and the moon for a steady heartbeat. There was a quiet thud, followed seconds later by another. His pulse was too slow, his heart too weak. My eyes found the blood pooled around my feet and rump and I began to shake.

That was too much blood to lose.

"Asta," I croaked, feeling everyone's eyes fall upon me. "What happens if he doesn't turn?" I already knew the answer, knew what the witch would say.

"He would die, Rhona." It was like death had come down to stand beside me and offered its cold and bitter caress. "I'm sorry," she finished, and I closed my eyes against the barrelling darkness in my mind.

"Then he must turn. He must stay alive." My words sounded out of tune in my own ears as I spoke them. "He needs to stay alive. He can't die."

"Rhona," my brother warned, his own voice straining.

"He will live, girl. Mark my words. He will live and he will hunt. He will obey and kill because he has been bitten." The Crone had spoken directly to me and anger flashed through me. I clenched my fist, digging my torn nails into the flesh of my palm. "The new moon is upon us. The first day in the new cycle is coming. He will begin to change soon. Begin to shift. There is nothing you can do. You'd do better to kill him now, before he kills *you*."

I looked down at Eli. His chest slowly rose and fell, with his eyes closed and eyelids fluttering. But he was still pale, still on the brink of leaving this world. My eyes burned as I thought of life without him. I pictured him turning into one of those foul things, unable to act upon their own free will. I heard Roman growl out a sob, as his thick fingers pushed me with force out of the way, as he knelt beside his friend, his brother-in-arms since they were small boys.

"No, it won't be like that," he growled, venomously.

"Roman," I sobbed, hunched on the cold earth, as Eli's blood that coated my trousers had seeped down to the flesh underneath and the winter night began to chill my skin down to my bones. Roman gripped Eli's hand tightly, both their blood-stained fists locking. Roman's broad hand was stretched white over Eli's slack unmoving fingers.

"You've done enough!" Roman's words were like being stoned. Harsh and quick. The animosity in me swelled and I bit back my retort, tampering down the spiteful creature now free within me, her bloodlust not yet quelled.

"That's enough!" Finian defended, coming to stand behind me.

The hateful creature had slithered back under the surface of my skin, leaving the broken shell barely breathing. My brother had never spoken to me like that or acted with such vehemence, to anyone and never to me. Something cracked within me, breaking away from the pieces I had been rebuilding all these years.

"You," Roman seethed, spitting angrily as he turned on Finian, "you lied to us. You told us the attacks were manageable. Where is your father, Finian? Has father run away from his pitiful son, leaving him and all his people to defend this fucking spit of land from the demons and monsters? Where's your royal allies? Your regal fucking friends? Why have none of them come to your aid, come to save you?" Every word held a bite, each word cutting and driving deeper than the last. Roman was impetuous, his scowl darkening. Asta's soft voice cut in, her eyes downcast.

"Brennan is on his way. We will take Eli back into the house."

"No, we can't, Asta, there are families there. Children," Jax rumbled.

Arguments erupted. Roman swore and growled. Finian was trying to reign in the outburst and objections. I closed my eyes, closing myself off entirely, locking the pain, the hurt and fear away, making everything recede until a numbness slunk over my skin and deep into my muscles. I stopped crying, the tears desisting entirely as I opened my eyes. The words I proceeded to speak were hollow, echoing out of the shell of me.

"Eli can be placed in my cabin, under my care. Not in the house. Finian, if Brennan is accepting of this, could he assist me in healing the wounds?"

"Of course."

"Then that is settled then. I will take charge of Eli. The estate and house will still be safe. He will not enter through the walls of the house yet. When and if he turns," I couldn't comprehend the thought, "we will deal with that."

"I will stay with you," Asta whispered, walking to me and placing a cold hand on my shoulder.

Jax protested but he was silenced by Asta's glare. I couldn't bring myself to look at Jax for stealing Asta's allegiance away on this. But I was grateful and selfishly prayed she would stay with me.

"And what of the bargain we made Rhona?" the Crone croaked, and all eyes slid to the eldest entity of the Trinity, to her puckered and lined face. "What of the debt you owe the balance. A life for a life, remember?"

I did remember.

How could I forget?

I couldn't feel myself stand, but the movement caused blood to flow and ignite my feet. "The debt still stands," was all I said, as people arrived, and Brennan rushed over to his Lord. I watched men gather Eli gingerly and place him on a wooden stretcher. Everyone's voices, the talk and snide comments, the arguments and objections, became a dull murmur in my ears.

"Is there a way to stop the change, grandmother?" Asta asked over the dim of voices. I watched the men as they carried Eli's motionless body away, back towards the stables, where my wagon would be.

"Yes, Rhona is already on that path. The life debt still stands and so does the boy and her redemption," the Crone hissed and with a crack, she too vanished into the night.

I followed, leaving them all behind, as I walked the shadowy path beside the grass and shingle that was stained crimson, and the corpses scattered everywhere in the aftermath.

Chapter 38

I didn't sleep for two days. I didn't rest or eat. I couldn't. Brennan had helped me bind the wounds across Eli's back. The open wounds bled and seeped through the bandages we changed every few hours and to my despair, the flesh wouldn't heal, clot or dry. Eli stayed in his sleeping state, unmoving and unresponsive to touch, sound or pain. Every hour was torture. Every hour I was petrified it would be his last. And for what? He had ended his life, to save mine. The thought made me sick, but I swallowed down the revulsion and the fear, and kept going. My own self-loathing, fuelling me.

Asta stayed with me, bringing me food and water. She talked to me as I worked and fussed over Eli's soundless form. I heard nothing of what she said and saw nothing of what she did as I moved and worked, unable to associate time as the constant candlelight held me in a fevered state of denial. I didn't connect with who entered and spoke, or who visited Eli. I had no idea. It wasn't until the third day, when Asta's words penetrated my haze, that I finally listened.

"The new moon is tomorrow. We will know then if he will turn."

"The wounds aren't healing. What does that mean?" The words scraped up and out of my throat.

"I do not know, Rhona. The blood isn't clotting." Her tone was careful. "The spell I used was to strengthen his heart. Which it has to a degree. But I do not know if tomorrow will make a difference." Her voice was too soft, like she was talking to a cowering animal. I swallowed down what wanted to burn and rumble up and out of me. "You need your rest. To eat, sleep, and bathe. You still have…" She trailed off. I slowly lowered my gaze to my hands, to the knuckles and wrists coated in rust. My trousers and coat were crisp and clotted with brown, the dried blood had stained the grey wool. Movement caught my eye and my reflection stared back at me hollow in the cracked mirror. Dried blood still coated my face, like a cracked mask, with white streaks blotted across my cheeks and eyes. "I will stay with him. I will call for Roman, whilst you tend to yourself. You need this, Rhona. You will be no use to him on the brink of exhaustion, nearly dead yourself."

I nodded, silently opening my chest, and searching for clean clothes. None were there. They had been taken to the room Finian had granted me. I looked at Asta then back to Eli. She was right, of course she was. I needed to sleep, and now my mind thought about it, every muscle, fibre and nerve ached. I moved to stand, weary and tired. The sheer shock and memory of what had happened pulsed deep.

"Rhona, if he does change, there may still be a way to save him. The Crone said so herself. If we kill the lycan, all who are turned, could potentially be returned," she pleaded, but I couldn't even fathom how we could kill such a creature. Not after what had happened.

"Call me if anything changes," I said. She nodded in response and I left, feeling her eyes trail me as I closed the door and walked out into the frigid day.

***

No hot water greeted me when I returned to my room. The copper tub and its contents were like ice water as I sank below the lip, dousing my body entirely. I gasped, but bit down hard on my lip, tasting blood as I forced my head under, the shock causing me to convulse and shake. I held my breath, filling my cheeks with air from my lungs until the water stopped stinging and I found the cold inviting. When my lungs burned, I breached the surface, cascading crimson water everywhere. I scrubbed and scrubbed, rubbing my skin until it was pink, and the water was useless. I called for more, the maids and women attending eyeing me fearfully at my request for more cold water. They obeyed, thankfully, and I was able to rinse the last of the blood and gore from my skin and hair.

I dressed in front of the fire, my other riding trousers and shirts now cleaned and mended. I dressed fully, in case I was called in the middle of the night. The shock and fear of before, of awakening to Roman and Eli barrelling in my room with that news, was enough to see me dress this way to sleep for the rest of my life.

I couldn't bring myself to sleep in the bed, smothered in the cotton sheets and pillows, so I sat down in front of the fire, now crackling in the small hearth. I watched the flames devour the logs, and my arms and hands automatically reached for the pile and threw on a new one. My eyes wouldn't close. My mind wouldn't rest.

That's how Finian found me, dressed and staring into the fire. I heard his light knock, heard him call my name and the squeak of the hinges as he peaked in when I would not answer. Surprise lit his face as he found me on the floor, highlighted and glowing in the firelight. I didn't look at him until his legs were beside me, the fabric of his trousers and the leather of his boots taking my focus from the burn setting into the back of my eyes. I turned, slowly, looking up at his cleaned and healing face. The cut on his forehead and gash across his cheek were still pink, the scarlet scabs and dark bruises were prominent against his fair complexion. He wore all black again, and I wondered if he only ever wore black, for that is all I had seen him in. Was it on purpose? Did he genuinely choose to wear the colour of his mother's magic? Maybe it was to remind his father or to remind himself. But I didn't care.

"Have you slept?" His voice was quiet, and he began to sit down beside me. I returned my attention back to the fire, to the flames licking up the blackened soot covered stones.

"Eli's wounds haven't healed at all and the new moon is tomorrow," was all I could say, all my mouth would function for.

"You need to sleep, Rhona. You do not know what tomorrow will hold. You need to be at your strongest."

Again, I didn't respond. Red burnished over my hands and exposed arms, the heat from the fire warming me through and through. But the heat couldn't warm away the ice within me. The ice in my heart.

"Look at me, Rhona," Finian asked.

I did nothing.

"Rhona, look at me," he ordered, but still my eyes burned and glazed at the orange and red hues that blinded me. Rough fingers grabbed my chin, pulling me away. Stunned, I focused, blinking severely. Finian's white feathered brows were creased, as he glowered down at me. "You do not get to give up. Do you hear me?" His voice was rough as his breath danced over my face. "You are strong, you are gifted with magic even the witches do not understand. You do not have to give up because of him."

I swallowed as bile rose. This constant sickness of nerves chaffed the depths of my throat. I tried to pull my chin away but Finian's fingers gripped tighter, as his other hand reached around the nape of my neck, pinning me in place. "I won't let you give up. I won't let you do this to yourself because of him."

My voice rose and bubbled up out of me, my anger suddenly free from its cage. "Do what to myself, Finian? You know nothing!" I spat.

"I see you, Rhona. I see you. See the pain, see the lies and the mask. You're just like me. Empty. Hollow. At war with yourself. Exactly like me. Because I've lost too many men and women to that fucking forest and those evil creatures. I've watched them turn and become something else entirely. The people they once were, now long gone." His voice was rising as each word rippled over my skin.

"It's not true," I gritted out, trying to shrink away.

"Yes, it is. And Eli will be the same. He will change and leave, and he will die. They will all die." My eyes stung, but no tears threatened to spill. My body was used up and exhausted from crying and aching and living. But still Finian gripped me, his pale silver eyes penetrating down to my soul. "You know it's true, Rhona. He will be gone."

Enraged, a moan escaped through my teeth. What he was saying was all true. I had thought it over and over again in my mind, until it was imprinted on the walls of my skull and eyelids but hearing it from him made it all the more real.

Finian's eyes darkened as he glanced at my mouth and his lips crashed into mine, sealing my lips with his own. I tried to break away, free myself, but his tongue swept in as I tried to shout. It flicked across my tongue, hot and sweet and for a brief moment I was stunned into submission. Eli's face flashed inside my closed lids and I tensed, as shame overcame me. My hands found Finian's chest and I shoved us apart and I gasped, my lips, finally free. I was panting wildly, wrath and something else clawing to get free. Finian's hooded eyes looked down on me, dominant and defiant as his thumb possessively grazed against my bottom lip.

"He didn't deserve you, Rhona."

White hot rage engulfed me, and I spat at him. It landed across his nose and left cheek, startling him as I seethed and writhed out of his grip. The muscles in my legs barely moved from pins and needles, and it felt like my bones had moulded to the stone hearth floor. When Finian looked at me again, whilst his hand smeared and wiped away my spit, a dark smirk played at his lips. The cold creature within me, revelled and purred at that look as his eyes became molten once more and he leaned in. The flames caught the remaining spit, shining on his cheek as he flashed his teeth in a wicked smile.

"You'll realise soon. You'll realise you deserve more than he could *ever* have offered you. And I'll be waiting."

I didn't dare move as the keys heated and the blue light filtered through the cuffs of my shirt. I was trembling. The rage and sheer venom that I wanted to ensue upon the man in front of me nearly erupted. But with another infuriating smirk, Finian stood and left the room, leaving me shaking. I was dazed as the phantom traces of his lips flickered into life and I felt hot and cold all over, unable to understand and decipher whether I was truly angry for the stolen kiss. But I understood one thing - the cold callous creature I had become for mere moments days before had slid back into my skin, and she was ready to unleash hell.

***

I awoke cold and bewildered on the stone floor, in front of the blackened fireplace. No embers were in the grate and by the chill of my skin, there had been none for quite some time. I stretched my aching arms and legs, clicking my spine and neck. I searched for my coat, needing the extra layers to warm the chill that had set in deep. I found it heaped on the floor, caked in all manner of blood, including Eli's. Seeing it only brought everything crashing back. I walked away from it and into the dressing room, my hands shaking out the tremors that threatened to overcome me on the way. I opened the mahogany wardrobe doors, so they crashed against one another violently. Several coats hung, unused, moth eaten and covered in a film of dust. Velvet and fleece, wool and leather. Some long dress coats were embroidered with flora and vines. Others were glittered with metallic thread like a night filled with stars. They were not appropriate for what I had to do, for the path that was snaking and becoming more vindictive with every turn or decision I made. My hands forced the hanging garments over, snapping each one out the way, not caring if I damaged them. It was a parade of ravaged beauty in fabrics a traveller could only dream of. Until I found one. The black wool piece caught my eye at the back. The mid length appealing to me. Its thick coarse wool was heavy, and the collar was lined with tawny animal fur. I pulled it from its perch, dusting off the shoulders and sleeves and dressed in it, buttoning up the brass buttons to the neck, the confinement making me feel strong, as though safe in armour. The fitted coat felt lightweight considering and I whirled and shifted my arms. I glanced at myself in the mirror as I walked past the dressing table and the callous creature stared back. Her dark blue eyes were shaded and bruised. Her lips were pale, and her dark brows and hair gave her the willowy look of death. I didn't see me, staring back through the glass mirror and I was glad for it. I didn't want to look at her.

Chapter 39

I heard my name being called from the hall, but it wasn't who I had expected to be calling it. A heavy fist beat at the wood and I rushed from the dressing room. Opening it, I found Jax panting, resting his arm against the frame as he gasped down a breath. I was instinctually alert with the sickening fear that washed over me.

"He's waking up," he gasped, his pale smooth skin shining. The auburn hair on his head was cut angularly and tufts were protruding at all angles. Air whooshed into my lungs and my knees weakened. I gripped the frame, unable to speak. After Finian's harsh words last night, I didn't know whether to be thankful he was alive or to dread it but I closed my eyes, sucking in the relief and fear that threatened to spill out. I would deal with that when it came. I had to.

"We need to go now," he said, and he grabbed my hand and pulled me out the room. We briskly walked side by side, both silent and fully aware of each other. No one on the estate knew Eli, a potential turned, was still on the grounds and yet it felt like it, as eyes trailed us, trailed me. The looks and glances sliced at my skin like shards of glass as they glazed over me and then to my hands and wrists, to the keys imprinted upon my skin. My eyes kept catching Jax and his narrowed expression. The freckles that dusted his pert nose and round cheeks were dark today and I heard him clear his throat, *twice*. I swallowed down the anger that wanted to whip from my tongue.

"Out with it, Jax."

"I don't like this. Not one bit," he replied, his voice quiet.

I halted, spinning on my heels to face him. "Jax, we've not known each other long. But I have known Eli my entire life," I spewed, my voice rising. "He is a good man. He has a strong heart. That is all I will say on the matter." I began walking again, leaving the muted man in my wake.

"Men can change, Rhona. People change," he called and there was no mistaking his distrust.

I continued walking, leaving Jax behind me, unable to think about such things, and unable to digest losing Eli.

Cold air washed over me as I entered the courtyard. Snow fluttered down from a darkened sky, the winter here still burdening the landscape. The aftermath of the attack was still evident in the lull and stillness of the camp and there was hardly any chatter, hardly any bodies roaming or walking about. The guards that had been stationed nights before were sparse, many of them dead or healing in the infirmary. The lack of men and women occupying the wall gave me pause. I hadn't asked how many we had lost. How many had been killed, or worse, turned? My empty stomach blazed, and I swallowed down the ache building up my throat.

I quickened my pace, until my legs were pounding against the hard earth towards the stables. I found them there, standing outside my cabin and home; Asta, Roman and Finian. All were talking hushedly, wrapped in coats and furs against the biting chill. It did not phase me, the cold. I walked past them and into the shadows of my home, leaving the door open.

Eli was shirtless, the bandages that I had meticulously changed repeatedly were gone. His skin glistened in the morning light with sweat and I noted what looked like week-old bruises on his chest and shoulder, not the dark ominous bruises that decorated his skin the night before. I leant over him, watching his eyes flicker under his dark lashes. He *was* becoming conscious.

My stomach dropped at the thought of him changing further. I steadied myself as my fingers carefully prodded his shoulder, whilst I keenly watched for any movement or stirring. I glanced at the fading scars from the lycan's teeth, the skin smooth as though the marks were years old. My jaw worked but I was unable to formulate words. This didn't make any sense. The open wounds and gashes that had kept Eli on the brink of death these past few days were gone. Healed. I watched the man in front of me. My friend, my betrothed. He *had* turned. The transition of his body and form were now at the mercy of a catalyst to the unknown. For him *and* me. My eyes continued to carefully watch the now, strong flickering pulse at the base of his throat. I swallowed the anguish, grinding my teeth to stop the thoughts that were hammering against my senses. The wooden steps up into my home creaked and I knew it was my brother before he even spoke.

"It is happening. His body is changing," I could only nod, still dumbfounded and silent. "We need a few days to see how he fairs. To see what happens." His words were weary as he stood, towering over me.

His shadow encompassed us, cloaking our small trio in shadow. A trio we may no longer be. The burn returned to my eyes, the ache and choking sensation to my throat, but I bit the inside of my cheek, forcing it away and down, and allowing the darkness within me to devour it all.

"We don't know how long he will have." Asta's cool voice filtered inside and the weight of my cabin shifted as Finian and her stepped in as well. My short fingernails were still lined with black as they gripped and moved a strand of hair out of Eli's eyes. His chest rose and fell with full breaths and his skin had returned to its usual golden hue. The muscles across his chest, arms and abdomen seemed as though they were straining under his tanned glistening skin.

"What do we know?" I asked, unable to face the party behind me.

"Not much, but we will look in the library. See if my family kept anything. Records, stories, anything that may help." It was Finian who had spoken and the sharp-fanged creature beneath my skin stretched and yawned awake at his voice. I pivoted, eyebrows raised. After last night, this was the last thing I expected from him. His silver eyes locked with my own dark blue, like the oceans crashing with a storm.

"What do we do when he wakes?" I dared, my voice strained.

"We've already discussed-" Roman began, but I cut him off.

"Discussed? Without me?" My words dripped with venom as the hollowness faded from me and the keys twinged at my wrists.

"You needed your rest, Rhona," Asta pleaded, but I hissed, and her metallic eyes turned wary.

"You've done enough," Roman spat, arms crossed, and I whirled, standing to face him, ready to battle this out as siblings. The wildness I knew shone in my face, didn't make him falter as he glared down at me. His dark brows gathered to a stern crease. "He wouldn't be in this position if it-"

"Had it not been for me? You think I don't know that?!" My teeth were bared, lips shuddering to contain my howl of rage. "I know, Roman. Know all too well why he did what he did. Know that he's been trying to save me, for a long time, before I even realised it. Before I realised why." My words were shrill and frantic, the urgency to speak the truth like that of water overflowing a ravine. "I know. It's like poison in my blood, sucking the very life out of me. What he did," words evaded me as my jaw quivered, "I can't have him die because of me, as well."

Eli's breathing hitched and he choked. I spun, wanting to face anything other than the questioning look on my brother's face.

"Roman, now is not the time for such talk." Asta was stern as she moved around both men, coming to my side. The witch knelt beside me, her face unreadable as her eyes slid to mine and I was grateful, so very grateful, in that moment for the woman beside me.

"I think now is the perfect time." But Roman's protest was silenced by Eli opening his eyes and jumping up, clawing himself away and up from the bed. His face was pained, eyes manic, as he scrambled, his muscles and arms straining.

"Eli, Eli..." I hushed softly, trying to coax and calm him back to the now.

The cords of muscles clenched on his neck and his wide eyes shot about the small room and the people within. I inhaled, shock gripping me, as his blue eye and brown eye shone with fevered light from within. I tried again, placing my hands cautiously on his neck, turning his face to see me. Black pupils contracted, as his breathing heaved and then settled. His hands and arms stopped thrashing as he looked at me, wholly new and healed.

I didn't know what emotion shone on my face as I moved closer to him, vigilant of what he now was and could become. But I had to try to see if he was the same person I had known, had come to look for and needed in my own way.

"Eli, it's m-me," I stammered but held his gaze, and couldn't help the terror that coated my tongue.

His nostrils flared, inhaling the stale air of the cabin. He processed his surroundings, the sights and smells, and the people here with him. As I beheld him, my blood turned cold as I glimpsed the animal shining behind his eyes. The beast was waiting to shed its skin and be free. I sat back as the terror within me heightened.

"Roman," I said, my voice wavering. But Eli surprised even me, as his hands swept up to my face, his warm palms gliding over the skin of my cheekbones and throat.

"Rhona?" Finian's worried voice called.

But I was trapped by the beast lurking just a breath away under Eli's very skin. As the man in front of me began to awaken fully, his eyes and mind found something in my face. A muscle flickered in his jaw and I stilled, like prey awaiting death, as his thick callus fingers glided down to the pulse at my throat. Heat flooded me at the memory of that possessive touch nights before. I dared not move, aware the beast within would be ready to pounce. But his forehead touched my own and I closed my eyes, shaking.

"Eli," I croaked, trying to depress the rising hope in me, sparking to life. "How do you feel?"

His eyes trailed up my pulse and along my jaw to meet my eyes again. The man and beast were aligned, even as I saw the creature within shudder. There was a darkness in Eli's eyes now that had not been there before, untamed and unyielding. Breathing through his nose again, he stilled, leaning back, brow gathered.

"Brother?" Roman asked, his voice subtle and assuring, unlike how he had spoken to me.

Eli's eyes shot to, and focused on, Roman. The beast within surveyed the weapons upon my brother, noting the stance behind me and the sword drawn at his side. I heard Roman sheath the blade, the metal kissing the strap and cover. There was a great sigh, loud enough to fill the entire cabin, as Eli relaxed slightly, his assessment done and hackles dropped.

"What do we do?" I asked anyone who had an answer that was something other than my own mind.

"For your protection, for ours and my people, I say we lock him in your room, Roman. For now. You can watch him." Finian was back to being the Lord once more, trying to control the situation.

I began to argue, but Roman interrupted, agreeing with him. "Ay, that would be better than a wooden box here."

"No!" I warned. "We can't lock him up in a room. It's not fair."

"It's the safest option, Rhona," Roman cautioned.

"It's the *only* option," Finian affirmed.

I looked to Asta, wanting and needing her input. But the witch looked at Eli and a line drew on her brow, her dark eyebrows raising. She inspected the man before me and found him dangerous. I could tell by the way her back straightened and her eyes shifted to Finian and my brother. I was defeated, unable to contend with the three of them.

When I faced Eli again, there was none of the softness I had once glimpsed, or the surety and sound man I had grown with. He was still and quiet, his skin and face the very same, but something coiled and snapped in his eyes, darkening them unrecognisably. With my stomach twisting, I stood, needing air. Eli's hands dropped from me and the cold air from outside caught me off guard as I beheld my betrothed. He watched me with no emotion, no warmth. He watched me with the eyes of a predator, assessing its prey.

The familiar tug pulled within me and the ache that had been building, built to a crescendo.

I had to try.

I had to try for Eli. To make the man trapped within, if he was trapped, know we were still here for him, his friends, and brethren.

"Eli." His eyes locked upon me once more as I spoke. "I know you're in there. I know you. You wouldn't hurt me or Roman, or Asta or Finian, for that matter." I gulped down the misery that was dulling the relief. "I need you to do what I tell you. So you don't hurt us, or yourself."

I waited for a look that told me he was still in there, and that he understood, but none came, even when he tilted his head with predatory intent and his nostril flared, inhaling deep. Someone began pulling me and my feet obeyed, shuffling backwards.

Before I could react further, Eli extended his neck and whiffed me, inhaling deep and quick. Whatever he had smelled made him shudder.

His lip curled at whatever he found, and I couldn't stop my bottom lip from trembling. Pale fingers gripped at the fabric of my waist, pulling me further away and I arced, finding Finian moving me, as his eyes were lined with unease.

"Eli, do you understand?" I asked. Eli moved his neck, cracking the bones of his spine and we all froze. But he began to sign. I dared not move, as myself and Roman read the word Eli was communicating. It was simple, divisive and did not clear the doubt riddled within me.

'Yes,' was all he signed.

***

Eli moved into the house with not so much as a flutter or flinch. I watched as Roman and Finian, accompanied by seven other guards, walked Eli into the house, up the stairs and into the room he had shared with Roman. No one asked any questions as Finian commanded the men into silence, even as they all eyed Eli warily. I couldn't imagine what they must be thinking, as the door closed smoothly on Eli's highlighted form and then men were ordered to guard the door. Eli hadn't turned to look at any of us as he walked into the room, leaving me cold and numb in the hallway as the door clicked shut and a key was twisted, locking him inside. Four guards were always to be stationed outside his room, with orders to alert us if anything else were to happen to him.

The angst and adrenaline pounding throughout my body was deafening and I fidgeted, unable to keep still in my own skin. Everything seemed too close and constricting, too loud or too bright, as we made our way up another flight of stairs and along a long passageway. I had heard brief murmurs of conversation as we walked, dazed and suffering. 'Library' had been muttered and I assumed that was where we were heading. My legs moved automatically, the muscles pushing me forward each step as though of their own accord, whilst in my mind I replayed the scene before over and over again.

I hadn't realised Asta had been walking closely beside me, her arm grazing my sleeve every now and then, until she whispered to me, "are you alright?"

I didn't answer.

"Rhona, this is the safest option for him for now," she whispered, grabbing my arm and stopping us both. "Don't go into the darkness, Rhona." I finally looked at her, her silver eyes shining. "Don't let it ride and take you. Be strong. Be strong for him, for yourself."

She struck a chord within me and the tug on my ribs pulled uncomfortably over my heart. The slight ache riffled down my sternum and I filled my lungs, the cool air of the estate clearing my mind. She was right, of course she was right. Eli deserved more than this person, more than me. Her slim hands raised to encase my face, as her umber thumbs softened and smoothed over my temples and forehead. I wrinkled my brow, pulling my head back. "Do not move. I am trying to calm you," she babbled as her full lips breathed and moved silently. Her thumbs moved down, smoothing the line, and then worked under my eyes, where the tissue was soft and tired. Tingles radiated across my face at her touch, at the feel of her soft, scarred fingers delicately touching me. The shadows that had been looming drew back and the ache in my chest eased to a more bearable tone. Astonished, I grabbed her hands.

"What did you do to me?" I asked.

"I dissolved some of your fear. Took it away and banished it. To make it easier," she said matter-of-factly.

"Thank you," I managed, feeling the air travel down into my lungs more freely. "I mean it," I whispered, feeling Roman and Finian eyes now upon us from up the lantern-lit corridor. "You have been a great friend. I didn't realise I could have such a friend in a witch," I admitted sheepishly, unable to look at her, but I continued. "You see me more than any other in my life, I think. And I thank you. And I see you."

A small smile tugged at her lips, but I did not reciprocate it. My mouth wouldn't allow it.

We continued up to the others, fully aware of my brother's glare, every step of the way. Reaching double doors of studded mahogany, Finian opened them wide, eyes on me the entire time. The doors yawned wide and the smell of stale paper and dust filled my nose. The space was dark; no lanterns or candles had been lit in this cavern of a room. In the thick shadows, I could just make out towering shelves, filled and thriving with hard-covered books. The smell of leather and wax crept over me, easing the tension smothering me.

Finian prowled in, looking left and right into the great room; no one seemed to be there.

"Asta, would you?" Finian asked and with that the witch walked over the threshold.

Her dark form was swallowed by the shadows deep within the library and we waited. Blinding white and yellow threads snaked out of the gloom, as Asta worked her magic. The lanterns began to spark and ignite and the smell of oil burning wafted out into the corridor to me. The room grew in light and size as each lantern glowed to life, highlighting row upon row of bookshelves and stacks, all teeming with books. Roman said nothing, did nothing, beside me other than brood. I couldn't deal with him and his temper, so I stayed quiet.

Dust motes swirled in the warm light in front of me as I walked in, moving myself away from him. The room was beautiful, the same dark mahogany theme of the rest of the house was also in the library. Tall shelves housed hundreds of coloured books, aged and covered in dust, maps and scrolls lined one wall and a large tapestry hung on the furthest one. I walked towards it, drawn to the subtle grey weave and knit. It was a map of the Continent, of all the estates, cities and villages that were spread across the land. As my eyes trailed across the lands that had been mapped and finely stitched, my fists clenched as I followed the borders from the south, my eyes passing the middle of the Continent. I saw Windmore stitched in elegant thread, then Oaknell. My heart thudded harshly at seeing the lettering for the last place I had seen my uncle and clan. My eyes roved up and across the map, seeing the Savage Vale and Neath Briar, continuing up to the north, towards the Fallow. But where I expected to see threads of trees and the vastness of the Fallow, scorch marks were in its place. The entirety of the area was a black, charred smear. The Fallow had been removed, purposefully. In fact, the entire north was completely blackened, now unreadable and unknown. My eyes lingered over the scorched fabric, barely clinging to the beam from which it was hung. My mind wandered, wondering why someone would burn a map, but then I swallowed, remembering why we were here.

We began scouring the rows upon rows of books for anything that could help us, well, help Eli. We looked for anything that could lead us to the lycan, to understand why the people that were bitten then changed and became 'turned'. Finian had a desk brought up and within minutes, it had been littered with books. Chairs were carried up from Finian and his father's chambers as well, and we all worked and read, trying to find something to lead us in the right direction. I didn't know how to beat the creature without Eli, or where to even begin in hunting it or trying to find it. Memories from maps we held within our camp, created by our traveller ancestors, showed the Fallow and the Fallow Mountain to the very north of the Continent. But in the tapestry, the scorch marks stretched further than I knew. If Asta was right, the Fallow wasn't just the forest outside these walls. It was this very land. This entire Continent. I ground my teeth, throwing the book I had been reading on local farming of Neath Briar into the ever-growing pile of useless texts that had been growing in the corner.

"This is useless," Finian hissed, tossing his away from him. "My father made sure nothing of magical origin remained after my mother..." His eyes blazed as he looked around the library, doubt lining his face.

"We have to try, there must be something," Asta sighed, her head in her hands over a large ancient looking book.

"The bastard made damned sure her legacy and others," he paused, eyeing the witch, "of your kind were wiped from our house."

More books on the Neath Briar estate were found, and books on Finian's family tree and the residing families of the estates nearest, as well as those no longer alive or on the map. Asta found information on creatures but found them to be nothing more than children's stories, the creatures and beings within hosting nothing of the monsters we had faced so far. Books on healing and anatomy were skimmed, as well as books on the land and the monarchy of the Continent. We read anything, hoping to find something. Every now and then, sighs of frustration echoed from each of us, the lack of material evident in the bland mortal texts.

Rufus and Jax had joined us, looking and noting things which could be of use. I said nothing, even when I heard the young boy's sniffs from the end of the table. His eyes were still rimmed with red and shadows darkened under his young face. I wondered then, if Jax and Rufus had a mother here on the estate or if she too was now dead like their father. I bit my lip as I watched them over the aged pages on the history of the county and land, seeing Jax pass his brother a white lace handkerchief. The boy took it timidly, his face suddenly hidden by a book of maps. After several hours, Rion and Daven came into the library bringing trays of food and drink with them for us all.

Roman left to check on Eli, returning several minutes later with eyes downcast. He fell into a heap on an armchair and picked up the nearest book from one of the collected stacks, not looking in my direction once.

I observed Finian look up and witnessed both men share a look. The grim line that set across his mouth as he returned to his own reading set my teeth on edge.

More hours passed, and shadows replaced the light from small windows in the dome ceiling, high above us. The fire in the grate was brought to life when a chill crept over the room, as our research took us deep into the night. Nothing I read was worth the time. Nothing mentioned the Fallow, the lycan or any magical creatures within. Finian's father really had done his utmost to eradicate any magic from within his home. I at least expected something to have been missed, something to have remained unnoticed. The crackling fire and quiet murmurings of the group filled my ears, distracting me from another bland text on the history of the Baltisse line. Watching from the corner I had placed myself in, Finian stood and walked over to Roman.

"Daven, check on Eli, will you?" Finian asked, and the man snoozing in the armchair nearest the fire stood, stretched, and left the room. Over my book, Finian and my brother exchanged hushed words and my stomach clenched as a fresh wave of anger pulsed in my blood.

Asta looked up towards me from where she was sitting in her soft chair beside the tapestry, with Jax sitting and leaning against her legs. Rufus dozed, his head resting on Jax's thighs as the older of the siblings stroked the younger's hair. Her silver eyes locked with my own before I left their haunting gaze, returning my attention to Roman. His back was to me, facing the fire. His dark hair was unkempt, with loose strands falling from where they were tied at the nape of his neck. Blood spatter was on the back of his shirt and I realised then, what I had not deemed to acknowledge. He was in as much pain as I was. I could see it, in the way his shoulders slumped, and his head bowed. He was angry and hurting. Eli was after all his best friend, and brother-in-arms.

My throat constricted, my breath invalid as my heart broke yet again for my brother, for what I had caused. Self-loathing was something I had been accustomed to for many years, but in that very moment, it had intensified to an intolerable level.

I wanted to cry, to scream, to fight and hit or beat something. I ached to release everything coiling and clawing under my skin. The door to the library clicked open again and Daven returned, shrugging his shoulders. I threw yet another book onto my useless pile, the spine breaking and pages flying, scattering their yellowing shells across the floor in front of me. Leaning back, I rested my head against the chair, eyes closed.

What must Eli be thinking?

What must he think of us, of me, trapping and caging him like an animal in that room? I wondered if he had moved, if he had slept or even eaten. Had food been brought to him? I rubbed my eyes, my fingers wanting to dig behind them and rip out the thoughts rallying in my head. Sighing heavily, my hands fell to the arms of the chair and dust clouded my vision. I coughed, swiping at the air. When the motes settled and I could breathe easily again, I stretched my neck, looking up into the gloom of the library ceiling and dome.

I thought back to the books and journals that had been kept in my wagon. The books and writings from hands long ago. My mother's hand, my grandmother's hand, and many, many before them. They must have housed something within their aged pages, and a small part of me realised they probably did have. A pang of annoyance swept over me, remembering that they were no longer in my wagon. We had moved and stored them in Roman's caravan, along with most of my other possessions to make room. I winced, frustrated. The air stirred above me, lint, dust, and fibres swaying lazily high above. I followed the sway of the drifting debris, following the way they floated across my eyes. Something shimmered beyond the waves of dust motes and I focused my eyes, searching the gloom. Painted shapes became clear in the shadows of the ceiling and my breath caught, eyeing two golden eyes above. My legs vaulted me from my chair, my feet landing swiftly. I catapulted around, looking above at the mural cast in shadow.

"Finian," I called, my voice bleak and unused for some time, "I've found something."

Chair legs scraped and all ran up and forward to me at the centre of the room. My eyes never left the ceiling, as they surrounded me. Finian's silver eyes skimmed my face, seeing my wide gaze fixed above. His eyes followed and I caught in my peripherals the sight of his mouth opening wide into a 'o' shape.

"Asta, could you light the dome please?" I asked, as all eyes were now scanning the gloom. Asta's voice rumbled a soft, breathy word and she plucked a white thread from the air, weaving it once, then twice. The circular light orb that bloomed before her rose, as though on a phantom breeze, up into the rafters of the domed ceiling.

"The old bastard missed that," Roman's voice growled, as the mural became clear.

Flora and fauna in delicate and detailed swipes of a paint brush were illustrated high above. The dome was a perfect circle, several feet above the towering bookshelves and small glass windows. Trees, animals and creatures were painted in glorious strokes of colour, embossed and detailed with eroded gold and silver. I marvelled at the painting, at the bewitching depictions of the creatures. They were the creatures of the Fallow. The mountain at the heart of the painting, the very peak of the dome, looked prophetic due to the thrashing strokes of greys and black.

Fairies, pixies, and spirits were painted flying with other creatures with wings. Trolls, like that of the Knarrock troll, were illustrated below the mountain, near a ravine of thundering waves and water. Wraiths, shadow people and daemons, were peeking through the dark and shadowed swathes of an area of the Fallow, red and black eyes glittering among shaded and glooming strokes of grey trees. Other creatures danced and played in rays of gold and green. It was a mural of the Fallow. A mural surrounded by seven large stretching trees, which all intertwined and connected about the rim of the dome. The seven gates. Next to the seven gates was a horned creature, garlanded and pictured in silver. The therns.

I swallowed.

Cool fingers encased mine and I jumped, returning to my own skin. I looked and found Asta's fingers, holding my own. She breathed a shuddering breath, her eyes shining as she looked up in awe at the beautiful display of colour.

"That's where we'll find the lycan," Jax breathed, lifting a freckled hand to point above.

All our eyes travelled to where he motioned to. Painted near the darkest leaves and beasts, was a crag of rocks; it was a gorge near the mountain itself. Golden yellow eyes blazed and the familiar form of the lycan was depicted. That familiar twinge pulsed and pulled at my rib and like death's cold breath, the hairs on my nape stirred.

"There's only one way to check." Jax's voice pierced the dim and haze in my head and I ripped my eyes away from the ceiling, to him.

His blue eyes were rimmed with pale lashes that fluttered as he beheld us all looking. I saw his throat bob and his cheek flush pink as we waited, not knowing what he was suggesting. "We bring Eli in here. See if he reacts to it?"

I heard Roman intake sharply through his nose and saw his jaw and the muscles of his neck tense.

"No," Finian snapped, his metallic eyes darting to me. I held my face placid, controlling the catastrophe within me.

"Jax is right, Finian, it would give us an idea. If Eli does react or does something to indicate that this may be where the lycan is…" Asta trailed off, her hands sweeping across the ceiling. "It's our only choice right now. We have to try."

Yet again, Finian's eyes tried to penetrate the wall I was hiding behind. His white brows gathered, his jaw tightening as he crossed his arms.

"I'll go get him," Roman replied.

***

I paced, awaiting Eli and Roman.

"Rhona, this isn't a good idea," Finian said as he charged at me, grabbing my wrist. I halted my steps, unable to react as his fingertips touched the rapid pulse there. The pound of my heart must have betrayed me, as Finian came in close, leaning over me. "Do you really think you can save him?" His breath brushed warmth over my cold cheeks and my eyes shot to his mouth.

I didn't know what I thought, didn't know what I believed, but I had to try and do something, anything, to keep me from going insane. The lump in my throat was nearly choking me, but I didn't move or shake off his grip. I closed my eyes, beating back the wave of wrath threatening to overpower the numbness. His rough fingers reached up and caught my face and I reluctantly opened my eyes, finding his own searching mine, as though trying to find the flaw in my mask.

"Rhona." My name was like a prayer on his lips as his thumbs brushed across my bottom lip. I tasted salt and smoke on it and the wrath within me became searing. Light danced in his eyes as he saw it bubbling beneath the surface of me. "There she is," he purred. "Fight. Fight hard."

His lips shaped into a harsh smile, which corrupted his beautiful face.

I began pulling away and out of his touch, just as Roman walked through the door accompanied by Eli. Both eyed me pointedly as I freed myself from Finian's overbearing closeness.

I walked smoothly, placing one foot carefully in front of the other, towards Eli, who stood motionless watching me. I saw the muscle flicker in his temple as I approached, saw his mismatched eyes glow and crease in the corners, in question. My emotionless mask was in place, although I wanted to crumble at seeing him again. I wanted to rip it away and run to him sobbing and begging for his forgiveness. But that girl was nothing but an echo within.

"Eli," I said, and his eyes locked to my own, his nostril flaring. "Is that where the lycan is?" I asked, raising my hand slowly to the yellow embossed eyes staring down on us.

We all watched him, paused and ready, waiting and assessing his every move. His eyes roved up to the ceiling, to the dome and mural above. Asta approached my side and with a deft flick of her wrist, the swirling orb above brightened further, sliding nearer to the painted beast at the crag of the mountain.

Eli's one blue and brown eye locked in place, finding their mark. I held my breath, afraid I would miss the quiver of his eyes as something like recognition hit. His apple at his throat bobbed and he blinked rapidly. His chest rose and fell, heaving great breaths as he remained transfixed at the lycan above. A gurgling moan escaped through clenched teeth and I heard Roman and the others draw their weapons.

It was confirmation enough.

Chapter 40

Eli had been escorted back to his rooms, accompanied by Roman and several armed guards. I had trailed behind them, my footfall heavy, my head a mess. Eli's response had been answer enough. The creature had come to the surface in that moment, beckoning him to follow and find others like him. If the mural was true, then we had a rough idea of a location. I couldn't bear it as Roman's angry gaze secured on mine, and he closed the door, shutting me out entirely.

We had an idea now, a plan, and with the keys on my skin we could access the Fallow and find our way to that darkened crack of rock and into the beast's lair, if we made it through the Fallow alive... But even with this new revelation, I felt more tiresome and defeated than ever.

"We will stay with you tonight," Asta said from behind me. I pivoted, catching her looking at Jax beseechingly. The man before me contemplated his refusal. I saw it waver across his mouth as he stared at the witch before him. I contemplated this person and I tried to understand who they were and who they had been. The man in front of me was sure and strong, and yet kind. His morals were true, his demeanour quiet. He only held her safety in regard, it was plain on his concerned face. His eyes roved over Asta's, and I saw him succumb to the feelings that shone through the void of doubt.

"I would appreciate the company, from you both," I said, swallowing the knots on my tongue.

"Then we will stay," Jax replied in earnest.

Sleep came easily once I had gathered myself on a chair in front of the fire. Asta and Jax had refused the bed, affronted and abashed at my offering, but I knew no matter what, they would sleep together in some form. I didn't realise that it was on the floor at my feet, curled into one another, pillows under their heads and a coverlet shielding their embraced bodies. I watched their peaceful slumber until my own eyes became heavy, then I gave in to the memories and dreams that haunted me. Screams echoed in my memory and I battled on, reliving the same scenario over and over in my head; my childlike body running across cobbled streets with tears stinging my cheeks, the cut on my brow burning as blood ran down my legs. The orchestra of screams from my past began to change from my girlish, shrill echoes of memory, until they were rampant in my ears. My skin crawled and itched, and as I surfaced from the depths of the nightmare, I realised with a start the screams weren't fading. My eyes shot open to find Asta and Jax scrambling backwards at the sight of a shadow messenger hovering before us.

It thrashed and groaned, making my ears ring, the sounds bouncing off the walls and floor powerfully. The screams were coming from it, screams so haunting and real as though they had been scratched up and out of my own throat. My blood turned to ice in my veins, my hairs standing on end, as the door to my room smashed open and Roman, Eli, Finian and Daven barrelled through frantically.

The shadow messenger thrashed one last time, it's high screeches piercing down into the chasm of my soul, before vanishing like smoke out the door and down the hall. The howls and cries echoed in its wake all the way.

My heart pounded in my chest, beating against my ribs and vibrating down to my empty stomach.

"What was that?!" Daven asked, his sword still held aloft as his eyes searched all our faces, horrified.

"One of my grandmother's shadow messengers," Asta responded, her voice shaking. Jax was on top of her, shielding her in a way I knew too well. The way Eli would shield me. Among the faces I found him and relief flooded me. No one dared speak as we listened to the stirring of people out in the halls.

"It was a warning." My words shook as I uncurled myself from the chair, my limbs creaking but obeying. "A warning of another attack." I was sure of it, sure the Crone would not send one of those things without reason. The screams were yet another cryptic message, but on this estate, with what had happened days before, it only solidified my thoughts as they settled. "Get everyone ready, as many as you can," I ordered, walking to the changing room, ignoring everyone's disorientated looks. Fire and adrenaline surged in my veins, as sheer terror animated me. The cruel creature lurking under my skin surfaced, fed and ready, from the days of repressed wrath and rage. It was now or never.

"Daven, awaken all the families, send word across the estate. Man the wagons with the families unable to fight. Get them out of here and far away," Finian ordered and Daven ran from the room, his steps beating down the hall as his shouts began alerting the residents of what was to come. Beyond the door, frightened voices began to respond. "Jax, go to the infirmary. Anyone healed enough to fight needs to get to the walls, anyone still injured should leave with the wagons."

I busied myself, strapping my knives and dagger to my calf and thigh, feeling the satisfactory weight of the steel on my body. Eli's curved cutlass gleamed deadly as I picked it up and belted it around my waist, before dressing in Finian's mother's black coat. I steadied my hands, ignoring the sounds of doors slamming shut and the thunder of the frightened people beginning their evacuation.

"What do we do?" Asta asked, coming into the dressing room after me. She wore another pale linen shift, her legs and feet bare. I threw her a pair of trousers and she scrambled to catch them, threading her feet through the legs and tucking her shift into the waist. I opened one of the wardrobes, finding a long coat of pale grey adorned with silver thread, I had admired earlier. I grappled it from its hanging, handing it to her, saying nothing. Taking the garment, her eyes glowed at the glistening threads.

"The lycan may be coming to us. This may be our only opportunity; we need to hunt," is all I said as I walked out of the small room to Finian, my brother and Eli.

"Put my brother on a wagon and get him away from here," I said, my voice and face stern.

"Fuck off, Rhona," Roman spat, stepping forward.

"I will not have you harmed because of me and this life debt!" I yelled, the rage rippling and snapping out. "You need to go back and find Baja. Tell our people to get off this Continent. Somewhere safe-"

"Rhona," Roman bellowed, but I held up my hand, silencing him.

"I will not be responsible for your death too," I confessed, pouring every piece of my heart out as I held his gaze.

Let him see the truth, I begged.

Let him see exactly the type of creature he has for a sister.

"I'm not going anywhere," Roman growled as his eyes darted over my face.

"We need him, Rhona," Finian pronounced as Rufus skidded into the room.

"My Lord, you-your f-father has returned," Rufus stammered, eyes wide and scanning the room for Jax.

"Good," Finian declared, his silver eyes trained on me. "We need all the help we can get."

The families had vacated their rooms within the hour, carrying and carting their only possessions out with them. Children were packed onto carts and horses whilst their parents and those unable to fight walked alongside, and they all made their way out of the estate onto the road, heading south. Anywhere away from the Fallow.

Lord August had demanded the gates be shut, and that all the people return to the estate where it was safest. None returned, and all who were able to, left with haste, running from the promise of the attack to come. After the slaughter from days before, who could blame them?

Word came that Lord August had travelled to a neighbouring county, returning sooner than anyone had anticipated. He had found no witches willing to help him on the road and had only returned with a handful of new men to assist on the wall. The promise of food and shelter had been offered as payment for the occupation. When they had seen the wide eyes of the people fleeing, dread and regret had replaced their optimism upon entering the estate. Finian had been called into a meeting with his father and council, and I could only imagine how the Lord would take the news that Lucius and many others had been slain. Eli was locked in the seclusion of his room, whilst myself, Roman and Jax helped prepare the barricades and the wall. Asta and Brennan were working through the infirmary, preparing what was left of the healer's supplies, rallying anything in preparation for more injuries and wounded. I prayed there would not be many, but my gut instinct told me there would be more than before.

The day crept on and my hands were sore with blisters from hauling logs and the remnants of trunks, furniture and tables from the estate house onto the wall. All who were left, and working were silent, the fear and anticipation of what was to come stealing their tongues. Roman hadn't spoken to me; he'd barely made eye contact and refused to be near me. I kept an eye on him as he worked tirelessly, only stopping for water and food.

The weapons that had been scavenged from the previous attack were being handed around by the time the afternoon swept into evening. All who had stayed were dressed for war I noticed, as I walked from the estate across the grounds. Fires were being lit across the walls, the cages of flames turning into beacons. I swallowed, feeling empty. My hands had begun shaking earlier and I hadn't been able to stomach the food that was passed around at supper.

A last feast, I thought, and I dug my nails into my palms, piercing the skin. The pain surged up my nerves and I heaved a breath, focusing on the ache and sting it brought.

Everyone was too quiet as the sounds of winds rustled the Fallow, beyond the wall. The snap and crackle of the fires set my teeth on edge as I walked along the stone, towards Finian. He was dressed in dark leathers, with twin blades strapped across his back. His white hair blew across his face as he surveyed the swaying trees and the Fallow beyond. He looked deadly, a pillar of stealthy muscle and commanding tone. A Lord, indeed.

I looked past him, catching the eye of Asta and Jax as they stood, motionless, looking out into the depths of darkness. Both their hands were entwined with one another's, both stood in solidarity to each other, like a brace against their own fear.

Lord August had not shown us any attention since he had conducted his meeting with his son and the remaining council still alive on the estate. From what Jax had informed me of earlier, most of the council had fled, all elderly and waning in health, and had abandoned the Lord and his demands to return. That fact alone had silenced the man and caused him to consider his son's speech at the meeting. A speech in which I was told, overruled the senior Lord's strategy of barricading the house.

Lord August and his men that remained, manned the embankment nearest the house. More men were stationed around him, protecting their liege more than any other part of the barricades and walls. Anger, hot and thrashing, flared in me as I watched the man walking up the length of the wall, towards us.

"Where is the one that has been bitten?" he demanded as he approached his son, his cold eyes creasing as he beheld me.

"He will be brought to the wall, Father. Soon," Finian replied, his tone laced with contempt.

"And you think the beast will attack again?" The question was trivial as Finian's father eyed all those around, hands behind his back.

"We received a warning," Finian swallowed, his silver eyes darting to me, "from the Crone."

"Why is their ilk meddling in such things?" Lord August spat, the discord evident in the sneer twisting his mouth.

"Because they wish to help us, Father," Finian sighed, rubbing a hand over his smooth jaw. His father only looked his son up and down, and then retreated up the wall to his small army of guards. Finian didn't watch his father retreat, instead he stood, breathing deep, leaning his hands on the wall, eyes roving the shadowed woodland surrounding the estate. The tension was palpable. This man, restrained and bucking under the command of his hateful father, showed no signs of defection, even from a father who despised him. My heart broke a little as I observed his jaw clench, imagining Finian as a small child, under the dominance and upbringing of that vile man.

The sky above was clouded, the shapes and wisps of vapour flying across the black sky swiftly, as the winds picked up, the cold gusts catching my curls and blowing them towards the Fallow. My brother was nowhere to be seen and some small part of me prayed he had fled with Balthazar, back to our uncle and clan. As if he had read my thoughts, Finian spoke.

"Roman is on his way, he's getting Eli," he said, eyes still trained on the forest.

"Why?" I rasped, my voice unused and dry.

Finian faced me, his muscled form, towering over me. "Because it's the only way to see where his loyalties now lie." His eyes traced my face as he spoke, and I knew what he really meant. The only way for *me* to see where Eli's loyalties will now lie. I ground my teeth, following the shadows of the trees. I could feel his eyes on me, but I ignored the urge to look back. "My mother's coat suits you," he offered, and I blinked. "I'm sorry, Rhona." I focussed then, finding his silver eyes boring into mine. "For everything. For all of this."

"This has nothing to do with you, you have nothing to apologise for," I breathed, feeling my spine tingle. "This was my own doing."

"This is everyone's doing," he replied and I stilled. "Magic has been suppressed and trapped here for too long because of us humans." I nodded in response, unable to say anything. The forest sighed ahead of us and my palm began to itch. The sound was inviting me in, inviting me to let loose the darkness building in me. "What happens if the lycan doesn't come?" he asked and I swallowed again, feeling my throat tighten at the thought.

"Then, when we survive this, I move onwards, to the Fallow, to kill that fowl creature and its spawn," I said, resolutely, needing to believe it myself. A smile crept across Finian's beautiful mouth, and it distracted me from the thought of what was to come next and of what could happen if we should fail here.

"Then I will follow," Finian announced, his eyes alight. I began to object but he stepped into my space, his chin and chest so close I could smell the leather and iron on him. "I will follow you, Rhona. I will follow you to the ends of the earth."

I couldn't move as his eyes blazed like stars and his head dipped. His lips pressed to mine for the briefest of touches and I closed my eyes, absorbing the warmth I so desperately craved. His kiss was slight, contained, as though leashed. My breath stopped as he pulled away.

"Give them hell," he whispered and the cold creature clawing under my skin, purred.

***

The depths of night had descended and other than the flames alight on the wall, no other light shone. The new moon and cycle had begun. The sky above was a bottomless sprawling scape of black that felt heavy above me. I stood vigilantly, the cold winter air seeping through my coat, but I did not shiver. Roman and a chained Eli had come up onto the wall, neither of them coming to me, still stationed by Finian, Daven and Rion. I felt eyes on me every now and then, but when I looked, I found none, only Eli's tense jaw and furrowed brow. I wanted to go to him. I wanted to hold him, smell him and feel the Eli I had known. But every time I looked at the man I knew, something had subtly changed. His eyes were brighter, the blue and brown ablaze. He wore no coat against the chilling bite of the night and yet his skin glistened with sweat. The change was still riding him, the new moon cycle was doing something unseen. I clenched my fists, eyeing him and my brother. Roman's face was brutish, his dark brows constantly crossed as he signed with his hands, questions to Eli. The man I shared moments with signed back one worded answers, uncooperative and distracted. He watched with swift eyes the forest stretching far beyond, the muscles of his neck flickering with the pulse underneath. The scars on his neck shone in the firelight, the pale tissue taught against his flushed skin. The memory of my fingers tracing those scars in the barn breathed into life. I felt his breath on my neck and my skin flushed at the memory of his lips crashing into mine, hungry. The longing in me careened, the memory sputtering out, lifeless. That could be the only time I would share such kisses with Eli again. The only time I would have been able to allow my heart its true wish and freedom. The thought scratched at me, digging deep and killed all hope we would ever experience such a coming together again. I watched him for several minutes, my eyes burning, as he twitched, his body vibrating. Roman noticed it too and I gulped down the bile rising in my throat as Roman checked the iron shackles at Eli's wrists.

Asta moved towards me and I sniffed, straightening and smoothing my features.

"How are you?" she asked, face concerned.

"Wonderful," I replied tartly, but regretted the comment as soon as I said it.

"I mean, how are you? Are you tired?" Her ghostly eyes shone as they darted across my face and down to my wrists. "The magic, are you-"

"Tired, but I am well," I said, trying to reassure her.

"Just try not to ask the keys for so much, to the point where they are using you," she said, her face still lined with worry. "You remember what I told you?"

I nodded, hiding the snarling, wrathful thing lurking under the surface. I was exhausted. I was frustrated. I ached and felt like I could crumble into hundreds of pieces and be swept away in the winds that disturbed the forest. But I didn't let it show. The creature that had stirred to life in me days ago, was not allowing that to happen. She hissed and snarled, fuelled by the rage and hurt of a lifetime, the rage and hurt I had hidden and vaulted into the recesses of my mind. They had come forth, ruptured from their chains and snapped at the bit, needing to be let loose on to the world.

A gurgling rasp rang out from along the wall and we both spun. Eli was straining against his shackles, the rivets of corded muscles surfacing at his neck as his eyes flooded crimson. He gasped and writhed against the chains. Roman grabbed his friend, my betrothed.

His words of comfort failed to reach their mark. Eli was panting with his teeth bared, eyes wildly searching the forest.

"It's time!" Finian bellowed along the line of the wall. A chorus of iron scraping and bowstrings echoed into the night.

I unsheathed the cutlass, still watching Eli, as three guards and Roman tried to restrain him. My stomach rolled as a growl ripped from Eli's throat, a sound I had never heard, or ever thought I would hear from my mute friend. His hands grasped the wall as he sagged, his skin pulsating and trembling. A sob escaped my lips as I tried to move towards him, only to be stopped by Finian's strong arm.

"No, Rhona," he cautioned, and I halted, frozen in place as Eli's blue and brown eyes locked with my own and a snarl escaped his mouth.

The men and Roman's swords shot up, ready to do what was needed, if he was to shift right here on the wall.

My lungs deflated as the world I knew fell away.

It was happening.

Eli was now a turned. He struggled again, snapping and growling against the chains holding his wrists and ankles. The weight of the heavy iron stopped even his muscled arms from lashing out. My hand rested on Finian's arm blocking me, but I needed to reach him.

"Eli," I called, my voice tight, "fight it. Fight it, Eli!" I begged, trying to push past Finian. Rion stepped up to me and Finian, blocking my path and holding me back as Eli's growls resonated loudly. "Eli, fight it," I pleaded, lashing out at the men holding me down. I began begging, my voice nearly screaming as the forest beyond filled with the howls and moans of beasts. "Fight it, for me!"

One glowing blue and brown eye found me, trapped and thrashing to reach them. Eli's growls ceased as every muscle shuddered as he fisted his hands, straining to contain the beast from ripping him away. Shouts rang out from the south wall, then the west, as the woods rippled with movement.

"Get him off the wall!" Finian ordered and the three guards grabbed a panting Eli and began to haul him from the wall, and down into the grounds. Roman moved, bringing his fist up to strike the nearest guard, but Daven got there first, his sword raised and aimed for Roman's throat. "Roman, think," Finian rumbled, still holding me. "It's for his own safety, as well as ours!"

Defiance shone in my brother's eyes, his lip curled, and neck strained. The forest boomed and the air around became a frenzy of screeches. Turned charged out of the shadowed trees, jumping and clawing at the stonework walls. Arrows flew, ripping the air in a symphony of strings as howls bellowed up to us from the gnashing creatures below. Finian released me, hauling my body to face him. "Be smart, Rhona, and live," was all he said as he ran from me, along the wall to a creature clawing its way over the battlement.

The air above me hummed and crackled as shapes began volleying from the depth of the forest, up and over the wall high above. Witches.

I followed the shadows as they landed in the middle of the courtyard. Five women touched down, black dresses and cloaks billowing in a phantom wind. Several men and women on the ground surged forward but were met by a mass of black glittering mist that crept over their faces, down their noses and throats, suffocating them. They fell to the ground, limp, faces blackened, mouths gaping in horror. A scream pierced the air and I recognised it instantly. Asta was glaring at the witches below, her hands grappling with the wall in front of her.

"Acer!" she screamed, and fury curved her face into something fierce. I looked back at the witches, finally understanding. Acer, the witch who had cast the deadly mist, was Asta's double, with sleek umber skin, elegant long fingers and brilliant silver eyes. Her hair was not shorn like Asta's but fell down her arm in black locks. Coal lined her eyes and mouth and I swallowed at the sight of her. Asta's twin was the darker side of the same coin. Darker, foul and the epitome of evil.

"Hello sister," Acer hissed and with a swift flick of her wrist, the wall below our feet exploded.

Chapter 41

I fell, my stomach dropping, as rocks and stone cascaded down to the ground, taking me with them. Booms ricocheted and deafened me as the witches began attacking the walls, desecrating the battlement. I landed in a pile, the air whooshing out of my lungs as debris and dust coated me. I shielded my head, the remnants of rocks and rubble still falling over me. My back pounded in pain as the dust settled and I tried to heave a breath, my tongue and airways gritty, as I forced my legs to stand. Stones tumbled away, the air a storm of dirt and earth. The wall had been obliterated.

Piles of rubble littered the ground, with bodies buried underneath. I dragged down a breath, trying to clear my airways, but it was no use and I coughed and sputtered dirt and blood.

Guards stumbled up, rising from the ashes of stone but the turned surged forward. Picking off the people as the rose from the ground. Warm blood dribbled down my face as I whirled, looking for Asta. She stood, covered in dust, eyes wholly white, snarling. Her ashen fingers began plucking glittering red and black threads from the settling air and in a quick flourish, a knot formed and blasted forward. The force blew back the dust in a wave of power that sent Acer and the four other witches flying through the air. Beasts crept up over the wall and the sounds of fighting became clearer in my ears. Metal glinted under the rubble at my feet and I scrambled for my cutlass. Sword in hand, I ran over the broken slabs and stones to Asta, towards my friend. Her white eyes turned to me and with a pale thread she whipped at me. I halted, stopped completely by an impenetrable wall of shimming air.

"Help the others, this is between me and my twin," Asta spat, her voice not her own.

Rough hands gripped my shoulders and I spun. Jax, covered in white dust, his blue eyes red and watery, glared down at me. "As much as I don't want to, we need to leave her, to help Finian and the others," he implored, dragging me away.

We ran, darting over and through the throng of fighting. I could see Finian, coated in debris, battling a turned with pale white fur. The beast snapped its huge jaws, its hackles triggered and green eyes glowing. Arrow shafts dotted its hide, but it continued gnashing and mauling at Finian. Its wounds healed over its broken skin, the broken and splintered wood surging forth from the muscle, until the arrow shafts and tips were pushed out. I couldn't believe my eyes, couldn't believe what I was seeing. The beast was healing itself.

Daven erupted from the rubble, dazed and unsteady. Rion ran to him, sword aloft as another turned pounced forth. Rion's blade swiped cleanly down the ribs of the beast and it howled as it fell, skidding across the stones. Blood spattered the ground as I stumbled, catching the side of the beast's flank. The sliced skin knitted together again, completely regenerated. My empty stomach roiled; the thought of the beasts not being felled sent a wave of nausea over me.

Why wasn't the beast dying?

Jax and I reached them all just as the beast began to rise, the forest beyond the wall visible and open. The keys and my wrists warmed, and the itch swelled across my palm and down my fingers. I raised my hand into the night, grasping the cold air, as though solid and pulled it down with a mighty holler. The tree nearest the wall uprooted and fell, groaning as it smashed to the ground, on top of the staggering white turned. A gruff moan sounded from Finian and I rushed to him, cutlass in hand. A beast had him pinned and I jumped, the magic of the keys pushing me in an arc through the air. I landed on its back, bringing the sword down between its spine and skull. With a wheezing whine, it fell and I rolled away from its imposing weight, as it collapsed dead.

The trees rumbled again with more beasts ready to come forth. Rion moved hastily to Finian, hauling him up from the ground, and brushing him off. He was unharmed but breathing hard.

"My Lord," Rion asked, eyeing his master for any bites.

"I'm fine, Rion," he replied, eyes glowing wildly. "Where is my father?"

"He retreated into the house, sir, when the witches came."

"Witches?" Finian asked, fearfully.

"Yes," I spat, my mouth filled with dirt. "It's not just the lycan and its spawn, we have to worry about. Something else is happening here."

Finian's eyes widened further at the battle happening behind us. Turned were barrelling over the remnants of the barricades, followed by other barbarous creatures. Milky wraiths, with long spindly arms and hooded faces, swarmed through the turned as well as three skineths. The skin snatcher's elongated limbs jutted out in ghoulish angles as they began savaging the men and women fighting.

"The turned aren't falling as easily, unless decapitated." I hissed, wiping my blade on the length of my coat. "We need more than just us humans and a witch," I said as I drove past Finian and his men, my hand seeking below my coat and shirt to the medallion hanging around my neck. I pulled out the silver disc and fisted it tightly.

We need your help, I pleaded, and my legs took me up and over the mountain of broken stone and into the beginnings of the Fallow.

When I reached the nearest tree, I slammed my empty palm to its trunk, and the keys at my wrist ignited brilliant blue as the bands pulsed. I closed my eyes, gritting my teeth, feeling the magic respond to my call. The forest shivered at my touch and command. The vibration radiating across the leaves deep within. I peeled my palm and fingers away, my flesh stinging from the magic and impact, and ran back over the wall to Finian.

A skineth had heaved forwards and Finian, Rion, Daven and Jax were fighting it. Swords arced and cleaved the air, all of the men swiping and slicing the creature at every turn. The skineth lashed out with its long, rapier-like nails just missing Jax's exposed stomach. Finian shouted my name as I ran, skidding to the ground, my side skimming the rough gravel as the skineth's claws swiped the air where I had just been. I jumped up, knees cracking, as Finian's arms surged forth and I grabbed it. He swung my weight around, spinning me and my sword through the air as the creature whirled on me. Rion roared at the vile beast's back, stepping up onto it to drive his blade down the back of the gruesome skeletal shoulders. Black putrid blood sprayed, as it stumbled back shrieking.

"What the fuck were you doing?" Finian roared at me, eyes fierce, as I faced him.

"Getting us help!" I yelled back, feeling the floor beneath our feet begin to tremble.

The forest beyond shook, as the trees swayed and rippled in the darkness. Bark and branches crashed and flew as three Knarrock trolls bounded out of the shadows, bellowing an ear-splitting roar. They clambered over the fractured wall, their monstrous arms beating the ground as they herded the turned that continued to swarm in. One of the trolls, with fractured antlers and ivy-coated skin, grabbed a turned by the scruff and threw the creature into the depths of the forest.

Another turned with russet fur, lunged forth towards me, but was snatched mid-strike by the boulder-like fingers of a troll and beaten to the ground, its skull and teeth smattering in a bloody mess at my feet.

"Rid this place of the creatures," I ordered, and the troll's beady eyes blinked in understanding. With a raucous clamour, they barrelled towards the other beasts, denting the ground as they went

A thundering crack rang out across the air and I saw Asta, battling her sister still. The four other witches lay dazed and unmoving whilst the twin witches cast spell after spell. Green sizzling threads rippled forth from Asta and her sister fell cowering, now caged under vines of thorns and shimmering green smoke. The witch, now caged, screamed and seethed from within. I saw Acer's fingers twist forth from the vines, the vaporous thorns piercing her skin. Blood swelled and flowed down her fingers, igniting, blazing into blue fire. The cage in which she was concealed went up in billowing sapphire flames, freeing her. Jax screamed Asta's name, his voice ripping high, as a skineth crept up behind Asta. The witch whirled, eyes white, and with a thread of black chain she beheaded the skineth before it could even swipe her. Pride swelled in my chest but was quickly doused by fear as her twin thrust forward, grabbing Asta by the throat.

Something streaked high above in the darkness and my skin prickled, recognising the shrieks. The air split with a snap as the Crone landed in billowing streams of mist. A wraith slithered forward, its milky white robes and gnarled hands swiping for the elder. The Crone snapped her dark rotted teeth, and with a sickening crunch and wraith dissolved into nothing.

"Rhona," the Crone gasped, turning to me, "I must speak with you." Another turned jumped forward and I raised my blade, aiming for the creature's hide. The cutlass sliced through the fur and flesh of the beast, and I welcomed the blood that spurted over my face and neck. "Now, Rhona," the Crone demanded, her blackened hands clawing as she struck the beast, blinding it. Finian pushed me back as a skineth began running towards us, shouting at me to '*go'*.

I stumbled to the Crone, lungs aching for clean air. "This is a diversion," she hissed as her wide eyes darted about the fray of beast and human fighting.

"I don't understand," I murmured, licking the blood from my lips, mouth tasting coppery.

"This is a distraction, something-" the Crone began but I cut her off, finally seeing Roman and Eli alive and fighting across the courtyard. No guards surrounded them as the battled creatures. Instinct propelled my legs forward and I ran, ignoring the shouts from the Crone.

Roman battled a smaller turned, his coat and face blooded and covered in dust. The beast snapped its jaws at Roman's extended, sword-holding hand whilst his other clutched Eli's chains. Jumping over rocks, something sizzled and singed the lapel of my coat. The spell that had been launched at me landed to the ground and red sparks scorched the earth. I could see them, see Eli struggling against the chains and shackles, his face distraught, as Roman continued to swipe his sword at the creature. I shouted for my brother, but when his eyes locked with my own, I screamed.

Eli held a rock the size of his fist, his arm raised. In the blink of an eye, my brother fell, the wound to his head already gushing blood from Eli's hit. I pumped my legs faster, seeing Eli grapple for an object in Roman's coat pockets, my throat hoarse from screaming.

Teeth snapped out at me to my left; I hadn't noticed the turned charging to me as I made my way across the ground. I dived, my body and face grazing the rubble. I rolled as gigantic paws, pounded the ground at my head. I rolled, looking up at the beast, as teeth and drool thrusted into my face. Someone growled in the distance and the beast was suddenly shoved off me with a whimpering mewl. Finian blundered over, sword out shielding me. I thrust myself up quickly, dazed. The tawny beast lunged at me again, its razor teeth snapping at us. I gripped Finian's arms, trying to measure myself better.

"Touch her again and I'll fucking end you," Finian snarled. I froze. "She's mine," he bellowed, teeth bared at the turned, swinging his sword, awaiting the attack.

The creature's ears flickered, as though hearing something we could not. It was poised to pounce, but with a deafening growl it jumped away, tearing the ground up as it headed back into the Fallow. I whirled, finding Eli unchained, eyes dark as he looked upon us, my brother's unconscious body at his feet.

"Eli, what have you done!" I screamed, aghast as all the blood drained from my face.

Eli's lips rippled and a snarl erupted out from his chest. I shuddered, unable to move as he stalked forward. A howl reverberated across the clearing, from deep within the Fallow and moans and howls from the turned rang out in answer to the lycan. Eli's head twitched and cringed in answer, his face twisted in pain. I moved around Finian, my limbs rushing with cold. Eli cowered back, growling and writhing. The turned about the estate were fleeing, running away back into the depths of the forest from where they had come.

"Rhona, don't touch him," Finian ordered as I staggered closer.

Eli's eyes shot open, the irises glowing as the animal began to surface. His teeth bared and I watched in horror as they began transforming, growing long and sharp. His hand swiped for me, as a growl that rippled through the air. I fell back, winded, as he stretched and moaned. His skin trembled, and his body buckled and bent as the contained beast started ripping its way free.

"Rhona!" It was Finian. He ran at Eli, his sword raised, prized to kill.

I felt myself screaming, screaming so hard that I tasted blood. The keys heated and illuminated at my wrists as magic of the Fallow answered my need. The ground rumbled and ripped as a cavern opened up, splitting the earth in two between Finian and Eli. The trees groaned across the Fallow and beyond, and the remaining creatures whimpered and mewled at the sound of the earth breaking. Everything shook, shook with my scream, until it rasped past my lips into nothing. The cavern stilled, the earth resting once more as the keys dulled and the magic took something from within me. Eli's eyes had stopped glowing, they were wide with shock as he beheld me across the small ravine. Finian was at my side, sword hanging loose as he steadied himself, his toes balancing on the cliff of the split. I darted up grabbing him and pulling him down to me and we both fell back to the ground, Finian's body on top of my own. Forcing my limbs to obey me, I pushed myself up from under Finian.

As I looked up, my heart and mind became an assault of chaos at the sight of Eli's wide-eyed, horror struck face. My lip trembled as I saw what remained of the man, my betrothed, crack and splinter. My lips began to call his name, but it was no use as he ran off into the darkness of the forest.

Chapter 42

The creatures continued to withdraw, barrelling back across the wall at the call of their master, the lycan. Our people still battled the remaining skineth and wraiths that stalked. I ran to Roman, skirting around the ravine to get to his fallen body. I fell on cracking knees, the pain shooting up my legs and causing me to bite down on my lip and split blood. My hand cautiously lifted his head, and my fingers raised his eyelids to see the dilated pupils beneath. I leaned in close to his chest and sobbed at the sound of his lungs filling and releasing. Blood had dried across his temple, but it wasn't a bad wound. I sent a silent prayer to the Mother above, thanking her. I smoothed his clotted hair away from his face, as tears began streaming down my cheeks. I shook him, trying to wake him from the state of unrest, until his eyelids flickered and, dazedly, he opened his dark blue eyes. My eyes.

"What happened?" he croaked and coughed. I lifted his torso up slowly, so he was sitting upright, and his hand found his head and he winced.

"Eli hit you over the head," I sniffed, as my hands continued to smooth away his dusted hair. "He freed himself and left," I whispered, still not believing it.

Roman stilled my hand, his thick fingers tight on my wrist. "Did he change?" Roman asked, eyes clearing.

"He nearly did-" I began but Finian cut in.

"-And nearly killed Rhona," Finian hissed, his pale brows gathered, eyes dark. Roman straightened, his jaw tense.

"We need to get you up," I said, before Roman could answer and with Finian's help, we lifted my brother to his feet.

Snaps and crackles of magic sounded out as Asta and Acer battled on, both witches bloody but undefeated. The other witches were gone, if their bodies were among the dead I didn't know. I saw Jax skimming the area by Asta, held back by a wall up protecting him from any spells or entering her space and interfering with her own battle. Guards gathered together to beat off the remaining wraiths and skineth, the creatures falling quickly. I stumbled forwards, my whole body aching from within. Something flashed, searing my skin at the base of my throat, and I gasped, my fingers searching the layers of fabric to the burning metal around my neck. The medallion of the Trinity was glowing hot and I ripped it from my neck, unable to take the burning pain. A cry bubbled up in the distance and my eyes searched the fray. My blood ran cold when I saw the Crone standing before a hooded figure, a black blade protruding from her chest.

A chorus of screams ripped through the night air, from myself, Asta and Acer, as we saw the Crone fall. The hooded figure dissolved into the night, their form eaten up by the shadows and mist sweeping out of the Fallow. I ran, my lungs protesting as I hurled myself to the falling witch. At that moment I knew. I knew the Shadow Messenger's screams had not been from the fight that had happened, but from this. Our screams. The screams of three. Ice coated my veins as skidded to my knees, my hands clutching the elder on the ground. Blood bubbled up and pulsed from the dark blade, the same blade that had stabbed the heart tree.

"Rhona," the Crone spluttered, her blackened teeth and tongue spitting crimson. I looked for Asta, finding her running towards us, her beautiful face twisted in dread. Acer's screams tore through the night, the witch distraught at the sight of the Crone, her grandmother. She bellowed, casting spells of black across the retreating men and women, killing them as they fled. With a thunderous crack, Acer shot into the depthless night, her cries streaming through the sky, echoing like a lament.

Asta skidded beside me, hauling her grandmother to her, her eyes once again silver and lined with tears.

"Grandmother," Asta wailed, the ache straining her throat. "Who did this?"

The Crone gurgled and spurted blood as laboured breaths began to overwhelm her.

"The Maiden," the Crone crowed, "she is the one. The reason." Bloody coughs wracked her as she tried to speak. Every muscle and nerve inside me froze like ice as my pulse slowed and the world came into sharp focus. "The reason for all of this, she is the one who desecrated the seven. She means to," another bout of coughs fluttered up as Asta held her grandmother steady through them, "means to raise the Fallen one. Her bloodline," she wheezed and Asta's eyes found mine. Rage burned within them, as Asta's eyes filmed over to that wretched white, otherworldly and wrathful. "She released the lycan and is using him. They have compromised the humans." The Crone's wheezing became louder, her chest rattling with every heaving breath. Her robes rippled around the fallen witch, the fabric floating on a phantom breeze. Alarm ricochet through me as pieces of her cloak began to breakaway, disintegrating into the night.

"Grandmother, stay with me," Asta pleaded, her voice thick with tears. Finian, Roman and Jax stood behind us, all silent and looking on ashen.

"Rhona," the Crone rasped, and I leaned in closer, her hands reaching for me. "I release you from the debt. I release you from the life debt," she repeated, stuttering, and blinking rapidly. As though a weight was lifted, the air around me shifted and shimmered. The winds blew around us and I filled my lungs, breathing easier. "You were never meant to have the keys." As though suspended, we all froze. "Another was due to receive them. Another was to wield them."

I swallowed, stunned and disorientated. Asta sniffed, her cheeks lined and streaked with tears. Her hands reached up to cup her grandmother's face, as the old witch's blackened fingers encased them. I saw grandmother and granddaughter share one last look, one last shared moment and with a shuddering gasp, the Crone's chest rose and fell and didn't rise anymore.

My ears were filled with the Crone's words, as my blood thrummed in my ears and the darkness within me slithered. The child of my memory cowered in the depth and despair of my mind. I saw Asta's mouth open, saw the anguish shape her face as she cried and blared into the night. But I heard nothing. My own head was filled with the words I did not expect to hear. The Crone's robes continued dissolving, as an otherworldly wind swept across the clearing. Fragments and fractures blew away, until the Crone disappeared in a haze of glittering stars on the breeze.

Chapter 43

I sat unmoving, for what felt like hours, as the Finian and his men laid the dead to rest. Upon entering the house, Finian and Asta had found his father dead on the floor of the entryway, his chest carved open, the gore trailing in bloody footprints out of the door. He shed no tears for his father, as the bodies burned on a pyre in the middle of the courtyard, the smoke billowing in black plumes against the early morning sky. The cold of the morning had begun to seep through, and my coat was scattered in dew. Roman sat next to me motionless, his head in his hands, eyes closed to the atrocities across the estate. Brennan had come over with hot tea and I took the cup offered, my eyes still fixed to the ground at my feet. The steam from the tea enraptured me and it wasn't until I raised the mug to my lips and tasted the cold tea, that I realised more time had passed. The keys of ink at my wrist felt cumbersome, and the magic I had used, called for payment. The throb pulsed in my veins and across my temples. I could use the Fallow, to replenish and build back the strength that had been exhausted. But I didn't. I couldn't. I fed the magic pieces of me, drip feeding my malice and rage. I broke off the fragments of my own internal darkness to feed it, as payment. It was the only thing I could control as I sat there raw and numb.

I was free from the life debt that had encased and engulfed me these past weeks, but something else called deep in me, pushing me further into the brink of the abyss. I knew what we had to do. The keys and my heart aligned resolutely. I had to get Eli back.

Asta sat for a time, rocking with silent sobs, and Jax and Rufus comforted her in hushed voices. The witch had washed her face, and her skin glowed richly in the rising daylight. Fresh welts and cuts framed her hairline and arms, the blood dried and brown against the pale grey coat she still wore. Rufus shivered, huddled against his brother, his face pale and freckles dark, whilst Jax stared with wide, glassy eyes at the smouldering remains of the pyre. Finian trudged to us through the haze of smoke, worn and beaten, his black leather covered with peeling blood. He sat gingerly next to me, gasping as he did so. Blood smeared his face, the cut on his cheek and brow raining maroon streaks down his high cheekbones. His white hair was washed pink. He would need to wash it.

"What do we do now?" Roman voiced gruffly as he rubbed a rough hand over his eyes and mouth.

No one answered, all contented not to think about the future and what it might bring now that the Crone was dead, and the Maiden was the new enemy.

Licking my lips, I downed the ice-cold tea, my mouth parched and gritty still. "We find the lycan and stop the Maiden," was all I said as I looked each of them in the eye, weathered and exhausted, and allowing the pain to shine in my eyes. I couldn't hide it anymore. I couldn't build up the mask that hid the shattered soul within. I let it through, let it crack and splinter the facade I had held in place for so many years.

No more.

"We can't just go traipsing through the Fallow," Jax quipped, frightened.

"No, we need to understand the extent of what's happened," I sighed, thoroughly drained and used up. I needed them all in this with me. There was no way I could do this alone now that I knew about the keys, and how they were meant for someone else. Someone else was supposed to carry this burden. The therns words echoed distantly in the back of my mind, bringing to life a fresh wave of fear, *'unwanted in name and nature'*.

"We need to know the truth about the Fallen Sister and about the Fallow." I said, trying to bring my attention back to the here and now.

"What do you suggest?" Finian asked, and I saw the shadows darken under his eyes.

"The Crone said they had compromised the humans and I think she meant the Crown." Everyone's eyes darted to me. "Finian, you said that your father had sent word to the King and Queen, and the other Earls and Lords of the land, in hope to help fight on the wall. To stop the creatures filtering through?"

"Yes, these past few months, we received nothing in return. You don't think-"

"That the Maiden has infiltrated the court? There's a reason no one came to aid you. That no men were sent to guard the Fallow. Among other things."

That internal tug and compass whirled to life as I began piecing together the chain of thoughts that had been a mass and blur days before.

"It would make sense," Jax agreed, deep in thought, "if the Crown didn't know about the trouble, about the raids, because someone was stopping the information from getting through."

"Exactly." I heaved a great breath feeling my hands begin their tremors.

"The Crown's library hosts the best scholars and records of the land," Finian said, blinking. "We could start there."

"How do we even get into the palace, let alone the royal library?" Roman taunted, raising his brows sardonically.

"Through me. I am now the Lord of Neath Briar. We can travel to inform them of my father's death, the raids and change of title for me. And besides, I've been invited to his majesties ball, for the winter solstice." I watched Finian's throat bob. The thought of his father, in wake of his death, caused him to recoil. He was, indeed, Lord of the estate now. The blood trails still lingering on the marble entryway were evident of that.

A ball or any celebration for that matter, was the last thing I wanted to think about. But it was as sound a plan as we could gather in the early hours of the morning. The sky had lightened enough, bringing about the water-washed landscape, smeared with the gore of men and women lost. I swallowed, unable to look further than that of my feet, ashamed and defeated. The shock from the past few days silenced us again into a stringent state.

"Are you really planning to do this, Rhona?" my brother balked, agitated and irate.

"For my grandmother," Asta whispered, her silver eyes shining with fresh tears. Moments passed as we all regarded the distraught witch, watching her tears fall down the smooth panes of her cheeks.

"For my father," Jax said, wiping his mouth as Rufus burrowed in closer to him. I waited, feeling the embers flare in my heart, but they were soon extinguished as Roman scoffed, shaking his head.

"It's not that easy," he huffed, face pained. "You really think you can stop her? Stop her from raising the Fallen Sister, a fucking god?!" Roman shouted, spitting through his teeth.

"You're right. It won't be easy. But if not us, then who else?" I asked, throat hoarse. Roman's dark blue eyes locked with mine, the same eyes battling a silent fight. I held my countenance. I would not balk or fall short here. He pursed his lips, looking away.

"For my people," Finian announced, and I looked to the Lord as his eyes captured mine intently, "to the ends of the earth."

Something swelled within me, as we shared a moment of solidarity and knowing. Whatever it was between us, fluttered to life and I knew then, Finian would not stray from this ask. From me.

I waited for my brother, for the brave man to come forth, to unite us and support me once again, the way he had always done, even when he didn't know who his sister really was at heart.

"For Eli," Roman said, finally defeated, and for the first time in what felt like an age, the warmth returned in my brother's gaze as he considered me.

Looking at the courageous people, these friends, I felt utterly crushed. I was completely torn and broken at the thought of the oncoming hell that awaited us all. I was free from the life debt the Crone had burdened me with, and yet I still felt the weight of its chains around my heart. These people were walking into something that we couldn't even comprehend or imagine. I didn't know how much more my weary heart could take. But one thing was for certain. No one else would die for me. No one else would be harmed because of me. I would fracture the world in two to stop that from happening again. I would rip and destroy myself entirely before I let that happen again. I knew this in the depths of my soul as I looked in the eyes of my family and friends.

For Eli.

Chapter 44

Eli

My skin shed, the remnants of my human flesh falling away, revealing dark ebony fur. The shift was agonising as my bones twisted and deviated from what they knew. My muscles tore and snapped, growing over wider and larger limbs. My eyes blinked as the light of the world fractured in a new distorted clarity. The woods beyond were defined in deep concentrations of lustre and light. I could see everything, every leaf and branch, every tree and rock. I could smell the rotted corpses of deer half a mile away, the sodden earth beneath my feet, rich with life, and the crocus bulbs awaiting to sprout and thrive from deep under the dirt. I could smell the charred remains of burning flesh and bones on the wind as it blew through the forest rustling fur that covered me. I could sense the forest around me as it churned in the early hours, the trees whispering their prayers to the wind for the fallen.

The voices in my head were deafening, the whispers and hisses of voices I did not know. They orchestrated together, overpowering one another in a frenzied rampage of noise. I shook myself, trying to ease the blaring tones and shrill calls. But one among them was stranger than the rest, and it beckoned something in my very blood, ringing and roaring at the beast to follow. I snapped and shook, not wanting to move, not wanting to follow the ceaseless urge. It was as though the call was embedded into the beast's bones, into my bones, and the pain I felt only intensified as I tried to deny it.

I thrashed and writhed against the bonds and fibrous shackles demanding me to heel, to obey. The symphony of voices escalated in my mind and I faltered, the beast cowering at the noise. I couldn't be the monster, held captive by the lycan and its throng rallying in my head, urging me to bow and surrender.

A rippling growl escaped from my jowls, the sound causing me alarm. I hadn't been able to make sound for a long time and to hear it from within, with these ears that were so sensitive and new, crashed over me in a wave of unchecked emotion. I writhed at the demand coming down upon me, unable to see the light of morning as the darkness caved in.

END OF BOOK I

Authors Thanks

This has been a long time coming. I started writing this in 2017, when it was nothing more than a fleeting idea driving home from work one day, listening to 'Seven Devils' by Florence and the Machines. Since the age of fourteen I knew, deep down, I wanted to become a writer and after many years, two different BTEC's and two very different university degrees, I finally began my journey into the world of writing. Believe me, I made some questionable choices along the way, but now here I am.

I always knew I wanted to do this indie. I wanted to control the publishing of my novel, from the story, the cover and the formatting. I started art again, so I could create a cover I felt breathed life into my story. I learnt and watched many hours of formatting videos to try and make the printed book as beautiful as possible. And now the time is here. My baby is in print and I have finally released it into the world.

I want to firstly thank my amazing husband. You have supported me throughout my life, not only with my writing but when I was at my worst and most broken. You picked me up and helped build and shape me into the woman I am today. All those nights after my 9 to 5, you allowed me the space and time to write. You brought me tea (more like red wine) and ordered takeaways when I didn't want to cook. You held my hand and cheered me on from the side lines as I began to build the foundations of this new venture and career. I am so thankful for you, every day, and I love you with all my heart. To the moon and back.

To my family, especially my sister, I love you. There's not much more I need to say, but we've been through hell and back. But we're still here and thriving.

To all my friends, Frankie, Meg, Rach, Ash, Vic, Becky, Lisa and Rosie. Thank you for our wine nights, for our times out on the town and the memories I will cherish forever and always. You are the best group of girls anyone could ask for. From weddings, to festivals, to garage raves and many more. I love you all and thank you all for being my best friends.

To my editor, Rozanna, thank you for your patience and your mad skills! Without you this would be completely unreadable. Thank you for helping me shape this into something worthwhile. Thank you for all the hours you spent amending my poor grammar. You were a dreamboat at Uni and even more of a dreamboat now. I can only hope and pray you still want to work with me come book two!

To all my BookTok followers, supporters, and BETA readers, I am extremely blessed to have found you in our nook and book community: Lizzie, Dan, Jenna, Katie, Jenna, Jordan, Mariam, Nicole, Hannah, Laura, Louise, Kim, Ellie, Morgan, Johanna, Neal, Perry, Cassie, George, Luke, Fatima, Kylie, Katrina, Lily-Louise, Charlotte, Vanessa, Gabrielle, Shelly, Thomas, Sam, Victoria and Hattie! Thank you for all the comments, likes and shares. Thank you for all your wonderful advice and amazing videos. You've kept me sane, in tune and grounded, throughout building my social media platform. I love you all.

And to you, reader, thank you for reading the beginning. It is only just the start, I promise you. You have made my dream come true. You are bringing my world to life.

About the Author

Marnie L. Norton lives in Hampshire, UK, with her husband and two fur babies. She has a bachelor's degree in Creative and Media Writing and has dreamt of becoming a published author since the age of fourteen. She enjoys reading and writing fantasy, all things Star Wars and listening to murder and crime podcasts. She studies herbs, the moon, crystals and thinks of herself as a green witch. She loves long walks at her local beach, cocktails with friends and spending nights sat on the sofa, with her husband and dogs, with a takeaway, watching Lord of the Rings.

If you have enjoyed her book, please follow her on her social platforms for news and updates coming to the 'A Path of Darkness and Runes' series.

IG: @authormarnielnorton
TikTok: @authormarnienorton

Printed in Great Britain
by Amazon